CONSUMED BY
FIRE

THE FIRE SERIES

ALSO BY ANNE STUART

ROMANTIC SUSPENSE

ROMANCE

Lazarus Rising / reprint as
Here Come the Grooms
Angel's Wings
Rancho Diablo / reprint
as Western Lovers
Crazy Like a Fox / reprint
as Born in the USA
Glass Houses / reprint as Men at Work
Cry for the Moon
Partners in Crime
Blue Sage / reprint as Western Lovers
Bewitching Hour
Rocky Road / reprint in Men
Made in America #19
Banish Misfortune
Housebound
Museum Piece

Heart's Ease
Chain of Love
The Fall of Maggie Brown
Winter's Edge
Catspaw II
Hand in Glove
Catspaw
Tangled Lies / reprint in Men
Made in America #11
Now You See Him
Special Gifts
Break the Night
Against the Wind

NOVELLAS

Married to It (prequel to Fire and Ice)
Risk the Night

HISTORICALS

SCANDAL AT THE HOUSE OF RUSSELL

Never Kiss a Rake
Never Trust a Pirate
Never Marry a Viscount

THE HOUSE OF ROHAN

The Wicked House of Rohan
Shameless
Breathless
Reckless
Ruthless

STAND-ALONE TITLES

The Devil's Waltz
Hidden Honor
Lady Fortune
Prince of Magic
Lord of Danger
Prince of Swords
To Love a Dark Lord
Shadow Dance
A Rose at Midnight
The Houseparty
The Spinster and the Rake
Lord Satan's Bride

CONSUMED BY
FIRE

THE FIRE SERIES

ANNE STUART

Published by Montlake Romance, Seattle

www.apub.com

Amazon, the Amazon logo, and Montlake Romance are trademarks of Amazon. com, Inc., or its affiliates.

ISBN-13: 9781477828472
ISBN-10: 1477828478

Cover design by Jason Blackburn

Library of Congress Control Number: 2014957576

Printed in the United States of America

For everyone who's been asking me for more Ice books. Here it is.

PART ONE—BEGINNINGS

Chapter One

Evangeline Morrissey sank down on the rock wall, hot, dusty, sweaty, and tired. Her legs ached from climbing the hills beyond the tiny Tuscan town of Cabrisi—she'd underestimated how far she'd gone, and the way back was daunting. It was early afternoon but the sun was bright overhead on this hot spring day, and she leaned forward and rubbed her sore calves.

She frowned at the sturdy sandals she'd worn. Usually they served her well, but right now her feet hurt, and she just wanted to find a place to curl up and sleep for a little while, just a fifteen-minute nap out of the baking sun.

Fortunately she knew just where to find such a sanctuary.

The church of St. Anselmo was rarely used, a sixteenth-century remnant of a once denser population in these hills. Surely no one would object to her presence; as usual she wore a knee-length denim skirt rather than shorts, wrapped a shirt around her waist that she used to cover her arms, and had a kerchief on her head to keep her ridiculously curly reddish-brown hair in place. It was her standard costume, guaranteed to appease even the most fundamental of clerics no matter what their faith, and had served her in Spanish mosques as well as ancient synagogues. While she'd been working on her advanced degree in Medieval Religious Architecture, she'd naturally ended up spending time in a lot of places of worship, and she'd kept the uniform ever since. She simply had to remember which places required her to cover her head and which didn't.

The last bit of road approaching the church was steep, and her calves were in agony by the time she topped the rise. She stopped, momentarily startled.

She'd never seen a vehicle in this place, never passed anyone other than Father Francisco as he glumly paced the empty aisles. This time there were three cars parked beside the small church— a Bentley, a smaller, more discreet black Lexus, and a humble Fiat. Were some sort of officials having some kind of meeting about the fate of the church? Would they abandon such a beauty, allow it to be ruined by vandals, its stained glass windows shattered by the Italian equivalent of street punks? Surely not. There was nothing particularly remarkable about the church or its architecture—she barely had a page of notes on the place—but it was a sanctuary of peace and respite on a hot day, and she was a pilgrim of sorts, wasn't she?

She crossed the graveled area that could barely hold more cars than were already there, stepped into the cool darkness of the narthex, the traditional front entrance hall of the church, and blinked at the dense shadows lit only by the sun beaming through the rich, jewel-like colors of the stained glass window at the far end of the nave. She could see one man in the pews, his head bent in prayer, and with surprise she recognized the balding pate of Signore Corsini, the friendly Italian businessman from the hotel. There was no sign of the priest or whoever had come in the other cars. She turned to her right, slipping into the shadows. The tiny chapel off to one side would provide the private respite she needed, and she paused to light a candle and put an offering in the box before heading in. She always lit a candle, never sure whom she was praying for. Asking God for money or success in her profession seemed totally crass, and everything else in her life seemed in decent shape, so she'd come to the decision she was paying it forward, at least in terms of prayer, and she was happy with that.

She sank into the last of the five rows of pews in the chapel, sighing with relief. She'd overestimated her energy; the remnants of the old town wall were much farther than she thought, and she was worn out. She'd trained her body to nap efficiently: fifteen minutes and she'd wake, refreshed and re-energized. She put her hands on the pew in front of her, rested her forehead on them, and fell asleep immediately.

The sound woke her. She jerked awake, blinking at the darkness, before she remembered where she was. She'd either slept longer than she should have, or not long enough—she felt disoriented, confused, and she shook her head, as if the physical act could toss off the cobwebs.

She tried to recall the sound that had startled her. It had been a strange, unexpected noise, almost human, and her skin prickled with the sense that something was wrong.

Pushing herself up, she quickly crossed herself, wondering as usual if she was doing it backwards, and stepped back out into the narthex, coming to an abrupt halt as she saw two people enshrined by the bright sunlight pouring in the outer doors.

The woman was model thin, model tall, and had an interesting rather than a beautiful face. She was exquisite, as so many Italian and French women were, and Evangeline had learned long ago not to feel inadequate, but for some reason those lessons vanished in her sleep-fuzzed brain, and she knew she was a grubby mess.

The man didn't help. He was just a bit taller than the woman was, perhaps six feet, and if the woman was gorgeous this man was simply . . . she couldn't think of the word for it. Unlike his companion, he was dressed casually, wearing khakis and an open-neck shirt, the sleeves rolled up to reveal tanned forearms: he looked like a beautiful, slightly decadent Italian nobleman come back to life.

He had an elegant face, black hair that flowed around it in artful waves, and the kind of dark, liquid eyes you could drown in. His mouth was made for sin, his lean body had a whipcord, tensile strength, and Evangeline was in love.

She shook her head and laughed softly at the notion, and the sound caught their attention. They'd been so deep in conversation they hadn't noticed her sudden appearance, and they both jerked their heads in her direction with lightning speed, making her feel even more conspicuous.

She straightened her shoulders, gave them a smile and a polite "*bongiorno*," and moved past them into the darkness of the main church. Signore Corsini was still praying, bent low, and although she didn't want to bother him, she didn't want to go back the other way. It would look extremely odd if she immediately turned around, and she preferred not to face the glorious couple again. She dipped her fingers in the holy water and crossed herself again, her back to them, and started up the aisle.

She could feel their eyes on her, which was ridiculous. There was no reason for them to watch her—she was obviously just an American tourist wandering around the hillsides, and she should be the last person to interest them.

She was mentally slapping herself upside the head. What the hell had gotten into her, to worry about what people thought of her? She didn't want to look like that woman, no matter how stunning she was, no matter what kind of man she attracted.

And she didn't want a man like that. He was too handsome, too elegant, too self-assured, and worse than that, there was a burning intensity behind those dark brown eyes that made her even more uncomfortable.

When she dated she preferred ordinary mortals, men who were slightly offbeat. She liked normal men, people you bumped into at the Laundromat, slightly awkward, slightly rumpled, though she couldn't stand academics, most of whom had the morals of an alley cat. A life in academia, following her parents' example, was not particularly conducive to romance if her fellow professors made her skin crawl, but Evangeline was fine on her own most of the time. She considered the fact that she even enjoyed sex to be a major triumph, and she no longer had anything left to prove.

But this man was something else. Maybe she'd been alone too long: one look at that decidedly dangerous man and she'd practically swooned at his feet. She wasn't sure why she thought he was dangerous—the only likely danger was to her heart. No, he wouldn't even get that far. Maybe he was simply a danger to her self-esteem. Whatever the problem, she didn't want to get any closer.

She approached the altar first, remembering at the last moment to do that sort of dip she'd seen others do, and then turned back. When her parents had bothered to take her and her sister to church at all, it had been to the local Unitarian church, and she wasn't that familiar with the arcane rituals each faith demanded, though she did her best.

She thought she heard the sound of a car, and some of the tension left her. They were gone. She needed to start back to town if she was going to make it to her hotel in time for dinner, and she was famished. Turning, she started back down the aisle, pausing to look at the man still bent in prayer. She hid her smile—he'd probably fallen asleep as she had. Sooner or later he'd wake up and drive himself home in one of those cars—the Bentley, she guessed. It was logical to assume he would be returning to the hotel; maybe if she asked him, he would give her a ride down. But who knew how long the old man might doze, and he might not be planning to return at all, but continue up over the hills.

She wrinkled her nose. There was an odd, almost sewage-like smell in the air. There was no plumbing up here, just an open well, and someone must have used the place for an emergency bathroom.

She shrugged. These things happened—she only hoped the priest was alert enough to notice and get whoever looked after the place to clean. But it wasn't her concern.

She turned back to the entrance of the church and halted. Someone was standing there, silhouetted by the bright sun. A man, and while she could hope it was a priest she knew fate wasn't with her. All right, she could handle it. Handsome men usually had very little brains, and she could outthink almost anyone. She kept walking toward him.

James Bishop watched the girl move toward him, wishing he still smoked. She'd obviously been clambering around the hills all day, and she was a dusty, dirt-streaked mess. She'd clean up well—he had an eye for such things—and she moved well. In fact, if this were simply a cover, then she'd done a good job with it. She could almost convince him, if he could afford to be convinced.

He couldn't. Claudia had been very clear.

"I don't care if she saw us kill Corsini or not, she saw us. When the news gets out that someone was garroted in the old church, she'll remember seeing us there."

He'd shrugged. "What does it matter? We'll be long gone, and we'll look completely different. No one will connect either of us with the hit—we've made sure of it. We just go ahead as we'd planned— spend the night in town and then move on. She's no danger to us."

"Since when have you become so sentimental? She's a liability, and I'm not about to endanger myself because you're feeling sentimental."

"Our orders concerning collateral damage have changed and you know it. We don't need to add to the body count," he'd said irritably. He'd had no choice but to kill Corsini's chauffeur—the man had tried to cut his throat—but he still had blood on his hands, and he was feeling like god-damned Lady Macbeth. There was only so much Claudia's perfumed wipes could remove, and even he couldn't bring himself to rinse his hands in the font of holy water at the entrance to the church. Too much of his ancient Catholic upbringing coming back to haunt him, he thought.

"Changed for the worse," Claudia had snapped. "I don't care how squeamish Peter Madsen is, I'm not going to feel comfortable until she's disposed of. If you're too much of a pussy to do it, I will."

Bishop had kept his temper under control. "I'll check her out. If I think she's a problem, I'll take care of it," he'd said shortly.

"She's a problem."

"That's for me to decide."

"No, it isn't. Cut her throat, dump her with the chauffeur, and then get your ass back down to the town."

He'd given her the silky smile that always pissed her off. "And what makes you think you're in charge here, Claudia? You're the operative, I'm the handler. You took care of the old man, but I'm overseeing the operation. I make the decision—you live with it."

Claudia had snarled at him before taking off in the Lexus, peeling out of the parking space and tearing down the hill at suicidal speeds. He'd watched her go for a moment. It would make things a lot simpler if she simply took one corner too fast. She was unstable, and that was always a concern. Sooner or later Madsen was going to have to do something about her, but that wasn't his problem. He was just going to have to put up with her bad temper back at the hotel.

Which was the least of his worries. If he had to silence this particular witness he was going to be in a thoroughly rotten mood himself.

She had stopped and looked at Corsini, and he wondered if she could see anything. She didn't look perturbed, just continued down the aisle toward him, and for a crazy moment he thought of a bride walking to meet her groom. Some bride, he thought, the trace of a smile tugging at his mouth. She looked as if she'd been rolling in dust, she had scrapes on her long legs, and her hair beneath the bandanna was a mess.

She finally reached him, and if there was a slight hesitation in her step only he would have noticed. She looked him in the eye, plastered a totally fake smile on her face, the same one she'd given them before, and greeted him as she had before, in American-accented Italian, though this time with a hint of a question in her greeting.

He answered in the same language, with a better accent. "Good afternoon, signorina. It's a very fine church, isn't it?"

She was definitely nervous, looking up at him uneasily despite her friendly smile, but that could be simply because she was alone in a deserted place with an unknown man. For Claudia that would be enough to blow her head off. He wasn't as trigger-happy. "Very fine," she agreed. "I've been studying it."

"You are a student?" He was stringing out this inconsequential conversation while he covertly watched her. She was looking at him as if he were a murderer, he thought resignedly. He was going to have to kill her after all.

"Sort of," she answered, and he wondered why she was prevaricating. It raised his suspicions. "If you'll excuse me, signor, I have to get back to town . . ."

"You're American, aren't you?" he said suddenly in English. Maybe he could get a better sense of her in her own language.

She looked startled. "Y . . . yes. And you?"

"From Connecticut," he lied, but an East Coast polish went better with his current incarnation. He was actually from the endless winters of Wyoming, from miles and miles of emptiness and spiky mountains and bone-deep cold. "What is your area of interest?"

She clearly wasn't in the mood for idle conversation. She seemed anxious to get away from him, and that might have sealed her fate. "Medieval clerical architecture," she admitted finally. "With an emphasis on walled towns. And now I really need . . ."

"You picked a good town for it then," he said, cutting off her excuse to leave. "I haven't been back home for a number of years, but unless things have changed drastically I wouldn't think there'd be a whole lot of jobs in that area."

"I teach college. I already have my degree, I'm just working on a project." She seemed to struggle with the words, and he wondered what she really wanted to say. What was she covering up?

"You're an academic?" he said, and she winced.

"I suppose so," she said reluctantly. "Excuse me, but I really need to go." She was already edging away, and he kept himself from reaching for her. If she ran he could catch her. That, or bury a bullet in the back of her brain with the same amount of care it took him to tie his shoes.

"Do you have a car?" he asked, stalling her as she turned to leave.

She blinked those gorgeous green eyes of hers. They were startling—a clear emerald color that had to be from contacts, just as his own eye color was.

She was looking at him warily, filled with distrust. Shit.

"I don't need a car."

"Look, I'm driving down into Cabrisi. You must be staying there—it's the only town in the area, and you're on foot. Let me give you a ride. Trust me, I'm perfectly harmless." He held up both hands in a surrendering gesture.

"I don't think . . ."

"Look, I saw you here, and I don't like to leave a single woman alone up in these hills with no protection. Not when it's getting dark." He gave her his patented engaging grin. "For all I know you're some kind of super-spy, with epic martial arts skills and lethal weapons all over you. But in case you're not, I just thought I should hang around and offer you a ride."

She was judging him, he thought, looking at him as if trying to decide whether he was as harmless as he appeared. When she said nothing, he simply shrugged. "It's no skin off my ass," he continued. "I'm trying to be the good guy here. I know, I'm a stranger—you have no reason to trust me, but I'm not about to hurt you. Just give you a ride into town before the storm hits."

She jerked her gaze to the sky, and he knew she hadn't even noticed the storm clouds swirling down on the Tuscan hills. "I wondered why it had grown so dark this early," she said inconsequentially. And then she met his gaze, and her doubt and distrust had vanished. "I was going to ask Signor Corsini for a ride when he finished his prayers but I think he's fallen asleep."

He froze, all sentimental weakness vanishing. If she was connected to their recent hit then he'd have no choice. "Signor Corsini?" he echoed. The less he said, the more she'd have to come up with. It was an old trick, but an effective one.

"The old man who's praying. He's staying at the same hotel I am. I see him at dinner. He's very sweet."

She was staying at the Villa Ragarra, the same hotel they were using. That made things both easier and harder. Easier if she really was a liability and he had to dispose of her. Easier for him to find out what she knew if they were staying beneath the same roof, harder to keep Claudia from going after her. Claudia liked to kill.

"At that age he's probably got a lot to answer for," he said easily. "I wouldn't count on him being ready before the storm hits, and maybe he needs to atone while he drives down the hill. He's probably got any number of Hail Marys to make."

She gave him a look then, her head tilted questioningly, and he laughed. "Recovering Catholic," he said lightly. "I was a close acquaintance with repentance when I was a kid."

She nodded, believing it. It was nothing more than the truth. "Good point," she said finally, then glanced at the threatening sky. She took a deep breath. "I'd appreciate a ride."

So far so good, he thought. She hadn't made a fuss over her friend Corsini—she hadn't noticed anything odd. She was also willing, albeit grudgingly, to accept a ride from him down into town. If she knew the old man was dead, he would be an obvious suspect and she would never get in his car.

She still might bolt, but he knew people, women in particular, and he could tell when her uneasiness began to fade. Either that, or she was a first-rate actress, and he doubted that. He pointed to the Fiat Claudia had left for him. "I'm afraid that's all I've got to offer, but it works." He walked over and opened the passenger door, waiting for her, every sense alert. If she suspected something now would be her time to run for it.

She barely hesitated, stripping off her knapsack before slipping into the front seat, looking up at him questioningly. He closed the door, very gently, and moved around to the other side. She was already fiddling with the seat belt.

"You can put your knapsack in the back," he suggested, starting the car. It looked like the classic European rental, solid, reliable, and boring. This one had a lot more under the hood than anyone would ever suspect, and he could give Claudia's Lexus a run for the money, but the girl was unlikely to notice.

"I'll hold it, thank you," she said politely.

He nodded, putting the car into gear, and then they were off down the twisting roads that led to Cabrisi at relatively sedate speeds. She was staring out at the countryside as they sped past, doing her best to ignore him, which gave him the luxury of watching her. She had a good profile—sweet lips, a firm chin, a high forehead, and gorgeous eyes. She really was darling, and he idly considered what he'd like to do with her, exactly where he'd kiss her, which way he'd move. He'd like to drive the shy wariness from those wonderful eyes; he wanted her screaming beneath him as she came. He'd taken one look at her in the front hall of the old church and wanted her, and the more innocent she was appearing, the more he was allowing himself to fantasize.

He was getting hard, and that wasn't a good idea, so he tore his mind away from her dusty, gorgeous legs and concentrated on the road. The Fiat could handle these twisty turns even better than the Lexus, and on impulse he let the car loose, just a bit, taking the next curve at a speed that would have caused a normal person to blanch.

The woman beside him didn't. She watched the countryside whiz past, and her eyes were shining, her breath coming faster. But her hands had let go of the knapsack and grabbed the cloth seat, her knuckles white, and there was no disputing that she was both terrified and exhilarated by his driving.

He immediately slowed the car. "I'm sorry," he said. "I'm afraid I drive a little too fast for most people's comfort. It comes from living in Rome for years." He'd never spent more than a week in Rome at one time, but it made for a good explanation for his excellent Italian, which he was sure she'd noticed. She was the kind of woman who noticed things.

She turned to look at him, giving him a wry smile. "I'm sorry. I'm a bit of a chickenshit. Though I have to admit it was fun."

"When you weren't terrified for your life?" he suggested.

"There's that," she agreed. "By the way, my name's Evangeline Morrissey."

"James Bishop," he replied, reaching out to shake her hand. Now what in the hell had prompted him to give her his real name? He really must be off his game.

It didn't matter. He was going to disappear as soon as he was certain she wasn't a problem. Claudia wasn't one for accepting his gut feelings anymore, but if he could just keep the girl safe until Claudia left then he wouldn't have to worry. The ancient Romans might have been into sacrificing stray lambs—he wasn't.

"Evangeline," he murmured. "That's very pretty. What do people call you? Vangie?"

She shuddered. "God, no. They call me 'professor.'"

He raised an eyebrow. "You want me to call you 'professor'?"

"No, of course not. Evangeline will do."

He smiled at her, and he watched her melt a little bit. He'd perfected that smile, that look, and it worked on everyone, male and female. "In that case, Evangeline, will you have dinner with me tonight?"

She'd just been beginning to relax, but those words made her tense up once more. Why? "I don't think that's a good idea," she said.

"Why not? We both have to eat, and there are only two decent restaurants in town. We've got a fifty-fifty chance of ending up at the same place. Why don't we just plan to eat together?"

"What about the woman who was with you?"

She'd been observant. She'd only seen Claudia for a minute, but he had no doubt she'd be able to describe her perfectly. She was a detail-oriented academic. A liability, Claudia would say.

Not if he could help it.

"Claudia is a business associate, nothing more. She already has plans for dinner, and I don't." He smiled at her, and her eyes widened at the force of his full frontal assault. No woman could withstand him when he was being charming. An insecure professor from the States would be child's play.

"No," she said. "It's not a good idea."

Bishop stared at her, momentarily silenced. He could get past this, call in a few favors once they got back to town. It would be easy enough to find out where she was, bump into her. He knew women well enough to know she was reluctantly attracted to him. But why the reluctance? He glanced at her hands. No wedding ring, no engagement ring, so it couldn't be that.

"Are you involved with someone and think it would be cheating? I promise, I'm only talking about dinner."

She hesitated, and he homed in on the weakness. "Come on, Evangeline. I hate to eat alone, and it's been so long since I've talked to another American."

She was no longer clutching the seat now that he was driving more sedately, but her fingers were playing nervously with the cord on her knapsack. For a moment he let his imagination go. She could be something far from what she appeared—Corsini usually traveled with a bodyguard as well as a chauffeur. Maybe she had a gun in that harmless-looking bag.

No, if she was a bodyguard then she was a piss-poor one, and she hadn't even checked to see if her employer was sleeping or dead. She would have shot him and taken the car, or at least she would have tried. He was becoming as paranoid as Claudia.

"Okay," she said finally. "It's just that I usually work in the evenings. Transcribe my notes, that sort of thing."

"I won't keep you out too late, I promise you," he said. They were approaching town. "Where are you staying?" She'd already given that away, but he had to appear oblivious.

"Villa Ragarra."

"Perfect. So am I."

"Oh." She didn't sound particularly happy about it. He couldn't dismiss her as harmless until he figured out her reluctance. He had no illusions—he could seduce a mother abbess if he put his mind to it, and Ms. Evangeline Morrissey was acting as skittish as a virgin. Which she wasn't—he was pretty sure of that much, though he suspected she hadn't had a great deal of experience. Made his job a whole lot easier—he wouldn't have to put himself out to show her a good time.

So he simply smiled at her, knowing the smile never reached his eyes, knowing that no one ever noticed that it didn't. "Very convenient," he murmured. "When you get bored with me you can just walk away."

As if she'd get bored with him, Evangeline thought. That was exactly the problem—he was too mesmerizing. His smile never reached those unreadable eyes—for all his abundant charm, there was something else, something dark, coiled and waiting behind that flattering gaze, and if she had half the brains her brilliant parents had bequeathed her, she would run far and fast.

But . . . there was no reason he should be a danger to her, not unless she made the mistake of thinking all that charm meant something. There was no reason she couldn't enjoy a meal with someone, no reason she couldn't even go to bed with him if she wanted. She prided herself on being a healthy, normal young woman, despite . . . everything . . . and she and Lester had broken up nine months ago. That was a long dry period, but not unusual for her. She was usually too focused on her research and her career to worry about dating. If someone appeared, fine. If someone didn't, more time to concentrate on work.

James Bishop had appeared, and he seemed to be interested in her. Unless his simple words had been the truth—that he'd just been longing to speak to another American. Because she found him incredibly attractive didn't mean the feeling was mutual. She suspected he was that flirtatious and charming with every single female he met, old and young.

He pulled up in front of Villa Ragarra, an expensive little hotel that Evangeline could ill afford, but where she'd stayed every year she'd come to Italy. It was her one indulgence, and she knew Silvio, the concierge and half-owner, would look after her.

"Shall we eat here?" James Bishop said, looking at her. "Say, nine o'clock? Or would you like to eat earlier?"

"Nine's perfect," she said, gathering her knapsack and opening the door. "I'll see you then." She didn't care if it looked as if she were running away. She was. He was overpowering, particularly in the confines of that boring Fiat, which wasn't boring after all. In an open room his effect on her might not be so potent.

She disappeared into the cool darkness of the hotel before he could say anything, breathing a sigh of relief. She had no idea what time it was—sometime after five, she suspected, but that gave her plenty of time to make up her mind, to come up with an excuse if need be. That, or put things in perspective and enjoy a meal with a handsome man. Surely there was nothing so risky in that?

But she couldn't rid herself of the feeling it was exactly that. Risky, dangerous, and the smartest thing she could do would be to run away. She could do it, too. There was a late-night bus to the next town, where she could sleep in the youth hostel. He'd never find her there.

What the hell was wrong with her? She'd been reading too many thrillers. He was simply a handsome man who was bored, and she was available, at least for conversation. She needed a nice hot shower and a rest and everything would fall into place.

Chapter Two

"Did you kill her?" Claudia was stretched out on the chaise longue, her slender ankles crossed, her solid gold ankle bracelet glinting in the late-afternoon sun. She was filing her already perfect nails, and she barely looked up at him, her question desultory.

He was tempted to lie to her, but it wouldn't take much for her to catch him in it, and there was no reason for him to bother. "I'm having dinner with her tonight," he said, stripping off his shirt.

Claudia looked at his bared torso with all the interest of a snake handler. They'd worked together for so long that dressing and undressing in front of each other meant absolutely nothing, though in her Claudia-mode she tended to be a bit more modest. "Why? You could have dumped her with the chauffeur and the *carabinieri* would just think it was an organized crime hit with an unfortunate witness."

"Which is nothing more than the truth," Bishop snapped. "As far as I can tell she noticed nothing out of the ordinary. I'm having dinner with her to make absolutely certain, and then we can move on without worrying about it."

"Killing her would be more efficient," Claudia pointed out, her eyes narrowing. Claudia was like a terrier with a dead rat—she never let go.

"In the short run, maybe. In the long run—who knows? No one likes unnecessary bodies complicating things, least of all the Committee, now that Peter Madsen is in charge."

Claudia shrugged, unconcerned. "The Committee doesn't like witnesses complicating things either. No one's supposed to know the organization even exists. I'd choose dead bodies as the lesser of two evils."

She didn't even realize the absurdity of that statement. Would he ever get so jaded, so lost that he'd feel the same way? That human life would hold no value at all, except as a means to an end? He was halfway there already.

"If I'm convinced she saw something, anything, I'll kill her, quietly and efficiently, after we have dinner," he said grimly.

"Before or after you fuck her?" she taunted. "You think I didn't see the way you looked at her? I know you better than you think."

He ignored her, heading into the shower. He was going to do everything he could to keep this one alive. If for nothing else, for the sake of all the ones who had gone before. And for her gorgeous green eyes.

———

Evangeline's tiny room on the third floor was sweltering, and she turned on the noisy fan Silvio had brought her. When the storm finally hit, the heat might disperse, at least a little bit, but until then she was sticky and tired. She couldn't afford the air-conditioned second- and first-floor rooms, and she liked the view up here. She was so tired that all she wanted to do was collapse on the snowy white bedspread. She'd probably leave her outline in dust, she thought, and sank into the small chair beside the window as she tried to pull herself together. She must have gotten a touch of sunstroke. Once away from that man's mesmerizing presence, she was having second thoughts. Granted, he was gorgeous, but she'd seen pretty men before, and good looks were of little importance to her. She considered herself a woman who looked for character rather than beauty, though his particular beauty had temporarily distracted her. She needed to sleep, she needed to shower, she needed to curl up into an embarrassed little ball like a hedgehog, not that hedgehogs got embarrassed, she thought dazedly. Maybe she'd just slip down on the rug and sleep there.

She had to come up with some excuse about dinner. It wouldn't be the first meal she'd missed in her life, and once she managed to talk herself into a shower she'd probably be so exhausted she'd sleep through the night anyway. It didn't matter that she was starving. Thinking she might indulge in a one-night stand was all well and good, but she knew that was the last thing she'd ever do. It took her a lot to decide to go to bed with someone, and those rare decisions were usually fueled by weeks of worry and a generous amount of alcohol. She had no intention of drinking, and even then it took her weeks to get comfortable in bed with someone. No, she was definitely not having dinner with Mr. Tall, Dark, and Irresistible.

It was a plan. She pushed herself up from the low-slung chair, grabbed her wrapper and the thin towels the villa supplied, and headed for the shower room two doors down. She didn't dare take a bath—she'd probably fall asleep and drown. A nice hot shower and she'd simply call Silvio to leave a message for her unexpected Romeo, and then go to bed and forget all about him.

There was no one in the hallway, and chances were he and his partner were on the first or second floor, with the ensuite bathrooms and the reliable air-conditioning. He looked like a man who went first class all the way.

The shower room was empty, and she breathed a sigh of relief as she locked the door behind her and began to strip off her dusty clothes, tossing them on the floor beneath the shower spray for her own particular variation on a laundry. She bathed quickly and efficiently, dried herself, and wrapped her robe around her. That particular purchase had been a mistake—she'd bought it because it was lightweight, but it was a little too flimsy to wander hotel corridors in. She had even looked into replacing it, but everything was too expensive, and the thing wasn't that indecent. She unlocked the door and peered out; the hallway was still deserted, and she dashed back to her room, her wet clothes in her arms.

The bed looked so inviting she wanted to weep—her legs were on their last ounce of strength and her head was pounding, but she still had to drape her clothes over the small Juliet balcony so that they'd get the last of the day's heat. Her window faced an alley and she leaned forward past the old fan to catch a glimpse of the hills beyond. She smiled briefly, taking in a deep breath of the soft night air. It smelled of olive groves and flowers and the distant storm, and she knew she'd remember that smell when she was ancient. She loved it here so much. Somehow she'd find a way to return, even on an untenured professor's salary.

When she turned, heading for the bed, she saw the tall green bottle in the ice bucket and frowned. What was a bottle of wine doing in her room? But when she drew closer she saw it was bottled water, and she reached for it, too damned thirsty to question its presence or even to look for a glass, twisting the cap and pouring a good long swallow down her throat.

It was bliss. It had to have been delivered by mistake, and it didn't even matter if she were charged Silvio's exorbitant prices for it. It was worth every drop.

She saw the card a moment later. *Compliments of James Bishop.* She wondered if she should spit the water out. *The hell with that.* She took another long slug. Even if the man made her wary, this was simply a thoughtful gesture and nothing more, and she wanted this water.

She sat on the narrow bed. If she fell asleep without doing something to her hair she'd wake looking like a crazy woman. She quickly braided it, stripped off the damp wrapper and lay down on the bed, letting the fan-driven hot breeze blow over her body. A moment later she was asleep.

She woke in deep shadows and fumbled for the tiny alarm clock she travelled with. Eight thirty. Half an hour to the dinner she'd forgotten to cancel. Half an hour to dinner and she was absolutely starving.

She pushed herself to a sitting position, blinking owlishly. She'd slept hard and deep, dreamless, and it took her only a moment to bounce back into full wakefulness. Her headache was gone, she was clean and rested, and she felt like an absolute fool. What was wrong with her? A gorgeous man wanted to take her to dinner and all she could do was wonder what hidden agenda lay beneath that gorgeous face. When in the world had she become so paranoid?

Well, for one thing she wasn't usually the object of the attentions of gorgeous men. A man like that could have anyone he wanted, and there was no lack of gorgeous women in the mountain town of Cabrisi. Why would he want her?

She was being ridiculous. He didn't *want* want her; he just wanted company for dinner. And for that matter, so did she.

She dressed for dinner when she was in Italy, except when she stayed in youth hostels. At home she'd eat a bowl of cereal in front of the television, but here she followed the custom and enjoyed it. She had one dress, a black wash-and-wear slip of a dress that skimmed her knees, and a pair of flat black shoes that were almost weightless. She unfastened the braid but her hair was still damp, and she did her best to comb it into submission, using barrettes to tame it before checking her diamond studs to make sure they were secure. They were so large they looked fake, which was just what she counted on. What would a penniless researcher be doing wandering around Europe with diamonds like those in her ears?

A penniless researcher who had an older sister with sticky fingers who'd always coveted the diamonds. The earrings had been a gift from her elderly aunt Evangeline, who clearly thought she deserved some compensation for being saddled with such a ridiculous name, but even the inherited diamonds didn't make up for her parents' idiotic choice of a name.

She glanced at herself in the mirror. The freckles were out in full force—a spattering of gold flecks from the bright Italian sun, and she'd developed a tan on her strong arms and legs. Her reddish-brown hair seemed relatively subdued, and at the last minute she grabbed the little bag that held her makeup and applied swiftly drawn lines around her eyes, followed by a couple of sweeps of mascara. It was light enough that no one would even notice. Then she gave in and pulled out the one lipstick she carried, a soft pink that was more a stain than anything else. She pulled back to look at herself. That was the best she could do, and it would have to be enough.

Enough for whom? She wasn't going to primp for Mr. Bishop. She looked for a washcloth, ready to wash the betraying makeup off her face, when she heard the muffled gong of the dinner bell. She was being an idiot, on every level. She was dressed, presentable, and hungry, and why she'd put on makeup was unimportant. Sometimes she just felt like dressing up. Tonight was one of those nights. She grabbed her featherweight shawl and left the room, ready to face the beautiful monster she'd created in her head and put him in perspective.

⌣

A slow cat-like smile curved Claudia's mouth as she watched from the barely opened door across the hallway. The girl hadn't even bothered to lock her room. Silly thing. She might think she'd left nothing of value in there, but Claudia knew better. Secrets, the information was far more valuable than iPods and credit cards, and could never be completely covered up. Let James play his little games with the creature—if it amused him she didn't care. As long as he fulfilled his part of the plan, nothing else mattered.

Ah, but it did matter. James needed to remember why he was here, as an adjunct to someone who knew him as well as anyone. Which wasn't much—James kept his secrets as did she, and he wasn't about to cozy up to her and confess all. That thought was horrible. For now she simply took him at his word.

Not that she cared. He could just as easily have been sent as the active agent, with her as backup, but the sad fact was he lacked her total ruthlessness. He let ridiculous things bother him, like compassion, and mercy, and forgiveness. Those things were weaknesses, and it was little wonder she'd been put in charge of this job. He might have seen Corsini with a child and suddenly decided he deserved to live.

As for Claudia, she didn't know why they had been charged with getting rid of Corsini, and she didn't care. The Corsini family was involved in a dozen illegal operations, from drug smuggling to sex trafficking, but the old man was simply an accountant, an important cog in the machine, but not the *capo dei capi*. The organization that she and James served, ingenuously called the Committee, believed in compartmentalizing information. Things worked better that way. James held one piece of the puzzle, she held another. Solving puzzles was a game for children. As long as she could use her skills and ply her trade, the rest was for other people to work out. She was a weapon. All they had to do was point her.

The Committee provided her with an outlet for her complicated desires. A covert, multinational organization centered in London, it ostensibly sought to stamp out terrorism and international crime in ruthless ways no public organization could ever get away with, supposedly making the world safe. Claudia didn't give a damn about politics, and she knew the world would never be safe. She preferred it that way.

She waited until the hall was empty. James had already baited his trap, and no one would be up here roaming the corridors. No one would see if she slipped into the girl's room. She might not care about the people she was sent to kill, but those she chose on her own were different. Besides, she might have to answer to Madsen if it were traced back to her, and it always helped to know a little bit about her self-appointed victims. She might need a plausible excuse, and target practice wouldn't do.

⸻

Evangeline was the last person down for dinner, late as usual, and she liked it that way. Most of the evening crowd was already seated, busy in conversation with dinner partners, and there was no sign of James Bishop. If he stood her up she'd be overjoyed, she told herself.

She glanced at the restaurant in the atrium of the small hotel. It was a Saturday night and the place was jammed—it was one of the best places to eat in Cabrisi and they took in guests from the various B and Bs in the town, even stealing diners from the Americanized hotel in the business district. There were a number of couples who were unfamiliar to her, and then the usuals. The American couple was on a trip to celebrate their retirement, and they held hands, so she assumed it was a second marriage. No one held hands after ten years. In fact, she couldn't imagine her cool, practical parents getting close enough to each other to spawn two children, but in fact they had. The physical resemblances were indisputable, even though as a child she'd often daydreamed that she was adopted.

The two British matrons were arguing, as they always did, in their crisp, bird-like tones. They wore tweed skirts, twinsets, and sensible shoes, and she imagined the British matrons, or spinsters, or whatever they were considered, had worn the same uniform for the last eighty years. They tended to fight about money—one of them was frugal, the other a spendthrift—and she wondered if they were lovers. She hoped so. They certainly treated each other with the air of long-term partners. Though they didn't hold hands.

The Italian couple from Rome looked amorous, and the elderly scholar who had little use for a mere researcher sat in his corner, reading. Was that what she'd be like in ten, twenty years? There was no sign of Mr. Corsini, which surprised her. The Italian gentleman liked his food and his company, and he usually occupied the seat of honor for the entire duration of the evening meals, from seven until close to midnight, or possibly later, but after then Evangeline had sought her bed. He had kind eyes, and he always treated her in a most decorous manner. She liked him, and she hoped he wasn't still asleep up in the mountainside church. Maybe he'd moved on after all—it was a good thing she hadn't waited for him. And in the end she'd had no reason to be nervous about accepting a ride from James Bishop, thinking he might make a pass at her. In fact, he'd stood her up.

At least she wouldn't have to worry about making small talk with a gorgeous man. She was absolutely relieved . . .

"You do clean up well, Miss Morrissey," came a low, liquid voice in her ear. "Clearly it was worth the wait."

So why was her heart leaping instead of sinking in disappointment? She wasn't going to think about it. She turned to face her dinner partner. "Are you chiding me for being late?" she asked him point-blank.

He smiled down at her, those dark eyes enigmatic. "Never. A beautiful woman is always worth waiting for."

"But the plain ones better be on time?"

He laughed. "In fact, Evangeline," his voice caressed her name, and she felt an odd little ripple inside, "I find all women beautiful. I don't discriminate."

"That busy, are you?" she said caustically.

His forehead wrinkled, that high, perfect forehead. "Why so combative? Have I done something wrong?"

She was being an idiot. "No, of course not. I'm just tired and hungry and crabby."

"I can take care of that."

She raised her eyebrows. "What, all three?"

"Well, at least two of them," he said.

The dining room was packed, the noise level high, which would help with having to make conversation. She wondered idly where they were going to squeeze in.

"Everything set?" Bishop said when Silvio arrived, his usually perfectly pomaded hair slightly awry.

"Of course. This way, signore and signorina," he murmured, moving away from the noisy dining room.

Evangeline immediately froze. Did Bishop think she was stupid enough to agree to dinner in his room this soon after meeting him? Whether she trusted him or not, whether she had an instant, reluctant, incredibly potent attraction to him, she wasn't going to . . .

But Silvio was leading them away from the stairs, and she felt at least the first few layers of icy distrust melt. She had layers inside her that would take one of those things that drilled into the arctic core to get past, but she wasn't worried. She was like a hedgehog— too much trouble to get to and not worth the effort.

She'd forgotten that the terraces on either side of the dining room could be set up as well. There was only one table there, set for two, candlelit and romantic, the smaller of the two fountains splashing behind it.

Silvio had already pulled out her chair, and she had only an instant of hesitation before she sank into it gracefully, fumbling with the heavy linen napkin Silvio draped across her lap. "This is lovely," she said, hiding her doubts. "The water you sent up was very kind as well."

"As well as what? I'm glad that you liked the water, but I wasn't aware I had done anything for you." He took his seat.

"Mr. Bishop," she began.

"Please. James. It's been a while since I've talked with a fellow American and I miss our informality. Relax, Evangeline. It's only dinner. Two strangers in a strange land, sharing a public meal. There's nothing to be nervous about."

"I'm not nervous," she said, a lie that fooled neither of them. "I'm just not used to small talk."

"Then we can dispense with small talk. Tell me about your work instead."

"You wouldn't be interested," she said, reaching for the glass of yellow liquid. Limoncello, her favorite.

He noticed her surprise, but then, she had the impression he was a man who noticed everything. "Silvio told me about the Limoncello," he said, answering her unspoken question. "Why do you keep looking at me like I'm Jack the Ripper?"

That finally made her laugh. "Hardly. But this is the third year I've spent a month travelling around Italy on my own, and I've learned that it only makes sense to be cautious."

"Is that caution I see in those gorgeous green eyes of yours? Or acute paranoia?"

She squirmed. "I'd look a lot less paranoid if you stopped trying to shower flowery compliments on me."

"Saying you have gorgeous green eyes is hardly overdone. Now if I said you had eyes the color of the heart of jade, now that would be flowery." She made a face, and he laughed. "I tell you what. I'll let you do the talking, and I won't say anything nice at all, I promise. Tell me where you come from, what you love, why the hell you picked medieval clerical architecture, in particular walled towns, to devote your life to. Tell me who your best friend is, whether you hate spiders, why you love Italy, who gave you your first kiss. I'll just listen. It's been so long since I've heard an American accent."

She looked at him. "There are tons of Americans overseas. You must hear it more often than you think."

"Then it's your accent I like. Pacific Northwest, I'm guessing."

Now that was unnerving. "I don't have an accent."

"Of course you don't," he said soothingly. "People in the US don't think they do. I like regional accents—I can usually tell where someone came from, if not the actual state. And in some cases, like Texas or Massachusetts, it's easy enough to even place what part of the state that person comes from. For the Pacific Northwest accent, it's a bit of Scandinavian with a touch of Venice, and I'm talking California, not the gorgeous city to the north of us. Which I hope you're going to see on this trip. There are obviously no walls, but lots of medieval architecture."

He was probing so delicately, and she wasn't sure whether it was wise to tell him her itinerary. "Depends how much time I have," she said carefully. "Venice has been overdone. And I grew up in Port Townsend, Washington."

"One can never have too much of Venezia." He leaned back, a faintly ironic smile on his mouth. The mouth she kept glancing at and then jerking her gaze away. He really was something else, she thought, momentarily distracted, dreamy. If he really put his mind to it he might be almost impossible to resist.

Except he wasn't going to put his mind to it. This was simply to ease his boredom, listen to an American accent, and maybe even make a desultory attempt to get her in bed, but it wouldn't really matter. She was used to men like him, though she seldom spent time in their company. Now she was glad she hadn't.

Because he unnerved her, seducing her when he probably didn't even realize it. Despite the emptiness in his dark, dark eyes, he had the most devastating smile, a soft, drawling voice that made her want to curl up inside it, a mouth so luscious it didn't bear thinking about. Maybe she should just give in, assuming he did make a pass at her, which was still up in the air. It wasn't as if she were frigid, or a prude. She'd had enough therapy to get past any lingering . . . issues, and her sexual relationships had been satisfactory. She knew the rudiments of self-defense if he got kinky, and besides, she'd read *Fifty Shades of Grey* with horrified fascination. It might be interesting . . . no!

"What in heaven's name are you thinking about now?" Bishop demanded good-naturedly. "You do tend to wander off when I'm talking to you. I never realized how boring I am."

She met his gaze, that dangerous, ironic gaze. He was trying to unsettle her, surprise her. Well, two could play that game. She gave him a stern look. "You know perfectly well how seductive you are, and you don't hesitate to use it," she said flatly, "and don't pretend you don't. You reeled me in like I'm some poor salmon, gasping for air, and even if I struggle I'm still flapping around on the floor, fighting to survive."

He laughed. "Do you think you'll need mouth-to-mouth? I've never kissed a fish before."

Trumped again. She fumbled for her lemon drink. She didn't need to be thinking about kissing him. Thinking about how she wanted to kiss him. She raised her eyes again. "I'm not quite sure what game you're playing, but I should make it clear that I'm not the type who goes in for one-night stands or hops into bed with any man I happen to find attractive."

"You find me attractive? That's a step in the right direction," he said lightly, and she could still feel the intensity of his gaze. "So what kind of woman are you? What kind of man do you hop into bed with?"

This was getting entirely out of hand. Why had she used the word "seductive"? Why had he talked about kissing her? "I got my PhD when I was twenty," she announced abruptly.

He raised his eyebrows—dark, arched, almost satanic eyebrows. "A prodigy, then. So if you've already got your doctorate, why are you scrambling around Italian ruins on your own?" He took her change of subject with equanimity, and she breathed a small sight of relief.

"Publish or perish," she said. "Besides, how can I teach if I don't have firsthand knowledge of what I'm talking about?"

"One should always have firsthand knowledge," he said innocently. "Do you like teaching? Do you like your students?"

"I do," she said, surprising herself. "They can be pains in the ass, but every now and then you find one who's genuinely passionate about learning, and if I can find the right hook I can draw the slackers in as well."

She couldn't keep from staring at his mouth, and the smile that flitted across it was different than the others—it somehow seemed more honest. "I can imagine," he murmured. "So tell me how you do it."

It was an odd interlude—she knew he was drawing her out just as she did with her students, and yet she was helpless to resist. No, that wasn't true. She'd never been helpless in her life, not if she could do anything about it. But he smiled at her, spoke in that low, easy drawl, and she could feel all her caution and doubts melt away beneath his practiced charm. She found herself telling him things she'd never told anyone—her stage fright when it came to teaching, her perfect older sister, her remote parents. She told him about the beauty of the Pacific Northwest, a beauty she'd left for Massachusetts, where she was alternately freezing and roasting, and he listened, his eyes on her, his attention never straying, and she felt herself slipping, slipping, underneath his lazy, tempting charisma.

No one could be that seductive by accident—he had to have had lots of practice, and he was exerting everything he'd learned on her. She knew it, and even though she did, it worked. She was melting, and she slapped down that tiny warning voice inside. Other women did this, all the time, and she could count it as another milestone in her goal of putting the bad things of the past behind her. She was hardly a romantic—sex was a pleasurable, physical sensation, one that was much more enjoyable with a partner. She suspected he'd be a very good partner. He knew what she wanted to drink, he'd ordered for her, and he'd chosen perfectly. He was attuned to what she liked, what she wanted, picking up subtle cues, and he asked just the right questions, ones that had her telling him far too much, more than she'd ever told anyone. They say the real opposite of talking isn't listening, it is waiting. Waiting to get in your own two cents, your opinion, your experience. Not with James Bishop. He seemed content with listening to her, gently prodding to keep her talking.

Having sex with someone like that, someone so keyed in to her, could be quite extraordinary, she thought, gazing at his elegant, unreadable face. Maybe too extraordinary. She considered herself an ordinary young woman, a little stubborn, perhaps maybe even boring. She was too practical, too wary. She wasn't made for grand passion, for throwing caution and responsibility, and even duty, to the wind for the sake of a man. She'd worked hard to get where she was, and she had more hard work ahead of her that she couldn't afford to jeopardize, even for one night, especially one that could go disastrously wrong given how skittish she could be.

But this man might be worth it.

"Now what are you thinking about?" he said lazily, leaning back as he stirred his espresso. "You haven't said anything since they brought dessert." The tiny, perfect pastries sat between them, delectable, and she had the sudden thought that she'd rather lick him. Color flooded her face—she must have had too much to drink.

"Just what a lovely evening this has been," she said with a good stab at nonchalance. It failed, but she deserved credit for trying.

Once more he gave her that enchanting smile, the one that didn't meet his eyes. "You're looking nervous again. I thought you'd gotten over that."

"I'm not!" she protested. What would his hands feel like on her body? No one had touched her in almost a year, and Lester had been more enthusiastic than skilled. This man would be both.

Wouldn't she like to have just one time with someone who knew what he was doing? She could feel the color mount her face again, and she was ashamed of herself. Of course Lester and the others had known what they were doing, and she'd been fine, orgasmic, once she'd gotten over her initial fears. She'd just longed for something . . . more.

She suspected the man across from her was an expert at providing that elusive *more*, if it even existed. Except that he didn't seem to be making much of an effort to offer her more—his gently teasing manner, his flattery, was probably unconscious on his part. It was just what he did. She was sitting there in an absolute pool of irrational longing and he was leaning back in his chair, sipping his espresso and smiling, perfectly relaxed. She felt like a tightly wound violin string, ready to snap, and he didn't even seem to want her.

Which was a relief, she told herself. Depressing, demoralizing, but a relief. She wasn't up to dealing with someone like him. She preferred safety, reliability. And besides, he wasn't interested.

She realized another silence had fallen while he watched her, a speculative expression in his unreadable dark eyes. She laughed, just a little nervously. "I'm sorry," she said, taking a sip of her own cappuccino. For some reason he'd known she'd prefer it to espresso. "I'm drifting off again."

"You won't be drifting off with that coffee in your system," he pointed out pleasantly. "And it's early. I'd suggest we go for a walk but I think the storm is about to hit."

She hadn't been paying attention—not when there was something else so gorgeous to look at. She glanced overhead into the night sky. The stars were gone, hidden by the black, scudding clouds, and the poplar trees swayed in the breeze. She could feel the ozone in the air, the approach of the rain, and she wondered how long it had been like this, and whether he knew she'd been too mesmerized by him to pay attention to an imminent downpour.

Here they were, sitting out in the open, about to get soaked. "I'm sorry," she said. "I've been talking my head off and you've been wanting to get in out of the weather. I've kept you . . ."

"Why do you keep apologizing?" he said lazily, not moving from his relaxed position. "You haven't done anything wrong."

Yet, she thought. If she didn't get away from him she was going to make a complete and utter fool of herself. She couldn't tell whether he was sending her mixed signals or if she was looking for signs that didn't exist. Italian men flirted. European men flattered. James Bishop had lived here long enough that he would have picked up both habits.

"Sorry," she said, and then gave a little laugh, annoyed with herself. "It's a bad habit of mine."

"Sorry, sorry, sorry," he mimicked lightly. "Come to bed with me."

For a moment she thought she'd misheard him. "I beg your pardon?"

"I said come to bed with me," he said, still that lazy voice that signaled no strong interest at all. "I could teach you not to be sorry about anything."

The words hit her directly between her legs, an odd sensation. Words had never been that arousing in her life. Odd, because her few healthy relationships had been with fellow graduate students and academics, supposedly good with words.

She stared at him in shock, but at least her mouth wasn't agape in astonishment. That was about the only blessing. "You're kidding," she blurted, feeling utterly stupid.

"Oh, I never kid about sex. You're the most delicious creature I've seen or talked to in so long I can't remember, and I've wanted to fuck you since I saw you in that church, which was very unholy of me."

"But I . . ." Whatever she was going to say was lost, as the gorgeous woman who'd been by James's side that afternoon suddenly appeared, dropping down into one of the empty chairs as if she belonged there.

"We've got a problem," she said abruptly. And then, as if she suddenly realized she was intruding, she turned to Evangeline and gave her a dazzling smile. "Hello, there. I'm Claudia Facinelli, James's associate. You're the young woman we saw at the church earlier, aren't you?"

The woman had just the trace of an Italian accent, and her eyes were a bright metallic blue as she surveyed Evangeline. The glance was slow and assessing, but there was no identifiable judgment in it. It was just that she was so elegant in a lean, flat-chested, greyhound kind of way that Evangeline immediately felt plain and clumsy.

"Claudia, you're interrupting," James said, sounding bored. "Whatever it is, it can certainly wait until tomorrow morning." He made no effort to introduce her to his partner, and Evangeline wondered whether she should do it herself.

"I don't think so," the woman named Claudia said. "Apparently our recent efforts came to someone's attention, and repercussions are going to be very unpleasant unless we do something about it. *Now.*"

James didn't move, but Evangeline knew he'd tensed. "I'm sorry," she said, and then could have kicked herself for another stupid apology. "I'll let you two deal with business. Thank you for the lovely meal, James. I don't expect I'll see you again—I'm leaving early tomorrow morning for the north, probably long before you wake up. But I've had a lovely time, even though all I seemed to do was talk about myself. But maybe that was why I had such a good time," she added, knowing she was babbling. She pushed away from the table and at that James immediately rose as well. The woman stayed where she was.

"Claudia has a habit of exaggerating things," he said, unruffled, ignoring the fact that Claudia was watching the two of them quite closely. As if there was anything to see, Evangeline thought morosely. She shouldn't have had the second glass of wine at dinner, nor the liqueur before coffee. "I thought we might go for a walk before the storm hits . . ."

"I told you this had to be dealt with now," Claudia hissed. He didn't even glance at her, moving from behind the table to take Evangeline's elbow with a light touch that made her skin burn with longing. Damn it, what was wrong with her? She didn't like being touched by strangers, and yet the feel of his hand on her arm made her want to lean against him.

Claudia finally rose, putting herself directly between them, breaking their contact, and for a brief moment Evangeline wondered why the woman seemed so determined. Evangeline was hardly any kind of threat to James's associate. She was just a fellow American he'd taken pity on.

No, there had been no pity in his dark, mesmerizing eyes. She wasn't sure what she'd seen there, but whatever it was, it made her nervous. Had he meant it when he asked her to go to bed with him? He'd sounded almost casual about it, like he was suggesting an aperitif.

She slipped away from him quite easily. "The storm is coming," she said. "Thanks again." A moment later she was on her own.

Bishop watched Claudia out of narrowed eyes. "Was that really necessary?" he murmured. He wasn't about to let Claudia see how much she annoyed him. "I was making progress. I'm almost certain she saw nothing, suspects nothing, but as you said, we can't afford to leave any loose ends."

"She's already a loose end," Claudia snapped. "And Corsini's body has been discovered by a couple of hikers. Someone came tearing into town a few minutes ago, and all hell is about to break loose while you're busy trying to get into that girl's pants. Shoot her and get it done with, and then let's get the hell out of here."

"So we disappear in the middle of the night when a murder victim is found, and you think that will throw suspicion off us? You're being ridiculous. We have nothing to worry about—we were at business meetings all day. Our alibis are already set up and they're airtight."

"Airtight unless your American plaything decides to put two and two together, something she seems entirely capable of doing."

"So she's found dead, bringing attention to the guests at this hotel?" he suggested. Claudia hated to be thwarted, but he wasn't about to let her get her way this time.

"Don't be foolish—we'd move her. Or I would, if you're too squeamish to deal with it. I've never known you to be sentimental before, Bishop. Or has she got some kind of supernatural pussy that's got you hypnotized?"

"You overestimate my charms, darling Claudia," he purred. "I haven't gotten her in bed yet."

"Either you kill her or I will."

He gave her a long, measuring look. Claudia enjoyed killing, and she used every excuse she could think of to do it. She'd wanted Evangeline dead since she first saw her, and the more arguments he came up with, the more determined she was. In the end there would be very little he could do to stop her.

"I'll take care of her," he said in a flat voice, evading a direct answer. "In the meantime you need to go up to bed, take someone with you who can vouch for your presence, and I'll do the same. No one can trace us to the church but Evangeline, and the more skittish you act, the more suspicious we'll seem."

"I'm never skittish," Claudia said haughtily. "And I can't pick up just anyone. You know my tastes are . . . specialized."

"It's up to you. I'll take care of Evangeline and arrange my own night's entertainment. Find someone and spend the night talking to them if they aren't fuckable by your standards. I don't care."

Her face was like marble, hard, white, beautiful, with no emotion or life in it. "Do not, I repeat, do not make the mistake of lying to me, Bishop."

He smiled down at her lazily. "I lie to you all the time, my sweet. It comes with the territory." The wind had picked up, and waiters appeared, clearing the table as the empty wine glasses were tipped over. He cast a gaze at the roiling night sky. "Evangeline is right—there's a storm coming. Best take care."

He strolled away from her, relaxed, at ease, refusing to let Claudia know how she'd annoyed him. He headed for the winding stairs in the lobby. The restaurant was crowded now, people were coming in to escape the weather, and he took a cursory glance to see if there was someone he should take to bed. He hadn't ruled out Claudia's demands, and it was best she thought he was being practical, so he allowed his gaze to linger. There was a Nordic blonde with endless legs and an athletic body, a gorgeous black woman with fiery eyes, and an elegant older woman who could be an enticing possibility. All three were with groups, rather than one man, but even if they had partners for the night that would prove little obstacle. Turning, he was ready to continue up the stairs when he saw Claudia watching him with her cold eyes. If she was that determined to see Evangeline dead, then sooner or later she'd have her way. There was only so long he could protect the girl, and for what? For all he knew she was just as much of a liability as Claudia insisted she was, particularly once she heard about the dead man in the church. He ought to be practical. He wouldn't leave her to Claudia's tender mercies—she liked to inflict pain, whereas for him, killing was simply part of the business. He had no emotions regarding it, but then, he had no emotions anyway. He was wasting his time with Evangeline, when he had things to take care of.

Claudia didn't follow him up the winding stairs to the first floor. She didn't see him head up to the second, and then up, up into the steamy third floor of the old hotel with its ancient walls and the sighs of a thousand lovers lingering within them. The hotel wasn't full, and Evangeline was the only guest in the cheaper quarters on the third floor. Silvio never stinted on information, even when it involved another guest. A very practical man, Silvio was.

Bishop reached the top floor and proceeded to unfasten his tie, stripping it from his shirt. How did she stand it up here? It was like a steam bath. He heard the loud thumping of an old fan from one of the rooms—that would be hers. Anything that made noise was an advantage in his profession, but the windows in the hall and the ancient skylights overhead were open to the night breeze and the sounds below, and he knew from experience that Italian police sirens were very loud. She would hear them, and she would wonder. And she would ask.

Her door opened. She was barefoot but still dressed, and she had clothes and towels over her arm. She froze when she saw him.

He didn't move either. He had been working her all evening, knowing just what to say to put her at ease, the best way to throw off her equilibrium, and he'd felt the pull between them with reluctant acceptance. He'd done everything he could to make her want him. Unfortunately he was far from immune from those desires. He wanted to push her back into her bedroom, down on the narrow bed he could see behind her, and fuck her blind. He wanted her naked breasts against him, her legs wrapped around his hips; he wanted to lose himself, just for tonight, in the sweetness she tried to hide.

Instead he was supposed to kill her?

Not this time. This was one piece of collateral damage who wasn't going to be sacrificed to the angry gods of world safety. One young woman wasn't going to make any difference in the long run, and if it came to a showdown with Claudia there was more than a good chance he would win.

None of this showed on his face. He stood in the shadows, but she knew exactly who he was, and she hadn't retreated into her room and slammed the door. She stayed where she was, looking at him, and he realized she didn't know what to do next. What an odd creature, this woman who didn't know how to claim her own sexuality. There was so much he could show her. If he had the time.

He didn't even understand why she was so attractive to him. She was far from his normal type, with her flyaway hair and stubborn mouth. He'd fucked women for business and for pleasure, and he was sure he could come up with a good justification to take this one to bed. He just wasn't sure why he wanted to.

Maybe it was because he might have to kill her, and he didn't want to do it until he was sure it was necessary. It was hard for a woman to hide anything when she was enjoying the best sex of her life, which he intended to give her. If she had to die, then at least she'd die happy, not even knowing what happened to her. If he decided she could live, then there was no way he was going to let Claudia's strong hands and perfect marksmanship get anywhere near her,

The only problem being, Claudia didn't take no for an answer.

"What are you doing here?" He could hear a faint tremor in Evangeline's voice. Christ, she couldn't be a virgin, could she? No, he would have picked up on that much uncertainty. She just wasn't used to hookups, to casual encounters, to instant attraction, to accepting sex as just one more appetite to be assuaged. She was a romantic, he realized. And he was hardheaded and practical, no handsome prince to seduce her.

He said nothing. If she backed into her room he would follow her, if she came out he would take her. Her life might hang in the balance of that small decision.

She stepped forward into the deserted hallway, closing the door behind her. "I was going to take a shower," she said, still with that trace of nervousness. "It's really too late for a walk. Besides, I spent most of the day on my feet."

"I can take care of that," he said softly. The bathing room was next to her room, and no one else would be sharing it. He crossed the hallway, slowly, deliberately, and she didn't retreat, even though he could sense that half of her wanted to. Her arms were full of her clothes when he caught her shoulders in his hard hands. Slender shoulders, delicate. He leaned down and pressed his mouth against the crook of her neck, breathing in her scent. In the distance he could hear the first jarring notes of the *carabinieri*'s Klaxon, and he slid his hands up her neck, covering her ears with his palms as he moved his head and kissed her.

Chapter Three

His mouth on hers was a shock. It was no tentative kiss, no preliminary exploration. The mouth that covered hers was open, carnal, wet, and for a moment she was too startled to do anything but stand there clutching her clothes to her breast like an idiot. He was cupping her face in his beautiful hands, blocking out everything but his mouth, his body up against hers, and then he lifted his head, his deep brown eyes glittering in the darkness. "You want this," he said, no longer sounding lazy. It wasn't a question, and she couldn't nod if she wanted to, not with him holding her head still for his kisses, so she had to be brave.

"Yes," she said, too caught up in the mesmerizing feel of his body against hers to be shocked at herself. "I want this."

His slow smile was brief, and then he covered her mouth again, pushing her up against the wall, and she kissed him back. She could hear the heavy rain begin, and in the distance a police siren, and then nothing mattered as he pushed open the door to the bathing room and angled her inside.

"This isn't my . . ." she began, puzzled, but he hushed her, pulling the towels and the nightgown from her arm and tossing them in the corner.

The shared bath for the third-floor guests was one large wet room, covered with marble tiles, and Silvio had proudly shown her the new overhead rainshower, as well as the many spray options now available in the most recent upgrade. She didn't pay any attention. The sounds of the sirens were growing louder, and she vaguely wondered what had happened, until James pushed her against the wall, both of them fully clothed, and turned on the spray overhead, drenching them, drowning out the noise and any other thoughts.

She tilted back her head and laughed, suddenly happy. This was ridiculous, crazy, and she didn't care. If she was going to throw caution to the wind for a night of passion, then the wilder the better. She could do this and take joy in it.

He moved his mouth down her neck, leaving a trail of tiny bites in his path. The knit dress was stretching in the water, soaked, and he pulled it over her head before she realized what he was doing, so that she stood there in nothing but a skimpy black lace bra and panties.

He paused, looking down at her appreciatively. "That's encouraging," he whispered in her ear, letting his teeth take hold of her earlobe and biting down, so that she arched against him with a soft moan. "You must have known this was coming."

She could protest—but this wasn't the kind of underwear she usually wore, and there was no need to wear it under the black dress. She'd chosen it deliberately, whether she realized it or not. He moved back, pulling her under the full stream of the shower, his thumbs brushing her cheeks, pushing back her long wet hair as he kissed her eyelids, licked the water from her cheekbones and her mouth.

She reached up and tried to unfasten the buttons to his shirt, but the fabric was wet and stubborn. She needed to feel his skin against her. She yanked it in frustration, and he laughed softly against her neck. "Patience, Angel," he whispered, covering her frantic hands with his. "I'll take care of it."

He released her, only for a moment, as he simply ripped the shirt open and yanked it off. She knew what kind of strength was needed to tear that wet linen, and she shivered.

"Are you cold?" he whispered, reaching behind them, and the shower heated up as he turned the dials, apparently knowing from instinct how to adjust them. He pulled his belt free and threw it in the corner, where the heavy metal buckle clanged against the tile. She half expected him to yank down his pants, but instead he put his hands on her, pushing her back beneath the water where nothing existed but his mouth, his touch.

She closed her eyes as his hands slid around her, and a moment later her bra came free, falling down between them. Her small breasts were tight and pebbled against his smooth skin, despite the warmth of the water. She felt his fingers on them, tugging, rubbing, and she heard a quiet moan of pleasure that echoed in the tiled room and knew it could only have come from her. His head moved down, his mouth latching onto her nipple, sucking, and she felt a spasm of reaction between her legs. She liked this. Men had always been so gentle with her breasts, so tender, and she'd felt nothing.

James Bishop was rough, demanding, and she could no more resist those demands than she could fly. He moved to her other breast, leaving the first distended and needy, and when she felt his teeth on her a spasm rocked her body, shocking her.

He pushed his hand down her stomach, beneath the black lace of her panties, finding her entrance without fumbling. Finding her clitoris when every other man had had to search. He knew where it was, and he knew what to do with it, rubbing his thumb across it, his mouth catching hers again as she cried out.

She fell back against the cool tile wall, and he followed her, reaching up to tilt the shower spray so that it poured down on them, drowning everything out but touch.

"Stay like that," he growled, and she blinked her eyes open for a moment, just long enough to see him sink to his knees in front of her, sliding the panties down her legs until they rested around her ankles. She stepped out of them, kicking them away, as he put his hands on her thighs and held them apart as his tongue touched her. A shudder ran through her. This was too much—this was more sex than she'd had in her last few months with Lester, and James wasn't stopping. He licked and sucked and bit at her clitoris as two long fingers slid inside her, filling her, and she couldn't stifle her sudden shriek of . . . was it passion? Fear? Need?

None of it mattered—she was well past the point of second thoughts. He was so good, so adept at this that she came immediately, her body jolting in reaction, a hard, sharp orgasm that was over too quickly, and she felt a wave of disappointment. She knew her body—she was done, and she'd been so turned on she'd been unable to hold back. She tilted her head back, letting the warm water splash down on her, waiting for her body to return to stillness.

He must have felt her climax, but he didn't move away from her. If he was expecting more response from her it wouldn't . . .

The next orgasm slammed into her like a freight train, and she screamed, every inch of her skin prickling, burning, as she arched back against the wall, shaking so hard she thought she might fall apart. He surged upward, covering her mouth with his, and she could taste herself as he swallowed her cries. When her hard spasms subsided into flutters he lifted his mouth. "You don't want to alert the entire villa, do you?" he said with a soft laugh. "When you need to scream again just bite me."

When, he said. Not if. She shivered in his arms. "I can't . . ." she began in a raw voice.

"Oh, yes, you can," he said. "You can't even imagine how much you can." He took her hand and placed it on his fly, and he was so damned hard she felt another shiver dance over her body. She wanted this. This part of him, and all of him besides. She wanted his cock, and she wanted it inside her.

She reached for the button, but he'd already unfastened it, and she just had to manage the zipper in the wet fabric. It stuck, of course, but he had narrow hips and she simply shoved his pants down, his cock jutting forward.

"While you're down there," he said beneath the pounding water, "take me in your mouth."

Sudden fear sliced through her, and she shook her head, trying to draw away. He caught her, pulling her up against him, moving her back against the tile, kissing her with such wicked intensity that her temporary panic melted away, and heat steamed through her body.

"You don't have to do anything you don't want to do," he whispered in her ear, then sank his teeth onto her earlobe, and she wanted to arch up against him.

"I'm sorry . . ."

"Shhhh," he quieted her. "There's nothing to be sorry about. No rules, just what feels good. And what I want now is you. I'm going to fuck you, fuck you fast and hard, and you're going to take it, aren't you?" His voice was low, intense, and he was doing something with his hand. It took her a moment to realize he was sheathing himself with a condom; she had no idea where it had come from and she didn't care. "You're going to let me fuck you blind, and when you come you're going to put your mouth on me and scream into my skin until you can't scream anymore. And then I'm going to take you into the tiny bed in your room and we'll do it all over again."

She stared at him, the water splashing down over them, clinging to his long, long eyelashes, and she knew she'd do almost anything he wanted. Even . . . that. "Yes," she said.

He slid an arm under her butt and hauled her up, pressing her against the wall, pulling her legs around him. She only had a moment to savor the feel of him against her, and then he pushed into her, hard, as he'd promised, and she started to come again.

"Not yet," he growled in her ear. "Don't come yet."

"I don't . . . know if I . . . can help it," she gasped.

"You can." He punctuated his words with a hard thrust that pushed her up against the wet, slippery wall. "You can do exactly what I tell you to do. You're going to let me fuck you, and you're going to fuck me back, and when I tell you to come then you will."

She wanted to tell him it didn't work that way, but she was past words. The pulse of him, the push of him, each time rocking her hard against the tile wall, was turning her brain to mush and her body into nothing but a mass of sensations. She could feel her climax struggling to break free, and she tried to think of something else, to prolong it, but all she could think of was him, inside her, that hard, veined part of him. She trembled on the edge as he thrust into her, again and again and again, their bodies slapping together, slapping against the wet tile, until she was panting, gasping for breath, suddenly afraid of where she was going, afraid of losing everything, of never coming back from this cataclysmic storm of desire.

He hauled her up tighter against him, going deeper than he had before, so deep she cried out with pleasure tinged with pain, her body beginning to spasm around his cock.

"Not yet," he said. "Not yet."

Her eyes had been closed in the darkened bathing room, but she opened them beneath the tumbling water, wanting to see his face as he took her. His eyes would be closed and he would be in some other universe, lost in the journey to completion.

But his eyes were open. Staring at her, so dark, so dark. "That's right," he whispered. "Look at me. Watch me as you fuck me. I'm not one of your polite academics, Angel. I'm something you've never seen before, and you need to know who you're with."

As if she could forget, she thought weakly, staring at him, into his eyes, shaking so hard she thought she would fall apart. She tightened her grip on his shoulders, and he moved closer still, his strong, wet body covering hers, and he was slamming into her, again and again and again.

"Put your mouth on my shoulder," he whispered in a tight voice. She obeyed immediately, licking the water off his skin. "Bite," he said, slamming her back against the tile, going rigid in her arms, and her pent-up release erupted, a scream started in the back of her throat, and mindless, blind, she sank her teeth into his shoulder, harder as each wave hit her, an endless trail of climaxes, each one stronger than the last, until she was sobbing, she could taste blood, and he was still thrusting inside her, slowing almost imperceptibly.

She let go of him, her head falling back with a gasp as she shuddered helplessly. He pulled her against him, and she let her forehead rest against his shoulder as he held her, his hands surprisingly gentle as they stroked her back.

Which was beginning to hurt, she realized dazedly. Everything was beginning to hurt, though she cried out in distress when he pulled free from her and tried to set her on her feet.

She couldn't stand. She sank to the wet floor in a little heap of exhaustion and overstimulation and closed her eyes. Would he leave her now? Walk out of the place in wet clothes? Or stark naked—she could see him being arrogant enough to do that. She didn't like arrogant men. She couldn't think of anyone but him.

He was standing over her. He'd removed the condom, and his cock was at eye level, still erect. She had just enough strength left to lift her head and look at him.

He was looking troubled, or so it seemed to her in her dazed state, but a moment later he'd leaned down and scooped her up in his arms, and his lazy smile warmed her bones. "Poor little angel," he murmured. "I've worn you out."

She realized the shower was off, their clothes in a wet heap in the middle of the floor. She dropped her head against him, so weary.

He carried her, both of them naked and dripping, through the third-floor hallway. She hadn't closed her door completely, and he kicked it open, slamming it shut and locking it while he still held her. The next moment she was down in the concave single bed, the big fan blowing over her, making its customary racket, and the hot air stirred around them.

She was so sure he would leave her. But he slipped into bed beside her, pulling her back into his arms, his tenderness a polar opposite of the fierce sexual possession. She wanted to cling to him; she wanted to cry. She'd never felt like this before, even remotely. He'd leave, and she'd get over it. But right now he was here, and that was enough.

She could feel his mouth at her ear, just as she could feel his chest against her tender back, feel the hard bar of his cock against her butt. He kissed her, very softly. "This isn't good," he whispered. "This isn't what I planned."

"What isn't?" she asked sleepily, snuggling against him.

"You. Me. This was supposed to be a one-night stand."

"It isn't?"

"No, it isn't. Go to sleep, Angel. We'll figure this out in the morning."

She pressed against him, feeling like a lazy kitten. "Why do you call me angel?"

It took him so long to answer that she was almost asleep by the time he spoke. "Your name's Evangeline. You're not an Eva, a Vangie, or a Lina. Angel seems to fit."

She felt a stifled burst of laughter. "After what we just did? I think I'm going to burn in hell. I'd better go back to the church and confess my sins."

Did he stiffen, just a little bit? No, she was imagining it. "No," he said. "We'll find a church in Venice."

That was enough to make her lift her head to turn and look at him. He was looking sleepy, at ease, as if he'd made up his mind about something. She wrinkled her brow. "Why should we find a church in Venice?" she asked.

"To get married, Angel. We're getting married."

Chapter Four

Bishop heard Evangeline's soft laugh before she sank back against him, and a moment later she was asleep. He really wanted to roll her over on her stomach, take her from the back, right then, but she was worn out, and he'd give her that. She clearly didn't have a lot of sexual experience. That, or she'd had phenomenally lousy lovers. Maybe both. He hadn't met anyone who was squeamish about going down on him, but he really knew very little about her. Maybe she was a religious fundamentalist. No, scratch that—she'd certainly liked his mouth between her legs. So had he. Keeping her in a kind of thrall would be easy enough. Getting her to marry him would be relatively simple. Love at first sight, he'd tell her, with a rueful expression, and she'd believe him.

It was a drastic solution, but the only one he could think of. There were few hard-and-fast rules within the ultra-secretive Committee, even under Peter Madsen's more reasonable rule, but one that held firm was that no one could kill a spouse. Only the operative himself. Occasionally there had been instances where people had married an infiltrator, intent on destroying the covert organization from the inside, and it had been up to that operative to take care of things. It had never been a problem.

But otherwise family members were off-limits, and if Claudia broke that rule, the punishment would fit the crime. She'd have no choice but to keep away. Claudia might be enraged, but she'd accept it. She knew the rules, and no one argued with Peter Madsen.

It would take a few phone calls to arrange things in Venice, but with Madsen pulling strings, it would be easy enough to cut through the red tape. He looked down at her, sleeping so peacefully in his arms. Marriage was nothing—it was simply another tool in an operative's arsenal. He knew of many who'd married half a dozen times, none of them legal. He would marry anyone the Committee told him to. He knew that marriage and family and a normal life were no part of his future, ever. If a legal marriage to Evangeline would keep her alive, it was no skin off his ass. He hated collateral damage, particularly when it involved women or children, and he'd do anything he could to prevent it. If marrying Evangeline was the only solution, then he had no compunctions, though it wouldn't have been his first choice. He didn't expect it would make any difference in his actions in the future—he'd never be able to maintain a normal marriage, not with his disaster of a life, so bigamy wasn't a problem.

It had to be legal, or she'd still be fair game. And they had to stay married, or Claudia could still go after her. He knew Claudia well, and she wouldn't give up easily—she could hold a grudge for years. But he sure as hell wasn't about to keep Evangeline with him, tell her who and what he was. No, he was simply going to sweep her off her feet, remove her from this town before she realized anything had happened to her old friend Mr. Corsini, marry her, and jilt her.

It was a pain, but it shouldn't take more than a couple of days, and it had amazing side benefits. He hadn't fucked such an innocent in . . . hell, he didn't know if he ever had. It was going to be . . . enjoyable to teach her.

He pulled her pliant, sleeping body closer, the noisy, weak

fan making little progress against the heat. It didn't matter. His throbbing hard-on didn't matter. He'd have to get her out of here early, but he could let himself sleep for a few short hours, his body wrapped around hers. He had a plan, and it was almost foolproof—he'd never make the mistake of thinking anything was totally without risk. He'd have a busy couple of days of bureaucracy and sex, and then back to business as usual.

He breathed in the scent of her skin and smiled against her flesh. He'd consider it a vacation, the first he'd had in four years. He let his lips drift against her temple. She was going to be quite a treat.

Three days later Evangeline rolled over in the huge bed in their suite at the Hotel Danieli, stretching luxuriously. She had no idea where the sheets and covers were—they'd kicked them off during the night—and she didn't care. For the first time in her life she liked her nudity. She felt sleek and catlike, her hair was a cloud, not a rat's nest, her body well loved and marked by him. It was nothing compared to the bite mark on his shoulder. She'd drawn blood and never realized it, and now it was a dark bruise.

It should have made her sick, but James liked it. He'd wanted her to bite him again if she felt the need to scream, but she couldn't bring herself to do it. She'd smothered her cries against his chest, against the pillow, against the mattress. She rolled onto her stomach, pressing her face against the sheet as she remembered. God, where had her brain gone? All she could think about was sex; all she could think about was James.

The last three days had been insane. He'd insisted on leaving Villa Ragarra at the crack of dawn, before anyone but Silvio was up. The clothes they'd left in the bathing room had been washed and dried and were waiting for them, neatly folded, at the front desk. James had tried to pay her bill but she'd emerged from her sex-dazed haze to insist it go on her own pathetic credit card. Then they'd headed off into the sunrise, taking the surprisingly powerful Fiat, and she'd slept beside him, not questioning anything. She'd been fully prepared to argue if he brought up the idea of marriage again, but when he woke her up, they had already parked in the Piazelle Roma, at the very entrance of Venice, and it was time for breakfast. He somehow managed to find something more substantial than the usual pastry and coffee favored by the Venetians, and then she found herself in a small church off the Campo Manin, with a kindly looking priest waiting for them.

She'd been too astonished to protest at first. And then James had kissed her, hard, said "Trust me," and she did. It was a ceremony, an act, but nothing legal or binding. It couldn't have been. They would have had to jump through hoops to do that, and James had assured her they'd have a real ceremony when they got back to the States. She'd gone along with it, not protesting, blinded by emotions she was hesitant to name.

She couldn't really imagine it. Couldn't imagine her stiff parents reacting to her impulsive behavior, her sister taking one look at James and erupting in jealousy. It was a game, a dream, one she was afraid would end sooner or later, but in the meantime she had every intention of living the dream in their luxurious suite at the Hotel Danieli.

She'd told him how ridiculous it was—they had three rooms and they never left the bed, even for room service—but he'd insisted, and her protests had turned to a silly distraction, and they were laughing and making love again, doing things she'd never considered doing.

This was the first time she'd woken in the huge bed and he hadn't been with her. She yawned, glancing at her wedding ring. At least there he'd been sensible—it was pink glass from Murano, narrow and pretty. He assured her he'd replace it with something more substantial when they got back to the States, but she was never going to let this one go. For one thing, she'd have a hard time doing it—once on, it had stuck. But it symbolized the strange, abrupt, fragile beginning for them, and she would always cherish it.

"James?" she called sleepily. There was no answer, but Evangeline didn't move. He must be in the bathroom that was larger than many New York City apartments. She had no idea what time it was, she wasn't even sure what day it was. They had all blended together.

In fact, she was feeling a little achy and sticky. A nice long shower would be lovely, unless James was taking advantage of the marble bath that was big enough to hold four people. They'd used it once already, and she wouldn't mind trying it again, except that she was hurting. Her body wasn't used to all this activity.

She climbed out of bed and peered into the bathroom. He wasn't there, but there was another, equally elegant bathroom on the other side of the living room, and he might have gone there so he wouldn't disturb her. She walked across the magnificent parquet floor to the other side, unconscious of her nudity, but that bathroom was empty as well. He wasn't anywhere in the suite.

She ignored the uneasy feeling in the pit of her stomach. He probably knew she needed a break, and he'd gone out so he wouldn't distract her. Besides, he'd ignored his cell phone, ignored messages that had been slid under the massive double doors to the suite. He must have decided now was a good time to catch up on things while she slept.

Suddenly she felt cold, exposed, standing in the middle of the massive living room of the luxury suite wearing nothing but skin. It was as if the sun had gone behind a cloud, which was ridiculous. She had only to look out the high leaded-glass windows to see it shining down on the water. It was only her imagination.

She took the fastest shower she'd taken in three days, the first one she'd taken alone, ignoring memories of what they'd done in the marble-sided shower stall, and dressed quickly. Her jeans and loose T-shirt weren't proper attire for a place like the Danieli, and James had promised to take her shopping for some decent clothes, but of course she'd refused. Even if they'd really been married she wouldn't have let him pay for her. It would have stretched her budget beyond bearing, but she could buy her own dress. Provided she found one on sale.

But they'd never gotten that far. Never gotten out of the bedroom, and she felt her skin heat as more memories flitted through her mind. His mouth everywhere, tasting, sucking, biting. They'd been with each other every second since he'd first walked into the shower at the Villa Ragarra, and this was the first time she had a chance to think. Had she lost her mind, going off with a perfect stranger?

No, he was hardly a stranger. She'd known that the moment she saw him, up at that mountain church. She'd looked into his deep brown eyes and known . . . something. He'd felt the same. He'd whispered about love at first sight, a ridiculous concept, but she grinned like an idiot every time she thought about it.

She was grinning now, her strange misgivings leaving her. She hadn't eaten since last night, and it was midday. What she needed was a good meal and a call home to her parents. Not that she'd tell them she was married, or even engaged. She'd just say she'd . . . met someone.

Without James the suite seemed vast, almost cavernous. Here she was in Venice and she hadn't even been outside. She pushed open the window and stuck her head outside. The walkways were packed with early-summer tourists, but the Grand Canal glittered in the sunlight as the water taxis and *vaporettos* rubbed shoulders with the gondolas. Could she talk James into taking her on a gondola ride? They were tourist bait, ridiculously expensive, and she'd never had any interest in such a ridiculous thing. With James everything was different. She knew what he'd do. He would slide his beautiful, strong hand beneath whatever clothing she wore and make her come, covering her mouth with his. She smiled at the thought, but for some reason her eyes filled with tears.

She shook them away. Had she suddenly become a silly, dependent woman? That wouldn't do at all. That wasn't who she was. Except when James put his hands on her.

She couldn't stay immured in their elegant suite, waiting for him, and the room-service menu, fabulous as it was, had its limitations. She wanted a Diet Coke and some Pasta ai Quattro Formaggi with the tang of gorgonzola. She wanted to sit by the canal and watch the pigeons and think about nothing at all.

There was no missing the disapproving looks as she walked through the lobby of the Danieli in her jeans, T-shirt, and Asics, and it took her longer than she expected to find a dress she could afford. She finally discovered one in a tiny shop with a cheerful mongrel curled up outside to greet her. The dress was a rose color, clung to every inch of her, and made her green eyes sparkle and her cheeks flush. She'd surprise James when she got back to the hotel. She'd make him wait in the salon while she changed, and then they'd end up back in the bed again, and maybe she wouldn't wear the dress out into the hotel for days . . .

She ate a late lunch in the bright sunshine, watching the tourists. She wasn't far from the hotel, and she kept her eye out for James, but there was no sign of him. He'd probably already gone back to the suite, and she was suddenly in a rush to finish, happiness bubbling inside her as she practically ran back to the hotel.

The suite was still empty. She searched the place, but there was no note from him, only her own left untouched. She shook off her unease and went to change into the dress. She should have bought stiletto heels but even for James she couldn't go that far, and her thin, strappy sandals would do. She even put on makeup, then looked for her diamond studs.

She couldn't find them. At first she thought she'd misplaced them—after all, she hadn't had a brain in her head these last three days, and she'd had much more important things to think about. But the more she searched, the colder she grew. She dumped her meager belongings on the neatly made bed but there was no sign of them.

Maybe James had found them lying around and put them away for safekeeping. She went for his suitcase, opening it, momentarily surprised to find it empty. No diamond earrings, no change of clothes, and yet he hadn't unpacked.

She didn't hurry. There was no need to rush, no need to find out the truth more quickly than she had to. His shaving supplies, his toothbrush were missing. She hadn't even noticed that when she woke up. Everything was gone except for the empty suitcase.

She went back to it, looking for some clue. There was a thin bulge in one of the outer pockets, and she pulled out his passport and wallet, and relief poured through her. The wallet had his American driver's license, credit cards, even a Costco card, and she wanted to laugh. She'd panicked for nothing. He'd tease her when he got back, tell her she'd promised to trust him, and then he'd kiss her . . .

She put the wallet down and picked up the passport. The picture was a good one—weren't passport photos supposed to be terrible? His was gorgeous. Except, why was his passport here? They'd had to leave theirs with the front desk when they registered. Of course she'd been so besotted with her new wedding ring on her finger that she hadn't been paying much attention, but surely she remembered being asked for hers.

There was something else in the pocket, wrapped in cloth and tied with a black ribbon. She ripped it open and felt her blood freeze.

More passports. Half a dozen of them, from the US, the UK, France—she didn't know all the myriad colors, but they each represented another country. She knew what she would find when she opened them, and she went through then, staring dully. Photos of James Bishop in every one, each with a different name, a different identity. He wasn't James Bishop at all. He was a liar and a thief.

She looked around at the elegant bedroom. Her father had had her earrings valued for insurance, and they'd been estimated to be worth thirty thousand dollars; two nights in this palatial suite would wipe out any profits. Why would he spend more money than the earrings were worth just to steal them?

She reached for the phone, then drew her hand back. She couldn't do this. Not this way. She went into the bedroom and ripped off the fucking dress, dumping it on the floor, and pulled on her jeans and T-shirt once more. Shoving everything in her backpack, she paused by the wide row of windows overlooking the Grand Canal. Then she yanked off her wedding ring and threw it into the dark, murky waters before heading down to the lobby.

It was early evening and the vast atrium of the ancient hotel was almost empty. She straightened her shoulders and headed for the desk.

"May I help you, miss?" the starched concierge asked, barely lifting his gaze from his paperwork. He'd taken one look at her clothing and known she wasn't worth his time.

"I wanted to ask if you'd had any messages for me from Mr. Bishop."

One elegant eyebrow rose, and with a weary sigh he went over to a computer station and began typing into it. "Your name, miss?"

"Morrissey. Evangeline Morrissey. We've been staying in the suite on the second floor."

That caught his attention, and he let his superior gaze run up and down her rumpled appearance. He was clearly not impressed, and suddenly Evangeline longed for Silvio's cheerful presence. "The Emperor Suite. Yes, I see. You're paid up till tomorrow. But there are no messages. And no Mr. Bishop is currently enjoying our hospitality."

"Then who have I been sharing a room with?" she snapped, her annoyance finally trumping her desperate anxiety.

"The suite was registered to a Monsieur Pierre Boussan, but he retrieved his passport this morning and checked out. He left no messages and no forwarding address."

She just stared at him, his words not making sense.

But they did. She'd been a complete and utter fool, prey to the oldest con in the world, and she didn't grieve the loss of her great aunt's famous diamonds nearly as much she grieved the loss of her heart, her soul.

"Miss Morrissey, may I do something for you?" The man suddenly sounded concerned. She must have looked like she was about to faint on his polished marble floor, she thought grimly.

"Just give me my passport. I have to leave."

"But you're paid up through tomorrow."

And who knew if the credit card was real? It almost certainly wasn't, and she'd end up in jail until she could get through to her father to cover the bill. That was one conversation she wasn't going to have. She summoned a calm smile. "And it's been lovely, but I really must leave. There's been a family emergency."

"I am sorry to hear that, Miss Morrissey," he murmured, all polite manners since he'd discovered which room she'd used. He was rifling through something, and belatedly Evangeline remembered how things worked in the US. He probably hadn't even run the credit card yet, waiting for any last minute room charges, and he would call the police . . .

"Here it is," he announced, her battered blue passport in his hand. "We hope you will return to the Danieli, Miss Morrissey, you and Monsieur Boussan."

Monsieur, he'd said. So presumably the passport he'd handed him was a French one, and he was no more French than she was. Out of the deepest, darkest part of her she managed to produce a tired smile.

"I doubt it," she said. "This was a once-in-a-lifetime occurrence."

"We will always be at your service. May we call you a water taxi? Our own launch to take you to the airport?"

She shook her head. The sooner she got away from them the better. "I have things to do in the city. I'll take the *vaporetto*."

"As you wish, miss."

She'd thought that she could find an empty spot in the *vaporetto*, duck her head, and cry. She didn't. She stayed dry-eyed and calm, through the interminable wait at the airport for the next empty seat. Through the short flight to Berlin and then the overseas flight to Boston. She didn't sleep, didn't eat, she just sat utterly still, utterly calm. If the authorities had the ability to recognize a human time bomb, they would have isolated her.

She reached her tiny house running on coffee and fumes. It smelled musty from being closed up for so long, and she moved across the living room like a zombie, opening the window to let in the muggy air. She turned and saw the beautiful copy of the David her parents had given her for her birthday. She picked it up and hurled it across the room, smashing it into pieces.

She went through the place methodically—the living room, tiny bedroom, bathroom, and kitchen. She broke everything she could find, she threw things, ripped things, smashed things, yanked her bookcases over, ripped her clothes out of her closet, upended her bed so that the mattress lay haphazardly on the box spring. And when there was nothing left to break, nothing left to destroy, she dropped down on the lopsided mattress and wept.

PART TWO—FIVE YEARS LATER

Chapter Five

Evangeline Morrissey Williamson pulled her battered pickup off to the side of the road, carefully maneuvering the ancient Airstream trailer into a stable position before switching off the motor. Merlin, her German Shepherd, cocked an ear but otherwise stayed up on the bench seat, used to her ways. She leaned her head back and took a few deep breaths, dragging the calm around her. She didn't want to go back. She'd spent the last three months in the Canadian wilderness, documenting the ruins of the luxurious lodges and railway hotels that had been built well over a hundred years ago, making sketches of what they once must have looked like, serving as an amateur archeologist when she came across shards of dishes, tools, abandoned detritus of a long-vanished lifestyle. It wasn't as if she didn't know where she was going next. The Laughing Moose Lodge near Glacier Park in Montana had stopped operating in the 1930s, and very little of it remained, much lost in the encroaching wilderness, and she'd allotted a full two weeks to study it during her sabbatical, with more time available if she needed it.

Changing areas of study had been easier than she'd thought. She'd lost her interest in ancient church architecture. When she'd told her department head and nominal boss, he'd looked at her, appalled. "You have all your research done!" he'd cried. "And you did it on your own dime, not even with a grant. You just have to write something, and we both know that writing comes easy for you. Don't throw all this work away."

But she'd been obdurate. She'd wanted to burn her research, but her friend, Pete Williamson, had simply taken the boxes and boxes of papers away from her. He was only five years older than she was, one of the university's shining stars, and he'd made it his mission to guide her through her new area of study.

The guidance hadn't been necessary, but she'd appreciated the thought. She'd thrown herself into her new work on ancient Adirondack lodges with complete abandon and eventually gave in and married Pete.

It was supposed to be the perfect marriage. Pete already had a book deal, he was handsome and charming, and half his students, male and female, were in love with him.

She'd always known he was too susceptive to flattery, to adoration, and she had no illusions about his fidelity. He needed that adoration to breathe, like air; she knew he took graduate students to bed during the time he was seeing her, while making her all sorts of promises, but having no illusions meant there were none to be shattered. As mistakes went in her life it was far from her worst one—that last summer in Italy won the prize. The following year, before she married Pete, was in its own way even worse. And after nine months of marriage, she and Pete had parted amicably enough. At the time.

The year before they'd married had been bad. She'd fucked anything in pants, trying to get James Bishop out of her system. It hadn't worked, but at least marrying Pete had put a stop to that. Once settled into the safety of a seemingly stable relationship, she found she could let go of her past.

She found she could let go of Pete, her safety net, quickly enough as well, and her work, so different from her previous area of study, was enough to finish the rest of her healing. She got grants, a quietly respectable book deal, then a job teaching at a small school in northern Wisconsin, and by the time three years had passed, she'd made a peaceful, if slightly wary, life for herself.

She'd never planned on getting a dog. They were too much trouble and her parents had never let her have one when she was growing up, even though she'd begged. But Merlin had found *her*, and he wasn't interested in her doubts. He'd just shown up on campus one day, was fed by everyone from the kitchen staff to the maintenance people to half the students, and wandered around with perfect manners, seemingly at random, until he happened to come across Evangeline walking to class.

He'd followed her. At first the large dog made her slightly nervous, but he simply kept at her heel, almost like a guard dog, and when she went into class he waited outside, lying down peacefully until the students left and she emerged. And he followed her to the library. To her car.

It took her three days before she began bringing dog treats, telling herself she would toss them to him to drive him away. He'd simply catch the treat midair and continue to follow her. She held out eight days before she let him in the car.

"This is a short-term thing," she'd advised him as he sat beside her, panting cheerfully. "Just till I find you a good home."

But there'd been no good home, and in truth, she hadn't made much effort to find one. She called him Merlin, because he was so damned smart, and he seemed to take it as his role in life to be her protector. He must have had some training at some point in his puppyhood, but if he missed his earlier home he made no sign of it. He took care of her. He wouldn't let her leave the house without him, or with her laptop and lunch still on the kitchen counter. He'd wormed his way into her life and her heart and she couldn't imagine life without him.

His overprotectiveness wasn't a particular problem. He was perfectly well behaved, even with someone he perceived as a threat. He never barked; he just bared his fangs and growled low in his throat and people backed off from her, from her car. Oddly enough, he seemed to know who was harmless. Children, slightly disorganized students, the dean were no imminent problem. He despised the college president, though Evangeline thought he must have picked up on her own antipathy, but what had really surprised her was his furious dislike of Pete the one time he'd visited her.

She'd asked for her research back. He'd told her he'd lost it. She'd said, "Find it." He'd told her he'd burned it. She'd told him he lied: he'd never burn original research. He'd finally showed up at her door one day, without warning or any boxes of notes and research, and Merlin wouldn't let him in, even though Evangeline had shushed him and calmed him. When Pete had tried to walk in, Merlin had lunged at him, and Evangeline had had to drag him into the bedroom, shut the door, and try to ignore his furious and unexpected barking.

Merlin was smarter than she was. Pete was there to confess his sins, his eyes full of crocodile tears. His new book was coming out, detailing his journeys through the walled towns of Italy, complete with her original drawings, and her name was nowhere on it.

"I'll pay you your share of the royalties, of course," he'd said eagerly, while she sat like a stone. "Not that these books ever make much, so it probably won't even earn out its advance. And if it goes into a second printing I'll make sure I put you in the acknowledgments, but you know that's unlikely as well. I feel just awful about this, Vangie. It was a moment of weakness. I needed something for the new book—you're at this shit backwater school, but I'm at Harvard now. Publish or perish is a serious business, and I was at my wits' end when I remembered your papers. You'd told me you wanted to destroy them, so I didn't think you'd care."

"Wouldn't care that you stole my research and put your name on it?" she'd said in a deceptively mild voice.

He'd winced. "It sounds so sleazy when you put it that way."

She said nothing, letting him make the obvious inference. "Listen," he went on, "I can cut you a check for five thousand dollars, just as a gesture of good will. I know it might not seem like much, but remember, I compiled all that raw research, organized it, wrote the narrative. It's really my book."

"With my research. What did you get for an advance?"

"That's not a fair question. The advance was based on my name, and how well the last book did, and of course for travel and living expenses . . ." his voice trailed off.

"The travel and living expenses that came out of my pocket," she supplied. "And your previous book didn't do that well. What was your advance?" He still hesitated, and with Merlin barking in the background it was hard to be subtle. "I can always call your publisher and explain the situation. They'll tell me how much they paid you."

"Fifty thousand dollars," he muttered.

She stared at him. That was a monumental sum for an academic treatise, but Pete would have turned it into a cocktail table book, with glossy photos and his own leonine good looks on the cover.

"And you offer me five thousand dollars of hush money? I suppose you'd have me sign something attesting to the fact that I had nothing to do with the book?"

"I said I'd put you in the acknowledgments. Come on, Vangie, you know how the world works. Be reasonable."

She smiled sweetly and rose from her seat. "I'm going to let Merlin out now. I would suggest you be long gone before I get to the bedroom door. He's smarter than I am, and he seems to dislike you even more than I do, which seems impossible but there it is."

"Vangie, don't be difficult . . ." he began, but she ignored him, reaching the bedroom door. Merlin hit the front door just seconds after Pete had closed it, and she could see Pete running for his rental car, a Lexus of course, like he had hellhounds on his heels. He would have had one after him, if she'd given in to temptation and opened the door.

"Fucking men," she'd said to Merlin. "Next time one comes around, remind me how much I hate the whole breed."

Merlin had looked up at her with his wise eyes, and she rubbed his head. "You're a very smart dog, you know that? From now on I'm going to let you tell me who's worth spending time with." He'd ducked his big head beneath her caress, making that whining little sound of pleasure. In the last two years he hadn't let a presentable male anywhere near her.

Merlin seemed to love camping and life on the road just as much as Evangeline did. Every night he would disappear for a half an hour or so, and it took her a while to realize he was patrolling the perimeter, even if they'd been in the same place for weeks. "You must have been a police dog," she told him, feeding him a slice of bacon. "Or part of a military canine unit. You are one damned fine guard dog."

He'd taken the praise and the bacon as his due, flopping down beside her, his big warm body pressed up against her leg, his work finished for the night; and she'd wondered what she'd ever done without him.

This sabbatical had been everything she'd dreamed of, with the slight hassle of dragging the damned Airstream everywhere she went the only downside. But she'd even gotten good at that, able to back it into a proper spot with only two or three attempts, and she loved it. It was small—a dinette at the back with all her research material spread over it, a bed at the front, a tiny kitchenette, and even a toilet with a shower. She loved her compact, solitary, happy life wandering around the Canadian wilderness where she had no cell phone coverage and no Internet. That part could be a pain when it came to research, but she worked her way around it, finding Internet cafes or campgrounds with Wi-Fi, and most of the time she found she could live perfectly well without it.

The path to success in research of any kind was to specialize, and if you managed to find something that sparked public imagination so much the better, as that dickwad Pete Williamson knew. In the increasingly stressed, urbanized world, the fantasy of remote frontier living with the luxuries of the Titanic and no danger of drowning was powerful. She'd had to pick and choose among the grant offers, and she'd let go of Pete's perfidy.

She'd had to. Not long after Pete's book had came out, he'd been mugged, beaten to an inch of his life, his perfect looks ruined; and his career had tanked when other instances of academic plagiarism had cropped up. Karma was a bitch, just like she was, and she could let go of it. She didn't even need to waste her time thinking about him.

"I'm not ready for this to be over, boy," she said to Merlin as she sat in the truck. "I don't want to go back home." It wasn't that her work and time were done. She had another six weeks on her sabbatical, and there were two sites in Montana, as well as one in northern Minnesota, that she had yet to study. But crossing the border between Alberta and Montana meant accepting the fact that her time was coming to an end, and sooner rather than later she'd be back in the classroom.

She liked to teach, she truly did. She liked the small, shabby Victorian house she'd bought and fixed up almost as much as she loved her tiny vintage Airstream with its silver bullet contours. But Wisconsin didn't feel like home. Nothing did, and the nights when she woke up sweating and shaking she knew she'd been dreaming of James Bishop, even though her conscious mind refused to acknowledge it.

She sighed, shoving her hair away from her face. She kept it short nowadays, and it had a ridiculous tendency to curl, making her look like a pixie, but at least it was out of her way and fit under her beloved Grumpy ball cap.

She yanked the cap back on, shoving her hair beneath it. It was a midafternoon in August, and the border crossing, while it was a small one, would be busy. She hated crossing borders—they always wanted to poke through Annabelle, her private name for the trailer, mess with her papers, hassle her about Merlin, observe her dirty laundry, and question her for hours. Merlin was always a perfect gentleman about it all, and she suspected he recognized a uniform as a sign of authority. As for her, she'd learned to pee before she got to the crossings, because God knew they wouldn't let her near a bathroom until they were convinced she wasn't carrying something dangerous in her vagina.

Nothing was going in her vagina but her battery-powered BFF, and chances were they'd come across that too if they searched intently. She was counting on this smaller crossing to be more laid-back, but there were no guarantees.

She looked at Merlin. "Do you ever get the feeling that something isn't right? Of course you do—one look at Pete and you knew he was a shithead. You've got better instincts than I do."

Merlin didn't disagree. Evangeline couldn't shake the quiver of uneasiness in the pit of her stomach. She felt as if something catastrophic was about to happen. It was probably nothing more than the end of her sabbatical looming on the horizon, but it seemed like something more troubling was ahead. She wanted to stop time, pull the camper up, and stay in the woods, away from prying eyes and prying hands.

She shook herself. It wasn't as if northern Montana was a hotbed of big-box stores and suburbia. Where she was heading wasn't much different than the wilds of Canada. It was just closer to the realities of her ordinary life.

"I'm being an idiot, Merlin," she grumbled. He simply looked at her. "We need to get to our new campground before it gets dark, and I can't sit around with my thumb up my ass brooding. Tell me to get a move on."

Merlin rose up on the seat, gazing at her intently. "Okay, message received," she muttered, making a face, as she pulled out onto the narrow paved road, heading toward the border crossing.

It was even smaller than she expected. One window, though she knew perfectly well they weren't going to just let her go through, not with a dog and a trailer. She was flagged over before she even approached it, and she pulled up behind the small building with a sigh, yanking the cap off her head and threading her fingers through her hair. It was going to be a long day.

She'd underestimated the border agent's zeal. He was a tall man, with a moustache and a lean build, but he still seemed to crowd her. Presumably that was the reason he was the first man in a uniform who Merlin immediately distrusted, and the feeling was mutual. He'd made her put Merlin in the kennel in the back of the building, then locked her in a room where she could watch him tear poor Annabelle to pieces while she listened to Merlin's mournful howl. Everything came out, even her granola and smoothie mixtures. She half expected him to upend the toilet, which wouldn't be that bad because she didn't like to use it, preferring the wilderness if given the choice. She'd gotten very adept at squatting.

It was going to take hours to put everything back together, and that wasn't part of the border agent's job. She wasn't getting out of here anytime soon, and she began revising her itinerary. Of course they'd taken her cell phone, but she had an almost photographic memory, and there was a little-used campground just a couple of hours past the border where she could stay for the night instead of her planned stop. She let a litany of truly obscene epithets run through her head as she looked at the sour-faced guard. One of the other agents should be questioning her while he went through the trailer, or vice versa, but the two other people in the building didn't seem to feel any more friendly toward her own personal border agent than she did.

And even though she'd taken precautions, she was going to need a toilet sooner or later. Plus, Merlin hated being away from her, and his howls were getting more determined. She lost track of time—there was no clock in sight and she used her smart-phone instead of a watch—but eventually her entire life was spread out by the side of Annabelle, and the unpleasant-looking guard was sauntering back toward the building. At least one of the other guards was repacking her trailer. She knew from experience they could have left it up to her, and she thanked heaven for small favors. Now if she could only have a bathroom.

She knew better than to ask. The border guard came into the room, pulled out a chair, and sat across from her, a sour expression on his face.

"Are you going to stop that damned dog from barking?" he opened the interview.

No attitude, she reminded herself. He was just doing his job. "I can't very well calm him if I can't even see him," she said politely enough.

He shuffled through her papers, screwing up her careful order, dropping a sheet on the floor and stepping on it before he picked it up, leaving a big boot print in the middle of it. "So your dog's papers are in order. Yours, not so much. There's no record of when you entered Canada."

She controlled her weary sigh. "They don't stamp passports when I drive through. I entered Canada on May twenty-seventh, as you can see from my notes and my records, and I've been there ever since."

"Doing what?"

It was right there, and she'd already explained herself twice, but she patiently did it again. "Research for a book on abandoned vacation lodges from the early part of the 1900s."

"You got any proof of that?"

Don't lose your temper, she reminded herself. "I have my identification card for Greenbough College, where I teach the history of architecture, I have pages and pages of notes and drawings, I have a letter of permission from the Minister of Canadian Heritage, I have camping receipts from the areas where I've been working."

He grunted. "There was nothing incriminating in your trailer. I'm just deciding whether to send you to the auto unit to pull your tires."

Alarm shot through her. Not that there was anything to see, but that would take hours, and Annabelle was finicky; and how damned long would it take before she could get a bathroom?

She kept her face stoic, knowing he was watching her for every tic. "Is there anything I can help you with?" she said politely.

He ignored her question, turning back to the papers. "I think that dog is dangerous. I'm thinking of having him kenneled till we can get a vet in to certify that he's not a problem."

"What?" Her voice rose in panic. She wasn't about to leave Merlin in their hands. "Why?"

"I don't have to give you a reason, Ms. Morrissey. And why do some of your possessions identify you as Evangeline Williamson, with another address entirely?"

Shit and double shit. "Because I got divorced."

"How long ago?"

"Three years."

"That should be time to update everything."

"I have a lot going on." She sounded a bit testy, and she cleared her throat. "Please don't impound Merlin. He needs to be with me."

"He stays here . . ." he began. Just then the door opened and one of the more pleasant looking agents poked his head in.

"Boss says no to the canine impound. The kennel is full," he said apologetically. "Unless he's bitten someone you have to let him go."

The first agent looked furious. "Have you seen that dog?" he demanded.

"Seemed harmless enough when I checked him out," the second man said. "Let the two of them go. We're about to get a bus of college students down from Toronto, and you know what a pain in the ass they can be."

The agent wasn't happy. He looked at Evangeline out of his oddly emotionless eyes for a long chilling moment, and then he rose, his chair scraping on the cement floor. "You're free to go. And take that hellhound with you. Just give us your destination tonight in case we have any follow-up."

She didn't want to tell him, but that was childish. It was just a campground. She would have given anything to snarl at him. Ever since . . . Italy . . . she hadn't been big on patience, but she knew when she was outclassed. She gave him a polite smile, rising and gathering her papers together, and told him the name of the camping area she'd decided on. "Thank you."

The second agent rolled his eyes, looking at his fellow worker, and some of Evangeline's anxiety faded. If they all thought the man was an asshole, then she wasn't alone. And she was about to get a bathroom, her dog, and her trailer, in that order. At this rate they'd make it to the camping area near Bear's Claw, Montana.

There was no sign of her nemesis when she emerged from her blissful time in the ladies' room, and once released, Merlin was a perfect gentleman as always. What had gotten into him, to be so aggressive with the border patrol? He seemed absolutely fine around the other two on duty, treating them with polite friendliness, even condescending to wagging his tail when one of them scratched him behind his ears.

"Fine dog you have there, miss," the man said. "Sorry you had to deal with Smith. He's a newbie and he's a little too by-the-book."

"That's one way to put it," the other man muttered, clearly not impressed with their new agent. "Do you need any help getting your stuff together?"

She smiled at them gratefully. Maybe all men weren't buttholes. "No, thanks. I'll be fine. I just want to make it to Bear's Claw by tonight."

"That's a pretty remote area, miss. You sure you'll be all right? Even this time of year there aren't many people around."

Merlin lifted his head, offended, and Evangeline laughed. "I've got Merlin. He's more than enough protection."

"Well, he sure as hell didn't like Smith, so the dog clearly has good sense."

Merlin paced beside Evangeline as she checked the trailer hitch, just to be sure, then opened the door of the old pickup. The dog hopped in and settled down on the bench seat before she could say a word, and she climbed in after him, grabbing a Diet Coke from her cooler and refilling the water pan she had strapped to the floor on the passenger side. A moment later she was off, the obnoxious border agent forgotten.

The roads were rough as she drove into Montana. For some reason Merlin seemed restless, glancing back at the camper every few minutes and whining softly. "What's up, Merlin? Something wrong with Annabelle? I checked the hitch and the tires, and everything's fine. We'll just put everything back in order when we camp for the night."

Merlin was only slightly appeased, and continued to look back at the trailer with an expectant expression on his face. As Evangeline took another slug of her DC, she turned on Grace, her GPS, programmed with the soothing voice of a British woman. For a while she'd called her Mary Poppins, but Mary Poppins was too grumpy and she ended up being Grace. Evangeline turned off onto a secondary road, and it took her almost two hours to find the campground in Bear's Claw, Montana.

"Remote" wasn't the word for it. It was as if she were on another well-forested planet. The sign was old, covered with moss, the cabin at the entrance was deserted, and she had the depressing feeling there'd be no plumbing or electricity.

It didn't matter. There was plenty of room to park, and a clear, fresh stream ran across the back of the clearing. She needed to set up, get something to eat, open up the trailer, and check the damage. She backed up carefully, jerked when she misjudged and bumped the back end of the camper into a sapling. Merlin was whining again, almost desperately, and she figured he had to pee. She put the truck in park and opened the door.

Normally Merlin was the most gentlemanly of animals, and waited for her to precede him. This time he leapt across her before she could get out of the truck, landing on the ground and heading straight for the trailer's side door. He didn't bark, didn't whine, but instead began scratching at the door.

"What's wrong with you, baby?" she said, climbing down and slamming the truck door. "Something spook you? That border patrol shithead won't bother you anymore. We're here to stay—nothing for you to worry about."

Merlin didn't look particularly worried—just determined, scratching at the door and whining softly, then looking back at her.

Evangeline shook her head. The sun was setting, but she'd manage to park in a position where it shone directly in her eyes. "Gimme a minute," she grumbled, and unfurled the canopy. It was always the first thing she did when she settled for the night, for the week, for the month. It made things feel more home-like.

"Are you hungry? Is that what the fuss is about?" she demanded. "All right, I'll get your dinner. Just wait." She put her foot on the metal step and turned the handle of her beloved Airstream, pulling it open. Given the state of the campground, it was a good bet there wasn't even any power, and her batteries would only last so long. She should have bought that generator. She climbed up into the trailer, then stopped, turning back to look at Merlin.

To her astonishment he seemed to have lost interest. The moment she opened the door, he took off on his customary patrol of the area. "You crazy dog," she said with fond exasperation, standing in the open door. "What's gotten into you?"

But he'd abandoned her, and she turned around, about to head into the back of the trailer, when everything froze: her heart, her blood, her very being.

She wasn't alone.

Chapter Six

The interior of the camper was shrouded in shadows. There was a table at the far end, one that turned into a bed, with the kitchen and bathroom in between, and her own bed was directly behind her.

A man was sitting at her table, the early-evening sun coming in behind him, turning him into a silhouette. She could see his general outline. She could also see the gun that lay on the table in front of him.

She'd already closed the door, or she would have simply thrown herself out of it and run. As it was, she started to edge toward it, very slowly.

"Don't do that." The voice that came out of the darkness was laid-back, casual, making the order even more chilling. "Why don't you take a seat on the bed and we'll talk."

She stopped moving. "I don't want to talk," she said. She should have been terrified, but she'd given up being afraid five years ago—she'd given up letting anything or anyone intimidate her after that debacle. "Whoever you are, I want you to leave. How did you even get in here?"

He leaned back against the banquette, his hand playing with the gun, and she got a better look at him. His blond hair was cut short, and he had several days of stubble that was either due to necessity or a fashion statement. For some reason she thought it was the former. He wore rough clothes—a denim shirt and jeans—and there was a certain implacability to his face that made Evangeline's stomach twist. She wasn't going to let him scare her, she thought firmly.

"How do you think I got in?" The man's voice held no particular inflection or accent, making it even more unnerving. "When you were being harassed at the border. I needed a safe way to get out of Canada and your camper was the perfect vehicle."

"Good. Now leave."

He laughed, and the sound made her stomach twist more. Was it fear this time? Or something else?

"Afraid I can't do that. I have things I have to do, and you're the only game in town."

She kept her back straight, her hands at her sides but curled into fists. "Are you an escaped prisoner?" she demanded flatly. With his clothes and his cool, expressionless face he could have walked off a work farm of some sort.

"Not exactly."

That wasn't much of an answer, but since he hadn't threatened her yet, except to play with that gun, she felt her courage harden. "What do I have to do to get you to leave?"

She didn't miss his slow grin. "What are you offering?"

She didn't react to his deliberate taunt. "My dog will tear your throat out when he gets back."

"I don't think so. Otherwise he wouldn't have left."

"Is someone else with you? He might have gone after something in the woods."

"So many questions," he said lightly. "No, I'm alone. Why don't you come closer?"

"I'm good," she said, not moving from the spot in front of the doorway. She still hadn't given up the idea of throwing herself at the door. If she managed it just right, she could hit the handle and the door would fly open, sending her tumbling to the ground. She could scramble to her feet fast enough, but he had a gun.

"Don't even think about it," he said, obviously reading her mind. "You wouldn't even reach the door. Now come here before I have to come and get you."

That idea sounded even worse. Maybe if she sat at the table and pretended to trust him she could talk him into leaving. The stranger was wrong about Merlin—he'd get the gun away, he'd get the man on the ground and hold him. She just had to placate him for the next few minutes while Merlin did his nightly reconnaissance.

"All right," she said, moving forward.

"And get me another beer while you're at it."

Her outrage grew. "You've been drinking my beer?"

"And eating your granola shit and anything else I could find. I'm afraid I haven't been able to get to any food in the last couple of days, and I'm starving."

She moved through the central galley, opened the tiny refrigerator, and pulled out a beer.

"Get one for yourself," he added.

"I don't want . . ."

"I don't give a flying fuck what you want. I told you to get yourself a beer."

She recognized the real menace beneath the casual voice, and she wasn't going to make the mistake in thinking he wasn't a very dangerous man. She grabbed the second bottle, shoved the door shut, and somehow managed to stalk the few feet she had to travel to get to the table. He looked up at her, still in the shadows. "Sit."

She considered balking, but he was holding the gun, and Merlin would be back soon. She sat, staring into the face of the intruder, getting her first good look at him.

He looked like a soldier. Or maybe a mercenary—there was something lethal about him, though she had no idea how she knew that. In her entire life she'd known assholes and saints, and assholes outweighed the saints by a ton, but this man was something else entirely.

His face was angular, but she wasn't going to stop and think whether he was handsome or not. It made no difference if he was model gorgeous or a monster. He was a threat, and she needed to get rid of him.

His jaw was strong beneath the scruffiness, but it was his eyes that drew her. They were a bright, absolutely compelling green-blue, like the color of Caribbean waters. They were deep and mesmerizing.

And oddly familiar. The wrong color, but she knew those damned lying eyes, even if she hadn't seen them for five years.

She leaned forward, seemingly casual, and before he realized what she was doing, she grabbed the gun from the table, turning and pointing it directly at his heart.

"You bastard," she said in a low, vicious voice.

If he was disturbed that she'd taken the gun he didn't show it. "There you go," James Bishop said calmly. "I was worried you'd forgotten me."

"I did my best. It was your self-satisfied smirk that gave you away. What are you doing here, James? If that's even your name. And what the fuck did you do with my diamonds?"

The man she'd known as James Bishop watched her, seemingly unconcerned about the gun she was pointing at him. "You may as well keep using that name. It's as good as any."

Damn, she wanted to pull the trigger. She wanted to blow a hole in him the size of the Grand Canyon; she wanted to shoot him with so much firepower that he was blown through the back of her very solid camper. The pistol was nothing but a .22, and while she could probably do some real damage, her ability to kill him even at close range was iffy.

She looked back at him, not bothering to disguise the hatred she felt. She thought she'd gotten past it. Damn it, she *had* moved past it. Only to have it dredged up with his shocking reappearance, with the wrong eyes and the wrong hair and the wrong everything. She really wanted to kill him.

"Why are you here?" Her voice was icy cold. She would have done anything to convince him that she felt nothing, not even anger, but that ship had sailed. "For that matter, how did you find me?"

He leaned back, watching her out of those familiar-unfamiliar eyes. "Are you going to shoot me?"

"Maybe." She kept a hard grip on the gun. "How did you find me?"

"I never lost you."

She almost pulled the trigger at that. It was a good thing for him that the safety was on. She glared at him. "Is there any chance you're going to explain yourself any time in the next twenty-four hours?"

"No."

She cocked the gun and pointed it at his head. "Leave," she said in a cold voice. "I don't want to get blood and brains all over my camper, but I'll do it, and I'll bury your goddamned body where no one will ever find you. Either that, or leave you for the scavengers. Save me a lot of trouble and just get out."

He looked at the gun, then to her eyes. "Oh, my angel, how you've changed," he drawled, and she pulled the trigger. Nothing happened.

His smiled widened. "Really, Angel? I didn't think you had it in you. You think I'd let you have a gun with bullets in it? I would have taken it away from you if it was loaded. But I have to say I'm charmed that you had the balls to actually try to blow my brains out."

"Sentimental, aren't you?" she growled. She didn't give up the gun, though.

"Always."

She wasn't going to ask him again, only to get another oblique answer. She sat very still, watching him as he drank the beer, not touching her own. She felt as if she were in some kind of swirling, Daliesque nightmare, spinning through her formerly safe world. How could he be there, appearing out of nowhere in her camper? Was he even real?

On impulse she reached out and pinched him, his warm, smooth flesh, and he didn't flinch. He cocked his head, amused. "You mean your second line of defense after shooting me is pinching me? I think you need a little training in the art of self-defense."

"I wanted to make sure you weren't a nightmare. Though in fact you are—every nightmare I've ever had wrapped up into one smarmy man."

"Smarmy?" he echoed. "Now that stings, Angel. My charm is one of my very best weapons."

"Weapons? Oh, that's right, your job is so dangerous. You seduce and abandon idiotic young women and take them for whatever they have. I'm surprised you even remember me."

His eyes were half-closed as he considered her. "How can I forget my sweet little wife?"

She glared at him. "What the fuck are you talking about?"

"Tsk-tsk. Such language, and from a professor, no less! Angel, you've grown bitter in the last few years."

"If you call me Angel one more time I will hit you over the head with this beer bottle," she said evenly.

He smiled benevolently. "You can try."

Bastard. "We're not married. You may go through the same ridiculous charade with all your marks, but that marriage was not legal and I knew it all along. It's not that simple to get married in a foreign country—there are papers and forms and waiting periods."

"Looked into it, did you? What you didn't take into account is that with the right amount of power you can cut through all sorts of red tape. We're married, in the sight of God, the rites of the Catholic Church, and the laws of Italy."

He had to be lying. There was no earthly reason for him to actually marry her, and if he had, she was merely one of many, making the marriage polygamous and illegal. "I don't believe you," she snapped. "And if by any chance you're telling the truth for once in your wretched, miserable life, then I'll get a divorce immediately."

"Italian divorce laws are notoriously tricky. You'll just have to put up with it a while longer. You've survived being married for five years—another few weeks won't harm you."

She focused on his last words and her stomach dropped. "Another few weeks?"

"You and I are taking a trip, Ang . . . my darling." He eyed the heavy beer bottle warily. "Think of it as a belated honeymoon."

"That's not going to happen."

He shrugged. "Well, be that as it may, but I need to get to New Orleans by Thursday, and we're using your camper. A number of very bad people don't want me to make it down there, so I need to use you to get me there. Ever been to New Orleans? It's a fascinating city."

"Fuck you. I'm not going anywhere with you."

"Yes, you are."

And just like that the danger returned, and the man opposite her truly was a stranger. He was cold, flinty eyed, and he could snap her neck in an instant if he wanted to.

He didn't seem to want to.

"Tell you what," he said, suddenly affable. "You've had a long day. Why don't you tell me what the hell you have to eat here and I'll whip us up some dinner. Believe it or not I'm a decent cook."

"I'd rather eat poison."

"Who's to say it's not?" he said sweetly. "I thought I saw some whole wheat pasta and tomato puree." He made the very dire mistake of turning his back on her as he reached up to the cabinet over the two-burner stove.

She didn't hesitate, and flew out of the seat, aiming the unopened bottle of beer at his head. A moment later she was being shoved against the stove, his body hard against her back, and her wrist numb beneath his iron grip. The bottle dropped from her nerveless fingers and she heard it roll away on the floor. He was all heat and lean muscle against her, covering her, and if her brain refused to think about it, her body remembered, and warmed in a despised, carnal response. She shivered, and he stepped back, not releasing her, and she spun around, glaring up at him.

She wasn't sure what she expected. A brutal slap, maybe worse. The deliciously wicked lover from so long ago had disappeared, and the man in front of her wouldn't hesitate. But he merely looked annoyed. "Now that beer will be undrinkable until tomorrow, and it will never be quite as good. You have excellent taste in beer, Angel, but you need to treat your beer with more respect." He took her other wrist before she could have the sense to hit him, holding both together in one hand as he started to pull her toward the bed.

That was enough to jar her from her stupor. She started to fight him then, kicking, struggling, and it was a shock to see how easily, efficiently he subdued her. "Don't get your knickers in a twist," he muttered, shoving her down on the mattress. "I'm hungry, not horny." He held her there, looking down at her in the shadows. He wasn't even breathing heavily, while she was panting from her exertions. "If you promise to stay still and not make any more ill-advised attempts to club me over the head, I won't tie you up."

"Take your hands off me." He was forcing her to lie still, and she hated the feel of his fingers digging into her shoulders, the unexpected strength of him.

"Then do as I say." There was no compassion in his face, no emotion whatsoever.

She didn't hesitate. He probably would tie her up if she gave him any reason. "Okay," she said, and the moment the pressure lightened, she squirmed away from him to the far side of the double bed. She thought about it for a moment. Stuck here would give her no options—if she were cooking for him there were knives, heavy cans of black beans and tomatoes, frying pans . . .

"Would you like me to cook for you?" she said in a defeated voice, keeping her furious eyes shuttered.

He laughed heartlessly. "And let you get at the hardware? I don't think so. Just relax on your divan like a princess and I'll make us something. It's the least I can do."

"The least you can do in return for trespassing, involving me in a felony, manhandling me, threatening me . . ."

"When I manhandle you, you'll know it," he said, turning away from her. She had no weapon, so she stayed still, thinking furiously.

But she did have a weapon. Merlin would be back from his patrol any time now, and he would rip Bishop's throat out, or at least take a good chunk of it. She'd seen him flatten a man in five seconds when he thought the man was going to hurt her, and now there was a real threat right in front of her.

She had no choice but to lie there, watching him as he rummaged through the neat little cabinets full of kitchen supplies. She'd forgotten his body. Too bad he hadn't developed a paunch; if anything he was leaner, stronger, not the elegant playboy with the well-toned body of a gym rat, but . . . the word "soldier" came to mind again. But there was no way someone like Bishop was a soldier.

She didn't want to watch him move—it brought back too many memories—but she couldn't roll over and turn her back on him. She couldn't let him know how much she remembered, how much it still bothered her. How much it still . . . hurt. He needed to think she was so over him . . .

Think? It was the simple truth. All she bore for the man was hatred. But it needed to be icy cold, not the scalding rage that filled her veins. She grabbed for one of her pillows, punched it, and tucked it under her head. All right, she could put up with him for now. Merlin would soon put an end to all this.

And then a horrified thought hit her. "Do you have a gun?"

He didn't bother glancing back at her. He was already busy opening cans, fiddling with things. "You just tried to blow my head off with one," he said mildly.

"I mean another one. One with bullets?" Merlin could still take him down, but she wasn't going to sacrifice her dog for her own safety. If Merlin got shot . . . It didn't bear thinking of.

"Somewhere. Not on me." He shot her a swift glance. "Any more questions?"

"Are you carrying a knife?"

He smiled then. "Angel, I don't need weapons to keep you in line—haven't I just proved that to you?"

Okay, that meant Merlin was safe to attack him. She was going to get out of this. Maybe she'd find that loaded gun and do what she'd tried to do earlier.

The memory made her feel slightly ill. It had been instinctive, pulling the trigger, but what if it had been loaded? What if she'd killed him, or even just wounded him? Not that he didn't deserve it, but she was another matter. She didn't want the psychic burden of shooting or killing anyone.

But she could use the gun to corral him. She could tie him up, then abandon him to the coyotes or the wolves or whatever. Let him get all the way down to New Orleans on his own—he would no longer be her problem.

"You got water?"

His voice roused her from her bloody thoughts. "I have a couple of gallons in the truck. I was hoping I could hook the camper up, but clearly this campground has seen better days." Two hours farther on the road was a good campsite with amenities like showers and electricity and flushing toilets. Thanks to the border agent, this abandoned campsite was all she got, and with her unwanted hitchhiker she would have preferred a crowd.

He nodded, set down the knife he'd been using to cut up an onion, and motioned to her. "Up and out," he said.

"Why?"

"Because I'm not leaving you alone in here while I go get the water, babycakes. I did a thorough search of this place while you were driving, and by the way, you are one fucking lousy driver. I could barely stand as you tore down these back roads."

"You aren't supposed to ride in the camper. It's against the law."

"I broke the law? Oh, my goodness." His sarcasm was even less welcome. "Get the fuck out of that bed or I'll join you in it."

That was enough to get her moving. "I thought you said you weren't interested." She swung her legs over the side of the bunk, eyeing him warily.

"I never said that. I just said I wasn't particularly horny. That was before I felt you up against the stove. Now I'm just as happy to take care of either appetite, but I don't imagine you'd like it much."

As a threat, it was pretty damned effective. She shot to her feet, but in the tiny camper he was closer than she realized, looming over her, and the knot that had lodged in the pit of her stomach tightened some more. She moved, the backs of her knees pressed up against the bunk. "After you," she said with mock courtesy.

"I don't think so, Angel. You're much too impressively dangerous." He reached over her head and pushed the door open, and in the distance, in the dusk-shadowed woods she could see Merlin's camouflaged coat.

She felt a cold triumph. "Certainly," she said, climbing down the steel steps onto the ground. She could make a run for it—he said he had no gun or knife on him—but the damned man could probably run faster. No, she was going to rely on Merlin, her savior.

He stepped down after her and closed the door, glancing around him at the campsite, the breeze rustling the canopy of leaves, drowning out Merlin's race through the woods.

Merlin cleared the trees, and James's eyes widened for a moment. It only took that long—he looked, and then Merlin had launched himself across the clearing with an odd growl in the back of his throat, flattening James.

She quickly moved out of the way, looking for another weapon to threaten him with once Merlin got the bastard subdued. James was trying to fight him off, pushing at him, and Merlin was making that strange noise, not the killer growl but more of an excited whine. To Evangeline's astonishment James managed to push Merlin off him, rolling over with him, and there were no snapping jaws. She realized with sudden horror that they weren't fighting: they were wrestling, tussling. Playing.

"Good dog," James said, struggling to sit up. Merlin jumped at him again, rubbing his huge head against James's shoulder and almost knocking him over, and James rubbed that special spot right beneath his throat that made him practically sing in ecstasy. Merlin tried to crawl into James's lap but he was shoved off. "That's enough for now, boy. I have to make dinner."

He got to his feet, brushing at his jeans, giving Merlin another absent rub as the dog pushed his head against Bishop's long legs, and he glanced at Evangeline. "Told you he wouldn't rip my throat out."

"What are you, the fucking Dog Whisperer?" she demanded.

He just smiled as he headed for the truck, Merlin trotting after him happily. He grabbed the two gallon jugs in one hand and pulled the door open. "You want to eat outside? It's a nice night."

"I want you to go away."

He rolled his eyes. "Haven't you realized that isn't going to happen? You know what they say when you're going to be raped—just lie back and enjoy it."

A combination of fury and remembered horror suffused her. "You disgusting, sexist asshole. You touch me and I'll castrate you."

"Tell you what—I'll give you a knife and see if you can go through with it. We can try right now . . ." He reached for the button of his jeans.

"You're forgetting that I pulled the trigger," she said with grim satisfaction.

"Not forgetting, Angel. You looked like you were going to throw up after you realized what you might have done. It's never easy to kill someone, particularly someone you've fucked."

"How do you know?" she shot back.

The look on his face silenced her. He did know. Her con man, faux husband knew what it was like to kill, and the knot in her stomach grew bigger.

"Personally I think reacquainting yourself with my mighty wang will render you frozen in awe and lust, leaving my balls intact, but I may be overrating my attraction. I'm willing to risk it if you are." He undid the button with one hand, still holding the water gallons. Merlin, the traitor, was watching both of them, his head moving back and forth, but he was sitting at James's feet.

"Stop it."

He raised an eyebrow. "Really?" He refastened the button with a show of reluctance. "Then come back inside and stop asking stupid questions while I cook."

"They're not stupid questions."

"They are because you know I'm not going to answer them. Come along, sweetheart." He crossed and batted her on the butt with the gallons of water. "And bring your silly dog."

Merlin no longer seemed much like her dog, but at that he turned and moved over to her, rubbing against her as well. Rubbing James Bishop's nasty, conniving, deceitful cooties onto her own jeans. "Traitor," she said, looking down at him. She squatted down, looking into his wise eyes. "He's a bad man. You were supposed to rip his throat out."

"He needs an attack order if he doesn't recognize an immediate threat," Bishop said, waiting at the door. "He's been professionally trained. Usually 'attack' or 'bite' does the trick, unless he's been trained in Europe. Then you'd have to figure out what language he was trained in."

She rubbed Merlin's head to reassure him she harbored no ill feelings for his sudden affection for strangers. "I'm pretty sure he's an all-American dog. Otherwise how could he have found his way to a tiny campus in northern Wisconsin?"

"There's always that," he said, noncommittally. "I'm hungry— get in the fucking camper or I'll put you there."

If he took a step toward her, Merlin should have attacked him, even without a verbal order. He had always taken his protection duties seriously, but Bishop seemed to have the ability to cloud Merlin's judgment. She moved past the man up into the camper, and this time Merlin came with her instead of keeping guard outside the door. At least he recognized that Bishop was more of a threat than anything that lurked outside in the deserted campground. She moved past him, sitting down at the dinette again, avoiding the bed for reasons she wasn't going to consider too closely, and Merlin dropped down to the narrow walkway with a sigh.

Bishop ignored both of them as he worked at the stove, and Evangeline made herself watch him, his efficient grace, the beauty of his lean body beneath the work clothes. Of course he was beautiful—it was his stock-in-trade. You couldn't be a con man if you didn't have anything to offer, and he used his beauty to lure women in. At least, she assumed it was only women.

"How many times have you done this?" she demanded suddenly, wishing she still had the beer that had gone rolling across the floor. He'd helped himself to another but hadn't offered her one— he probably didn't want to risk having his head bashed in while he cooked. He didn't realize she'd stored her cast-iron frying pan, the one she used for campfires, beneath the seat of the dinette.

"Done what?" he said without looking at her.

"Seduced someone in order to rip her off? Do you have any particular criteria? Do your victims have to be presentable, young, or do you go after older women in search of a boy toy? I would think they'd be more profitable. And what about older men? I would think anyone would like a pretty young thing like you."

She saw the side of his mouth quirk up in a half smile, but he was concentrating on cooking. "You still think I'm pretty? That relieves me." He took a swig of his beer. "I don't think you'd believe me if I told you the truth, though I could certainly make up some fascinating stories. In the meantime why don't you just sit there and see if you can come up with some way out of this. You won't be able to, but it should keep you occupied."

"Fuck off."

"Bad girl," he murmured in mock reproof. "What would your students think?"

She ignored him. "If I can talk my suddenly pacifistic dog into attacking you, how do I get him to stop? Assuming there's a slight chance I don't want him to kill you. I assume I yell at him to stop."

He shook his head. "If you'd had any sense, you would have signed up for classes once you realized you had a trained attack dog glued to your side. But you're not terribly sensible, are you? If Merlin attacks and you want him to let go, you say 'out.'"

"'Out'? That makes no sense." She looked down at the dog at her feet. "Attack, Merlin."

Merlin whined unhappily, looking between her and Bishop. She tried again, as Bishop watched with the supreme confidence of a man who knew he was safe. "Bite, Merlin."

Merlin sat up, put his head in her lap, and whined some more. Evangeline gave in. "That's all right, boy. We'll wait until he threatens me again. Then you'll get him."

"I don't think so," Bishop said. Somehow he'd managed to unearth the plates she'd brought with her, and a moment later he'd placed one in front of her, heaped with beans and vegetables and strips of what had to be pork if she knew the contents of her tiny freezer. It smelled divine, even in her current state of fury and something that was uncomfortably close to fear, but she knew if she took one bite, she'd throw up. She'd managed to get her hand beneath the cushion that covered the hinged seat in the back, but the handle of the fry pan wasn't on top, and she couldn't very well lean down and get it.

Or could she? He'd turned his back again, presumably to retrieve his half-empty beer, and she dove for the cabinet, yanking the frying pan out with a cry of triumph.

Except it was the smaller one of the set, big enough to fry a couple of eggs over a fire and not much more. She sat there, staring at it in dismay, and then looked up at Bishop.

He was leaning against the counter, perfectly relaxed as he watched her. "You don't give up easily, do you, Angel?" he said, and the name hardened her resolve.

"I never give up," she snapped. "And stop calling me that stupid name. You can call me Ms. Morrissey, or Professor Morrissey, or if you really must, Evangeline. I don't like nicknames."

"I'm afraid it's Mrs. Bishop," he corrected lightly. "And I'll call you any damned thing I please. You're forgetting I have the upper hand."

She weighed the cast iron in her hand. Granted, it wasn't quite the weapon a full-sized one would be, but she didn't really want to crush his skull, just knock him out, and this was probably better suited to the task. It was damned heavy. "You don't have any guns or knives," she said smugly. "I could break your hand with this thing. Or your face."

"You think a little thing like a broken hand would stop me?" His voice was soft, musing, at odds with his chilling words.

"Who *are* you?" she said. "What are you?"

He leaned forward, plucking the frying pan from her hand, twisting it so quickly that she cried out in pain, and shoved it into the cold oven. "You already called it, Angel. Your worst nightmare."

She threw the plate at him.

He ducked, though the food went everywhere, and a moment later hauled her up from the banquette, his hands rough and impersonal. "I've had enough," he muttered, manhandling her back toward the bed, and her panic increased until she remembered his earlier words. He wasn't interested in her—he was hungry, not horny.

He shoved her face down on the mattress, putting his knee in the middle of her back, and her struggles were useless. He grabbed one hand, pulling it behind her, paired it with the other, and she heard a ripping sound. A moment later he was wrapping something around her wrists, and the more she struggled, the harder he pressed with his knee, so that she could scarcely breathe. "Merlin," she tried to cry, but her face was pushed into the mattress and the sound of her voice was muffled beyond recognition.

He moved his knee and flipped her over, with the casual efficiency of a short-order cook flipping burgers. Then he grabbed her ankles, wrapping them as well with her cheerful Mickey Mouse–patterned duct tape. "You son of a bitch," she spat at him.

"I haven't decided whether to gag you or not," he said, looking down at her. "Trust me, it's even more unpleasant than having your hands and feet bound. It makes it hard to breathe, especially if you start crying."

True outrage filled her. "I'm not going to cry."

"Good. Then lie there and be quiet while I eat my dinner. I don't remember when I last had a real meal, and I'm tired of you annoying me."

He turned and headed back to the dinette, where he began to eat from the huge plate mounded with food in front of him.

Merlin was beside her, whining. He licked her face, her tear-free face, and made distressed noises, but he'd done nothing to help her.

"Merlin, eat." Bishop said, and Merlin immediately turned away from her and began clearing up the food that was splattered all over the floor and walls.

Evangeline fell back on the bed, shaking with frustration and fear. The man she'd supposedly married, the lying, cheating bastard, had returned, a stranger now, with the wrong eyes, the wrong hair, the wrong everything.

It was growing dark in the cabin, but he'd turned on the wall lights at the dinette and was looking at a crumpled piece of paper. Not hers, so she could only suppose it belonged to him.

He turned to glance at her through the gathering shadows. "I don't suppose you get Internet out here?"

She didn't answer, but simply turned her face away from him. She wasn't going to speak to him again, not when everything he said was lies and more lies. She stared at him as he ate with calm efficiency, and fury burned within her.

Calm down, she told herself. *Calm down and consider the situation and your alternatives. If you keep fighting him, he'll overpower you. If you run, he'll come after you. You need to be reasonable, to appear as if you're going to cooperate. Otherwise he'll just keep you trussed like a chicken. He even managed to mesmerize Merlin . . .*

She looked up at him. "How did you know my dog's name?"

Chapter Seven

It was a reasonable question, Bishop thought as he shoveled food into his face. It was a slip, but he was always good at fast responses. "His name is on his collar," he said, pretending he wasn't looking at her. He couldn't keep his eyes off her. Five years. Five endless years.

He'd seen photos of her, surveillance video. There'd never been a time when he hadn't known exactly where she was and who she was with. The only time he'd seen her from a distance was at her wedding to that asshole. He could have told her the guy was a fuckhead, but of course he didn't go anywhere near her. If Madsen even knew Bishop had been there he would have blown a gasket. But Bishop couldn't let Evangeline get married without getting a good look at the man.

Part of him had really hoped he'd be a decent human being, an all-American good guy who'd love her and treat her the way she deserved to be treated, who'd give her a safe life full of love and babies.

His delight in knowing Pete Williamson was a sneaking, lying asshat told him he wasn't even close to getting over her, and he'd kept his distance for the next three years, doing his best to avoid the photos that were passed on. Knowing she was safe was good enough for him.

But she wasn't safe anymore. He wasn't about to tell her that—he wasn't about to tell her anything more than he absolutely had to. The less she knew the better—this time when he disappeared she wouldn't be in any danger. He was going to make sure of it, no matter what the price.

She was practically vibrating with rage as she lay tied up on the bed, and damned if he wasn't even more turned on. He'd never seen her furious, but for some reason he found it encouraging. It was a sign she could take care of herself. When she had pulled the trigger to shoot him in the face, he could have kissed her.

She'd be all right, once he took care of things. Until then, she was going to have to put up with him, and learn that resistance was futile. He laughed to himself. Even after all these years, the life he lived, he was still a Trekkie.

He took his empty plate to the tiny sink, then grabbed her plate from the floor and added it in. He glanced over at her. "You got a dishwasher?"

It was supposed to annoy her, and it did. "That would be you," she said.

He cleaned up efficiently enough, heating water on the stove and methodically washing everything he'd used. He dried it all and put it away, then turned to his little problem.

Shit. He would have given ten years off his life to climb into that bunk with her. Unfortunately, kinky bastard that he was, he even liked the Mickey Mouse bondage. Touching her like that was probably the last thing he should do, for his sake and hers. Just that moment of shoving her up against the stove had left him with a hard-on that hadn't subsided completely.

God, he needed a shower. He'd been in the woods for weeks, hiding out until Corsini's men had given him up for dead. It took a lot more than that to kill him, which they'd find out soon enough. Unfortunately somewhere along the way they'd discovered

Evangeline's connection to him, which doubled her risk, and he knew they'd been looking for her as well. Otherwise he would have left Canada through Washington and returned to his current persona, Charles Edmunds.

He wasn't going to get pissy about it—life had a habit of throwing curves, like the time she'd walked into the church where he'd just assisted in an execution. It would have been so much simpler if she'd never been there, never seen what she'd seen. He still hadn't decided if he would have preferred that simpler version of life.

Fortunately it wasn't up to him to decide. He leaned against the sink and looked at her. Her hair was in her face—he'd always loved her soft, flyaway hair, and he wanted to push it out of her eyes. He didn't.

"Well, don't you make a lovely little housewife?" Her voice was caustic.

He grinned at her. No matter what happened, she wasn't going to give up easily. "I was a Boy Scout."

"I don't believe you. Boy Scouts don't seduce and rob helpless women, they don't kidnap them . . ."

"You're hardly a helpless woman. If it had been your choice, you would have still been scrubbing my brains off the dinette."

She shuddered, trying not to show it. He was okay with her reaction—violence was difficult to process, especially if you weren't used to it. He still knew she wouldn't hesitate to pull the trigger again if she felt threatened.

He pushed away from the stove and leaned over the bed platform, resting his arm against the overhead framing, staring down at her. Deliberately intimidating. "I've got one question."

"Why should I answer yours? You don't answer mine."

"You get one, I get one. Go ahead." He was being stupid. His question was so reasonable and so important he shouldn't waste time with her. But he couldn't resist.

"Okay." She glared up at him, not hesitating. "Exactly who are you? Because even though you bear a resemblance to the man I met in Italy, you aren't the same man."

"That one's too easy, Angel." He loved watching her stiffen every time he called her his pet name for her, the name he'd only spoken on rumpled sheets smelling of sex. "My real name is James Bishop, and I'm your husband."

"Liar."

"It's not my problem if you don't believe me," he pointed out. "Now for my question, and it's important. Did you tell anyone at the border crossing where you were headed?"

She looked up at him, her delectable mouth stubborn, and for a moment he was distracted, remembering the feel of her mouth on his skin. Ignoring it, he leaned over her, all menace. "I'm going to need an answer, and I don't mind what I have to do to get it. The truth would be a good idea as well, considering your life is at stake as well as mine."

She looked startled. She still hadn't figured out what kind of world she'd suddenly stepped into, just as she hadn't known in Italy. He couldn't protect her completely this time, though, and trying to might mean the difference between life and death. She had to know he wasn't playing games.

"Yes. I told the asshole who was giving me such a hard time. I bet he was one of your friends, holding me up so you could sneak into the camper."

He pulled back. "Shit," he said in a low voice. "We're getting the hell out of here."

"Not a friend, then?" she said. "So unfasten me and we can go."

He shook his head. "I think you're better off right where you are. It's a bouncy ride but you'll survive." That way if Clement caught up with them she wouldn't be a visual target. And she wouldn't see him kill the man.

"I don't want to stay here!"

"Yeah, well things are tough all over," he said heartlessly, reaching for duct tape. "Maybe next time you'll keep your mouth shut. Or lie."

"I'm not a good liar." She was eyeing the duct tape warily.

He gave her his most affable smile. "I'm an excellent liar, as you well know. I'll teach you. In the meantime I'm strapping you in so you don't fall around inside the camper. I'm going to be driving fast and I don't want you hurt."

Her eyes widened in alarm. "You're going to what?"

"You heard me." He ran the duct tape across the bed, row after row, trapping her. He'd survived any number of stormy seas using the same principle, lashed to his bunk. She'd be fine. "Do I have to gag you?"

"No." There was just a note of breathless panic in her voice. Even if she had agreed, he wouldn't have gagged her. People could choke to death on fear, and he couldn't quite calculate how frightened she was. She was determined not to show him.

He leaned over and brushed her hair out of her eyes. "I'll keep you safe," he said. "I promise."

He pulled back before he could say anything more, do anything more. She was his personal Kryptonite, and he had to remember that.

"Merlin, heel," he said. The dog had been curled up on the floor by her bed, and he rose obediently, whining softly as he looked back at her. "With me, Merlin," he said.

He locked the door from the outside.

⌣

Evangeline heard the sound of the lock, and for a moment absolute panic raced through her body. She was trapped in here, and even if she managed to get free from this ridiculous spider's web of duct tape, she'd have a hard time getting out. There was an escape window, but it was dark, and she didn't remember the instructions. She had a flashlight somewhere . . . no, it was in the cab of the truck, so no help there. She squirmed, trying to free herself, but she could barely move.

A moment later she was just as glad. She heard the roar of the truck engine, and then they shot forward with a jerk. The camper bumped and bounced over the rough terrain, and Evangeline lay very still. Poor Annabelle—her trailer wasn't used to such rough treatment, and suddenly she remembered tearing up and down mountain roads beside the man calling himself James Bishop, a name she didn't believe for one moment, any more than she believed in this specious marriage. Annabelle couldn't withstand such treatment . . .

The camper jerked and swung hard to the left, and Evangeline let out a grinding moan. At least they were on a paved road now, though it wasn't in the best shape. Bishop—she couldn't think of anything else to call him and *that asshole* got tiresome—was driving like a bat out of hell. She had no idea her elderly truck was capable of such speeds, particularly when pulling her ancient camper.

It was pitch dark in her bunk. They didn't pass any streetlights, or other cars for the matter, and the darkness was a cocoon, exacerbated by the bonds. She could hear things crash in the cabin as he went over bumps, took corners too fast, and she closed her eyes, praying the trailer wouldn't whiplash and come loose, sending her over some cliff.

She took a deep breath, and then another, trying to center herself. She'd learned proper breathing as well as yoga after she'd left Pete. It had taken her too damned long to figure out that she couldn't change anyone else, couldn't change men. She could only change herself and her reaction to things.

So she lay in her bunk and breathed calm, steady breaths; slowly her body relaxed, sinking into the plush mattress she'd treated herself to when she'd bought Annabelle. She visualized the breath flowing through her body, she visualized every joint, every muscle, every inch of her body relaxed and at peace. She pictured James Bishop tied to a tree so she could have target practice. And then, unbelievably, she slept.

She woke slowly, her eyes fluttering open. Some time in the night they'd stopped moving, and if she could judge by the light filtering in through the curtain, it was early morning, just a little past dawn. She tried to sit up, forgetting she was trapped in her bunk, and she fell back in frustration. Her entire body hurt, but most of the pain was focused in her shoulders, and she bit back a cry of pain. As she began to see more clearly, she realized Bishop had converted the dinette into a bunk, and was asleep there, with Merlin lying on the mattress beside him.

That put her over the edge. "Hey, Bishop, or whatever your real name is," she called out.

He didn't move. He would have been exhausted after driving through the night, and she didn't give a damn. "Bishop!" she said again.

He remained motionless, though Merlin had lifted his head, alert.

"I heard you." His voice came from the bed. He didn't sound particularly tired, just long-suffering, and she wanted to snarl. If anyone was suffering, it was her. "I was hoping you'd take pity on me and let me sleep."

"Pity isn't in my vocabulary."

"And you're a college professor!" he mocked, turning over.

She ground her teeth. "What the fuck are you doing with my dog?"

Merlin jumped down, pacing the small length of the camper to press his cold nose up against her face, whining.

"He didn't like the duct tape. Neither did I."

"You could have cut me free." Too late did she realize what she'd said, and she scrambled. "So Merlin could join me, not you."

He sat up, his lean body silhouetted in the early-morning light, and she watched as he rose and worked the kinks from his body. The convertible dinette made a cramped bed, and he was a tall man. At least there was some justice in this world.

He paused by her bed, looking down at her. "Do you have to pee?"

Jesus, what a question! "No," she snapped.

"You always did a have a bladder like a camel's," he said affably. "We're about two hundred miles from Bear's Claw, and this isn't a formal campground, which means the wood's our toilet and the river's our bathtub. Since you're in no particular hurry, I'm going to clean up. You got towels?"

"Not for you."

He shrugged. "Suit yourself. I have no problem with nudity if you don't." He was out the door before she could protest, but Merlin stayed where he was, sitting on his haunches in the guard position she was used to.

"Great good that is," she said to him, her voice full of affection. "He's the one you're supposed to be protecting me from."

Merlin gave her that look. It was one uniquely his, one she'd never seen on another dog, a canine expression that roughly translated to "you've got to be kidding me."

"I don't suppose I could talk you into chewing through the duct tape?" she said.

Merlin's whine could have been expressing his regret. She sighed. He'd simply met another alpha dog—it wasn't his fault.

"Give me a kiss, baby," she said, and Merlin licked her nose with his long tongue, snuffling at her with sympathy.

She needed the sympathy. In her annoyance she hadn't realized just how much she had to use the facilities, or lack thereof. Bishop would take his own sweet time, and in the meantime all she could do was lie there and try to figure out what the hell was going on.

She had very little to work with. Her thieving gigolo of a phony husband had popped up out of nowhere, in the middle of the wilderness, with a gun and a ruthlessness that was a far cry from the slow-burning sexuality that had once kept her in such a haze of desire that the rest of her brain had stopped working. He'd given her some cock-and-bull story about keeping her safe and matters of life and death, and she wondered if he was batshit insane. Why the hell had he shown up now? Could she believe a damned thing he said?

She already knew the answer to that. He was made of lies, and there was no way she could ever trust him. She couldn't outthink him—he was too flat-out ruthless. She wouldn't put anything past him, including using that gun on her.

She flinched at the horrible memory of pulling the trigger. It had been a moment of sheer rage, all the hurt and betrayal and misplaced love exploding in one violent moment. What if the gun had been loaded?

He'd called it. She'd be cleaning his brains off the dinette. She hadn't been able to think of any way to threaten him, any leverage. So she'd pulled the trigger—he'd known perfectly well how horrified she'd been at her own action. He knew she wouldn't carry through with it again, not unless her life was in danger.

Oddly enough, she didn't think she was in any danger from Bishop. Sane or not, lying or truthful, he wasn't going to hurt her. Physically, that was. He'd already hurt her so much in every other way that there was nothing else he could do to her.

She also wasn't going to play along with whatever fantasies or lies he was spinning. Since she couldn't fight him, and she didn't even consider the option of asking, of begging him to go away and leave her alone, then her only choice was to run. She could make it in the woods on her own for a good long time; she could walk to civilization no matter how long it took her. Anything that awaited her in the woods was less threatening than the return of James Bishop.

"So what are you going to do, baby?" she said to Merlin. "Are you coming with me, or staying with that slimy bastard? And if you stay, are you going to rat me out?"

Merlin looked at her out of those wise black eyes, but his answer was anyone's guess. She suspected he'd come with her—he was still in his protective mode, even though he seemed have a case of love at first sight with Bishop. She couldn't blame him there— the same disease had hit her long ago in Italy, much to her shame.

Bishop took too damned long doing whatever he was doing, and she was ready to scream in rage when he finally opened the door and climbed in. She'd been sure he'd be naked, but he was fully dressed in clean clothes, similar to the ones he'd been wearing. His blond hair was wet, but he hadn't bothered to shave, and his stubble looked good on . . . what the fuck was she thinking?

He tossed a backpack onto the dinette/bed and paused by her bed, an eyebrow lifted. "Still got an iron bladder?"

"If you don't cut me free I'm going to pee in the bed and I'll make you sleep in it."

"Kinky." He already had a knife out, one that was far too big for the job, and it was all she could do to keep from flinching as it slid against her skin. She suspected he did it deliberately—the flat blade of the big knife a subtle caress against her, and she wanted to jerk away. If she did she could get hurt, so all she could do was lie perfectly still as he cut the bonds away, finishing up with the tape wrapped around her ankles. He caught her arm in one large, strong hand, pulling her upright to get at her bound wrists, and despite her best efforts to keep still, she cried out in pain.

He frowned, but said nothing as her hands were suddenly free. She wasn't even aware of the tape ripping away from her skin—the pain in her shoulders was blinding, and she closed her eyes and sucked in her breath, trying to still any more sounds of distress.

She felt his hands on her shoulders, and much as she wanted to jerk away, she couldn't. He was kneading her flesh, his thumbs pressing into the joints, a slow, sure massage that was working out the knotted muscles that had felt frozen. Feeling rushed back to her arms like an army of fire ants covered her skin, and she let out a little yelp. His hands slid down her bare arms then, rubbing, and the memories of Venetian nights overwhelmed her. She forced her eyes to open.

Big mistake. He was too close, and he was looking at her from those damned sea-blue eyes that were so wrong yet so familiar. Suddenly he stopped, looking at her, so close, too close, and he was going to put that gorgeous mouth on hers, and she had no idea what she'd do if he did. Would she kiss his damned lying mouth back? Or would she sink her teeth into his tongue?

She didn't find out. He dropped his hold on her and got up from the bed, moving away from her as if she had rabies. "Go ahead and use the facilities," he said, as if they hadn't shared a tight, yearning moment.

Maybe they hadn't. She was nothing to him, nothing but a mark, and he'd been everything to her. She climbed out of the bunk, stiff and sore, and moved carefully, holding on to the bed for support. "If I want to wash can I trust you not to look?"

His derisive laugh made her remember the missing .22 fondly. "Feel free to prance around the camp in your birthday suit, Angel. I'm going to explore the area—take your time. I'll leave Merlin on point."

"You're expecting an enemy attack?" Her voice was derisive.

He ignored her question. "Don't make the mistake of trying to run. Merlin won't let you."

She doubted it, but she wasn't about to say anything. Merlin had had her back since he showed up on campus, and even if he irrationally adored Bishop, he still knew who his real master was.

She yanked open the drawer beneath her bed, pulled out clean clothes and a towel, and left the trailer before she could be tempted to say anything more.

The clearing was small, the sound of rushing water off to the left, hidden by the woods that surrounded them, and she made a beeline for the thickest growth, relieving herself with a groan of relief. She rose from her uncomfortable position, her legs unsteady, and gathered up her amenities. She had a bottle of Campsuds in the truck, and getting clean would go a long way toward restoring her equilibrium. It was a lot easier to feel hopeless and defeated when you were tired and dirty and sticky. And hungry. She'd been a fool to throw her plate at him last night, she realized. She needed to keep her strength up if she was going to have any chance against him.

The river was little more than an enthusiastic stream, but it was swift moving and the water was cold, even in the little pool it had formed. She glanced around, but there was no sign of Bishop, or Merlin for that matter. If Bishop was watching, then he could go ahead and get an eyeful. It wasn't anything he hadn't seen before, though her body had changed in the last five years. She was stronger, leaner, tougher. She'd lost any softness in her skin, and in her soul.

She stripped off her filthy clothes and stepped into the waist-deep pool, shivering as goosebumps covered every exposed inch of her flesh. She hadn't brought a washcloth with her, so she squeezed the biodegradable soap into her hands and began scrubbing her body, washing away his touch, washing away the grime of the last few days. She'd really counted on the campground showers, but this would just have to do.

Even her scalp itched. At the last minute she ducked her head underwater and scrubbed it with the soap. As a shampoo, Campsuds left a lot to be desired, but the unpolluted water would go a ways toward softening her hair. Her shorter hairstyle had its advantages, but she no longer had the option of braiding it into submission.

She waded out of the stream, shivering, and grabbed her towel, rubbing it briskly over her cold body, when something made her pause. Someone was watching her. It was no surprise—she never considered that Bishop would be trustworthy.

But it didn't feel like Bishop watching her. Bishop wouldn't lurk in the wood—he'd just walk boldly into the clearing and make comments about her body while she tried to dress.

She was imagining things. They were alone out here in the middle of nowhere—she didn't have any idea where they were, if they were even still in Montana.

It was only then that she realized Merlin hadn't reappeared. He was probably patrolling, but the knot in the pit of her stomach grew. She wouldn't have thought her situation could get any worse, but she suspected it was about to.

"Merlin!" she called, out, whistling for him. "Here, boy!"

There was no answering crash through the underbrush. Merlin had excellent hearing, and if he were anywhere nearby, he'd be pounding his way back to her. All she could hear was the sound of the stream behind her, the soft rustle of the wind through the leaves.

And she was standing there in her birthday suit, instead of getting her goddamned clothes on like someone with a particle of brains. Knotting the towel around her for added security, she reached down for her underwear—suddenly an arm snaked around her waist, trapping her arms against her body.

It wasn't Bishop's hard body. This man was almost as tall, but he wasn't as strong-looking, and he was dirty, smelling of stale sweat and garlic. "I wouldn't scream if I were you," a low, vicious voice whispered in her ear, and she realized that there was a knife against her neck, one that would give Bishop's blade a run for the money.

Evangeline froze. "What did you do to Merlin?" Her voice came out in a choked whisper.

"Fuck your dog. It's your partner I'm interested in, and I don't need a big-ass German shepherd getting in my way. You think I don't recognize a trained attack dog when I see one? You just behave yourself and after I take care of Edmunds you can go on your way."

It had only taken her a moment for her panic to subside enough to recognize his voice. It was the surly border guard from the day before, the one Bishop had driven like a bat out of hell to escape. Apparently he hadn't driven fast enough.

"If you've hurt Merlin I'll kill you," she snarled.

"You and what army? Just be glad I'm not going to kill you."

That was a lie. He was going to kill Bishop, or Edmunds, or whatever his name was, and then he'd kill her to tie up loose ends. She didn't want to die, and to her shock she realized she didn't want Bishop dead either.

Think, Evangeline, think. The man was too strong—she'd never be able to break free. If she were fully dressed, wearing her boots, then maybe she could have kicked him, but for all intents and purposes she was bare-assed, and for some reason her almost nudity made her feel weak, unable to fight back.

Which was crap. She was just as strong, just as smart with or without her clothes, and if she couldn't beat him with her body, she could use her brain. "Do you have to hold me so tight?" she complained. "I can barely breathe."

He didn't loosen his iron grip. "You'll survive."

No, she wouldn't. She had to get him talking. Was there any chance in the world she could play Mata Hari, seduce him into carelessness? Not hardly likely—even Bishop was no longer interested in her, and for all his lies and treachery, there'd been no doubt that his desire for her had been real.

"What did you do . . . ?" she began, and the sharp, slicing pain in her neck silenced her. She could feel the blood sliding down her chest, dripping into the towel, and she wondered whether he'd cut her throat, whether she was about to bleed out.

"Shut the fuck up," the man said. "Or I'll make sure you never say another word." She could still feel the steel pressed against her, and she let herself feel a moment's relief. Death might be imminent, but it wasn't there yet. "Where's your friend gone off to?"

"Now how can she answer you when you told her you'd cut her throat if she talks?" Bishop's lazy voice seemed to come from nowhere, and she jerked, trying to see him, but there was no one around.

"Come out, come out, wherever you are," the man holding her said in a singsong voice that was chilling. "Unless you want me to cut her throat right in front of you, you'll come out with your hands in the air."

"Now why would I do that?" Bishop drawled, his voice coming from another direction. "You're just going to kill me."

"Don't you want to save your lady friend?"

"You're a sick bastard, Clement, and we both know it. She'd be better off if you cut her throat—a quick, clean death. I wouldn't want to leave her behind for you to take your time with her." The voice had moved again, now to their left.

"If you say so, old friend. I can always find someone to play my games if this one has to be sacrificed. You have any last words for her? You want to tell her you love her? Give her the lie so she can die happy?"

"How do you know it's a lie?" came the voice, and the man Bishop had called Clement turned, pulling her with him, the knife blade still resting against her neck, as he peered between the brush.

"I've known you for years, Edmunds. People like us are missing something. We can't love, we don't feel guilt, and we do what needs to be done. You need to die, and if she won't work to draw you out, then she's of no use to me."

Evangeline felt the blade bite in deeper, and more warm blood spread down her chest, soaking into the towel. She was going to die, naked, in the middle of nowhere, and they'd probably never find her body. It was a lousy, ignominious fate for a tenured professor, and one more thing she could blame on Bishop.

"Don't be so quick, Clement. That's always been your problem—too fast off the mark. You get many complaints about that from your women?" Bishop's disembodied voice was soft, taunting.

"My women aren't usually in any shape to complain when I'm done with them. So this one is important to you? I thought she might be, though I admit it surprises me. I've never known you to give a shit about anyone."

"I don't." He seemed farther away now, and Evangeline wondered if he was just going to disappear and leave her with this monster. "But have you taken a good look at her? Why waste all that gorgeousness if you don't need to?"

She felt the man's head move as he looked down, and then to her horror he pulled the towel away from her, dropping it on the ground. She clenched her jaw. If she didn't get out of this alive then she was going to haunt James Bishop into madness.

Clement shrugged against her, and it made the knife bite in again, and more warm blood slide down her body. "She's not my type. Not enough tits and ass. But if she's yours, then you'd better show yourself or there's not going to be much left of her. I'll count to ten . . ."

"Don't bother, James," she called out in a caustic voice. "He's going to kill both of us, so don't waste any noble gesture on me. It would ring false."

"I'm incapable of noble gestures, Angel," Bishop said, suddenly close at hand, and the man holding her was yanked back.

She went flying, landing on the hard ground. She was stark naked, covered with blood, and she lay there, stunned for a moment, until her eyes focused on the men.

Bishop and the erstwhile border guard were rolling in the dust, grappling with each other. Bishop had a knife as well, though his wasn't as big as the guard's weapon, and they looked like strangers, people she'd never seen before, as they rolled and grunted and fought. It was far from a clean fight—the guard kept trying to knee Bishop in the crotch, and Bishop was equally vicious, the violence so thick in the air that it made her ill.

The border guard had his lips drawn back from his teeth in a feral grin as he straddled Bishop, but a moment later Bishop tossed him off as he rolled away, and there was a patch of blood beneath Bishop's arm. He was the one who was truly scary, fighting with such icy calm and determination that she never once considered he might not win.

They broke apart and were both on their feet so quickly, it was almost synchronized. Then they circled each other. Bishop was edging closer, keeping his body between her and Clement, and without looking at her, he growled, "Get the fuck out of here, Angel. This piece of trash won't take long to deal with, but you don't need to watch."

She was still slightly dazed, but she knew a lie when she heard one. For some reason he wasn't sure he could stop the man, and he wanted her out of the way. She wanted to be out of the way as well, whether he won or lost, and if the two men kept each other busy, she could make her way to the truck; hopefully he'd left the keys in it. Even if he hadn't, she could manage—she had a spare hidden under the seat. The canopy was out on the trailer, and the road that had brought them to this clearing was little more than a path. The thought of driving out of there wearing nothing at all wasn't enough to stop her. She and Annabelle would make it.

"I won't leave without Merlin," she said, shaking off her stupid wish that she had something, anything, to cover her body.

"What'd you do with the dog, Clement?" Bishop's voice was silky. "If you hurt him, I'll make you very sorry."

Clement snorted. "You think I'm an idiot? Killing dogs causes more trouble than it's worth. Even Colombian drug lords get sentimental over their dogs, and if I got the reputation that I off animals, I wouldn't be able to get a job anywhere."

"Sweet of you," Evangeline muttered.

"I said get the fuck out of here," Bishop said again in a cold, hard voice she would never have recognized. "I'll find Merlin after I finish with this prick and we'll come after you."

Now why didn't that thought fill her with dread? She should do what he told her to do—get the hell away from there and just hope he wasn't able to find her later. Except . . . she wasn't going to leave Merlin.

In fact, she wasn't going to leave Bishop either. If Clement got the drop on him she could always leap onto his back, distract him long enough to give Bishop the advantage again. "I'm not going anywhere."

"I'm going to beat you after I kill Clement," he said through gritted teeth, never taking his eyes off the other man.

Clement laughed. "You can't even make your woman obey you, Edmunds? I thought you had more balls than that. She'll appreciate having a real man take care of her after I kill you."

Bishop was still moving, always keeping her guarded. "You're a real man, Clement? Then why do you have to fuck women you're going to kill? No one else hold still for you?"

"I like it when they fight. Don't you?" Clement licked his lips, and Evangeline felt sick.

"Oh, sometimes. As long as they're into it," Bishop said in a conversational voice. "But are we really here to talk about sexual variations, or are you going to put your money where your mouth is and try to kill me?"

"If I take a run at you, it puts me at a disadvantage. You've killed enough people to know that," Clement purred. "I think you should come to me."

She saw Bishop's broad shoulders shrug. "Have it your way." He moved so fast he was no more than a graceful blur, kicking Clement in the side of his head. Clement staggered back, stunned, slashing out with his knife, but Bishop dodged him, moving to Clement's side and kicking him in the back of the knees. Clement went down hard, his head hitting the ground with a thud, and he didn't move, dazed.

Bishop went to stand over him, kicking the dropped knife away from him. Then he knelt down, grabbed Clement by the hair, and yanked his head up. "You cut my woman," he said, "and you hurt my dog." And to Evangeline's horror, he took his knife and slashed the man's throat.

Evangeline turned her face into the dirt and vomited. She could hear the gurgling sounds as the man bled to death, but Bishop didn't move; he dropped the man's head back and watched as he died.

She didn't have enough in her stomach, and she was racked with dry heaves by the time he rose and turned toward her. He was going to kill her as well, she thought, no longer caring. What had the dead man said . . . "You've killed enough people . . ." Bishop the liar, the thief, the *murderer*, had no reason to keep her alive. She was a witness . . .

He scooped her up in his arms, and she fought him, her arms flailing, but he managed to subdue her with quick, brutal efficiency. She gave in, too sick and exhausted to continue the battle, and he carried her past the body, pushing her head against his shoulder so she couldn't look. A moment later they were in the camper, and he was setting her down on the bed with exquisite care. She knew she should jump up, hit him, run, but for the moment she was just numb, and there was no way she could stop him from doing whatever he wanted to do.

He moved away from her, and she closed her eyes, trying to disappear into herself. But then she remembered she was naked; she reached for the sheet, pulling it up around her and curling into the fetal position.

Bishop came back. "Sorry, that won't do." She felt the mattress sink beneath his weight, his strong hand catch her shoulder and force her to face him. It wasn't worth the struggle, and as she let him pull the sheet away, she told herself she didn't care. It wasn't as if he hadn't seen her body before.

She opened her eyes then, looking up into the face of a killer. It was the same face. The high cheekbones, the familiar-unfamiliar eyes. She looked at him, and it hit her with the force of a blow.

She wanted to fuck him. For a crazy, irrational moment she wanted to pull him down over her, take him between her legs, rut with him in the blood that covered her, and it didn't matter how sick she felt: she wanted him. She wanted to wipe out death with life, she wanted to change everything. She stared up at him and said nothing.

"I'd wash you off in the stream but you'd be more likely to pick up an infection," he said in a flat voice. He had a wet cloth in his hand, and he was washing her, cleaning the blood away from her skin. He worked with impossible gentleness, and all she could do was lie still and watch him, keeping her face expressionless. He found a place that hurt, and he frowned, his touch even more gentle. "It's not that deep," he said. "I think I can close it with butterfly bandages. I'd rather not have to stitch you up—I'm not very neat with my needlework."

I'm supposed to smile at that, she thought. She couldn't. She lay still as he rinsed out the cloth and drew it down her body with the impersonal attention of a doctor, as if her body had never meant anything to him. Finally he pulled back. "You've got two gashes, both of them shallow, and they bled enough that they should be fairly clean, even though you ended up rolling in the dirt. I'm going to put some disinfectant on them and bandage them . . ."

"What about Merlin?" She could finally talk, though she almost didn't recognize her voice.

"As soon as you're taken care of, I'll go after him. Either it's too late or he'll be fine—five minutes won't make any difference." He must have brought her first aid kit over to the bed with him, because his hands were on her again, and she felt the sharp tug as he closed her torn flesh with the butterfly bandages. One slash was on her collarbone, the other was across the top of her breast. Any lower and it would have been across her nipple. She shuddered.

"You're cold," he said, finishing with the second wound, his cool hands on her breast, and she wanted to cry. But she didn't cry anymore, she reminded herself. He flipped the sheet back over her, and she felt an odd, disjointed relief. "I'll get you something for the pain."

"I don't need anything, I just need Merlin."

He ignored her, moving away, and when he came back, he had a bottle of water and a pill in one hand. It wasn't from her medical kit, and she looked at it dubiously. "I'm not going to . . ."

"If you want me to go after Merlin, you'll take it," he said flatly. "I've got other things to take care of out there, and I need to be sure you're all right."

"I'm all right without drugs . . ."

"Take it." His voice wasn't just implacable, it was dangerous. She wanted to protest again, but something in those blue eyes stopped her, and she took the pill. She had every intention of tucking it in her cheek, but she ended up swallowing it by accident.

She was too tired to glare at him. She sank back on the blood-stained sheets and closed her eyes. "Bring Merlin to me." Her voice was barely audible. "No matter what."

He said nothing for a long moment, and she was tempted to open her eyes again. She didn't. "Rest," he said finally. "I'll bring him back."

James Bishop stared down at Evangeline, controlling his need to touch her again. He had had better days in his life. He really hadn't wanted Evangeline to know just how dangerous things were. He'd been a fool to think he could outrun Clement—even though he'd checked to make sure there'd been no tracker planted on the truck or the camper, he somehow must have missed it. It was unforgivably sloppy on his part—the kind of mistake a rookie would make. He'd been so determined to get Evangeline out of harm's way that he'd almost gotten her killed.

He wasn't used to making mistakes—another reason why he couldn't risk being anywhere around her. The Corsinis knew she was a way to get to him, and they were as relentless as the Committee. It had taken five long years to bring the Corsinis' filthy sex trafficking to its knees, but the rest of the crime family continued on like some overbloated octopus—the other arms slimy and lethal.

He never should have left Evangeline's side earlier—that or, even better, he should have made sure Clement never got near her in the first place. He'd been searching for Merlin, whose sudden disappearance should have alerted him, and he'd played right into Clement's hands. He'd fucked up, and he'd ended up with Evangeline's beautiful, creamy skin marred by that bastard's knife, with Merlin out there, possibly hurt or dead despite Clement's assertions that he didn't kill animals, and worst of all, he'd ended up with Evangeline knowing exactly who and what he was, a calm, methodical killer. It was no wonder she'd thrown up in the dirt.

There was nothing he could do about it now. He stared down at her as she lay beneath the bloody sheet, and he could see the outline of her body perfectly. He'd never wanted to fuck so badly in his life.

He was used to it—the normal aftermath to taking a life. But he'd never wanted to fuck anyone else he'd worked with or been with, and he'd killed more people than he wanted to remember.

The problem was, he did remember. He knew all the faces, every sound as their life left them. He knew the finality of it, and it gave him no sense of power, as it did for people like Claudia or the other operatives, like Matthew Ryder. He usually just felt empty.

But he hadn't killed when he'd been around Evangeline. Evangeline, who could put her arms around him and hold his head against her breast, who could take him into the warm, wet, peace of her body and bring him to a ferocious climax that was life itself, a spit in the eye of death.

He was hard, and it was a good thing she was too wiped out to notice, or she'd probably throw up again, and he wouldn't blame her. He rose, surreptitiously adjusting himself. First off he had to find Merlin, and then he had to get rid of the body and wipe out any trace of their short, fierce battle. Then maybe he could take care of the slash in his side that had finally stopped bleeding.

She hadn't noticed that either—a good thing. She was on the ragged edge already, and it would give her a good target to punch. She was ruthless, thank God. That ruthlessness might very well keep her alive.

The drug he'd given Evangeline would likely knock her out for hours, which would give him more than enough time to deal with things. They needed to get the hell out of there—while Clement liked to work alone, he was no more than a hired gun. His Eminence and the Corsini family had sent Clement after him—somehow they had found Bishop's connection to Evangeline. Clement's employers would expect a report, and if they heard nothing, they'd know that Clement had failed. And then they'd send someone else.

But for the next few hours Evangeline could sleep while he took care of business.

He looked down at Clement's body, and remembered the slashes on Evangeline's chest. He slammed his boot into the man's head, just because. Then he went in search of Merlin.

Chapter Eight

It was dusk when Evangeline awoke. Bishop had turned on one of the lanterns and set it on the dinette, and he was busy with something. His back was turned to her, and his shirt was off. She stared at him for a long sleep-dazed moment, and then realized something heavy was beside her. She turned, and Merlin lay there, in one piece, wagging his tail slowly. She reached out a hand to touch his head, and he snuffled and slept on.

"Clement clubbed him on the head and left him for dead. Lucky for him Merlin's got a harder head than most humans." Bishop's tight voice came from the dinette, but he hadn't turned to look. He was still doing something with his back to her, and she stared at him.

He had scars on his back. She remembered some of them from five years ago, and he'd given her the easy excuse of an accident-prone life when she'd asked him. She'd kissed and licked every one of those scars.

He had new ones. A slash across his hip that had healed to a pale pink line, and a deeper score just below his shoulder blade that would have come much too close to his heart. He could have died and she never would have known.

Never would have cared, she reminded herself. She didn't need this new information about the man who'd lied to her, tricked her, robbed her. Presumably he'd graduated to bigger targets, who were more lethal, since his penny-ante time with her. The stakes were a lot higher than a measly pair of diamond earrings. What he'd stolen from her hadn't been thirty-thousand-dollar earrings—it had been her trust, her heart, her soul. Her reaction to his betrayal had been just as lethal—she simply hadn't had the ability to claim revenge. Whoever had sent the dead man must be another one of his victims.

"Are you admiring my back, Angel, or did you have something to say?"

She didn't move. "Was he another one of your victims? What did you steal from him?"

"From whom? You mean Clement? No, he was just a middle-man. A hired gun, so to speak." Bishop's voice was cool, clipped, as if killing a man was an everyday affair.

"Then who was it you robbed?"

"No one." He turned to look at her, and she realized with a mixture of sickness and awe what he was doing. He had a slash across his ribs, and he was sewing himself closed.

She sat up too quickly, and her wounds screamed in protest, her head spun, and Merlin stayed asleep. "That man hurt you." It was a stupid thing to say—obviously he had.

There was an air of hidden tension about him—the violence of the afternoon still hung in the air, but he answered her anyway. "I should have been faster. I was trying to get him away from you before I killed him." He paused. "Violent death is never easy to witness, and I was trying to spare you. But would you fucking listen? Of course not." He stabbed himself with the needle again, not even wincing.

"Why are you doing that? Aren't there any more butterfly bandages?"

"This one's a little too deep for bandages, and you don't have surgical glue or staples on hand, which would have made things a lot easier. I didn't expect we were going to run into this kind of trouble when I came after you."

"You came after me?"

He looked up again. "You didn't think it was an accident, did you? I thought you were brighter than that. Clement and his buddies were looking for a way to get to me. I thought disappearing into the Canadian wilderness was a smart idea, and then I could meet up with you when you were crossing the border." He stabbed the needle in again, and Evangeline winced.

"And you expected a warm welcome from me?" She wasn't about to show him any sympathy, even with the odd mood he was in. Tension was coming off him in waves, and it was washing over her, but she had every intention of ignoring it. She wasn't going to tiptoe around his feelings.

"Not particularly. I've always been a realist. But I figured I could handle you." He pulled the thread through, pulling his torn flesh together, and then wiped the blood off with a paper towel. He was doing a lousy job of it and she wasn't sure how he could even reach the end of the long slash.

She pulled the sheet from beneath the sleeping dog, and Merlin didn't move. She wrapped it around herself, tying it at the neck so it made a makeshift toga, and then slipped out of the bunk, her feet on the floor of the camper.

Weakness shot through her, and for a moment she thought she was about to collapse. She heard Bishop curse. "Get back in bed," he snapped.

As if she was going to obey his orders. She held on to the stove, then the narrow kitchen counter, as she made her way back to him, and he glared down at her with profound distrust. "What do you want, Angel?"

"I want you to stop calling me angel," she said. "Move."

"Move where? There's not a whole lot of room in this trailer. Couldn't you have chosen something a little more spacious? Some nice cushy RV instead of this vintage tin can?"

"Annabelle is a treasure," she said, moving past him and perching herself on the seat of the dinette. The medical supplies were spread out on the table, some of which she'd never seen before, and the Formica was littered with blood-soaked paper towels. His shirt lay on the other side of the dinette, and it was soaked with blood as well. "You're making a hash of that. Come here."

He stared at her in disbelief. "Don't tell me you're offering to stitch me up?"

"I'm not offering, I'm ordering. You're doing a terrible job of it."

"And just how many people have you stitched up?"

She shrugged. "No one. I can't do a worse job than you're doing, and any squeamishness I might have will be wiped out by the pure joy I'll get from stabbing needles into you." She found a pair of gloves and began pulling them on. "Not that I don't trust you," she added in a limpid tone, "but I don't intend to expose myself to your doubtlessly tainted blood."

He looked at her for a long moment, then moved closer, right up against her, handing her the needle. She hadn't taken that part into account, that she would have to be so close to him, touching him. She looked at the torn flesh in front of her and considered throwing up.

"If you're going to do it, then stop farting around. I don't want you puking all over me. It helps if you look at it as something other than human flesh. Think of it as repairing a rip in a tarp." His hostility was aimed directly at her, and she tried to think of some terrible thing she might have done. He was the bad guy here, not her. He had a lot of nerve dumping all that anger on her.

He was also wounded and probably in a lot of pain, even

though he didn't show it. She could give him just a little bit of slack. She swallowed, then stabbed the needle through his skin. He didn't even blink as she pulled it through.

"So tell me," he said. "Why do you call your camper Annabelle?"

She frowned, concentrating. He was trying to distract her, and probably himself as well, and she was willing to let him. "It seemed like a good name for her. She's a little old-fashioned, very sturdy, nicely retro. I like to personalize inanimate objects—it makes life pleasant. My GPS is Grace, my truck is Dolores." She bent her head. She could smell the coppery scent of his blood, could smell the familiar scent of his skin.

"That way you can be surrounded by machines you've turned into people and not have to deal with anyone at all. Is that particularly healthy?"

She jabbed the needle with a little more force, but he still didn't react. "I find that inanimate objects are more trustworthy. They break down, but you can always fix them, and if they really screw up, you simply replace them. Much easier than putting up with humans." She grabbed a paper towel and wiped more blood away, then took another stitch. "I've learned people are dispensable, and I'm mostly better off without them."

"Including your family?"

"Most especially my family. My parents couldn't care less, my sister dislikes me and seems to want everything I have. Maybe I should send you to her."

"You think you still have me?"

She ducked her head, feeling heat flood her face. "Oh, she likes anything I ever had. I think you two deserve each other."

He said nothing for a moment. "So if you don't like your parents, why did you become a college professor just like them?"

That made her jerk her head up, and she was much too close to him. She was breathing him in, and it was like a drug, like hashish fumes clouding her senses. "How do you know about my parents? Why would you remember something like that?"

"I know everything about you," he said.

She tied off the knot, then surveyed her handiwork. Very neat, and the bleeding had stopped. "I sincerely doubt that," she said, making her voice cold, even as her body warmed. She set the needle down on the table and looked for bandages.

He had gauze pads and strips of surgical tape already prepared. "I can handle this part."

"Shut up and let me finish." She covered the long gash with antiseptic ointment, smearing it on lightly. "I assume you cleaned this properly before you started sewing?"

"Rinsed it with your bottle of rum."

Her eyes shot up. That had to have hurt like hell, and he hadn't made a sound. "Just as long as you didn't touch my Scotch," she said, applying the bandage, smoothing it carefully over his torn flesh.

"I'm not a complete savage. That's an unopened bottle of a very fine single malt you have. My brand, in fact. You never used to like Scotch—I had to drink it alone. What made you change?"

She shrugged, and her shoulder protested at the unexpected movement. "Maybe I developed a taste for quick oblivion."

"Now *that* is a terrible waste of Scotch." He was watching her. She could feel the heat coming off his body, seeming to surround her, and she needed to get away from him. She applied the second strip of tape with a little too much force, but he didn't even blink.

"Since it's my Scotch, I don't worry about it." She pulled back, then looked up at him. She couldn't move—he was blocking her, keeping her trapped on the dinette seat, and there was something menacing about him, a menace she hadn't felt before. It was sex and anger, and her nerves tightened. She had to wait until he moved away, and he didn't seem to be in any hurry to do so. "And you didn't know I started drinking Scotch five years ago. Clearly you don't know as much as you think you do."

"Five years ago? That's interesting."

"Why?"

"Just that you started drinking my brand of Scotch right after I left you. Seems like a kind of sentimental, romantic thing to do."

"Romantic?" She was outraged, partly because when she'd started drinking it she would close her eyes and taste his mouth on hers. "There's nothing romantic about Scotch. I was trying to scour you out of my system."

"Did you try prune juice?"

"We never did it that way."

His laugh was cold. "Well, if you're interested . . ."

Instinctively she shoved him, not caring if she hurt him. It was a mistake. He caught her hands the moment she pushed at him, and he held them against his skin, staring down at her, his eyes hooded. "You need to be careful, little girl," he said softly. "I'm not in a tolerant mood. I don't like killing, even when it's necessary, and it makes me impulsive."

After her first attempt at pulling away she stayed still, knowing she was no match for his strength. She could always butt her head against his wound, but he seemed impervious to pain, and it would only annoy him. Or worse. "Impulsive, how?" she said, but it came out in a breathy tone.

"Impulsive in that I could easily turn you around, shove you against the dinette, and fuck you senseless. It would take very little to make me do it, and you wouldn't stop me." His voice was flat, expressionless, as if he were talking about math equations or directions to the nearest Walmart.

"You mean I *couldn't* stop you," she said, her voice cold, her body flaming.

"No, I mean you *wouldn't* stop me. And you know it as well as I do." They stayed motionless, staring at each other, her hands splayed across his warm, muscled stomach. There was nothing between them but anger, she told herself, and she didn't want to make him any angrier.

Aggression was rolling off him in waves, and he would turn that aggression on her. If she admitted the truth, he was right, she *would* let him. She lowered her gaze and her head, like a submissive bitch, she thought bitterly, but it worked. He released her hands and backed off. "Get your clothes on," he said, "and grab some extras. We're getting out of here, and we're leaving Anastasia behind."

"Annabelle," she corrected automatically, able to breathe now that he had stepped back. "And I'm not leaving her anywhere."

"You don't have a choice in the matter. She's too noticeable. You and Merlin and I are going ahead on our own. I need to be in New Orleans in three days, and I've already wasted too much time."

She didn't bother arguing—she wouldn't win. She had no intention of agreeing either; she wouldn't give him that satisfaction. She simply started toward the bed and the drawers of clothes built in underneath it.

The trailer was very small. She practically had to rub against him in the narrow passageway, and she found she was holding her breath. All that skin. All that firm, golden, muscled flesh. "Is there any chance you could give me some privacy?"

He looked at her, and for a moment she was sure he was going to say no. But then he said, "Five minutes," and left without another word. She dressed as quickly as she could, taking care with her wounds. They were already looking better, but she didn't want to do anything to aggravate them. She could hear Bishop unfastening the coupling between the trailer and the pickup, and she bit back her fury. There was nothing she could do about it right now.

Her only real decision was whether or not to bring her research. In the end she tucked it beneath her mattress. A lot of it was scanned onto her computer and safely tucked in the Cloud, including the first month of her notes, but she'd left the two American sites for the end of her trip, and that was looking iffy. Then again, her ex-husband could always show up and steal everything again, though right then Pete didn't seem like much of a threat. He hadn't published anything since he'd put out her research as his own, so she imagined he must be feeling a little desperate.

God, she had lousy taste in men! Most disturbing of all was her reaction to Bishop's presence. She could thank God he had no idea what she was feeling, what she was thinking. It was weak, shameful, unutterably stupid, and she hated herself for it. He was the enemy, she reminded herself, on every single level. He'd as good as kidnapped her, and she'd watched him commit murder. The man had been stunned, helpless, and Bishop had simply cut his throat with a horrifying efficiency. And she'd ended up wanting to fuck him.

She needed to get away from him, she'd always known that. That wasn't likely to happen anytime soon, but if she behaved herself he might lower his guard. She had credit cards, money in her wallet . . .

In the truck. It was in the glove compartment, and there was always the chance he hadn't looked there. A chance in hell, she thought.

Merlin was awake, trying to sit up, his legs wobbly underneath him, and she knelt on the bunk, helping him. Merlin was more important than a thousand Bishops. As long as he was okay, she could deal with a trifling annoyance like her ersatz husband.

The door slammed open, and the trifling annoyance stood there, a damned sight bigger and more annoying than she'd hoped. "You ready?"

"Merlin needs help," she began, but he stepped into the camper and caught her arm, spinning her around and pushing her out the door.

"Get in the truck," he said tersely. "I'll bring him."

She stayed on the bottom step. "I don't want to go out there."

"For God's sake, why not?"

"Is . . . is that man still there?" If he was, she would get sick again, and that was the last thing she wanted. She couldn't remember when she'd last eaten, and as far as she was concerned she could wait a hell of a lot longer. The thought of dry heaves, however, made her think twice.

"I don't know what you're talking about," Bishop said flatly.

She blinked. "Clement. The man you killed. He was lying in a pool of blood just outside the camper."

He shook his head. "I didn't kill anyone. You must have been having nightmares."

"But I . . ."

He came up to her, caught her chin in his hard hand, and his face was grim. "There was no one here, Evangeline," he said slowly, deliberately. "You saw nothing."

After a moment she nodded. She was being unusually dense. Clement had tried to kill both of them, after all. Even if Bishop's remedy was a little extreme she couldn't really fault him. "I saw nothing."

"Now get in the fucking truck."

There was no blood in the dirt, no sign of a struggle, no sign of any disturbance. She didn't want to know what he'd done with the body—there were plenty of scavengers in the north woods who could take care of things. She didn't want to think about that either, and she moved across the small clearing to climb into the driver's seat. Sure enough, the keys were gone, but she found her spare set beneath the seat. If only she could talk him into putting Merlin in the cab; then she could take off before he got in. She leaned over and opened the glove compartment to retrieve her wallet. Of course it was gone.

She leaned back, holding on to the steering wheel as she took deep, calming breaths. He rapped at the window, and she would have locked the doors, ignoring him, but he was holding Merlin's shaking body, and she had no choice. She opened the door.

"If you think you're driving, then you've lost your mind somewhere in the last five years," he said. "Move over and let me put Merlin between us."

At least that was a blessing. She didn't want to be cuddled up against him, thigh to thigh in her small pickup. She didn't bother to argue, sliding across the bench seat to a perch at the far end. If she could bring herself to leave Merlin, she could easily escape. It was clear Bishop liked the dog, would keep him safe. But for how long? You didn't abandon your family in times of danger, and Merlin was the only family she had.

She slid over as far as she could go. Merlin collapsed against her, whimpering happily, his big head in her lap, and she stroked his fur, almost ready to cry.

Bishop had climbed into the driver's seat, and a moment later they were bumping along a makeshift road. She buckled herself in, then looked over at Bishop. "You need your seat belt."

"Why? Because I'm such a cautious man with a concern for human life?" he shot back.

"No, because if we hit something, you'll be flying all around the cab like a frog in a blender, and you'll probably kill Merlin and me when we would have been perfectly fine."

His grim expression lightened slightly. "Frog in a blender?" he echoed. "You do have an interesting way of looking at things." To her surprise he fastened the seat belt. "There. Does that make you happy?"

"Where's my wallet?"

"In a safe place. I don't want to tempt you into taking off. It would just waste time while I went looking for you, and trust me, I *would* find you." It sounded like a threat, and she wasn't fool enough to think it was only her imagination.

"Why don't you just let me go?" she demanded.

He hesitated, as if he were considering options, and then he looked at her out of those beautiful, wrong-colored eyes. "Because they'll find you, and use you to get to me. If I ignore their demands, and I might very well have to, then they'll torture and kill you, probably send me bits and pieces of you until they give up and just put two rounds in the back of your head. And you'll be praying for it by that time."

She couldn't say anything. She leaned against the door, staring at him while he drove. She wanted to tell him he was delusional, but she'd seen the dead man, seen what both of them had been willing to do in that vicious, deadly fight. This was no fantasy.

Her mouth felt dry as dust, and she swallowed. "Why would you give a good goddamn what happens to me?"

She didn't think he was going to answer, but eventually he did. "You're my wife. If anyone's going to kill you, it's going to be me."

"Oh, for Christ's sake, just give me an honest answer for once!" she snapped, exploding in fury and impatience. "You know as well as I do that we weren't ever married."

"Of course we were."

"That would make my marriage to Pete bigamy."

He didn't even blink. "Yes. I checked very carefully to see if he was in the business, but he was clean, just a slimy college professor with a taste for coeds and plagiarism. Look at it as a gift. You were never really married to that piece of shit."

"I'm touched," she said acidly. "I'll need some proof."

The first glimmer of a smile lit his brooding face. "My, how you've changed, Angel. You used to be such a trusting soul."

"That was before I met you. Nowadays I wouldn't trust my own mother."

"As far as I can tell you never trusted your parents, and with good reason. Face it, Angel, you're my wife."

"I told you, I need proof!"

"You won't take my word for it? I'm wounded."

"Damn right you're wounded, and if you give me any more shit I'll smack you in your stitches."

"I would strongly suggest you keep from hitting me," he said in a calm, unsettling voice. "I might react . . . badly."

She believed him. He'd protect her, but he could also hurt her. A lot. She took a deep breath, trying to shake off the chill his words had brought. "I need proof I was married if I want to get a divorce."

"Do you want to?"

"Want to what?" She was feeling cranky, upset, confused.

"Get divorced. It'll be harder than you expect—Italian marriage laws are fairly rigid, and we had a cardinal perform the service."

"Yeah, right," she said. "That was either an actor or some poor seminary student looking to make a quick buck."

"He was a little old for a seminary student, wasn't he? And there was a certain gravitas to him . . ."

"All right, an actor. A good actor. In fact, I don't even remember him or what he looked like." She regretted those words the moment she said them.

He wasn't about to let that slip by. "Something distracting you, Angel?"

"You were probably feeding me an aphrodisiac to keep me compliant." Her voice was sullen. Embarrassment did that to her. She wanted to change the subject, fast, but she should have known he wouldn't let it pass.

"No aphrodisiac. Admit it, you were besotted with me. Back then I could make you come just by looking at you."

Jesus, why didn't he stop? She turned her face toward the window, watching as the scenery sped by. "If you believe that's physically possible, then some woman must have fed you a load of crap at some point."

He laughed, and she felt just a bit of the tension leave his body. "Well, you came close. I can prove it to you."

"No, thanks. I'm not interested in your soulful looks. I just want to get away from you."

He grunted in annoyance. "Still on that? How about this? As soon as I think you're safe, I'll let you go. First we have to get to New Orleans and then I can reevaluate things."

She wasn't going to get her hopes up. "Exactly why are we going to Louisiana? It's the most corrupt state in the union. Or is that why it attracts you? That would make sense."

"Keep on trying, Evangeline," he said lightly. "Sooner or later you'll manage to get to me." It was a warning. "We're going to New Orleans because the people I work for have decided to set up a branch in the United States, and New Orleans seemed an obvious choice. It's an international port, the local laws are . . . elastic, and to top it off, it's got a strong connection to my current project."

"The people you work for? Your project? Exactly what is it you do?" She made no effort to keep the disbelief from her voice.

He turned to look at her. She could see his reflection in the window, the assessing look on his face, and then he gave her his charming smile, the one that was full of shit. "I'm a consultant."

"Who kills on the side?"

"Competition's a bitch," he replied.

"But . . ."

"Just shut the fuck up, Evangeline." She'd managed to get on his nerves, a dubious triumph. "We've got a long drive ahead of us, and I don't want to spend the next ten hours bickering. Not when there isn't a bed nearby to resolve things."

That stopped her. He punched the stereo she'd had put into Dolores, and music filled the cab. He cast a glance at her. "Punk?" he said in disbelief.

She bit back her annoyed retort. *Don't poke the sleeping tiger*, she told herself. "There's country, classical, rock and roll, some opera, African music—just about every kind of music with the possible exception of polka music. If you don't like punk I can change it if you tell me what the . . . what you did with my iPod."

"Punk is fine. It fits my mood."

It didn't fit hers. She'd taken cocaine once, at Pete's urging during one of his faculty parties, and it made her feel nervous, jangled. The circumstances and the music were doing the same thing to her, and she kept one hand in Merlin's fur, as if it were a security blanket, as she tried to take stealthy, calming breaths.

The Dead Kennedys were pounding away through her Bose speakers, always a great choice for long, fast drives but getting on her last nerve at the moment, though she said nothing. She breathed again.

"I find it works best if you breathe in through the nose and out through the mouth," he observed.

She ignored him. He was right, of course—she'd been too anxious to even remember that much. She'd make it through this.

The song finished, and X Japan came on. "All right, you've managed to surprise me," he said. "Japanese punk?"

"You said you didn't want me to annoy you," she muttered, refusing to look at him directly. She could see him well enough in the window as the sky grew lighter. "I don't think we can have a discussion without it."

"You're probably right." He seemed perfectly content with J-rock when he finally found a paved road; then the driving style she remembered so well came into play, and they were barreling down the thankfully empty road. They had gone through the

Ramones and classic Stooges, with "I Wanna Be Your Dog" leaving her feeling itchy, when he straightened slightly and reached into the pocket of his jeans, pulling the fabric tight against his crotch. He pulled out her iPod, and glanced at her. "Got any requests?"

For you to go to hell, she thought fiercely. "Van Morrison," she muttered. Van the Man would give her strength.

"Good choice," he said, and she immediately regretted it. He glanced down at her iPod Classic, navigating it faster than she could, and a moment later "Days Like This" came on the stereo. It was a cynical choice but she didn't care; she let the music slip under her skin, shutting him out. He stopped trying to talk to her, instead concentrating on the road, and she finally, finally began to relax. There was nothing unsalvageable in a world with Van Morrison in it.

She drifted into sleep, on and off during the endless hours, and when she woke with a start, she needed a bathroom, and damn, did she need some food. At some point they'd gotten on a wider road. Tall, spiky mountains appeared on one side as they headed toward a depressingly flat landscape. "Where are we?"

"Halfway through Wyoming." While she'd slept the music had changed, and he must have set it to shuffle. At the moment it was Richard Thompson.

"If you don't stop soon I will start to chew off my own arm."

"Hungry, are you? I'm not surprised. Maybe next time I cook for you, you won't throw the plate at me."

She gritted her teeth. "I'm afraid I can't wait that long. I need a bathroom and I need food. You need to stop in the next town."

"There aren't many towns in this part of the country."

She looked at him. Some of that tension had left him, but not all, and she knew she should still tread carefully. She wasn't in the mood. "Find one," she said flatly.

"Yes, ma'am," he said sarcastically. Merlin was lying at her feet, marginally more alert, and he added a whining noise to her request.

"You need food, old boy?" Bishop said, sounding a lot more affectionate toward her dog than he had been with her, and for a moment Evangeline couldn't decide who she was jealous of, which was patently ridiculous. Bishop had taken over her life five years ago, and now he'd come back and taken over again. He was even trying to steal her dog from her.

"He hasn't eaten in a long time either. We'll need to find a pet store, if possible, or at least a grocery store. He doesn't eat people food."

"He'll be fine with people food."

"I only give him a very expensive blend for big dogs with delicate digestive systems," she said sternly.

"What makes you think he has a delicate digestive system? He'll be fine with a couple of hamburgers."

"Why the hell do you think you know more about my dog than I do?" she demanded, thoroughly pissed.

He didn't answer, and his words to Clement came back. *You cut my woman, and you hurt my dog.* Not that she was his woman, but she had the sudden, horrible, unavoidable feeling that Merlin really was his dog.

"You bastard," she said under her breath, leaning back against the seat.

He sighed wearily. "What did I do now?"

"You know what you did. You took my diamond earrings, my trust, my . . . my love, and disappeared with all of them. As if that hadn't hurt me enough, you give me a dog so you can have the extreme pleasure of ripping him away from me."

He didn't bother denying it, the bastard. "Figured that out, did you? Took you long enough. Don't be so melodramatic. I hate to tell you, but he no longer considers me his owner. He obeys my instructions because I trained him, but if he was given the choice, he'd always come back to you. You have that effect on dumb animals."

Merlin lifted his head, as if to protest the description, and Evangeline rubbed behind his ears in his favorite spot, wondering what other dumb animals had supposedly fallen under her spell. There was no way he was talking about himself.

"So why don't you tell me why the hell you dropped your trained attack dog in the middle of a Midwestern college campus and expected him to find me and stick to me?"

"That was the easy part. He's trained to guard, but even a soldier like Merlin has a mushy heart in the center. That's part of what makes him so good—if anyone comes near you who means any harm, he'll rip his throat out."

"And that's why he didn't rip your throat out," she said, feeling stupid and trapped and manipulated. "I should have realized that from the very beginning."

He shrugged. "I know you're used to being the smartest person in the room, but there are times when even you can't figure something out." She gave him a contemptuous glare, one that left him completely unmoved. "As for finding you, it was easy enough. You remember that practically transparent wrapper you wore a couple of times for approximately two seconds? It contained enough of your scent to train him to home in on you."

She jerked her head to stare at his cool, emotionless face. "How in the world did you get that? I threw it in the trash when I left the Danieli."

"I retrieved it. I figured it would come in handy. If I ever ended up missing you, I could always jack off into it."

"You're disgusting," she said.

"So you've said."

He pulled off the road, and she saw a truck stop, with a dozen big rigs parked outside, and her hopes rose. She loved country music and trucking songs. Maybe they really were the knights of the road, and they'd come to the rescue of a damsel in distress.

His gorgeous blue eyes were on her. "Don't even think about it, Angel. I can kill, remember? Kill without remorse, without thinking twice, and trust me, I can be very efficient. You want to be responsible for the death of one or more of those truckers inside?"

He knew her too well. She refused to admit defeat, but she was going to have to think very hard before she put anyone else in danger. "Just feed me, Seymour," she said, "and I won't give you any more trouble."

"*Little Shop of Horrors,*" he said, recognizing the quote. "That would be wise on your part." The menace was still there. The man who'd tended her wounds, who'd protected her, had disappeared, leaving this cold-eyed stranger in his place. She'd been a fool to forget exactly who he was, seduced by the familiar body and the familiar touch. "Stay here while I walk Merlin."

The dog lifted his head at the sound of his name, turning to look at Evangeline expectantly. "I think he wants me to come."

"Tough. To me, Merlin," he said in a cold voice.

But Evangeline was stroking under his neck; along with all his hidden training, she'd done a little of her own, and that was her signal to relax and play. Merlin turned and climbed into her lap, an impressive feat for a ninety-pound animal. Evangeline gave Bishop a limpid smile. "He thinks he's a lapdog," she said. "He may have started life as an attack dog, but after three years with me he's become an absolute pussycat." She was exaggerating, but it was basically the truth. Merlin loved to wrestle, to curl next to her, to climb into her lap. The only thing he wouldn't do was sleep on her bed—he insisted on sleeping by the door, always on guard. He'd slept on Bishop's mattress in the trailer, and it had only increased her anger.

"Don't push me, Angel," he muttered. "Get out of the damned truck then. We can all go for a walk."

She gave him her best smile before reaching for the door.

"Walkies, Merlin!" The dog jumped off her in excitement, waiting for her to climb out before he followed, dancing around.

"'Walkies'?" Bishop said in tone of deep loathing. "You've ruined my dog."

"You forget, he's my dog now. You gave him to me."

"Wouldn't hold up in court," he muttered.

"And of course you're comfortable with the legal system."

"If I want him you can't stop me from taking him."

The thought filled her with fear, but she was determined not to show it. Merlin was busy marking everything around them, and she hoped he'd lift his leg against Bishop's faded jeans. "If you take him, he'll do whatever he has to in order to get back to me. Ever seen *The Incredible Journey*? He'll find me."

She should have kept her fucking mouth shut. Bishop was on the ragged edge, and pushing him over would be a very bad idea. For some reason she couldn't help it. She wasn't going to be a victim, ever again.

"Do you want to eat?"

It wasn't a question, it was a threat, and she could already smell hamburgers and bacon on the air.

"Eat," she said with appropriate meekness, mentally giving him the finger.

He didn't say anything more, but she got the message. She walked behind him, a deliberately demure ten paces as they made their way through the grass-covered space next to the diner. Merlin kept running ahead, then turning around, shooting straight back to her, cavorting in joy, bypassing Bishop each time, and any doubts she had vanished. Merlin would swim oceans to get to her, and she'd do the same.

Bishop got back to the pickup truck first, and by the time Evangeline and Merlin arrived he had a bowl of water for Merlin to inhale before the dog jumped into the truck, the cab windows open. He wouldn't leave, and he'd make sure no one would come near the vehicle.

It was a cool evening in the late summer—the endless day had brought them through Montana and into the flat part of Wyoming, and she hadn't been awake to appreciate the jagged peaks of the mountains. Would they get back in the truck and drive all night, or were they going to stop at a motel . . . ? She didn't want to think about it. She needed to fill her stomach. After that, she could come up with a plan. She'd been fantasizing about revenge for the last five years—surely she could adapt one of those scenarios to her current situation?

Food. She was planning to follow Bishop into the diner, but he caught her arm in a grip that looked casual but was going to leave bruises. "Smile at me, sugar," he muttered. "Or you're on bread and water."

She gave him her most brilliant smile. "Fuck you," she said sweetly, and walked into the truck stop like the most docile of wives.

Chapter Nine

Bishop took in a deep breath as he checked out the diner. It was crowded, noisy, and bright, filled with the smells of everything cooked in fat, and all those strangers made him feel twitchy. Evangeline was being relatively well behaved beside him as they took an empty booth—he'd scared her. Good. He wasn't in the mood to fart around, and it would take very little to push him over the edge. He'd never hurt her, but right now he didn't mind her thinking he would. In fact, the smart thing to do would be to keep her on edge, afraid enough to obey his commands without hesitation, not ask any questions, not think for herself.

But that wasn't the new Evangeline. In fact it wasn't even the old Evangeline, though she'd been a damned sight more trusting. She'd still been reticent, but he'd been able to smash through any of her doubts with sex, blinding, mesmerizing sex that left her shattered and compliant.

There was only one problem with that. It had left him shattered as well, and he hadn't been able to replicate the experience in the last five years. No one felt like her, no one took him to the places she did, and he'd eventually given up, at least for the time being.

A good long period of celibacy would probably whet his appetite, make him appreciate the simple pleasure of getting off.

He hadn't factored in having to rescue Evangeline.

He'd thought she was safe enough at her backwoods little college, particularly with Merlin dogging her heels. Bullets wouldn't stop Merlin—nothing would.

He had no idea how Corsini's people had found out about Evangeline. He'd done his level best to break every single tie he had. He'd trained Merlin for her, but Ryder had delivered him, and it would have been almost impossible for him to be traced back to Bishop. "Almost" being the key word.

He must have made a mistake, one of many as far as Evangeline was concerned, which was why he'd kept away from her. His brains were in his pants when it came to her—it was purely sexual and he knew it, but even that knowledge couldn't diminish his need for her.

Now the Corsinis were after her, and he suspected he could thank Claudia for that. She could have leaked the information to the crime family. That way they'd use Evangeline as a way to draw him out, and if he wasn't careful, they'd both be dead. He'd never be able to prove Claudia's interference, but once the Corsinis made the connection, Evangeline's days would be numbered. Thank God she'd been off in the hinterlands doing research, out of reach of everyone, not even an Internet connection or cell phone service to track her. It had given him long enough to come out of the woodwork to protect her.

He'd married Evangeline to keep Claudia away from her, and it had infuriated his sometimes partner. There'd been nothing she could do about it, and he'd assumed that after five years she would have forgotten all about her. He should have known better than to make assumptions. Claudia had become more and more unstable in the last five years and their boss, Madsen, knew it. Getting rid of an operative like Claudia wasn't as easy as handing her a pink slip—she was too much of a loose cannon, and too skilled to be taken out easily. He didn't envy Madsen—it was going to be a bitch no matter how he decided to handle the situation.

Problem was, Claudia was too damned smart, even if she was caught up with maintaining her cool, unemotional focus; and getting rid of her, the only viable way to control her, wouldn't be easy. In the meantime all bets were off, and Claudia might or might not continue to follow orders. She'd never forgiven Bishop for ensuring Evangeline would live, and if she couldn't kill Evangeline, she'd find someone who would. All his complicated schemes and hard work might come to nothing. He should have realized there was no way Claudia was going to let it go. If he'd really wanted to ensure Evangeline's safety, he should have killed Claudia during that mission. But he didn't kill easily; he'd worked with Claudia on a number of occasions, and he'd made the mistake of thinking she was more stable. Maybe back then she was—after all, Evangeline had survived five years. It was the rest of his wife's life that was in jeopardy.

Evangeline wasn't looking very happy about his efforts to keep her alive. She was staring at the greasy, thick menu with the concentration of a scholar, her forehead wrinkled beneath her loose, flyaway hair, and he wanted to reach across and brush the curls away. He did no such thing. It was shorter than it had been when he first met her, and he liked it. He liked it longer too. In fact, he liked every damned thing about her.

Things had happened so quickly she hadn't picked out the anomalies of his story. She'd questioned him, of course, and circumstances had forced him to reveal too much already, but if he kept doing his best to scare her she might be smart enough to back off and behave herself.

And hell might freeze over.

The middle-aged waitress, with the appropriate name Alice

emblazoned across her generous bosom, was already pouring wickedly dark coffee without request. "Hey, honey," she said to him. "What can I get you?"

"Lumberjack Breakfast," he said. It came with three fried eggs, a double order of bacon, sausage and ham, home fries, six pancakes, and a steak on the side.

She looked at him, impressed. "You got it. And what about you, sweetheart?" she applied to Evangeline.

He waited for her to order something like a chef's salad or a mushroom omelet, but she didn't even blink. "I'll have the same," she said. "And Diet Coke and keep it coming."

Alice grinned. "My kind of woman," she said. "I'll put that order right in."

Bishop glowered. He hadn't eaten in too damned long, and his temper wasn't feigned. "You're never going to eat that much."

"Can't afford to treat a girl to an expensive meal? I can always call Alice back and tell her my 'husband' says I can't have it. It wouldn't be the first time she's heard it."

"And it wouldn't be the first time that a husband busted his wife across the chops in a place like this," he growled.

She gave him a demure smile, unthreatened. "Yes, but I'm a sweet, helpless little girl and you're a big, nasty brute, and all these truckers would come to my rescue. If I were fat and middle-aged they'd probably cheer you on, more's the pity, but in my case I don't think they'd let you get away with it."

"You've gotten cynical in your old age."

Her eyes flashed. "I'm twenty-eight."

"I know." The coffee was so strong it was guaranteed to keep him up all night, driving, but he hadn't decided whether that was the way to go or not. Having Clement find him had thrown his plans into the crapper, but he was good at improvising. If he found a motel that felt right, he'd stop; otherwise he'd just keep going.

He knew how to go without sleep for days, and he wasn't even tired yet.

A large, icy glass of Diet Coke appeared in front of them, along with a plastic pitcher filled with the stuff. "You drink all that and you'll be peeing all night long, and I'm not making a dozen stops."

She shrugged. "You forget—I have an iron bladder. Anyway, it's my truck. I'll pee in it if I want to."

He couldn't let himself smile, much as he wanted to. He shrugged. "Your problem, not mine."

"Oh, I think when we get farther south and warmer it'll be your problem too."

"Drink your damned pop and shut up."

Her eyebrows raised. "Aha. You're from the Midwest."

"What makes you think that?" he said lazily. Wyoming was a far cry from the Midwest.

"Only Midwesterners call soda, pop," she said smugly.

It wouldn't do any harm to spike her guns. "Well, you're wrong. I'm from Wyoming, and we call it half a dozen names, like liquid poison and pig swill."

"What part of Wyoming?" she countered. "Are we near your home?"

"I don't have a home anymore, and any connection I have to this place is long gone. And stop asking me questions you know I won't answer, Angel. The less you know the better." He used his name for her deliberately—he liked the way it made her bristle.

"I hardly think that's fair, since you supposedly know everything about me. Including my birthday and where I was born," she added, taunting him, clearly doubting him.

"You were born September tenth, at seven twenty in the evening, at Jefferson General Hospital in Port Townsend, Washington. You weighed seven pounds, fifteen ounces, and . . ."

She looked slightly ill. "Enough," she said. "I believe you."

"I also know the name of every man you slept with when you first came back from Italy and tried to fuck me out of your system." The resources of the Committee were far-flung, and he'd been able to find out anything he wanted while keeping his distance, even though it had driven him crazy.

If he was hoping his words would cow her some more he was mistaken—she met his gaze fearlessly, and he allowed himself a moment to fall into her green eyes. "Now that's impressive," she said, a challenge in her voice. "There were a lot of them, and I don't think I even remember them all."

"Well, if there's anyone who particularly annoyed you, just describe him and I'll go beat him up when this is over," he said lightly.

Shit. Shit shit shit. How stupid could he be? The woman he was in . . . the woman he was protecting was smarter than should be legal, and her eyes had narrowed.

"You had Pete beaten up, didn't you?"

He stalled. "I don't know what you're talking about."

"Right after our divorce went through, and I found out he'd taken all my work and passed it off as his own, some random stranger backed him into an alley and beat the shit out of him. Was it you?"

"Now what makes you think I'm a knight errant?" He took a delaying sip of his coffee.

"Because you just offered to do the same to anyone else I slept with. It's not a major leap." She was watching him intently.

"Maybe I just like an excuse to hit people." He had the vague hope she'd only hear the threat in that, but she ignored him. For someone so damned smart, she was really fucking stupid. "So drop it."

She was going to test him, and he tensed. "Well, there was this guy in Boston. I forget his name, but he was six foot six or something, and a total asshat. He thought he was God's gift to womanhood and he couldn't even get me off."

149

She said it deliberately, and he'd warned her. He kicked her, hard, beneath the table, enough to hurt, and she stifled her squeal of pain, her eyes dark at his betrayal. She probably thought he'd never hurt her. It was past time she knew that he'd do whatever he had to do.

"You keep forgetting I'm the enemy, Angel," he said laconically. His appetite had vanished. She had to do what he told her, or they'd never survive, but he'd kicked her harder than he'd meant to, and it made him sick. He didn't let it show, and kept his expression bland. "I have nothing to do with the man you met in Italy five years ago, and you need to remember that."

"Then why do you keep insisting we're married?" Her voice was small, subdued, and he felt guilty, which was flatly absurd. He killed people, beat people, tortured them when ordered to, and women weren't exempt. Some of the most vicious, deadly creatures he'd ever met were women. So why was he feeling guilty about a little kick?

"John Hall," he said suddenly.

She blinked. "What?"

"John Hall. He was the tall jerk in Boston. Shall I send a hit team after him?" he said sarcastically. Except that he wasn't really sarcastic—at the time he wanted nothing more than to kill every man she'd slept with during that period when she first got back to the States, and he'd never had a jealous bone in his body until then.

Before she could reply, their food arrived, a massive feast covering the table with dishes of toast, eggs, pancakes, breakfast meats, potatoes, and steak. Evangeline had already worked her way through most of the pitcher of Diet Coke, and Bishop was on his third mug of the sludge they called coffee. "I'll get you a refill," Alice promised him after she'd unloaded her tray, and returned in a moment with the pitcher, A-1 sauce, and more cream. "You just call me if you need anything, sugar," she said cheerfully.

He gave her a tight smile of thanks before turning to the food laid out before them.

"I want to know . . ." Evangeline began, but he interrupted her.

"I don't give a shit what you want right now," he growled. "Just shut up and eat."

He expected her to give him more trouble, but after that kick, she did what she was told, the lure of food, too much for her to resist. There was so much food, they'd end up taking half of it with them, and he still had to order a couple of burgers for Merlin, but right then all he cared about was shoveling eggs down his throat. Whether he wanted to or not he had to fuel his body, and he dug into the meal with grim determination.

He was halfway through his pancakes when he finally looked up and froze. She was chewing on a piece of toast, and everything else was gone. She'd eaten the eggs, the pancakes, the sausages and bacon, even the mediocre potatoes were gone. The steak was mostly gristle, and she'd left that part behind, but somehow she'd managed to devour the huge meal so quietly and efficiently that he was left dumbfounded.

"Want your bacon?" she asked.

"You can't still be hungry," he said in a flat voice.

"I was thinking of Merlin. I don't think meat would hurt him, but I draw the line at hamburgers."

"Too bad—I already ordered them, and if you won't let me feed them to Merlin, then you'll have to eat them yourself."

Aha! She was more stuffed than she pretending to be, because the mention of eating more food turned her gorgeous skin slightly pale. He needed to remember she had a weak stomach. "You've already eaten too much on an empty stomach," he continued. "And I don't want to be holding your head over a toilet."

"I'm fine," she said in a tight voice. "And speaking of toilets, I have to go."

"Yeah, I'm sure you do."

"Listen, fuckwad, you can't come into the ladies' room with me, so just chill! Where could I go? You know I'm not going to ask anyone for help and risk getting anyone caught in the crossfire. I've just had about a gallon of Diet Coke, and the time is now."

He believed her. She wouldn't risk anyone else, and there really was nowhere they could go. They were at a truck stop in the middle of nowhere and had been on the road for sixteen hours. Even she had her limits.

"Go ahead," he said. "Just don't think you can sneak out the back with that extra pair of keys you found. You wouldn't be able to start the truck, and you'd end up pissing me off for nothing."

She didn't bother to hide her annoyance. "I don't have my wallet or driver's license anyway."

"And we're just about out of gas, and there's no way you're going to get any without a credit card."

"Won't a credit card lead your so-called enemies to us?" she said caustically.

"Did Clement look like a so-called enemy?" he shot back.

Repeating his own words, she said, "Clement? Who's he? I don't remember anyone named Clement."

She was really pissing him off. He couldn't risk stopping for a rest when he was in such a volatile mood—he was inches away from . . . no, he wasn't even going to allow himself to think about what he wanted to do with her. "For someone who has a full bladder, you don't seem to be in any hurry," he said instead, ignoring her taunt. "The offer is time-sensitive."

She stomped off, radiating fury. He watched her go, as did half a dozen truckers, and he wanted to smash every one of them. She was wearing loose, raggedy cutoffs and an oversized t-shirt with "Come to the Dark Side, We Have Cookies" emblazoned on it, which he viewed with wry amusement. He had no idea whether she'd chosen it on purpose—he hadn't delved into her clothing—but the geek t-shirt was a little too close to the truth. He was the Dark Side, all right, though it wasn't cookies he was offering her, and she wasn't coming willingly.

But man, she had gorgeous legs. Long, tanned, strong-looking. Her ass was gorgeous too, even beneath all that loose denim. She'd been all soft innocence and sweetness five years ago. Now she was hard.

So was he.

He knew how long it took a woman to empty her bladder, even a very full one, and he was on the verge of going after her when she reappeared; and all the truckers got to enjoy the front view. She put her hand on each empty booth as she approached him, and he frowned. Was she hoping to leave her fingerprints all over the place? It wouldn't do her any damned good.

She slid back into the seat, an unreadable expression on her face. That was new too. He'd always been able to read her. He had that ability with most people—it was part of his training—but she'd been able to put up blinders every now and then. "What next?"

The leftover food—his leftover food—was already boxed up, as well as Merlin's hamburgers. He looked at her for a long moment. She looked too closed in—she'd done something. "I think I should make use of the facilities since we're here."

He could feel the tension shoot through her. "You're a man. You can just piss by the side of the road," she snapped.

He smiled sweetly. "Yes, but I thought I'd save your delicate sensibilities. If you're not sitting here, waiting, not looking at anyone when I get back, I'll shoot you."

"No, you won't."

No, he wouldn't, but he didn't like her knowing that. "I'm on my very last nerve, Evangeline." With that warning he headed to the restrooms.

Chapter Ten

He was going to find it, Evangeline thought, trying not to panic. No sense of decency would keep him from going into the ladies' room: he'd see the note she'd scrawled on the mirror with the crayon she'd stolen from one of the tables set up for kids, complete with kids' placemats. That was probably why Bishop had chosen this table—someone had been in the midst of cleaning it off and would know not to put kids' stuff out. She wouldn't put it past him—he seemed aware of the smallest details.

She didn't like thinking about what his reaction was going to be. She could hope someone had gotten there first, but there were only two other women in the place, plus two waitresses, so it was unlikely anyone had gotten in there that quickly.

So far her luck had not been good. There was nothing she could do this time, just face the music. He wouldn't shoot her, they both knew it, but after that she wasn't sure what his limits were. She stretched her leg out on the banquette seat and rubbed her shin. His kick had *hurt*, damn it, enough so that she was having a hard time not limping when she came back.

Someone slid into the seat opposite her, and she looked up, expecting Bishop, only to find it was one of the truckers who'd

been watching her while she ate. He'd been at the end of the counter, so Bishop, with his back to the wall, hadn't been able to see
him, but she had, and it had been uncomfortable. Worse when she
came back from the restroom.

"Hey, little lady, you don't look like you're too happy," he
drawled in a cigarette voice just two packs short of cancer. He
stunk of them, as well as sweat and diesel. So much for her Knight
of the Road fantasy. "Your man been giving you trouble?"

"He's not my man," she said instantly, then regretted it as the
trucker smiled, exposing nicotine-stained teeth that hadn't seen a
toothbrush in weeks, maybe months.

"Well, then, sugar, I'm your man. How'd you like a ride to
Vegas? Lots going on there. Pretty girl like you could get work, no
problem."

Shit, Bishop was going to be furious. He'd told her not to talk to
anyone, but this wasn't her fault. "No, thank you," she said politely.

"But why not? If he ain't your man, he still treats you like shit.
Couldn't hear what you were saying, but I know when a women
ain't happy."

I bet you do, she thought. She thought fast. "He's taking me to
see my grandmother. She's dying. Of lung cancer," she added for
good effect.

"Damned shame. Where's she live?"

Fuck, she wasn't good at instant lies. "Albuquerque."

"Well, hell, honey, why didn't you say so? I'm my own boss,
and this load's supposed to end up in Albuquerque. I can bypass
Vegas for a pretty little lady like you."

"No, thanks. He's my brother, and we never got along."

"He doesn't act like . . ." His words trailed off, and Evangeline
knew why. Bishop was back, and he'd be in a very testy mood after
seeing the message in the ladies' room. Especially when he'd told
her not to talk to anyone.

She turned and looked up at him. His face was completely blank, which made him very dangerous indeed. He wouldn't shoot her, but she couldn't count on him not shooting the trucker. "Hi," she said brightly. "This gentleman sat down with me and offered to take me to Albuquerque to see Grandma, but I explained she's your grandmother too, and even though you and I never got along, I'd still rather go with you. But he was very nice, and you don't . . ."

"Get up," Bishop said in a soft voice, and Evangeline was about to move when she realized he was talking to the trucker, who, idiotically, didn't look afraid.

He was a burly man, with big, ham-like fists that he'd probably used on those unhappy women he'd mentioned, and he rose, all belligerence. Bishop was taller, but lacked his bulk, and all the other truckers had stopped eating, stopped talking, as the scene unfolded in front of them.

"You got a problem with me?" the trucker demanded. "Just passing time with the little lady. Didn't look like she was too happy with you, and I was offering her an alternative. Out of the goodness of my heart," he added.

Bishop didn't speak, didn't move. Then he did, and it was so fast Evangeline couldn't see what he did, but the trucker ended up on the floor of the diner, groaning.

Bishop turned to look at the men who'd been following this. "Anyone else?" he said in an amiable voice.

They all looked away, mumbling denials. Bishop scooped up the containers of food and shoved them in a plastic bag he must have gotten from the waitress, and then he grabbed her arm and hauled her to her feet. At least that was what it felt like—the others would see it as a combination of ownership and solicitude. Fortunately he'd taken her left arm, and it was her left leg that was aching, so she didn't have to worry about trying to disguise her limp.

No one said anything as they left the diner. No one said anything when he took her to the passenger side of the truck, opened the door for Merlin to jump out, then shoved her up into the seat, some of his temper coming through. "If you have an ounce of sense left in your overeducated brain, you'll stay put and keep quiet. I don't want excuses, I don't want apologies, and I sure the fuck don't want any more attitude. I'm going to feed Merlin, give him some exercise and then we'll be off. Do I need to bind and gag you? Just shake your head—I don't want to hear you speak right now."

She should be afraid, very afraid. She'd never seen him this mad, and she knew just how dangerous he could be. She had to make that try in the bathroom—surely he'd understand that? She wasn't some helpless female about to go gently into that dark night.

She did as she was told. Her arm hurt where he'd grabbed her, and she'd probably have bruises, but that was the least of her worries. Her leg was still aching, but she knew better than to complain, and watching Merlin caper about almost made her smile. Almost.

Several of the truckers left while Bishop was off with Merlin, including her erstwhile suitor, who was being helped by a friend, but they studiously kept their gaze away from her old gray truck. Bishop was lucky the bunch of them didn't decide to ambush him, she thought, but then remembered the looks on their faces when they saw how swiftly Bishop could take a man down. No, no one was coming near them.

She leaned back and closed her eyes. There was nothing she could do about things—she'd tried her best and been shot down. She was just going to have to take her medicine.

She jumped when Bishop yanked open the driver's door. Merlin leapt in and greeted her with the joy of someone returning after a year's absence, and Bishop slid in beside them, leaning down and fiddling with something under the dashboard, presumably whatever would have stopped her from driving off. She reached in her pocket for her extra key and dropped it in his lap.

It landed on his crotch, which was unfortunate, but she refused to be sorry. If it were up to her, that was where she'd kick him, good and hard. He scooped it up, shoving it in his pocket without looking at her, and started the truck, pulling out of the parking lot and setting out on the road at his usual insane pace.

Instead of turning left, getting back on the interstate, he turned right, onto a road that seemed to lead into nowhere. There were no town lights that she could see, nothing but miles and miles of flat prairie. He was going to kill her and bury her in that prairie, she thought, suddenly panicked. Why did she refuse to think he meant her any harm? Simply because he said so? Simply because she'd once loved him?

It was a long time before she finally got up the nerve to speak. "I'm sorry I wrote on the mirror," she said meekly. "But I had to try, you know that."

To her surprise he didn't snap at her. "What mirror?" His tone and his face were expressionless.

Relief and hope swept through her. "Uh . . . nothing. I mean . . ."

"You mean you're sorry you wrote a note on the mirror that gave your license plate number and asked for help? Not a problem. It was easy enough to clean off."

Her hope deflated like a balloon. "You bastard," she muttered.

"Don't push it."

"Push what? Are you going to shoot me and bury me in the desert?" she demanded. "I'm tired of being afraid of you. What are you going to do with me?"

"You're afraid of me? You don't act like it," he said in a low, affectless voice. He seemed to consider it for a moment, and she wondered if her life hung in the balance. "I'm not going to shoot you, I'm not going to hit you, I'm not going to torture you. If I have to tie you up and gag you I will, but that's the worst that will happen. Unless I lose my temper, and then I might spank you, but that's unlikely."

She turned to him, outrage wiping out her fear. "Spank me?" she said. "I'd like to see you try, you demeaning sexist bastard."

To her amazement there was a slight lift to his mouth, as if he found her funny. "Would you? I'll keep that in mind."

She didn't know how he did it. There was nothing sensuous in his voice, nothing suggestive in his expression, but all she could think of was sex—dirty, sweaty, nasty, lovely sex—and she could feel her temperature rise, feel her unwilling body react to her arousal in all the familiar ways.

She crossed her arms over her chest, more to hide her hardened nipples than to assuage them, but the sudden pressure made things worse, and she slid even farther away from him, trying to think of unpleasant things and failing entirely. She leaned her head against the window, with Merlin pressing up against her, offering her comfort.

What was it Laurel and Hardy used to say? Something like, "That's another fine kettle of fish you've gotten yourself into." She could relate. She was in a fine kettle of fish, the sharks were circling, the water was coming to a boil, and she was drowning. She closed her eyes.

It didn't help that she was so impossibly conflicted. It should have been so simple—she hated him. He'd lied to her, and cheated and stole. Worst of all, he'd ruined her for any other man, though she'd done her best to test out a replacement that first year, as he seemed to be fully aware. She'd married Pete because he was energetic and undemanding and he could make her come. After Pete she hadn't even bothered—she could do it faster and better by herself.

The man who had caused all that grief, the man who had disillusioned and defeated her for the first time in her life had returned to make her life even more miserable. He'd essentially kidnapped her; she'd been stabbed, drugged, and a witness to a brutal execution, and it was only going to get worse. And she was sitting here trying to will her body into behaving.

What the hell was wrong with her? She'd never been into bad boys, though she'd tried a few to see if that was what was lacking. The only bad boy she'd ever loved was James Bishop, and she'd known he was a bad boy beneath the elegant clothes and lazy charm. You only had to look into his eyes.

Not that she'd really loved him, she reminded herself firmly. If he'd been who he said he was . . . if he hadn't been after her jewelry . . . if he'd loved her . . .

But none of that was true and it didn't matter. The dismal truth was that her body was remembering the things he'd done to it, the way he'd touched her, and her body wanted him. That was it, she thought. It was her body that was betraying her. Her head and heart weren't involved.

Bodies could be kept under control. Physical hungers could be ignored. She moved even closer to the door, remembering how to breathe. In through the nose, out through the mouth, quietly, so he wouldn't notice.

"Don't get all nervous again," he said as he turned down an even narrower road. "You're going to like it."

She had no idea what he meant by that, and she was damned if she was going to ask. He said he wasn't going to kill her and she believed him. That was the best she could do, but it was good enough for now. He drove in silence, and she began to close her eyes, ready to sleep again, when something made her glance at him.

He was fiddling with a machine that looked as if it came from Star Trek, though a lot smaller, some kind of uber-cell phone. "Don't text while you're driving," she said, crankily. "It's probably against the law."

"We're in Colorado. Everything is legal here, even weed," he said, still moving his thumb over the keypad. "And not only is there no traffic, there's nothing on either side of the road to hurt us if I go off the side of the pavement. So chill."

Chill, she echoed to herself, almost laughing at the absurdity as they continued down the narrow road at breathtaking speeds. Dolores's air-conditioning had never been one of her strong points, and it was working overtime. Even night on this flat plain was ridiculously hot, and the engine was probably overheating as well. The vents just seemed to be blowing warm air in on her, and she started to lower the window when he stopped her, simply by overriding the controls on the driver's side.

"The AC is dead," she said in a grumpy voice.

"I noticed."

"I think we're burning oil," she added pointedly.

"We are."

Shit. She couldn't afford to replace Dolores—not with a truck sturdy enough to pull Annabelle. Then again, she might never find Annabelle again. "If you drove a little slower, you might save the engine you seem determined to destroy."

"Killing an engine isn't something that preys on my soul, Angel," he said. "I just need five more miles out of it and we'll be good."

"Her," she corrected. "And her name's Dolores."

"Good to know, so she can have a decent burial," he drawled. "And that helps. Women like to do what I tell them."

"They just want you to believe that," she scoffed.

This time he did look at her, and the lights from the dashboard danced across the angular lines of his face, reflected in his eyes. If she didn't know better she'd think it was a smoky, sensuous expression that didn't quite meet his mouth. "Oh, I don't know. Once I got you in bed, you were pretty amenable to almost everything I suggested. Though I can still think of one thing we haven't tried . . ."

"Shut up!" Damn, she sounded a little hysterical. He would read that as sexual interest, and she wasn't admitting to it. It would be her little secret and she'd take it to the grave with her. She continued in the calm, flat voice she'd wanted to use. "I'm really tired of your empty sexual innuendos," she said firmly. "They don't frighten me. You might kill me, but you'd never rape me."

To her surprise and annoyance he laughed at that, really laughed. "Evangeline, my darling one, I don't think it would be possible for me to rape you. You'd give in far too easily. Fortunately for you, rape is not a game I'm interested in playing."

"Rape isn't a game," she said fiercely.

His smile vanished and he looked at her again. "Did I miss something?"

She'd said too much again. "Miss what? You know everything about me, didn't you say? Surely the great James Bishop, or whoever you are, couldn't have missed something."

He was watching her far too closely for the speeds he was driving. "Did someone rape you?" His voice was sharp.

"Watch the road," she said, taking a deep breath. It was no one's fault but her own—she'd brought it up. The sooner she got it out in the open, the sooner he'd drop it. "I was underage and the records were sealed."

"How young?" His voice was grim.

"Don't worry about it. I was sixteen, fully capable of making my own decisions. And no one threw me down in the dirt and had me against my will. It was more a case of . . . inappropriate seduction." She felt a little shiver under her skin at the memory, and she had to hope he didn't notice. But he would have—he noticed everything.

"This happened before we met." It was a statement, not a question.

"Obviously."

"Who was it?"

"You know, I'd really rather not talk about it. My point was that rape isn't a joke or a game or . . ."

"Who was it?" he rapped it out, and she turned stubborn.

"None of your . . ."

He interrupted her again. "I can make you tell me. There are dozens of ways to do it, and I'll use every one of them, no matter how unpleasant, so you may as well give it up."

"Ve have vays of making you talk," she said in a heavy, mock-German accent.

"I thought this wasn't a joke."

Shit, she didn't want to think about this or talk about it. She took a deep breath and spoke rapidly. "He was a professor friend of my parents. He always had an eye for the freshman girls—he was notorious for it. So are most of the others, but he decided to branch out and experiment on me, and I . . . I was too in awe of him to do anything but go along with it. I didn't like it, but he didn't hurt me, at least not after the first time, didn't threaten to kill my parents or any of that crap. He was just the kind of man who had that power over people. He had incredible charisma, but he was as insidious as a snake, and of course I did what I was told."

"What about your sister?" he said in that cool, emotionless voice he used so much of the time. "Why didn't he go after her first?"

"Oh, Leslie was much too pretty. Everyone wanted her, and she thought too much of herself to be easy prey. Not like me."

He nodded, not correcting her assertion that Leslie was the pretty one. Of course he wouldn't—he knew everything about her. But he'd missed the most important, most devastating piece of her past.

"How old was he?"

Telling him she didn't want to talk about it would be a waste of time; he'd already ignored it. "He was sixty-three."

"Jesus, how did he even manage?"

She was already too deep in the mire and he wouldn't let her climb out. "He had me help," she said. *Would he put two and two together? Of course he would.*

"I see," he said in a voice that made it clear he saw everything. "You said was."

"What?" She was trying to pull herself out of the muck, but it was clinging to her.

"You said your professor was the kind of man who had power over people. Is he dead?"

"Yes. Heart attack in his early seventies. He was in bed with a nineteen-year-old."

"At least she was the age of consent." His voice was absolutely bland, and her curiosity got the better of her.

"Why do you care if he's alive?"

"Because otherwise I'd have to kill him."

It was lightly said, and it sounded like a joke. It wasn't, and she knew it.

"Does he have any children?" he said casually, and her eyes flew open in shock.

"You're not touching them. I won't tell you his name."

"Angel, with the little you've told me I can find out anything. Apparently it had hardly any lasting effect on your interest in sexual matters."

"It was boring. I didn't care one way or the other." A small lie, but he couldn't prove otherwise.

She'd given something away again, she thought as his jaw tightened. She should just shut up and deal with whatever torment he tried on her. "What's that?" she said, thankfully distracted. Something large and white had loomed up in front of them, and Bishop slammed on the brakes, yanking the wheel to the left. She could smell the burning rubber, and she put her hand on Dolores's dashboard, gentling her, a thank you and farewell. She suspected she wasn't going to see her again.

Fortunately Bishop was also distracted by the large vehicle, forgetting his questions, and he slammed the truck to a stop, turning it off. "What are you doing?"

"Saying good-bye to Dolores."

If he thought she was crazy, he didn't bother to say so, and simply nodded. "Your dreams are about to come true."

"You're letting me go?"

"That's not what you want," he said quietly. "And you and I both know it. Climb down and check out your new ride."

Merlin hopped out of the driver's side after Bishop, and slowly, carefully Evangeline slid out the opposite side. Her bruised leg gave way for a moment, but she managed to disguise it behind the open truck door. When she finally got a good look at the monstrosity, words failed her.

It was a Winnebago. Not a brand-new, gorgeous RV, but a very old, very rusty Winnebago with a cracked windshield. It was covered with dust, and she looked at it dubiously. "We're taking that? An old wreck we found by the side of the road?"

"Don't judge a book by its cover. And we didn't just find it—it was waiting for us." He'd taken a flashlight . . . her flashlight . . . out of the glove compartment and he was shining it over every rusty inch of the damned thing. There was even something that looked like an old analog antenna, which would do them absolutely no good.

"It probably leaks," she said morosely.

"Looks like it, doesn't it?" he said, sounding more cheerful than he had in a long while. He pointed his ridiculous cell phone at the door and she heard a click as it unlocked. That was certainly a lot more high tech than this old wreck should have been; Bishop moved past her to open the door, then stepped aside and gestured her to go in.

She didn't want to. For some reason it felt like crossing some border, past the point of no return, and she held back for a moment. It was a waste of time to hesitate—he'd simply overpower her—but something held her back.

"You want me to carry you across the threshold?"

That was enough to move her. She walked carefully to the door, trying to disguise her limp, and reached for the handhold, pulling herself up into the wonders of Annabelle's cousin.

Chapter Eleven

Inside, the RV wasn't much bigger than Annabelle had been when you took the front seat into account. The U-shaped dinette was on the right side of the camper, as well as the stove and sink, followed by an angled door that signaled a bathroom at the end. On the left side was a single bed, more kitchen equipment, a chair on the other side of the door, and a bed platform above the front seats. They were fairly standard features, except that everything inside was brand-new, and state of the art, instead of rusty and broken-down as the outside suggested. There was also a built-in flat screen with machines beneath it, and she suspected it wasn't for watching movies.

He gave her a little shove from behind, and she almost stumbled. Merlin, being much more of a gentleman, waited for her, then paced past her and stood guard behind the driver's seat. Bishop followed her in and shut the door behind her, closing them into utter darkness.

It happened so fast she couldn't control it. From out of nowhere panic clamped down over her like a smothering blanket, freezing her in place.

"What the hell's wrong with you?" Bishop demanded.

She pushed back against him, suddenly desperate. "I have to get out of here," she said breathlessly.

"Too fucking bad. This is your home for the next few days and I . . ."

"You don't understand," she choked out. "I can't breathe. I have to . . ."

He opened the door, and she rushed past him, forgetting the pain in her leg. She tripped and landed on her knees on the hard dirt, but it didn't matter. She could breathe, and she felt the warm night breeze begin to wash the clamminess from her skin.

Merlin was making distressed sounds, but Bishop must have ordered him to stay in the RV. He was looming over her in the darkness, and she knew she should get to her feet, to lessen the height difference and her own horrible sense of powerlessness, but she couldn't. What the hell *was* wrong with her? She was strong; she didn't suddenly fall apart like this.

Bishop was looking down at her, and she could sense his irritation but she didn't give a damn. "Since when have you been claustrophobic?" he drawled. "I'm not in the mood for games, Angel."

She was having trouble talking as well as breathing, and it took her a moment to find her voice. "Never," she gasped. "It just hit me."

"How convenient." He reached down and hauled her up, and she managed to get her feet under her. His hands were tight on her arms. "You're getting in there and you're going to behave yourself or I'll tie you up again, and this RV comes equipped with more advanced things than duct tape."

She'd gotten at least a portion of her self-control back. "I'll be all right." At least she hoped so. She had no idea where this sudden panic had come from. Not that she didn't have a dozen or more reasons, including the man beside her. Apparently the human mind and body could only take so much stress before cracking open.

There was a quarter moon in the clear night sky, giving her enough light to see him, his eyes glittering. He was a total stranger. He was the man she loved. The knowledge hit her like a sledgehammer to the heart.

He said nothing. A moment later he scooped her up, throwing her over his shoulder and carrying her back into the darkened camper as if she were a sack of potatoes. He tossed her onto the bed at the back with even less care, but the mattress was thick and cushioned, and Merlin immediately paced over and took his position by her head. "Move again," Bishop said, "and you'll regret it."

He stalked to the front of the camper. She tried to breathe through her tight throat, forcing calm on herself bit by bit as she heard him start the engine. It purred like a Jaguar. Who the hell *was* he? What kind of person had something like this at his fingertips?

He pulled onto the road and took off at his usual breakneck speed, faster than any Winnebago was supposed to go, and Merlin flopped down on the floor beside her. She knew better than to try to get him up on the bed with her—he'd always refused to. He was standing guard, even if he allowed himself to lie down, but damn, she wanted to comfort herself by burying her face in his fur.

She turned to face the side of the RV. The window just above the bed wasn't curtained, and air-conditioning was blowing through the unit. At least in this vehicle he couldn't hear her, couldn't see her, couldn't sense her in the darkness as long as he was driving. She turned her face against the wall, dry-eyed and desperate.

If she could cry, it would make things better. This happened occasionally—the tension, the anger, the grief and betrayal would build up until she felt helpless, and the only way to break the emotional roadblock was to put on the saddest movie she could find and weep buckets over some fictional character. *Beaches*, *Steel Magnolias*, any Nicholas Sparks movie . . . Any of them could break the dam and she'd be fine.

All she could do now was lie in this bed on top of the thick mattress and shiver, not from the cold, but the blocked, conflicted emotions. Her only respite was common sense.

She shouldn't have any emotions about her current situation, much less conflicted ones. The magical appearance of the deceptive RV was one more bit of proof that Bishop wasn't the gigolo and thief she'd presumed him to be. Her diamond earrings were small change when it came to equipment like this.

And a petty thief, or even a grand thief, would hardly be able to dispose of a man as quickly and efficiently as he had with the man who had been sent to kill him. And her.

Who was James Bishop? Who was he working for? The little bits and pieces he'd told her made no sense. Given his ruthlessness when dealing with Clement, why had he bothered coming after her? They weren't married—she knew that much, no matter what he said. He was just playing mind games with her, and he was very adept.

Who was he? What did he want? For that matter, what had he wanted with her in the first place? She was an adjunct teacher on a bare-bones research trip and she had no delusions about herself. She was no troll, but Bishop, with his almost sublime beauty, was supermodel territory.

She closed her eyes. Merlin whined softly, sensing her distress, but it was quiet enough that Bishop wouldn't hear. Would he drive all night? Probably—he was more machine than man. She'd just have to survive—she was holding on by her fingernails, and the pit yawning beneath her was terrifying. There wasn't a damned thing she could do about it.

She didn't sleep—tension was threading through her body like barbed wire, pulling tighter and tighter. She simply lay there in the bunk, hugging herself. If she turned on her other side she'd be able to see him up there in the driver's seat, she'd see his reflection in that huge windshield. She stayed where she was.

She'd lost all sense of time when she felt the RV leave the highway once more, as they drove over a pitted road, too fast, of course. There was anger in the way he took the corner, she thought, burying her face in the pillow. She'd pretend to be asleep—that's all she seemed to do anyway when she was around him. At least there was a bed up over the driver's area, and he could just climb up there if he'd stopped to sleep.

The RV came to a stop with a lurch, one that would have woken her up if she'd actually been sleeping. She couldn't tell if the sky was lighter or not—not without lifting her head, and the only way she was going to make it through this overpowering miasma that seemed to have come over her was to keep very still, keep away from *him*.

He made no effort to be quiet. "Fuck," he said, and she could hear him getting up from the seat. To her horror, instead of heading outside or climbing up into the bunk, he headed straight back toward her.

She was having a hard time controlling her breathing enough to simulate sleep. She was practically vibrating with tension, but it was still very dark, and the tremors were so slight he wouldn't see them; if he'd just go away, she'd be all right, she'd manage to get through this . . .

"Fuck," he said again. "What's wrong with you? And don't tell me it's claustrophobia, or fear of the dark, or any shit like that. And stop pretending to be asleep—you wouldn't fool anyone. I've been listening to you shiver and shake for the last few hours."

She opened her eyes, but she wouldn't turn to look at him. Couldn't turn—every muscle felt frozen in her panic. That's what it was, she realized to her complete shame. It was a panic attack, and she hadn't had one since she'd been a hormonal teenager.

Recognizing what it was should have stopped it, given her enormous willpower, but she still felt caught in its grip. "Evangeline," he said in a quiet, dangerous voice.

Don't touch me, she thought desperately. *Please don't touch me.* She managed to grind out the word in a raw whisper. "Don't." He didn't listen.

The moment she felt his hands on her, pulling her from the bed, something snapped inside her, something dark and dangerous that terrified her. She went wild, hitting him, kicking him, slapping him as she tried to break free from his iron grip.

He simply wrapped his arms around her, tight, so tight it cut off her breath, which made it worse. She wanted to scream, but when she opened her mouth no sound came out, and his body was clamped against hers so that she couldn't even struggle. She was trapped, caught, there was no escape . . .

He held her a little bit away from his body and he shook her, hard, and it felt as if her bones were rattling inside her; but if he thought it would shake her out of the panic, he was wrong. He loosened his grip slightly, and she tore herself free, throwing herself toward the door.

He caught her, and she clawed out at him, her fingernails raking across his chest as he yanked her back, and she was screaming. She heard her voice in the back of her head, and she couldn't even guess what the words were. A small, shamed part of her was standing apart, watching this with shock and horror, but she couldn't stop, she had to get away from him before he devoured her with his darkness.

The battle was short-lived and dirty: she thought she heard Merlin's bark, Bishop's curse and a short, sharp order, and then it seemed like she was flying through the air, through the darkness, only to land in a dark, enclosed place with Bishop all around her, trapping her, closing her in, devouring her, his body on top of hers, holding her down as she fought.

It stopped so abruptly that for a moment she thought she was dead. One second she was fighting for her life, the next everything had drained from her body and she went limp beneath him, all her desperate fury vanishing.

But she was still breathing—her chest was rising and falling against his, and their hearts were pounding in a rapid counterpoint. Why was his pounding? He'd subdued her with little effort. It had to be something else—she could swear he didn't even have a heart. He was a cyborg, an android, a little green man from Mars, and she wanted to laugh, but if she started she wouldn't stop, and that was even more terrifying.

It took her a moment to realize where they were—in the sleeping compartment above the driver's seat. The mattress beneath her cushioned her as the other one had, even with Bishop's weight on top of her, holding her down, holding her prisoner, and she felt her breath begin to speed up once more.

"Open your eyes, Angel," he said, his voice soft but implacable, and she realized she'd kept them tightly shut during their short, fierce battle, as if by blinding herself she could pretend it wasn't happening. She should have known better—closing her eyes on a roller coaster only made it worse.

She opened them, and she could see his face, closer than she expected. She could see the glitter in those eyes that were all wrong, she could feel his breath on her skin, the familiar-unfamiliar weight of him pressing her into the mattress, the hard ridge of his erection pressing at the juncture of her thighs, and then realization struck her.

"*That,*" he said, reading her perfectly, "should be the least of your worries. It seems to have become a permanent condition ever since I found you again. I want to know what the fuck is wrong with you."

She opened her mouth, but she had no voice and no words. Her throat felt raw, and she realized she'd screamed enough to have hurt it. And how could she explain what she didn't understand herself?

It finally came out in an almost inaudible rasp. "Don't . . ." she managed to begin, and she could feel the anger and frustration in the body plastered so tightly against hers.

"Jesus Fucking Christ, Angel, what do you think I'm going to do? Cut your throat and bury you in the woods like Clement? Rape you? I told you I wouldn't hurt you."

"Don't . . ." she tried again; he was so close, and she didn't want to be here, she didn't want to be trapped underneath him, she didn't want all these clothes between them. She wanted him inside of her, she wanted him hard and fast, pounding into her, driving all thoughts and fears from her tangled brain, and her breathing began to speed up once more, as tremors danced across her skin. She took a deep breath, forcing herself to calm down as much as she could, forcing the rest of the words out. "Don't . . . know."

"Is that 'don't' and 'no'?" he said, his voice harsh. "Or is that 'don't know,' as in you don't know what's wrong with you?"

She managed to nod. She was so cold, and so hot, trapped here in the enveloping darkness with Bishop on top of her, all around her. If he'd go away she'd be able to pull herself together . . .

He'd pushed himself up on his elbows, and was looking down at her in the inky darkness; and for a moment they were suspended in time, staring at each other. "Fuck it," he said finally, sliding one hand behind her neck to pull her mouth up to his.

His kiss was air to a drowning man, oxygen to an asthmatic. His open mouth closed over hers and his breath filled her lungs and her veins, and she was alive again, blood pumping through her body as he kissed her, his tongue sliding against hers with such perfect intimacy that she wanted to weep.

She made a sound, and whether it was protest or surrender didn't matter, because she kissed him back, hungry for him, desperate for him. She reached for his shirt and began yanking it free from his jeans, needing to feel his skin against her, needing to lose herself in him.

He'd been a carefully banked fire, but with her hands on his skin he seemed to explode, and his patience vanished. He reached down and tore her cutoffs open, the strength in his hands shocking her as the zipper and denim gave way, yanked them down her legs, complete with her underwear, and threw them into the darkness. Her uneasiness returned—this was Bishop, this was a stranger. This was her husband, this was a thief and a liar. This was the man she loved, this was the man she despised. This man was a lover.

This man was a killer.

He shoved her legs apart, and she wanted to say something, to stop him, but things had gone too far in that short time. She heard the rip of his zipper, the quick shove of clothes, and for one brief moment the head of his cock against her, large and heavy, and it had been so long . . .

He thrust into her, hard, and she cried out. Not in pain, though it hurt, but with a pleasure so powerful it shook her. He was so big, filling her, and it seemed as if she'd been empty forever, needing him, only him, and no one could take his place.

She wrapped her legs around his tight butt, her hands caught up in his shirt, and he thrust again, and it was too much, too hard, too fast, and she couldn't get enough of him. The shirt ripped open beneath her desperate hands, buttons flying into the darkness, and she didn't care. She needed his skin, she needed to put her face against his chest and breathe him in again, that rich, clean smell of his skin.

It was the same. That scent that was peculiarly his own, and she pushed the shirt off his shoulder and licked him, licked the sweat off him as he pumped into her, over and over again.

The orgasm hit her like a shock—she'd been so caught up in the devouring pleasure of his hard thrusts that she hadn't even thought about needing more. This was what she wanted, and the climax that washed through her, sending her into spasms of choking pleasure, had come too quickly.

He pulled out of her, and she screamed in protest, hitting him. He was panting in the darkness, and his hands were rough as he flipped her over, yanking her hips up. "This way," he growled, and pushed in again, deeper than ever, and she wanted more. The pain wasn't important, the feel of him deep, deep inside her was what mattered, and she let go, taking his fierce thrusts with such raw satisfaction that she might die from it. This was life, this was what she needed, only this, forever, in the darkness. His body covering her, his hands yanking her bra up so he could slide his fingers over her breasts, rough with her tight nipples, and she buried her face in the mattress to silence her cries of fierce release, her body squeezing his cock as climaxes rocketed through her. So fast she didn't know where one ended and the other began, and it didn't matter. She was weeping into the sheets as he fucked her, and when he thrust home, holding himself there, his own climax hit him; then he slid his hand down to find her clitoris, and she lost it completely, sobbing into the mattress.

The climaxes wouldn't stop. He pulled out, too fast, and she lay face down on the mattress, letting the spasms race through her body.

She felt his big hands slid up her legs, and when he came to her hips, he turned her onto her back, more gentle now, and she could hear the sound of his rough breathing perfectly in the night air. She was panting, struggling to regain control, when he slid into her again, in deep, and she realized with a shock he was still just as hard. She'd felt him come, and he was still hard.

"I can't . . ." she managed to choke out, but he pulled her legs around his hips.

"You can," he whispered, moving into her, slowly now, rhythmically, the initial frenzy passing. They were both slick with sweat, and she felt weak, shattered, unable to do more than wrap her arms around his waist, bury her face against his skin and hold on. She would do this for him, let him . . .

The small climax hit her and she cried out, a shriek of surprise, certain that she'd had nothing left, and no sooner had it passed than she was afraid again. He was taking too much from her, there would be nothing left. She dug her fingernails in, pulling him closer, as she teetered on a precipice, terrified of the darkness beyond, certain she'd disappear completely.

"Let go, Angel." His voice was a rasp in her ear, and she heard the name with a twisted kind of joy. "Let go of it all."

She shook her head, beyond words, fighting it, fighting him, fighting to survive. He was stripping everything from her, she would die . . .

"Let go, Angel," he whispered again, and it sounded like love. "I'll catch you."

With those simple words he ripped away the last of her defenses, and she was open, naked, raw, and bleeding before him. She convulsed, and he was inside her, surrounding her, there was nothing but James in the velvety darkness as he joined her in that final climax. James and Angel in a cocoon of sweat and sex and endless pleasure pushed through the crucible of pain, back into love once more, and there was nothing left. Nothing.

She was vaguely aware of him pulling away from her, rolling onto his side beside her in the small space, and she felt abandoned. She realized with a shock that he was still wearing his jeans—he'd just shoved them down—and his shirt was half on. She was wearing her T-shirt and her bra was pushed up to her shoulders, and if she could she would have laughed.

She couldn't. She shuddered. The night air was suddenly cool as the sweat dried on her skin, and she started to turn, wanting nothing more than to curl up in shame, when she felt his hands on her body, unexpectedly gentle. He pulled her T-shirt over her head, found the clasp to her bra with unerring expertise, and unfastened it, tugging it free, and she was naked. He slid off the bunk, and she started to turn again, but his hand caught her, held her. A moment later he was back in the bunk, nothing but skin against skin as he pulled her into his arms. He said nothing, but simply wrapped himself around her, holding her tight against him. His heart was still thudding heavily, or maybe that was hers, and he pulled her leg over his hip to get her closer, tucking her head against his shoulder.

Now was the time to whisper words of love, of guilt, of reassurance. Now was the time to comfort her.

"Sleep," was all he said as he pulled a quilt over their rapidly cooling bodies.

She slept.

Chapter Twelve

Bishop let himself sleep for three hours. It was a luxury that his body accepted gratefully, and when he awoke, precisely at seven as he'd programmed himself to do, he felt better than he had in a long time. Better than he had in five years.

She still lay curled in his arms. Not that he'd given her any choice—in his sleep he'd sensed each time when she'd tried to pull away, curl in on herself, and he hadn't let her. He'd held her until the very last bit of resistance left her, and she clung to him as if they belonged together, needed each other to survive. Crazy, of course, but he needed that feeling. Just for a short while, he needed to indulge in that impossible fantasy, before he had to let her go again.

He slid away from her, hard as a rock, of course, and dropped his feet silently on the narrow floor of the Winnebago. Merlin sat up, immediately alert, and Bishop opened the door, heading out into the light with the dog.

They were parked in a remote corner of forest on the edge of the foothills of the Sangre de Cristo Mountains, one of the satellite-safe zones he'd been briefed on. There was even running water, though in late summer the river wasn't much more than a narrow stream. Merlin leaped ahead happily, signing everything as he went, while

Bishop thought dark, depressing thoughts as he waited for his erection to subside enough to relieve himself in the bushes. There were times when he wished he had half of Merlin's energy. Right now he felt . . .

He wasn't sure what he felt. Immense physical satisfaction, of course. How could he not? That it felt more than physical was something he wasn't ready to consider. Besides, what good would it do? Home was the Committee, not the arms, the soul, the snappishly sharp mind and welcoming body of his erstwhile wife.

He'd been too rough with her and he knew it, but he'd been holding his hunger, his absolute starvation for her, at bay for so long that when he finally cut loose from his restraints, he was like an animal, one that she met fully, not pulling back. He still wanted to kick himself. He would have been gentle with her, would have forced his body back under his rigid control, but she'd dug her nails into his skin and took everything he gave her and more.

He *should* have been gentler, eased her back into it, but he'd forgotten the almost incendiary passion that flamed between them, and it had torn his resolve into pieces. He might have hurt her—he couldn't be sure—but he was reasonably certain he could have stopped if she'd wanted him to, needed him to.

Shit, he thought, suddenly morose. Merlin was enjoying himself, sniffing everything, reveling in being off duty for a time, but when he glanced back at Bishop, it was as if he'd sensed his master's conflicted emotions. He shouldn't be having emotions. And he wasn't Merlin's master anymore. The dog he'd raised and trained had switched allegiance far more thoroughly than Bishop had ever imagined he might. He'd sent Merlin on a job, and the dog had fallen in love.

"Oh, Christ, Merlin," he said, his voice thick with shock. "You're as bad as I am. That woman is practically lethal."

Merlin immediately sat now that he was being addressed, and he looked at Bishop questioningly. "Yeah, I know," Bishop said. "We're both in trouble. I can get myself out of it easily enough"—at least he hoped so—"but I think you're in it for the long haul."

Merlin cocked his head, not looking troubled by this revelation. "Lucky bastard," Bishop muttered, stretching in the morning light.

He rinsed off in the icy water of the stream, then opened one of the outside storage compartments on the Winnebego to catalogue the supplies. There was enough fire power to fight a small war, a duffle bag with clothes, and a crate of the food he'd requested. Neither of them had eaten much—well, not counting that massive meal Evangeline had devoured at the diner—and they couldn't afford to skip meals. Maybe he'd climb back into the revamped Winnebago to find that the astonishing sex that always erupted between them had made her sweetly domestic and docile.

He doubted it. He'd kept close tabs on her for the last five years, watched her as she changed, known that he'd done it to her. Losing her naïveté had probably been inevitable, but it hadn't needed to be so extreme. She'd lost that incredible, slightly wary sweetness, and he missed it. Now she was snarky, and sarcastic, and it made him hot as hell. He'd been charmed by the semi-innocent young professor roaming Italy on her own. The new woman she'd become was even more irresistible.

He yanked on clean clothes—jeans and a deliberately stupid T-shirt—and stretched out on the grass. He'd give her a little time—they could afford that much. They were on the border of New Mexico and Colorado, and they'd be heading across the vast expanse of Texas. It was Tuesday, and he needed to be in New Orleans by Thursday. Ryder had been given the task of finding the perfect setting for the new American branch of the Committee, and he'd found the right spot. The new arm of the Committee would be just as covert, and who was funding it or the original branch in London was anybody's guess. As far as Bishop could tell it was probably a conglomerate of millionaires and western countries with the kinds of national budgets that could hide the Committee's expenditures. Ryder couldn't sign papers without him, and the real estate people were getting itchy; even though Bishop had suggested Ryder simply shoot the broker, they'd both known it was nothing more than a black joke. The sooner they got everything in place, the sooner they could put a stop to His Eminence and his hideous business, and Bishop wasn't in the mood to wait.

It was about twelve hundred miles between where they were and New Orleans. He could drive it straight, no problem, and the reconfigured engine on the Winnebago, not to mention the secondary gas tank, would make it fast and painless.

But an ancient Winnebago driving anything past sixty would look suspicious. Besides, once they reached New Orleans he had to let her go. Once Ryder assured him she was safe.

He still wasn't sure what his best move was. Just because Clement was dead didn't mean he was—they were—safe. The hierarchy of the far-reaching Corsini family had a long memory, and while Dimitri Corsini had been only a senior adviser and accountant, the rest of the organization had reacted to his execution with rage. His death had sent their complicated accounting system into chaos, and he'd been family. The Corsinis didn't deal with that sort of thing very well. They wanted Bishop, believed he was the executioner, and he had no interest in telling them otherwise. He could have garroted Corsini just as easily as Claudia had, albeit with lingering Catholic guilt about committing such a sin on holy ground, but he wouldn't have taken pleasure in it as Claudia had.

He would be in danger until the Corsinis' ugly trade was smashed, and they were close, so close. The Committee still didn't know if the corruption stopped with His Eminence or went higher, but once they'd taken care of business, things should ease off a bit.

The problem was Evangeline. Claudia was no longer trustworthy, so his original legal attachment to Evangeline would do little to protect her. At least Claudia was in Japan, trying to push her way in on Taka's mission, and he could be counted on to keep her busy. By the time he dissolved the marriage, Evangeline would have faded back into the woodwork.

Severing any connection with Evangeline would go a long way toward destroying her value as a hostage to anyone who wanted to get to him. He should have seen that coming sooner, done something about it, but since he never went near her, apart from her bigamous wedding day, he would have thought no one would realize he had that one connection. It was almost impossible to hack into the Committee's tangled power structure, but, just in case, he'd had several of his friends take turns keeping an eye on Evangeline. That way no one person could be traced if someone was lucky enough to get past all the firewalls and security.

Committee operatives needed to be free from entanglements— otherwise they were too vulnerable. Not that people hadn't worked around it: Peter Madsen, the head of the original British-based organization, was the first leader who had not only a wife but two children. They were kept safe through a combination of surveillance, discreet guards, and Madsen's reputation. It would take a madman to attempt to get to Genevieve Madsen or his precocious daughter Izzy—and his five-year-old son was almost more terrifying than Madsen himself.

Most operatives left the business when they made the mistake of caring about someone too much. Some worked on a contingency basis, like Bastien Toussaint, some had disappeared into the ether, like their previous boss, Isobel Lambert and her true love, Serafin the Butcher, aka Thomas Killian, the former CIA agent. And some carried on as always. The Japanese contingent, Reno and Taka, had the backing of the Yakuza as well as the Committee, and they were untouchable, but Finn MacGowan, after three years as a prisoner in the Andes, had settled down into relative domesticity. Falling in love was a definite problem in the Committee—lone wolves like Claudia and Ryder were much more effective.

Not, of course, that falling in love had anything to do with him or his current mess of a situation. He'd been thrown together with Evangeline when he'd expected never to see her again, and the reverberations could be felt all the way to London and beyond. He had to get her back, secure in her backwater college, with the assurance that no one would connect her to him, no one would touch her.

He wasn't sure how he was going to manage that, but Ryder would help. The two of them had their hands full—not only did they have to track down and terminate the Corsinis' New Orleans operation, but also they had to set up the framework of the Committee in the United States. Having London serve as the hub was getting more and more complicated, and it only made sense to branch out into the US. If there was a situation going on, a group that was causing trouble, planning some atrocity, it was almost always connected with his country, and Bishop had fought long and hard for a US branch. All they had to do first was to track down the man behind this particular horror scene and kill him.

He leaned back, looking at the bright blue sky. Merlin had finished with his territorial concerns and flopped down beside him, at exactly the right position for Bishop to rub his head. A flash of regret went through him at the thought of Merlin disappearing from his life forever, but then, he'd already been gone for more than eighteen months. Just because he hadn't gotten rid of his bowl and his dog bed didn't mean that he thought he was coming back. He *wanted* Merlin with Evangeline. As long as one of them was with her she was safe, and he knew he wasn't going to be anywhere around.

Fuck, he thought savagely. He wasn't going to bitch about the unfairness of life—he'd chosen this, he was still choosing this, and there was always a price you had to pay for the decisions you made.

He pushed himself off the grass, getting to his feet, and Merlin followed, moving to the door of the Winnebago to stand guard. Bishop needed to walk off his edginess. They weren't going to set off until early afternoon, and in the meantime he needed to keep his distance from Evangeline. Last night, or was it this morning, had been too intense, and he needed to keep focused on the job at hand. He looked at Merlin, who was sitting patiently by the steps up into the RV.

"Come on, boy," he said.

Merlin didn't move.

Bishop stared at him in surprise. Merlin was too good a dog to disobey a direct order. "Merlin, come!" he said, making his voice stern.

Merlin whined slightly, but he didn't move. Bishop shook his head. He wasn't going to sink that low, he wasn't. But Merlin wasn't moving, and there was no need to guard Evangeline right now. Merlin had no intention of leaving her.

He had no choice, though it galled him to do it. "Come on, Merlin. Walkies."

Merlin did a little dance in place, but apart from that he wasn't doing anything Bishop suggested. "Traitor," Bishop muttered beneath his breath, and then headed off into the woods, leaving his wife and her bodyguard behind.

———

Evangeline didn't want to wake up. She was curled up in bed, a soft, fluffy duvet wrapped around her, and as long as she stayed there, she didn't have to deal with him. She didn't even have to deal with facing her own culpability—she could just hide. It seemed a perfectly reasonable thing to do, until she heard Merlin whining at the door, and while she could ignore calls of nature, she couldn't ignore her dog. Wrapping the duvet around her nude body, she stepped out onto the floor. Directly onto her discarded shorts and underwear.

Kicking them out of the way, she opened the door, steeling herself to face Bishop. But he wasn't there; it was only Merlin waiting to get in. She backed up and let him past her, then looked out into the thick forest of pines. There was no sign of Bishop. With extreme luck he'd left her there, safe in a camper with all the comforts of home. Was he expecting her to drive for help? Or sit there quietly, waiting for his return?

If so, he was in for a surprise. Bishop wasn't the only one who could hotwire a car around here. She shoved the bed platform up and out of the way, refusing to think about the state of the sheets, and moved to the driver's seat. One look told her she was shit out of luck—this wasn't really a 1970s Winnebago, no matter what it looked like. The dashboard was a computerized nightmare, and while she was relatively good at technology, she was iffy when it came to upscale vehicles, never having been able to afford one herself. Besides, she could hardly drive off stark naked and wrapped in a duvet.

"Where's your asshole friend, baby?" she asked Merlin, who cocked his head. "No, you don't think he's an asshole, do you? It takes a woman to appreciate his full asshattery." She headed into the back of the camper to investigate. She hated using toilets in RVs—nothing could keep them from eventually permeating the living space. She hadn't taken into account the space-age facilities someone, or something, had supplied Bishop, and she took a look at the tiny closet-like room with awed appreciation.

A quick shower went a long way toward restoring her battered self-respect, clean clothes helped as well; but most useful of all was Bishop's absence. If he'd left her, and she only hoped he had, then eventually someone would come back to get them out of there. Maybe it wouldn't take that long for her to walk for help, and she'd try that eventually. First, she needed food.

The kitchen was another marvel, and it didn't take her long to cook up a frittata with fresh zucchini and mushrooms. She accidentally made too much, and she would have fed it to Merlin, but despite that asshole's assertion, human food wasn't good for him. She even found the high-end kibble she fed him, leaving the rest of the frittata on the counter while she continued her exploring.

She couldn't believe her luck when she found a laptop tucked behind canned food, and she pulled it out with a cry of triumph. She slid onto the bench of the dinette and opened it. Password protected, of course, providing nothing but a blank screen. The damned thing would probably explode in her hands if she did the wrong thing; but she had no intention of giving up without trying, so she started with the passwords, including the obvious "user" and "guest." The computer belonged to someone called Edmunds, which she assumed was either Bishop's real name or another alias, so she went on with the slightly less obvious "B1sh0p" and "Us3r."

No good, so she moved on to forms of Merlin interspersed with numbers, Winnebago, anything she could think of. In frustration she typed in "asshole" and "a55h0l3" but obviously it didn't work.

"I can do this," she told Merlin, who was lying peacefully at her feet. "I'm good at stuff like this." The problem was, everything she knew about James Bishop was a lie, so she sat back, racking her brain for anything that could possibly be true. She tried "Claudia" and its permutations, and at last, in total frustration and fury, she typed in "Evangeline."

"Stupid idiot," she muttered to herself. If she was going to be an idiot, she might as well go all the way. She threw in numbers for every vowel, cursing herself, then finally tried "EvANGELin3."

The screen opened. She stared at it in complete astonishment, then glanced down at Merlin. "He did this on purpose, didn't he?" she said severely. "He made the computer easy to find and did this to keep me busy. Asshole," she muttered.

That word was getting tiresome—she had to think of something new to call him, but right then she wasn't feeling terribly creative. She turned back to the screen and let out a frustrated curse. The laptop was demanding another password, and it sure as hell wasn't going to be "Evangeline" again.

She could play with that later. The screen also offered a shining golden opportunity. You could sign on as a guest, which she immediately did, only to be confronted by a generic Windows interface. She spent an hour searching through every possible path to documents, hidden files, and Cloud files, but it was as if the computer were absolutely clean. She knew it wasn't—getting past Bishop's next password would open a world of answers, but that wasn't going to happen. She could only make do with what she had, and she gave in to the curiosity that she'd always refused to indulge. Google was her friend, and she went back to the tiny village of Cabrisi, the hotel, Claudia and James, and at the last minute threw in the tiny church of St. Anselmo to see what she came up with.

She was so engrossed in her discoveries that she didn't even hear Bishop return. The side door slammed, and suddenly he was looming over her, shoving the laptop closed and yanking it out of her reach. "What the fuck do you think you're doing?" he demanded in a dangerous voice.

So much for morning-after love talk, she thought, eyeing him warily. "You didn't think I'd just curl up in a little ball and hide, did you?"

"That's what you wanted to do last night."

She knew her face whitened. He was prepared to fight dirty, was he? What else could she expect? He didn't know she could fight dirty too.

"It's a new day," she said brightly. "How do you happen to have Internet access here?"

"Trade secret." He shoved the laptop back where it came from, then slid into the dinette opposite her.

"What trade, may I ask?"

"You may not ask. At least I know you couldn't get anywhere on the laptop. It's password encrypted."

She looked at him directly. It was hard, staring into his sea-blue eyes that were so flat and expressionless. "I got through the first one," she said.

She expected him to be defensive, angry, but instead his mouth quirked up in a tiny smile. "Bet you liked that."

Asshole, she thought. "Of course that's as far as I got. You must have two or three more levels."

"Seven," he said flatly. "So exactly what did you discover? I know you couldn't have gotten anything off the computer itself, and the Internet wouldn't be much more helpful."

Ah, triumph, she thought, warming. "Oh, not much," she said. "There was no trace of a man named James Bishop who resembled you in any way."

"That's not true. I know for a fact that there are at least five James Bishops in this country alone who are thirty-four, six feet one, and about one seventy-five. They have similar facial structures, and hair and eye color can be changed."

"So it can," she said. "But at one point I knew you very well, and

I can tell the difference. Is that the reason you picked that name? Because you could have so many doppelgangers?"

He ignored her question. "So you didn't learn anything, did you, Angel?"

Crap. She hadn't tried "Angel" as a second password. Then again, he said there were seven layers of encryption, and it wouldn't have gotten her very far.

She smiled at him sweetly. "Not a thing. Until I decided to look up the tiny chapel of St. Anselmo in the mountains just outside the town of Cabrisi. You remember that, don't you? It's where we first met. And what do you think I discovered? That nice old man, Signore Dimitri Corsini, was murdered up there. I have a good memory for dates, and just imagine, it was the very day you and I were there!" she said in a mock innocent voice. "I must have missed seeing his murder by just a few minutes."

His cool expression didn't change. "Less than that," he said. "Claudia had just finished with him and we were leaving when you popped up."

"Oh, you're telling me you're not a murderer?" She batted her eyes at him. "I'm so relieved."

"Didn't your research tell you about the dead chauffeur found in the courtyard? He was my work."

He said it so calmly, but for some crazy reason it hit her in the stomach like a blow. She could only hope she kept her face unreadable—she didn't want him to know she cared. "Killing someone in church is a pretty rotten thing to do," she said.

He shrugged. "Not necessarily. Think of *Hamlet*. Signore Corsini went to meet his maker in a state of prayer. He might have flown straight to heaven. Somehow I don't think so, but you never can tell."

"Hamlet was an asshole." Apparently that was her word for the day. "If he'd killed his villainous uncle then and there, he would have saved a lot of lives, including his own."

"But it would have made a very short bad play."

"Why are we discussing Shakespeare?" she demanded.

He shrugged, then glanced over at the tiny kitchen counter and the food lying there. "You made me breakfast!" he said. "What a good little wife you are."

"I'm not your wife!" she snapped, tired of this mock civility. "And I just happened to make too much."

"Sure you did, Angel. Looks like you managed to get a shower too. I gather the plumbing facilities are adequate."

"Adequate," she agreed, not about to tell him how wonderful they were. "So what next?"

He was shoveling food in his mouth like someone needing fuel. He probably didn't even taste it. "You mean, now that I've had my wicked way with you?" he said between mouthfuls.

"If you don't mind, I'd rather not discuss it," she said stiffly.

If he hadn't been eating, he probably would have given her that infuriating grin, but he changed the subject. "Now," he said, "we drive to New Orleans. We'll take it in two stages—I need to be there by Thursday and it's about twelve hundred miles, so we can go at a leisurely pace."

Twelve hundred miles in a day and half was hardly a leisurely pace in Evangeline's opinion, but she wasn't foolish enough to think she was going to have any say in the matter. "And you're not going to drop me off anywhere along the way, are you?"

"Nope."

Okay, he'd be too busy driving to go for a repeat of last night, and if he tried she wouldn't be so fucking needy that she'd respond. "Are you going to want me to drive?"

He laughed at that. "Not that I'm not impressed with your ability with the truck and camper . . ."

"Annabelle," she broke in.

"With your ability with Annabelle, but the sad fact is, I don't trust you. You'd probably ram us into the first solid object you came to."

"If only that were you," she said dreamily. "When do we leave?"

"Now."

"May I take Merlin out for a moment before we go?" She hated asking him, but she needed fresh air even more than Merlin did.

"Are you stupid enough to think you can make a run for it?" he countered.

She shook her head. "You're safe. You don't have a willing hostage, but you've got one nonetheless, and there's nothing I can do about it." She slid out of the booth, hiding her wince as sharp pain stabbed her calf. "Come on, baby."

"Baby?" Bishop said in a pained voice. "You've ruined my dog."

"My dog," she said, and started the short pathway to the door.

"Hold it!" he said sharply.

She froze, careful to put her weight on her other foot. She turned her head. "What?" she said impatiently.

"You're limping."

"No, I'm not!" she said.

He stared at her for a long, thoughtful moment. "I should change your bandages."

"No need. At least the first aid kit was easy to find. I put new ones on after my shower." A sudden thought struck her, and her hostility vanished temporarily. "How are your stitches? I forgot all about them. Did you . . . I mean, did you . . ." Words failed her.

"You mean did I pop any stitches while we were fucking? I bled a little bit, but it was worth it."

She felt her face flood with heat. "You are such a sleaze!" she snapped. "And you're trying to distract me. I should check your stitches."

"Tell you what. I'll let you look at my stitches when you tell me why you're limping. I need to look at your leg."

"After I take Merlin out . . ." She let out a little whoop as he picked her up and deposited her on the narrow bunk, moving so fast she had no warning. She tried to squirm away but he put a hand in the middle of her chest, holding her still.

"Keep fighting me and I'll put my hand on your tits to hold you still," he growled.

She froze. "You're crass."

His smile was seraphic. "Yes, I am," he agreed, releasing her to turn and examine her legs. She knew what the right one looked like, and she'd worn long pants to hide it, but all her pants were loose, and he had no trouble pushing up the cuff to her knee, exposing the swelling purple bruise.

He sat back, for a moment all artifice disappearing, and looked shocked. "How did that happen?"

For some stupid, stupid reason she didn't want to tell him, to throw it in his face. "It doesn't matter," she mumbled, turning her face away.

But his hand caught her chin and drew it back, so she couldn't avoid his gaze unless she closed her eyes, and she wasn't that big a chicken. "Did I do this when I kicked you?"

Everything had shut down with him again, his face unreadable, but for some reason she still wanted to protect him. "It was a fluke. You didn't mean to kick me that hard, and you just happened to hit me at the wrong place and . . ."

"I meant to kick you that hard." There was a strange note of bitterness in his voice.

"Well, it worked." What else could she say? "It'll heal."

"It's a problem. You never know when you might have to make a run for it. This makes you a liability."

So much for tender regret, she thought, wondering why she felt crushed. "Then just put a bullet in my brain and leave me behind. That way I can't tattle on you."

He shrugged dispassionately. "That's protocol."

"Is it? Then why didn't you just kill me at the church and have done with it? Why go through an elaborate charade . . ."

He'd been examining the bruise, pressing against it, but at this he turned away. "It's not broken," he said, ignoring her question. "If you look hard enough, you'll probably find ice. Put it on the bruise, keep your leg elevated, and it should be fine eventually. We'll just have to hope we don't run into any problems."

It was a waste of time to glare at him—he wouldn't even notice. She sat up and gave a long-suffering sigh. "All right. After I take Merlin out."

"Merlin doesn't need to go out. He can hold his bladder for hours. Find something to entertain yourself with while I drive."

He started toward the driver's seat, and she slid off the bunk, starting after him. "Look, just let me get some fresh air." She hated the pleading sound in her voice.

She found herself talking to his back. He was ignoring her, of course, about to move between the two front seats to take his place behind the wheel, when she made the dire mistake of putting a hand on his shoulder.

He turned, in no particular hurry. "You can open a window," he said callously. "Go ahead and play with the computer if you're bored. You won't find anything interesting."

"The Internet is full of interesting things if you know how to look," she said, which was patently stupid. She wanted access to that computer again. She had barely begun her research.

"Fine with me, Angel. Do your worst." He reached over her and pushed one of the buttons over the door. She heard the locks click in, place, and she had no illusions that she'd have any way of getting out of this tin box without Bishop's permission.

She glared up at him as he started past her, into the cockpit of the RV, when he paused. "Oh, and one more thing," he said in a flat voice.

"What?"

His answer was to yank her into his arms, so fast and efficiently that she didn't have time to react. He shoved her up against the locked door, his hips pushing against her, pinning her there, his hands holding her head, his long fingers cupping her face, tilting it up for his mouth.

His mouth. She was so surprised she didn't try to close her lips against him. The feel of his body drained all her defiance, and she let herself mold to him as she opened her mouth for his kiss, her arms going around his waist to hold on, afraid she might fall.

He used his tongue, sweeping into her mouth, as if he wanted to taste everything, to suck the air out of her, and she sank into it, into the unbearable glory of his mouth, of his kiss, of his kisses. He pulled back and kissed her again, more gently this time, luring her, seducing her, and then he changed again, the kiss so hard she wanted to slide to the floor in a little puddle of desire. It was a good thing she had the door behind her. She released her hold on him a mere second later, putting her hands flat on the surface behind her, staring up at him, fighting her conflicting emotions. He moved away, a cocky grin on his face as he slid into the driver's seat, and if she'd been anywhere else, she'd have thrown something at him. In the RV there were no loose articles she could fling, only her tongue.

"Asshole," she said.

It was definitely the word for the day.

Chapter Thirteen

Bishop drove. He set the cruise control for a reasonable sixty-five, though that was unlikely for a Winnebago of its supposed age, and headed south until he hooked up with Interstate 40 and the broad, flat plains of Texas, where he pushed it up to seventy.

He hated Texas, at least most of it, and he'd considered changing his route. He had a couple of possibilities and he took this one that would bring him into Louisiana the quickest, or he would have headed through the wheat fields of Kansas. Either way, going from the Rocky Mountains to the delta would require a lot of flat landscape, and he was inured to it, even though he knew this seeming bucket of bolts could safely travel a hell of a lot faster and not have a problem. He was going to have to fill up the tanks eventually, have to let Evangeline get something to eat, though damn, that egg thing she'd made had been good.

He didn't know if she'd be easier or harder to control after last night. He wasn't going to think about it—driving across Texas with a hard-on wasn't his idea of heaven. Thinking about that ugly bruise on Evangeline's leg wasn't much better. He wasn't squeamish about hurting women—you did what you had to do, and there was no room for chivalry in a business where a sweet young thing could put a stiletto between your ribs, and in his case, had. But Evangeline was a different matter. Everything he'd done, he'd done to keep her safe from harm. And then he'd ended up being the one who hurt her.

He was being melodramatic, but the long straight line of the highway wasn't doing much to distract him. Clement had hurt her a lot worse, though she was well on her way to healing. So was he, despite the way he'd ignored his stitches last night.

Last night again, he thought, just when his erection was just beginning to subside. He adjusted his jeans again, grimacing, then laughed to himself. So the little wife could cook and sew? He wondered what other talents she was hiding.

Of course he shouldn't have kissed her this morning. He'd done an excellent job of making sure they were enemies again, but her presence had just been too tempting, and he'd wanted nothing more than to slam her against the wall and take her standing up. He didn't, but he gave in to the temptation to kiss the shit out of her. She was still just as vulnerable to his kisses—he'd felt her body soften, relax against his, and if he'd reached between her legs, he was sure she would have been wet.

She'd always been incredibly responsive to everything he did, and he used to wonder how many ways he could make her come. With his mouth, of course, with straightforward fucking, with his hand on her clit. Her tits had never been that responsive, but he hadn't had time to give them the attention they deserved, and he wondered whether she was one of those rare women who could come simply by having him play with her beautiful breasts. He wanted to catalogue her and their time together in the crudest possible terms. He liked to fuck her, he liked fucking. For some damned reason the term "making love" kept creeping in, and he ruthlessly shut it out, coming up with the rudest words he could think of, but he kept going back to her breasts, not her tits.

He wouldn't have the chance to find out about them, he reminded himself. Last night had been bad enough—there would be no repeats or variations.

He'd never been able to talk her into going down on him, and he'd accepted her refusal easily enough. He could get a blow job anywhere.

That was before he knew about her ancient, molesting professor. She said she'd had to *help him*, and she'd had disgust in her voice. She would have used her mouth on the old bastard, and it was just one more reason it was a good thing the man was dead, or he'd rip him apart. He knew how to kill, quietly and efficiently, but he also knew how to make it hurt, make it last, and he would have outdone Claudia in inventiveness if he'd been able to get his hands on the old man.

No, she'd never take him in her mouth, and he wouldn't ask her. Besides, he intended to make sure they never ended up in the same bed again, so the question was moot.

He had to stop thinking about it. He switched on the satellite radio. Part of him was in the mood for heavy metal, but that would probably get him worked up again. All he had to do was hear Nine Inch Nails sing "Closer" and he'd be on her like white on rice. Cool jazz was the safer choice. He didn't have to worry about it putting him to sleep—he'd developed the ability to go for days without much more than a couple of hours' sleep, and the three he'd gotten this morning, after the time he'd spent between Evangeline's legs, had left him relaxed and refreshed.

Okay, the erection was an annoyance but there didn't seem to be anything he could do about it, short of parking somewhere along the barren Texas landscape, going into the back of the camper, and fucking the shit out of her, which was a very bad idea on both their parts. He'd sleep alone tonight, assuming he even slept at all. He wasn't sure whether he'd go with the farmhouse or the RV— it depended on his usually reliable instincts. Wherever he and

Evangeline were, they'd be apart. He'd wait till she fell asleep on the narrow bed before going to bed himself, and if she heard him, she'd ignore him and pretend to be asleep. He knew her so damned well.

He heard her moving around in the back, and he wanted to tell her to sit the fuck down, but he knew she wouldn't, so he didn't bother; instead he tried to concentrate on the landscape, on the road, on the music, and on what was waiting for him once he reached New Orleans.

He'd been looking forward to it, but that was before he'd come close to Evangeline again. He hadn't counted on being so affected by her, though he'd done his best to hide it. At least she was keeping her distance. He had another three hundred miles to go before he reached his planned stopping place north of Dallas—an abandoned farmhouse on an abandoned road that required all-wheel drive to traverse it. This vehicle had the mobility of a tank—it could go anywhere despite its appearance—and they'd be safe for the night, safe long enough for him to check in with Ryder and Peter Madsen; and if the place was habitable, there'd be enough space to keep away from Evangeline, from making her want things she shouldn't want. It was easy enough to keep her hating him—getting her in bed was a little more of a challenge. He had to remember what was best for both of them, and that didn't involve the exchange of bodily fluids.

Speaking of which, he didn't have any condoms on hand. He already knew she was using a monthly contraceptive pill, though given she hadn't slept with anyone in the three years she'd been divorced, he wondered why. Probably to regulate her periods. He hadn't checked into her medical records but there'd been no red flags in the general surveillance, and he wasn't worried.

He'd been a bit more diligent when it came to the men she'd gone through. In his spare time, simply out of curiosity, of course, he'd checked out every one of the men she'd gone through the first year after he disappeared, and they were all clean, at least when she'd gone to bed with them. She'd been self-destructive, but she would have insisted on a condom—he knew that much. Same with that dickwad she married.

She hadn't said a word about a condom last night, which was a good thing because he deliberately hadn't brought any, thinking that would keep him out of her bed. He'd overestimated his will-power. Problem was, he already knew he was clean and that she had been conscientious and was protected from pregnancy. There would be no dangerous aftereffects from last night.

At least, not physically. The fact that he couldn't take his mind off his dick was a disadvantage, but something he could move past easily enough if there was the slightest hint of danger. His instinct, his ridiculously primal urge, was to protect Evangeline at all costs. He'd married her, he'd watched her, he'd given her his best friend, Merlin, all to keep her safe.

Which begged the question, what the fuck was wrong with him? Why did she matter when so many people had to be disposed of, regretfully on his part, but necessarily?

Peter Madsen had never questioned him, never begrudged him hijacking the state-of-the-art surveillance network to keep a close watch on her. He'd made no comment when Bishop had decided to go to Canada to lure Clement out of the woodwork, and if he knew Bishop's plan involved crashing into Evangeline Morrissey's life again, he hadn't said anything. The argument that getting rid of a threat like Clement, tied as he was to the Corsinis, was justification enough.

Of course Madsen knew. He was one scary bastard, and he knew everything. An injury had sidelined him to a predominantly desk-job position, and when he'd taken over the Committee, things ran even more smoothly than they had under the Ice Queen, Isobel Lambert. Madsen trusted Bishop and Matthew Ryder to complete their mission—dispose of His Eminence for one thing, and set up the new branch of the Committee for another. This branch was going to be different than Peter Madsen's Committee—there would be no old-boy MPs looking over his shoulder. Of course, Madsen paid absolutely no attention to those MPs any more than Isobel had, but they were still a pain.

New Orleans would be more self-contained—Madsen had no intention of informing his so-called overseers of its existence until absolutely necessary. After all, it was nothing more than one covert operation. Just one that was a little permanent, and considering how fucked-up New Orleans was, the American branch could probably find enough to do just taking care of local stuff.

But it was also a busy port, where drugs and guns and sex slaves could be shipped all over the world, or be off-loaded to the US, not to mention the holds full of illegal immigrants that came in. Once the Committee succeeded in smashing the Corsinis, they'd still have their hands full with the increasingly inventive and dedicated terrorists, both foreign and native-born.

With Dimitri Corsini's death, they'd only dealt a glancing blow, and in the last five years, they'd been at a stalemate. Their task in New Orleans would deliver a crippling strike, but it wouldn't destroy the Corsinis completely, simply because he, Madsen, and Ryder still didn't know how far the human trafficking reached into the organized crime community, if you could call anything, including crime, organized in New Orleans. It was a free-for-all when it came to corruption.

He couldn't afford to let himself get distracted by Evangeline Morrissey's magic twat. She was a woman, nothing more, and he had no idea why she stirred some random protective instinct in him, any more than he knew why she seemed to have a supernatural power over his dick. There were so many women who were more beautiful and far less trouble, and yet he couldn't keep away from her.

One more night on the road and he'd be home free. Once they made it to New Orleans, he could hand her off to someone—anyone.

Ryder would know someone who could take over, make sure no one could get to her, and then Bishop could concentrate on his job. Once he made sure his connection to Evangeline disappeared, she could return to her safe little world of academia, where no one would breach her ivory tower. And this time, when he left her, he wouldn't look back.

The man slid down in the seat of the rental car, his forehead creased in frustration. Where the fuck had Bishop disappeared to? And he'd taken that woman. Why, after five years, had he gone back for the woman he'd supposedly married and then abandoned? It made no sense.

Not that he'd ever believed the marriage was real. Problem was, he couldn't prove it was a lie, and until he could, little miss Evangeline Morrissey was off-limits. To Claudia, maybe. But not to him.

Evangeline Morrissey was a ticking bomb, and letting her go was a mistake of major proportions. The last five years the girl had been living on borrowed time, whether or not she'd put two and two together or had any idea what she'd seen.

Everything was taken care of; no problem existed as far as anyone else was concerned. The girl knew nothing, everyone was safe, or so that pussy Madsen had decreed.

Except he didn't agree. He knew there was a fucking problem, and it had been eating at him for five years. Now, finally, he'd been given the chance to do something about it.

He knew exactly where they were going—intercepting Bishop's reports to Madsen had been dead easy if you knew where to look in the vast galaxy of cyberspace. She'd already had someone try to kill her—the Corsinis had sent that fool Clement, who'd always tended to underestimate his enemies.

He was just as happy Clement had failed. After so long the man figured he'd earned the right to snuff out her inconvenient life himself, and he had every intention of taking his time with it. She owed it to him.

All he had to decide were the details. Was he going to try to get her away from Bishop, finish her off and disappear? It would be better that way—Bishop was damned good at what he did, and the Committee wouldn't work as well without him. Besides, Bishop was going to be stationed in the US from now on, and their paths would be unlikely to cross.

But if the man went with that plan, he'd have to kill Evangeline Morrissey silently and swiftly, and that didn't work with his long-put-off desires. He shrugged. He could play it by ear. Bishop and the woman were spending that night at a safe house outside of Dallas, one that was just about impossible to get to. He'd be waiting there for them, and if he could pick off the girl without involving Bishop he'd do so, even though he owed Bishop a 9mm bullet between the eyes for getting in his way one too many times.

By tonight this would be over. If he ended up having to make explanations to Peter Madsen, so be it. He would only be doing what he had to do, and he suspected Madsen would agree. Madsen had put new rules in place, new protocols for minimizing collateral damage, but the man suspected that deep down Madsen would be just as glad to get this loose end tied up, even if it cost him one of his best operatives.

Maybe that wouldn't have to happen. Maybe he could spin it so well that Madsen wouldn't even realize the man had been behind it, though Madsen was scary-smart. He'd deal with all that when he came to it.

For right now, he was looking forward to Evangeline Morrissey's last few minutes on this earth. She was already five years overdue to meet her maker.

Evangeline tried to ignore Bishop. He had jazz on the satellite radio, something a little too cerebral, but anything else would have probably gotten on her last nerve. And yes, she only had one left, and it was hanging by a thread.

Why had he kissed her like that? Her mouth still burned from it, she could feel him, taste him, and her body was in an uproar she had every intention of ignoring. So he had a certain practiced effect on her. So what? Sometimes people just struck sparks off each other. It was entirely possible to have insane sexual chemistry and hate each other the rest of the time.

At least she assumed so. When she'd returned to the US five years ago she'd been broken in every sense of the word, and she'd done what she could to wipe James Bishop out of her system. After that wretched year she was hardly an innocent—she should know a thing or two about sexual attraction and desire. She'd lost count of the men she'd slept with, but she did know she hadn't liked any of them. Surely that was proof she could have sex with Bishop and still despise him.

Except there was a big difference between those awful one-night stands and the kind of conflagration Bishop aroused in her.

She turned her back on him and headed for the refrigerator. They had bottles of Guinness there. She had no idea if these mysterious Powers That Be knew it was her favorite mass-produced beer or whether she happened to share that preference with Bishop. If so, she was going to pick a new favorite beer immediately.

She pulled out a bottle and opened it, breathing in the thick, yeasty scent of it. If she ever became gluten intolerant she'd kill herself, she thought, taking a deep swig.

"Bring me one while you're at it."

Damn, the man had ears like a bat. Assuming bats had ears. Or didn't they communicate by sonar? "You're driving," she tossed back, heading for the dinette.

"And you seriously think a beer is going to impair me? I can be dead drunk and still shoot the heart out of an ace of spades at five hundred yards."

"A regular Robin Hood. Why do you need to shoot cards?"

"So I can shoot people and not miss."

She felt a chill run over her at his flat words, starting with the icy beer in her hand. "It's probably against the law to have an open container . . ."

"We're in Texas. You really think they have a law like that? They're worse than Colorado. And you really think I'd give a flying fuck if they did? Bring me a beer and join me."

"When pigs fly."

"If you do, maybe I'll answer some of your questions." She knew he regretted the words as soon as he said them, but she also knew he'd stick to them. She was beginning to realize he had a peculiar sense of honor. He might have killed people—she didn't want to think how many—but he wouldn't go back on his word.

Opening the tiny stainless-steel fridge again, she pulled out another Guinness, opened it, and carefully made her way to the front of the camper. She dropped into the passenger seat, then glanced around her. The front of the Winnebego looked its age, though she knew that was deceptive. The vinyl seats were cracked and mended with duct tape, the dashboard was dusty, and some of the dials were cracked or simply not working. There was no such thing as a cup holder.

Without taking his eyes from the road, he reached out and took the Guinness from her, taking a long pull before settling it between his legs. Naturally her eyes followed, and she jerked them away, determinedly staring out the window. She didn't want to be looking at his crotch, thinking about his crotch.

"I thought you were a dedicated believer in seat belts," he drawled easily.

Of course she looked back, surprised to see he was wearing his, and she hastily reached for hers. She had no choice but to tuck her bottle between her own thighs, and the icy chill of the glass was an odd stimulation, one she had no intention of letting him see. She leaned back in her seat, took another drink, and glanced over at him. At his face, not where he'd set his bottle of beer.

"You said you'd answer questions."

"I did, didn't I?" He sounded faintly disgruntled.

"So let's start with the most obvious one. Exactly who and what are you?" She made it sound like he was an alien artifact or a lost species of snake, which wasn't far from the truth.

"I think we'd better get some ground rules established. If you think I'm going to while away the next five hours telling you the story of my life and a whole lot of the kinds of secrets I'd need to kill you for, you're mistaken. I didn't go this far to protect you only to have to turn around and cap you myself. I'll give you . . . let's say five questions, which I'll answer to the best of my ability, as long as it won't put you in more jeopardy."

She stared at him, his elegant profile so familiar and yet so different without that mop of dark hair. His short blond hair was growing out a bit, and the roots were darker, but not the mahogany shade his hair had been in Italy, and his scruffy beard was brown and flecked with bits of gray, which shocked her.

"Exactly what color is your hair?" she demanded. "Your eyes, for that matter? Sometimes you look like a complete stranger, and other times I know you far too well."

"My real hair, last time I saw it, was a sandy brown and I'm not wearing contacts right now. What you see is what you get. That's two."

"Two what?" Of course he'd end up having gorgeous eyes. The deep ocean blue of them was almost unbelievable, but she'd somehow known they were the real thing.

"Two questions, Angel. You've got three more."

"That's not fair!" she said, outraged.

He shrugged. "Take it or leave it."

The cheating bastard. "I'll take it," she said, reaching for his beer bottle without thinking, planning to grab the beer back. Reaching between his legs.

He moved his hand so quickly, she had no time to pull back, and held her hand against the bottle nestled in his crotch, against his zipper, against a part of him that was indisputably hard.

She yanked her hand back as if it were burned, moving to unfasten her seat belt, ready to stomp back into the cabin, or as close to stomping as she could manage with her bruised leg, when his words stopped her.

"You still have three questions. You aren't going to have this chance again, so you'd better take advantage of it while I'm still in such a cooperative mood."

She stayed put. She had little doubt he could drink any number of beers and be unimpaired, but the same couldn't be said for her. One beer was her limit—pathetic, but there it was—and hers was already half gone, relaxing her when she didn't want to be relaxed.

"All right. But I don't want you answering until I tell you it's one of my questions. I need to think about this."

"Take your time," he said affably. "We've got miles of highway between us and our next destination, and your company is, as always, delightful."

She didn't give in to temptation and call him a nasty name, mainly because she believed, in a strange sort of way, he actually meant it. Or maybe she was just telling herself that, but she didn't care.

"I want to know who and what you are."

"That's two . . ."

"I told you, no answers until I tell you what my actual question is. I want to know who James Bishop is. Who do you work for, and what in God's name your job is that you'd know how to kill people? Are you CIA, FBI?" She realized her first guesses would immediately make him one of the good guys, and she quickly added, "Or are you a criminal, which seems more than likely. Don't answer!"

He took another drink of beer, then draped his strong, beautiful hands comfortably on the steering wheel as they headed into the infinite flatness of the empty countryside. His eyes seemed to be on the road but she knew he was somehow managing to watch her. Maybe he had fabulous peripheral vision or hidden mirrors; somehow he was acutely aware of her every expression. Which meant she had to be more circumspect, or he'd catch her looking at him like a love-starved kitten . . .

Where the hell had that idea come from? Too much beer—probably because she'd had so little to eat in the last few days. There was no place to set the bottle, but she needed to be careful, not let maudlin emotions interfere.

"Tell me who you work for," she said abruptly. "That's a real question. If you feel like throwing in your real name free of charge that would be nice, but it's not an official question."

He waited so long that for a moment she thought he wasn't going to answer. She'd almost given up hope when he spoke, reluctantly. "I work for an organization called the Committee. They're based out of London, but they're planning on setting up an American office and one in the Far East. And my real name happens to be James Alexander Bishop. I don't use it very often, but I happened to use it when I met you. And yes, I'll give you that one for free, since I've already told you that one many times. You just chose not to believe me. That's three."

She thought for a long time. She needed to shape the questions in just the right way as to elicit the most information—Bishop would give her as little as he could get away with. Bishop. James Bishop. She believed him—in her own mind no other name fit him.

"What *exactly* do you do for this Committee?" The "exactly" ought to force him to tell her enough to get a sense of whether he was a good guy or a bad guy.

"You don't want to know," he said grimly.

She wasn't letting him get away with that. "I asked, didn't I? Question number four. What do you do for the Committee?"

"Kill people." His voice was hard, but she was prepared. He wanted to shock her, frighten her, and even if he did, just a little, she wasn't going to let him see it.

"That's not a complete answer," she said. "If all you did was kill people, then I would have been dead five years ago, and you wouldn't be wandering around Texas in a Winnebago."

"How do you know I'm not headed toward a target?"

"You may be, but it's an awfully elaborate cover. What else do you do, and this is still question four."

"I keep the world safe for democracy," he said mockingly.

"England isn't a democracy, it's a constitutional monarchy."

"Don't be ridiculous. The monarchy has absolutely no power—it's a social position and nothing more. It's a democracy."

"Well, tell me what you do to preserve democracy, then. Still question four," she reminded him, not trusting him for a moment.

He rolled his eyes, but she wasn't going to be intimidated. He started this—she'd play it to the end.

"I do anything they ask of me. I go undercover and pretend to be any number of things. Mostly I watch people, which can get fucking boring after a while. Bad guys aren't that interesting—you'd think they would be, but they aren't. Sometimes I kidnap trouble-some young women and have sex with them in a Winnebago."

He was trying to intimidate her, but he'd given her one very useful piece of information. "Or a hotel in Venice," she countered smoothly.

He glanced over at her deliberately, heat in his eyes, darkening them. "I'm not sure which I prefer."

To be truthful, neither was she, but she wasn't about to tell him that. She'd be an idiot not to prefer the suite at the Danieli, but right now her body still remembered the fast, hard passion of the night before, and it still tingled with need.

But he'd said *bad guy*. Which meant, whether he would admit it or not, that he considered himself one of the good guys. Whatever this Committee was, they thought they were on the side of the angels.

But didn't most villains think they were the heroes? People had a tendency to justify their worst behavior. Everyone was a hero in his own life, the star of his own movie.

So this so-called Committee thought they were good guys; and if they had an ingenuous mission statement like "Making the world safe for democracy," it meant they were an antiterrorist group, even if they sometimes behaved like them. She only had one question left, and she didn't want to waste it; while there were so many things she wanted to know, it really boiled down to one thing.

"Why me?"

He drained his beer, then reached over and took the bottle between her legs, the one she'd been ignoring. Maybe it was accidental that it pressed against her sensitive parts for a moment, another stimulation.

Who was she kidding? Nothing he did was accidental—he was the most deliberate man she had ever met.

"You want to clarify that? Considering it's your last question, you ought to make sure you get what you want."

Why did that sound sexual? Then again, to her battered mind almost everything he said sounded sexual. She took a deep breath. "Here's what I know so far. I accidentally witnessed a murder you committed, one I didn't realize I'd seen. Instead of automatically killing me, you took me back to the hotel and . . ."

"Fucked the shit out of you," he supplied affably.

"Stop it!" she said before she could stop herself.

"You want me to be more romantic about it? I took you back to the hotel and seduced you, made love to you until you were so infatuated you couldn't see straight? Is that more accurate?"

She gritted her teeth. "You fucked the shit out of me," she said. "Why?"

"Obvious answer, babe. You were hot."

"Don't be ridiculous. The woman you were with was gorgeous, and there were any number of other, much prettier, women who would have happily fallen at your feet. The reason you took me to bed had something to do with the murder."

"Claudia isn't exactly my type," he said obliquely. "The reason I took you . . . not to bed, but in the shower, in case you've forgotten . . . was to find out exactly what you'd seen. I kept you away from newspapers reporting Corsini's death, I distracted you from the sound of the police sirens, and I fucked you until you were incapable of telling me anything but the truth. If you'd seen anything, suspected anything, you'd have hardly let me go down on you with such enthusiasm."

She sat there like stone, determined not to react. His deliberately coarse words were like blows, hammering away at something she'd still been fool enough to treasure, like someone taking a sledgehammer to a classic marble statue. She hadn't realized she still kept even an ounce of emotion about that entire time once he'd betrayed her, and that was another wound. She wasn't the strong, iron lady she'd envisioned herself to be.

She wasn't going to let him know. She could keep that much to herself. And she had to keep him talking. He could shut down at any time—he'd answered more than five questions and he was hardly the soul of cooperation.

"All right, so we've established we had a night of sex. That was never under debate. You knew I'd seen nothing. Why didn't you just dump me the next day? Why worry about me?"

"Because Corsini's death was splashed all over the papers, and you'd seen both of us up there at the hillside chapel and could identify us. I needed to distract you until the big rush of publicity had gone by and Corsini was no longer front-page news. Your Italian wasn't that good, and you'd have no reason to pick up a local newspaper and try to read it. The Corsini family is a big deal in Italy, but the family is not well-known out of the country. Corsini's death barely made a paragraph in the English newspapers."

"Okay, I can understand that. I can even understand the Danieli—anyone who could go to the best hotel in Venice on an expense account shouldn't hesitate. But why bother with that sham marriage?"

He hesitated, and she was afraid he was going to stop talking. His eyes were straight ahead on the wide, endless highway in front of them, and he didn't even glance at her. "I had my reasons."

"And they were . . . ?"

"A question I'm not about to answer."

She wasn't ready to give up. "Okay, then tell me this. Why didn't you just kill me in the first place? It would have been tidier, and I don't get the sense that your organization is worried about collateral damage."

"You know shit about my organization. I don't happen to like 'collateral damage,' as you put it so professionally. I didn't want to kill you. Not if I didn't have to."

As a declaration of love, it left a lot to be desired, but it still thawed some of the cold that had filled her as he deliberately broke down their relationship in the crudest possible terms.

"Why not?" Her voice was softer than she wanted.

He shot her a glance, and then that slow, lazy grin resurfaced, telling her that honesty was over. "I'm afraid that's all you're going to get out of me right now, Angel. Unless you want me to remind you of everything we did in the shower, and then in your bed, in exact detail. Or what we did in the Danieli, or in that bathtub, or even . . ."

"Why do you remember?"

That wiped the smile off his face, she thought smugly, so she pushed it. "Why would you remember a few days from five years ago in such painstaking detail? You obviously were very experienced, knowing just how to turn me from an intelligent woman into a lovesick idiot, so it couldn't have been that unusual a way to spend a few days. You must have had tons of mindless sex before and since then. Why do you remember the time with me? Why the fuck am I here? How did I happen to get mixed up with you all over again when you should have been out of my life for good?"

She hadn't noticed they were nearing an exit, but all of a sudden he jerked the wheel and they headed off the highway with a squealing of tires. "That's a discussion for another time," he said amiably as he pulled up at a truck stop, one that didn't look all that different from the first one. "Time to feed you."

Refusing to go with him until he gave her answers would be a total waste of time, and she was starving. The cooking facilities in the Winnebago were limited, and she had a craving for pancakes, comfort food at its finest, slathered in butter and nothing else. No fake sweet syrups to ruin the taste—if she couldn't have Vermont maple syrup, then butter was an admirable substitute. And she'd eat meats full of nitrates and not give a damn. She'd work on him once she was finished.

Chapter Fourteen

Dealing with Evangeline was really quite simple, Bishop thought as he headed down the highway, a mammoth cup of strong, bitter coffee between his legs. All he had to do was feed her—preferably carbs—and fuck her, and she wore herself out. She'd slept for hours in the back of the camper after threatening him that she wanted more answers or else, and he had watched her in one of the rearview mirrors, curled up on the smaller bunk, sleeping like a baby. He would have given ten years off his life to park this sleekly reconfigured bucket of bolts and climb into bed with her, but the landscape was so spare and unforgiving that he hadn't seen much more than a short bush in a hundred miles. There was no way they would get any privacy, and besides, he was going to keep it in his pants, wasn't he?

Having sex with her last night had ended up being a very smart thing to do, even if his brain hadn't been working at the time. It had unsettled and confused her, left part of her both aroused and compliant, even though she was fighting that effect, and she'd go out of her way not to let him get close enough to pull her into bed again. As long as she kept her distance, he'd be able to concentrate on business, and they just might make it through the next few days safely. By late tomorrow they'd be in New Orleans, she'd be safe in someone else's hands, and he and Ryder could do what they had to do without any distractions.

He was going to need to answer some of her questions. She had to understand why she was in danger, or she wouldn't be able to keep herself safe. Even with the divorce and approaching execution of His Eminence, her safety wasn't guaranteed—he had too damned many enemies. It had never bothered him one way or another, but when it came to endangering Evangeline, it was another matter entirely. It would be better if he stopped keeping tabs on her—better for her, a hell of a lot better for him. He would have had no trouble forgetting all about her if he hadn't felt it necessary to keep an eye on her.

He let out a low, mirthless laugh. Yeah, sure. If only it were that simple. For some ridiculous reason Evangeline Morrissey had gotten under his skin, in his blood like some fucking plague, and he couldn't get rid of her. Even when he went months without checking on her, he couldn't keep from thinking about her.

There must be some kind of unfinished business between them, but he didn't know what it was. Not that he'd been thinking last night, but he'd kind of hoped that taking her to bed again would get her out of his system. That hadn't happened. And if he didn't get his shit together, they were all going to be in trouble.

He glanced back at her again. Her hair had come loose, that familiar cloud of coppery brown, and he wanted to bury his face in it. She smelled so damned good, so familiar. She smelled like coming home.

He needed to remember he had no home, and never would. It had been his choice, a logical one. Most of his family were long dead, he had no siblings, and because his father had been in the military, they'd moved so much that there was no place on earth he had any ties to. He was the perfect Committee operative—a lone wolf with no connections, nothing to hold him back or make him think twice. He was a weapon, albeit a very advanced, skilled weapon, and setting up the New Orleans office would be a piece of cake. Just as long as he got Evangeline safely stowed and out of his life forever. That was all he asked of a fate that had never treated him too kindly. He needed her gone.

He kept driving down the flat, endless roads, and it was almost a relief when he started having to deal with traffic. It meant he was nearing the Dallas-Fort Worth area, and the abandoned farmhouse that the Committee had used a few years ago. No one knew about it except the few operatives under Peter Madsen, and most of them would have forgotten it. It would be a place to unwind, to hide out, and there were half a dozen bedrooms in the place, which meant he could keep his distance from Evangeline.

All he had to do was piss her off enough that she wouldn't let him anywhere near him; then he could spend the night doing what he had to do—checking in with Ryder and Madsen, making sure his journey to the old house in the Garden District was still an option. He could hardly do that if he was rolling in the sheets with . . .

Shit. He had to stop thinking like that. She hadn't slept long, and during the last few hours he'd been intensely aware of her every move, the sound of her footsteps, followed by the soft click of Merlin's paws. She needed to make sure his nails were cut—short enough not to make noise, long enough to give him some purchase. With an attack dog it was a fine line, though he wasn't sure if Merlin could be called an attack dog any longer. She'd turned a canine weapon into a lapdog, and if he didn't have faith that Merlin would defend her with his life, he'd be annoyed.

Hell, he was annoyed. He'd put a lot of time and effort into training Merlin, and now that was shot to hell. But then, he'd trained the dog for her, and it only made sense that Merlin would adapt. They'd been comrades together, he and Merlin, but now

Merlin wasn't a soldier; he was a civilian with a highly honed sense of protection.

And he was going to have to let go of him.

Evangeline was up and about, rustling through the cabinets, looking for something to eat. "You don't have to worry about dinner," he said, probably the first time he'd spoken since their desultory and entirely phony lunchtime conversation. "There'll be food waiting for us when we stop."

He felt her come closer, close enough that he could feel her, close enough that he could reach behind him and grab her, pull her down. He kept his hands on the wheel.

"Just where are we stopping? And when?"

Questions. Why the hell had he ever offered to answer her questions—he'd told her more than he wanted. "We'll stop within the hour, and as for where, it's an abandoned farmhouse off in the countryside with an impossible road leading in to it."

"If it's impossible how are we going to get there?" Her voice was skeptical. Of course.

"Nothing's impossible for me," he said in a calm voice. *Except letting go of you.*

"Good to know," she said wryly, slipping into the passenger seat. "I may as well see where we're going."

"It won't do you any good. We're already off the main road, and there are so many twists and turns to get to this place you'd never find your way out, if you were fool enough to make a run for it."

There was a long silence. "Make a run for it?" she said finally. "That sounds rather ominous. What would I be running from? Besides your obnoxious company?"

He grinned. "That's it, babe. I even promise to keep my hands to myself. I gather there are maybe half a dozen useable bedrooms in the place—it's huge, and like this rust bucket, it's a lot nicer inside than out. You'll have a safe, solitary night's sleep."

He gave her a slanted side glance. Her expression was stony, showing nothing. What had he been hoping for? A look of disappointment? Or even better, relief?

It was a relief to him. He'd told her he wouldn't touch her, and he wasn't a man who broke his word when he gave it. There were few things sacred to him, but his word was one of them. She would sleep in celibate splendor, like a nun, while he stayed awake thinking about her.

He let out his breath in exasperation. What did it matter what her reaction was? What did anything matter? *Let go, you stupid bastard*, he told himself grimly. *Let her go before you get both of you killed.*

As they drove in silence over the increasingly narrow, rutted roads, it grew into a strangely comfortable silence. He stole a glance at her. She'd lost that stony expression, and she looked relatively peaceful. Merlin had pushed his way between their seats, leaning against her legs, and she was rubbing his head absently while he drove. Jesus, they were like an old retired couple on the road in their big ugly RV, exploring the country. The thought made him incomprehensibly sad.

That was patently ridiculous. For one thing, he wasn't going to make old bones, as his grandmother would have said. If he made it to forty he'd be lucky, given his profession. Evangeline wouldn't be anywhere near him. No aimless journeys into the great unknown, safe in their tin box of a vehicle, camping in the woods, grilling freshly caught trout. He hadn't been fishing in more than ten years, and he probably wouldn't go for another ten. He'd been damned good at fly fishing when he was younger.

"You like trout?" he asked suddenly, out of the blue. "Or are you one of those people who can't stand seafood?"

He expected her to ignore him, but instead she laughed. "So you don't remember everything from five years ago. I love seafood. I even ate the disgusting Venetian concoction called *squassetto*, which had to have every kind of seafood as well as God knows what else in it. And technically trout's a freshwater fish, so you can't call it seafood."

"Spoken like an academic," he said easily.

She didn't bristle. The sun was moving toward the trees, and things were oddly peaceful. "When I was camping in Saskatchewan there was a couple nearby who were into fly fishing, which I gather is a very tricky thing. They gave me one of the trout they caught, and I cooked it over the open fire. It was the best thing I ever ate. Including those amazing meals in Venice."

He felt a smile tug at the corners of his mouth. "It probably was. Did they clean it for you?"

"What kind of wimp do you think I am?" she said in lazy, mock outrage, her fingers threading through Merlin's short, rough fur. "I cleaned it myself. I happen to be very handy with a filleting knife."

He didn't know what that ache in his chest was—probably indigestion. "That might come in handy," he muttered, thinking of what lay ahead.

Her peaceful mood vanished, and he wanted to kick himself. "Oh, yeah? Who do I have to kill?" She kept it light, but he knew their few moments of amity had disappeared.

"Anyone who comes after you."

"And is anyone coming after me? I thought they were more interested in you. I was just a way they thought they could get to you. Whoever the hell 'they' are."

"It worked," he said shortly. He took a left turn, heading down a narrow path between fields of tall grass. A tractor had gone before him, so his path wouldn't be noticeable following the heavier tread of the tractor tires. At the end, about half a mile down, he'd reach the river that ran through this rare, untouched piece of country-side. The crossing was a couple of miles farther down. It looked so bad even Indiana Jones wouldn't have tried it, but there was no other access to the place. The fast flowing rush of the river was too deep everywhere else.

"Why?" She asked it like she didn't really expect an answer, and she wasn't getting one.

"I said five questions," he said. He didn't want to get her riled up—when she got mad he got mad, and when they both lost their tempers he put his hands on her, and then they were lost.

She wasn't particularly ruffled by his response. "That was question number four."

"Then I answered it."

"Not satisfactorily."

He grinned. "I didn't satisfy you? Now that surprises me. What were those interesting sounds you made? Something between the yowl of a bobcat and the scream of a peacock. Not that there are many peacocks in Texas."

He'd pushed it too far, and he realized he'd done it deliberately. She sat up straighter, her body tight with tension, and Merlin rose, his instincts responding to hers. "I guess we'll never know, since you aren't going to be hearing those sounds ever again."

"Oh, you never can tell," he said lazily. "You might find someone you want to get it on with while you're still being guarded by the Committee. You're noisy enough that if I'm in the same building, I'll hear it." Funny how he didn't like that idea at all.

"Despite what you know of me, I don't tend to fall into bed with men at the drop of a hat." Her voice could have frozen anything, even the steamy Texas evening.

He said it before he could think twice. "What about the year after I left you? I counted nineteen, but I might have missed one or two . . ." His voice trailed off when he saw her face, and he wanted to kick himself so damned hard he wouldn't be able to walk for days. "Sorry," he muttered, before he could help himself.

The damage was done. It was a good thing, he told himself. Her shattered expression was as good as any brick wall between them.

"You didn't miss any," she said in a hollow voice. "It took me a while to come to my senses, and I didn't realize how many there were until a couple of years later. I couldn't bear to think about it for a long time. I still don't like to remember, but I should. I need to remember so I'll never get so broken, so needy, again. Sex doesn't fix anything; it couldn't push you out of my system and make me forget." She turned to look at him. "I take it you were spying on me. Do you have any interesting videos you could put on the Internet?"

In fact, he did. It was a mistake, and he'd watched it once. Then he had taken his laptop and thrown it against a wall, destroying it. He'd thought it would help him let go. Seeing her in another man's arms had made him furious, seeing the desolate look on her face had almost sent him after her, until he remembered what being around him would do to her. He'd made sure all copies were destroyed, and there was no reason she had to know one had ever existed. "Of course not," he said.

She had almost the same expression on her face now as she'd had in that fucking video as she lay beneath a man who wasn't him. Shattered. Empty. He'd betrayed her, once again. Good, he reminded himself. It was a good thing.

She slowly unfastened her seat belt. "I'm going to lie down for a little while," she said. "Wake me when we get there."

"We're five minutes away." He didn't want her to go, he wanted to make things better, but he didn't know what to say.

"That's good," she said in a dull voice, rising and moving past him into the small cabin of the RV, Merlin trotting happily behind her.

Leaving the world's worst bastard alone in the driver's seat, driving into nowhere.

Chapter Fifteen

She didn't cry. At first Evangeline had wanted nothing more than to get away from him before he saw how raw his words had made her. She expected to fall on that bunk and bury her face in the pillow and weep, and then face him again with the calm expression that drove him crazy.

There were no tears. She wanted to throw up, as that sick, desperate feeling filled her again, reminding her of that horrible year. She could see them, smell them, hear the mindless buzz of their lame come-ons. She'd never gone to bed sober, not with any of them, but it still didn't wipe out the snippets of memory, and her stomach churned with disgust. Disgust with them, disgust with the situation, most of all disgust with herself. She thought she'd made peace with it, but just a few words from Bishop and she was an angry little ball of shame once more.

She felt Merlin's nose nudge her, and he made a soft whining noise of support. She laughed, a weak, rusty sound, and slung her arm around his neck, burying her head in his fur. "You don't think I'm terrible, do you, baby?" she murmured, low so that Bishop couldn't hear her. "I was just hurting so badly, and I was trying any way I could to feel better." Her voice almost broke on that one, and she couldn't decide whether throwing up or weeping was a better choice. Stoic non-reaction was what she should aim for. Bishop couldn't know how he got to her. Couldn't know that deep inside she was just as weak and stupid for him as she'd been five years ago.

She felt the camper tip and rumble over something that could scarcely be called a road, and then move through water, and she knew a sudden panic. Her cousin had died when his car had been swept away in a flood, and she'd always been nervous about vehicles and water ever since. Then again, if the Winnebago was carried away in a flood it would solve all her problems.

She sat up, looking out the narrow window beside the bunk. It was sunset, and she could see a farmhouse in the distance; it looked like the Bates Motel—derelict and depressing. It was probably the Taj Mahal inside, she thought grumpily. At least he'd promised a separate bedroom, which had somehow felt like a slap in the face. He didn't want to get involved with her any more than she did with him, and he wasn't hindered by foolish emotions. In his case it was simply lust, something he could control.

So could she. She could control everything about herself until she got away from him. Then she could let go, scream and rail and throw things, get rid of everything she had ever kept locked tight inside her, and he wouldn't know what he did to her, how he made her mixed-up and crazy and fragile and furious. How she still loved him.

She sat up abruptly. *Jesus, where did that come from?*

It was the simple truth: no matter how much he had lied, used her, no matter how dangerous a man he truly was, she still loved him, and the more she tried not to, the tighter the bonds grew.

She'd thought she was over him. She had barely thought of him in the last few years, and when she did her reaction had been fury, pure and simple. Hurt and betrayal had vanished in her righteous rage.

But now it was back full force, reminding her of just how much she still felt for him.

One day away from New Orleans, and he'd happily pass her off to someone else. One night in the creepy-looking farmhouse, a day on the road, and she could say good-bye to him forever. She just had to hold out that long.

He stopped the vehicle, then came back into the camper. She met his gaze stonily, which clearly didn't bother him. "Stay put," he said. "I need to check the place out first, then I'll come back and get you."

"All right." It was shadowy enough that he wouldn't see the tears on her cheeks. She glanced at the dog beside her. "I think Merlin wants to go with you." The German shepherd had risen, his body tense, almost like a soldier standing at attention.

Bishop raised his eyebrows. "You mean he'll leave your side? Miracles never cease. What kind of magic potion did you put in his food anyway, to turn him into such a pussycat?"

"Love." The answer was out before she could think twice, and the silence in the cabin was as thick as the humid Texas air coming in the open door.

Finally he spoke. "Well, I'm fresh out of that." Merlin bounded past him into the gathering darkness. "Stay put," he said to her again, and he was gone.

⌣

Shit. He'd made her cry. He was every bit the asshole she'd called him. He'd heard every word she'd whispered to Merlin—*You don't think I'm terrible, do you? I was just hurting so badly*—and he wanted to punch something. Why the fuck had he done that, thrown it in her face like she'd done something wrong? He didn't give a shit how many people she'd fucked.

Well, he did care, because he begrudged every damned one of them, and because it had hurt her. And still hurt her, even though she'd been looking for something to ease the pain. The pain he'd caused her. Around and around it went, in circles of cruelty he hadn't planned on, but it didn't mean shit whether he planned it or not. It had happened, and he couldn't fix it. He only made it worse.

The air outside the camper was so thick with heat and humidity that it felt like a steam bath, and it was well past the heat of the day. What would it be like midday?

Probably just what New Orleans would feel like, the city he'd chosen to house the new branch of the Committee. He'd picked the city; Ryder had picked the house. Bishop was impervious to weather—it took him just moments to acclimate, to move from the refrigerated cool of the RV to air so thick you could eat it with a fork. Would Evangeline be able to adapt as easily? Then again, she wouldn't have to for long. As soon as it was safe, she'd be back in her ivory tower in northern Wisconsin with a brand-new camper and truck thanks to the Committee, and she'd never have to think about him again. He just wished he could say the same thing for himself.

He couldn't stop thinking about her, worrying about her, and he was destroying her. Huge live oaks surrounded the front of the farmhouse, and he wanted to punch one. He'd break bones in his hands and put them in more danger, he reminded himself. No, he didn't have the luxury of taking his frustration out on inanimate objects. He had to stay on task, shut out any extraneous feelings he might have. *Feelings*. He wanted to laugh. He wasn't allowed *feelings*, and he damned well didn't want them.

Merlin returned from his pace around the building, which meant the place was clean, but the dog was still unusually tense. "What's up, boy?" Bishop murmured, squatting down beside him. "Something wrong?"

Merlin looked at him for a moment, then toward the RV, and Bishop sighed. "Yeah, you don't like being away from her, do you? She's got you suckered good. Join the club."

All the security measures were still in place when he climbed up the sagging front porch and unlocked the front door. The air-conditioning had been turned on, and cool air spilled out into the evening air.

His search of the place was deliberate, despite the security measures and Merlin's approval. He never took anything for granted, and they were up against very smart, very dangerous people. When he was finally convinced the house was safe, he headed down the stairs to the front hall.

Evangeline was standing there, the door shut behind her, her backpack in one hand, Merlin resting against her side, and he wanted to explode in fury. Why the fuck couldn't she ever do what he told her to?

He closed his eyes and counted to three before acknowledging her presence. He didn't want to make things worse by yelling at her.

"I told you to stay in the camper," he said in a dangerously calm voice.

She'd gotten her second wind, and no longer looked so fragile. "You took too long, and that place is like an oven when the air-conditioning is turned off. I figured if you weren't done by now you were probably dead, and I would be too, and I wanted a shower before I died. I decided that wasn't too much to ask from the universe."

"You think too much," he growled. "We'll keep to the first floor—there are three bedrooms on this level and I don't intend to sleep, so take your pick. No, take the one at the back. It's closest to the door if you need to get out fast."

Of course she picked up on it. "You don't intend to sleep? You've been driving nonstop for two days, and you plan to drive . . . what . . . another eight hundred miles tomorrow?"

"It's only about five hundred miles. And I don't need much sleep."

"I believe it. But that doesn't mean you don't need any. If this place is as safe as you say it is, then there's no reason you can't get a few hours' sleep."

"I'll think about." He pinned her with his stare. "Why do you care one way or another?"

"I don't," she said immediately, and he knew it was a lie. "I'd just rather not die in a fiery crash on the highway when you nod off and drift into oncoming traffic."

"Sensible," he said evenly. "Dump your stuff in the third bedroom and take your shower. I'll see what we have for grub."

"I think I'll take the front bedroom . . ." she began, but before she could finish he leapt down the last few stairs, picked her up, and threw her over his shoulder.

"You'll do what I fucking tell you," he muttered, absorbing the feel of her, the smell of her skin, the sweet softness of her. The damned hardness of him. He dumped her in the third bedroom while she was still sputtering in protest, and nodded toward the door at the back of the room. "There's the shower. I'll have dinner for you by the time you're done."

She glared at him. Good. Getting mad at him was much better, much healthier than that stricken, shamed look on her face.

And he had to get the hell away from her before he pulled her back into his arms and moved her over to the double bed. He kept his hands at his side, determined not to touch her again.

"I'll do . . ." she started in a rebellious tone of voice.

"You'll do exactly what I tell you to do," he snapped. "I'm trying to save your fucking life, not make it miserable."

"Lucky for you you're doing both," she said sweetly.

He slammed the door as he left.

That dog was too damned smart, the man thought from the safety of his hiding place. Granted, the fucking canine had missed him, as had the invincible James Bishop, but they'd come too close, and he didn't think either of them were entirely convinced. The farmhouse was basically an island—the river had changed course years ago and ringed the land, and the only place shallow enough to cross was so rough that you'd need four-wheel drive and even then you'd be lucky to make it across. Of course he hadn't driven.

Bishop knew the Committee had come up with something to cover tracks, strong enough to fool even a bloodhound, but then, he didn't realize it was the Committee who was after him. That he was being stalked by someone who had access to all the secret weapons and tools most covert organizations didn't even realize existed. He'd believe the dog, believe his own eyes, but he would still be alert.

The man heard the muffled sound of distant thunder. He'd been listening to it for hours, paying it no mind, though it sounded like it might be getting closer. Probably just heat lightning. If it did rain, it would make the path off the island impossible. He'd be trapped there with the three of them: the dog, Bishop, and the girl. In that case he might have no choice but to kill all three.

He'd start with the girl, maybe get away before the rain hit, before Bishop even realized she was gone. He could tell they weren't fucking—the anger between them was palpable. Typical—Bishop hadn't stayed with a woman for more than a few days, if that. In fact, Bishop tended to be less interested in pussy than most of the men he knew. The man shrugged. It didn't matter to him one way or another. Bishop was a good agent, a brilliant shot, and too valuable to be killed unless it was necessary.

Same with the dog. He'd never killed one before, and he wasn't sure if he could do it. But if either of them came between him and his quarry, he wouldn't think twice.

He would wait as long as he could, until the girl had gone to sleep, until Bishop had relaxed his guard. Bishop wouldn't sleep— the man had worked with him often enough to know that Bishop was relentless. The best he could hope for was a span of less focused attention. Hell, Bishop was only human—he might even fall asleep.

But the man doubted it. He was going to have to be very quiet when he went in to get her. *Piece of cake.*

———

Evangeline sat down on the old iron bed, and realized it had a memory foam mattress, her favorite kind. She pulled back the threadbare chenille cover and found heavy cotton sheets, and she sighed in pleasure. She looked up and saw a bathroom through the open door that was so big it had probably been one of the bedrooms. She pushed herself off the bed and went to investigate. It was huge, white tiled, with the biggest shower she'd ever seen, and a soaking tub large enough to hold two. She shut that thought out immediately.

The only problem, as far as she could tell, was the other door, the one that led to the hall. Which meant, presumably, that she was sharing this oasis with James. There were locks on the doors, and she was willing to bet there were other equally luxurious bathrooms around the place. He could damn well use one of those. She turned the lock and pulled the key out, pleased to see it wasn't a skeleton key but something more specific, something he couldn't override.

Who was she kidding—James could pick any kind of lock. Not that he'd bother. He didn't want to have anything more to do with her. Who could blame him?

She did her best to use up every ounce of hot water in the place as she scrubbed herself, over and over again, trying to clean something that had disappeared long ago. The shower in the Winnebago had been sybaritic, but size had its limitations.

Her skin was raw and red by the time she finally gave up and turned off the water, and she wanted to smack herself. She took a look at herself in the mirror, the haunted expression, the circles around her eyes. "You're being self-indulgent," she said in a quiet voice, just for her own ears, to break the deafening silence of the high-ceilinged, tiled room. "Get over it. So you spent a year trying to fuck him out of your system. It's in the past, it's done, and you're being a baby. Let go."

The woman in the mirror wasn't listening, so Evangeline stuck her tongue out at her. Reliving ancient nightmares wasn't worth the time, not when her life was at stake. Much as she hated to admit it, James was right. She was going to do exactly what he told her to do; she wasn't going to fight back and annoy him or ask him any questions. The best way to get through the next twenty-four hours in one piece was to keep quiet and follow orders. It would be easier on her soul as well. She wasn't going to think about James, about the past, even about the empty future. The only way to get through today was to live through it, and she intended to do just that.

She hadn't brought much when they'd abandoned Annabelle and her clothing choices weren't encouraging. There was a cotton sundress, a pair of cutoffs that were too short, a sweatshirt, a cropped top, and two oversized T-shirts, one that said "Nerds need love too" that she'd taken from Pete because it was so damned comfortable, and another with the word "No." on it. No, period.

She made do with the sundress, not liking the choice, the way it flowed around her legs and hugged her breasts, but it was better than cutoffs, and James wasn't even going to notice. Besides, the dress was comfortable. She didn't have to wear a bra with it, and it was soft and easy. As for the "No." T-shirt, she could just imagine Bishop's contemptuous reaction. She washed her face with cold water, then paused for a moment as thunder rumbled overhead. It was an ominous sound, creeping into her bones. She usually liked storms, liked the drama and the downpour, but not tonight. Not alone on this deserted island in the middle of Texas, with only James for company.

And Merlin, she reminded herself, glancing at the dog as he lay curled up beside her bed. Merlin would look out for her.

Speaking of which, she'd better check James's wound. Her own had healed over nicely, faster than she would have expected, but James had insisted on using some weird ointment on her and it had done wonders.

She pushed open her door, half expecting to find James out there, leaning against the wall like a neo-James Dean, but the hallway was empty. She could smell chili, and at the end of the hall she could see the glow of electronics. She paused for a moment, taking a deep breath. She could do this. She could be docile and pleasant for twenty-four hours or however long it took him to dump her.

"What are you lurking for?" His cranky voice came to her, and she jumped. He must have ears like a bat or some sixth sense to know she was out at the far end of the hallway.

"I'm waiting for Merlin," she lied, as Merlin paced ahead of her, looking back impatiently as if to say, *What's keeping you?*

She walked down the hallway at a brisk pace, trying to ignore the way the dress danced against her bare legs, and entered what must have been the kitchen in a businesslike manner. Sure enough, there was a row of computers, way too many for her piece of mind, and James was sitting in front of the monitors, staring at them intently. The kitchen was newly renovated, and the results were iffy. Clearly the rehab had been designed by men. Instead of the huge gathering place that it had probably once been, the space had been turned into a stainless steel laboratory, efficient and soulless.

James was still staring at the monitor, his hands flying over the keys, not turning. "There's chili on the stove. Don't worry—I didn't make it. They had stuff waiting for us, and since it's Texas I chose the chili. If you're too fainthearted for it, you can find something to suit your palate. I believe there's fettuccini Alfredo and . . ."

"Chili will be fine." In fact she liked spicy food, another thing he had yet to discover. He claimed he knew everything about her. Ha! He might know the names of every one of the men she had slept with when she came home, something even she didn't know, but he didn't know she liked spicy food. It was a small, lonely triumph, but she'd take what she could get.

She moved into the sterile kitchen. The chili was bubbling away on the gas stove, smelling divine. She opened the giant refrigerator and found avocados at the perfect stage of ripeness, a block of Monterey Jack, bottles of Guinness and . . . oh, praise God, Diet Coke.

She set to work, grating cheese, peeling and slicing the fat avocados. James was probably a purist, eating his straight, but she liked all sorts of things in her chili, including crushed tortilla chips, and he was going to have to take it that way. She filled two bowls, grabbed one and a bottle of Guinness, and plopped them down in front of him.

"Eat," she said. She had no idea why she was taking care of him . . . oh, yes she did. She needed him in decent shape to get her to New Orleans so she could get away from him. She was only being practical.

He finally glanced up at her, about to say something, but the words stopped in his mouth. His eyes ran the full length of her, the unfortunately low-cut bodice, the long, flowing skirt, her bare feet. He stared at her feet for a long moment, as if he'd never seen them before, and then when he lifted his eyes, he had his usual sardonic expression on his face, the one she wanted to slap.

"I see you decided to dress for dinner. Should I be flattered?"

"You should shut your mouth and eat," she snapped.

"Now if you could explain how I can manage that I'd be much obliged," he drawled, leaning back in the chair.

"You shove it up your ass." She stomped back to the kitchen to grab her own bowl, ready to retreat to her bedroom, but the passageway was too small and he simply blocked it with his long legs.

"Where do you think you're going?"

"I think eating around you would spoil my appetite."

"Stop being a baby, Angel. I don't need any added drama right now." He rose, all fluid grace, and took the bowl and the soda from her hand. "Get us silverware and a bottle opener. There are some peppers in the crisper—bring those too."

She would have felt ashamed of her pettish behavior if he hadn't started flinging orders at her. She was being childish, and that only gave him more power over her. "All right," she said evenly, heading back into the kitchen. There were fresh jalapenos, serranos, and habanero chilies, and she took one of each and rinsed them under water before putting them in a bowl and setting them in front of him, along with the utensils.

The small area adjacent to the kitchen had clearly been meant for a breakfast nook, but the table in it had been shoved against the window to make room for the computers, and he'd already set their food down there. She took her seat, then met his eyes.

For a moment she froze. His expression, which he quickly shuttered, was hotter than the habaneros, and it shook her. She'd been telling herself he didn't want her. No matter how quickly he hid that look, she couldn't pretend it hadn't existed. He might have nothing but contempt for her, but that didn't mean he didn't want her, at least on an elemental level.

"You want to say grace?" he drawled, breaking the uncomfortable silence.

She bit back her instinctive wisecrack. "No," she said, opening her soda and taking a good swallow before digging into the chili.

She'd give it a pretty mild rating—she'd once made a study of the Scoville scale and chili peppers in her undergraduate years and things tended to stay with her, deep in the recesses of her brain. If James was going to eat any of the freshly washed peppers, he was going to need an iron constitution. Jalapenos were very hot, serranos were blazing, and habaneros were nuclear.

He looked down at his bowl, loaded down with avocado and cheese and crushed chips. "What is all this?" he asked with a faintly derisive tone. "Can't manage your chili straight on? Tell me you don't put it on top of spaghetti and sprinkle cinnamon on top."

"Cincinnati chili doesn't deserve the name." This chili was delicious, but relatively mild, and she contemplated the hot peppers in front of them.

He took a bite. "Yeah, well this stuff is too fucking bland."

"Don't blame me. I didn't make it."

He reached out and took the jalapeno. With deliberation he bit off the end, then followed it with a forkful of chili. He didn't break a sweat. "That's better."

"Is that supposed to impress me?" Before she thought better of it, she took the jalapeno from his hand and bit into it, where his mouth had been, taking a larger piece. The seeds were the hottest part, spicy and delicious against her tongue, and it blended beautifully with her next bite of food.

He raised an eyebrow, taking a swig of beer. "It looks like you're the one who's trying to impress," he said. He rose, headed back to the fridge, and a moment later returned with two more beers. He opened one and shoved it at her, keeping the other one for a refill. "Chili needs to be eaten with beer, not belly wash."

"We should have Dos Equis, not Guinness, if you want to be a purist." She took a drink of the beer. It did blend better with the hot spices.

"You can't have everything." He reached for the serrano chili, then glanced at her. "Just how tough are you?"

"Obviously tougher than you ever realized. So much for knowing everything about me," she said sweetly. "That's not another jalapeno in your hand."

"I know." He bit off the end of it, ate a forkful of chili, and then drank almost half the bottle of Guinness. It was a good thing he'd brought himself a second bottle. He then held the pepper out to her in a deliberate challenge.

One she wasn't going to back down from. "You do realize that biting off the end of it doesn't give you the full heat. There are more seeds in the second bite." She took a healthy bite, and felt it sear her mouth. She had to go for the beer before the chili as she felt her face flush and tears fill her eyes, but at least this time she wasn't crying over him.

Was he going to up the ante? Habaneros were too much for her—she knew from experience—but she was damned if she was going to let James win. They ate in silence for a while, letting the residual heat in their mouths flavor the chili. James finished one bottle of beer, then started in on the second. She was almost at the end of her bowl, feeling comfortably replete. The fire in her mouth had died down to a pleasant buzz, her own beer empty, when she saw James reach for the remaining small yellow pepper.

He picked it up. "There are so many peppers that are hotter than this one," he said in a voice that was almost musing. "Particularly in Thailand and the Far East. I've spent a lot of time out there, you know."

"I don't know anything about you," she said, unable to help herself. "And everything you tell me I don't believe."

He smiled, holding the pepper by its stem. "You don't think I've gotten used to food a lot hotter than this pepper?"

Oh, shit, he was going to make her eat it. She'd do it, she wouldn't let him win, but she wasn't going to be happy about it. She usually stopped at jalapenos, and she was accustomed to a lot less than that ridiculously generous bite she'd taken, but there was too much at stake to back down now.

And then she laughed in relief.

"What's so funny?" he asked in a voice far milder than the chili.

"It's a fucking chili pepper, not the fate of the world. Go ahead and eat it. I don't have to prove how tough I am by burning my mouth out."

"It's not that hot," he said, his voice soft with reproof, and popped the entire thing in his mouth.

She was vindicated by the faint sheen of sweat on his forehead, and the fact that he drained almost the entire bottle of beer when he finished chewing. She laughed again.

"It's not that hot," he said again, the slight flush around his eyes belying his words. Before she knew what he was doing he'd leaned over, caught her chin in one strong hand, and put his mouth over hers.

He was on fire. His lips were blazing, his tongue was like a firebrand, turning her own mouth into a conflagration, her entire body shooting up in white heat, melting her from the inside out. She wanted to sink into the fiery heat of his bones, lose herself in the fierce demand of his mouth, and she wanted to burn, burn forever in that heat.

He drew back, and her own reaction was stronger than his: her heart pounded, her face flushed, her eyes watered, and sweat beaded on her forehead. Or maybe that was just how she reacted to his kisses, she thought dizzily. Wanting more. Hating herself, but wanting more.

"Here," he said, handing her half a cut lime. She had no idea where it came from—he must have brought it back when he'd replenished his beer supply. "It cuts the heat." He took the other half and bit into it.

She did the same, letting the citric acid fill her mouth, calming the flame his kiss had started. She was almost sorry to feel it lessen. She had the melancholy feeling that every time she tasted lime in the future, she would taste him leaving her.

"Better?" He acted like he'd never kissed her. All right, she could play that game as well.

"Much," she said, her voice slightly raw from the power of the chili peppers. "You get to do the dishes."

"No need. We just dump them in the sink and the magic fairies will come in and take care of things after we're gone."

She didn't bother to hide her outrage. "You're going to let the dishes sit out all night?"

"As if you haven't done the same thing," he mocked her.

Of course she had—she hated doing dishes and her house-cleaning skills were sadly lax. Only in the camper was she neat, and that was out of sheer necessity. And of course James would know that, damn him.

"Then you can put the leftover food away. And don't tell me there's no need for that either. Your 'magic fairies' might be hungry. There are children starving in China." She brought out the old cliché deliberately.

"There are children starving in Texas, and this isn't going to help any of them."

"No, probably not. But we're not wasting this." She rose, scooping up the dirty dishes and heading into the kitchen.

He followed her, and in the tight space, so much larger than anywhere in the campers, he seemed to crowd her. He put the food in the refrigerator, and she was just about to move past him when he suddenly blocked her exit, trapping her into the corner of the kitchen counter.

"Did you wear that dress on purpose?"

Lucky she was already burning from the heat of the peppers. "What? No, of course not."

"That's a shame," he said in a low voice. "Because I would so like to pull it up your long legs and find you wearing nothing underneath it."

She swallowed. "I've got granny panties underneath. You'd be disappointed."

"That would only make it more fun," he whispered. "And I like the way your nipples stand out when you eat something that's spicy. I'd like to lie you down on the bed and experiment with you, see what makes your nipples hard, see what makes you wet."

She was already wet from the sound of his soft voice. Wet and burning, as if he'd put that searing mouth between her legs. He wasn't even touching her, and she was melting, ready to fall, wanting an excuse, any excuse, to go into his arms. All he had to do was touch her and she'd give in. It was their last night, what more harm could it do, she wanted him so badly . . .

Then he moved away.

Turned his back on her and headed back to the computers, as if he'd said nothing incendiary at all. "I've got work to do," he said without looking at her. "There are a bunch of movies and a portable DVD player in the first room on the right. You should find something to occupy yourself with before you head for bed. We're going to have an early start, so don't stay up too late."

It wasn't a slap in the face. It wasn't even a gentle rejection. It was a dismissal, as if she were not worth thinking about. He had more important things to do.

And the thing was, she couldn't fault him. Oh, she could blame him for cornering her in the kitchen, getting her all hot and bothered, but the stuff he was doing at the computer was keeping them alive.

She left the room without a word, slipping into the hall. She wasn't going to watch movies, she wasn't going to read, assuming she could find something that interested her. This house had everything, but a collection of good romance novels seemed unlikely, and racy sex scenes were the last thing she needed right now. Her mouth burned, her body burned, outside the thunder shook the sky, but there was nothing she could do to get through the long night but get through it, she reminded herself.

Merlin had stayed behind with James, and for just a moment she felt bereft. Merlin was as wise as his name—James was going to be up for a while. He was the one who needed company.

She closed the door behind her. She wasn't particularly tired, but she needed some solitude. She'd forgotten to check his wound—she'd meant to breeze into the room and demand that he remove his shirt, but she'd forgotten all about it. Well, he could just fester if he was too noble to ask for help.

But he wouldn't. This house would have everything he needed to take care of any wounds. He was probably doing better than she was, and she was almost healed.

She flopped down on the bed, limp as a rag doll, worn out by the emotions, the tension, the danger. Overhead the thunder seemed to be closing in on them, danger from the sky as well as the world around them, and she shivered in the ozone-laden air. Maybe she needed to turn down the AC. The thunder was getting on her nerves, and every now and then lightning would spear through the sky. She rolled over on her stomach, pulling the pillow over her head. She wanted her old life back. This hurt too much— she just wanted to return to her boring world in Wisconsin where James Bishop was nothing more than a distant memory. That was a damned lie—James Bishop had been with her always, every day, an empty place in her soul that nothing had ever filled. Maybe this time she could finally forget him.

And maybe children weren't starving in China. And Texas. And everywhere, and . . .

For a moment she thought the arm that slid under her was James's, but the hand over her mouth held a reeking cloth in it, and before she had time to strike out, she was gone, into a scary darkness as the thunder shook the world.

Chapter Sixteen

Bishop pushed himself back from the computer and grabbed another beer. He was almost tempted to take another habanero chili. All he could remember was the taste of her mouth, not the explosive heat, and he didn't want to be thinking about her mouth. He glanced at Merlin, sound asleep beneath the computers. He'd fed him earlier—the Powers That Be at the Committee had provided the same designer dog food Evangeline used—and Merlin was conked out, as if he'd spent the day racing around, not in a cramped RV.

"Wake up, Merlin," he said, closing the refrigerator door. "I'm surprised you haven't been making a fuss about being with her. When I trained you to look after her, I didn't expect you to fall in love with her."

The silence that followed was deafening. Not that he expected conversation from Merlin, but why the fuck had the word "love" come from his mouth? And why the fuck wasn't Merlin moving?

He crossed the room in two strides, leaning under the table to put his hand on Merlin's neck. The dog didn't even twitch.

Bishop wasn't a man who panicked. He spent less than two seconds checking Merlin's heartbeat and pupils—he was alive but heavily drugged. And then he was down the hall, crashing into Evangeline's bedroom.

It was dark, but he already knew the bed would be empty. He turned on the light, staring at the open window. The rain had started an hour ago, but he'd barely paid any attention. It was pouring in, the wind whipping the wet curtain across the room, and for a moment he wondered whether she'd run away from him again.

He knew she hadn't. She never would have endangered Merlin by drugging him—she would have taken him with her. How the hell had someone managed to get into the dog food? Merlin wouldn't eat anything that didn't come from someone he trusted, but whoever had taken Evangeline had managed to circumvent that precaution.

Taken Evangeline. The words slammed into his head as he crossed to the open window, but he could see nothing through the torrent of rain. Who? Why? Her main value had been as a way to get to him. If they found her, they found him, and a sniper's bullet would have taken care of him. That, or blowing up the whole damned house to get rid of both of them.

Instead they'd taken Evangeline, someone who had no enemies, not even that asshole of a not-real husband who'd cheated on her and ripped off her work.

No enemies, except for Claudia, who never forgot a potential threat.

He didn't want to waste time, but calling London was a necessary evil, and he wasn't going to go through the computers.

Claudia was in the Far East, Madsen told him in the voice of a man who didn't like to be called at the crack of dawn. He had Takashi O'Brien's word for it.

Bishop didn't even bother to consider what time it was in Japan. Taka picked up the phone at the first ring, and he could hear the fretful cry of a hungry baby in the background, quickly silenced.

He'd lost count of how many children Taka and Summer had, and he wasn't about to waste time asking.

"Have you seen Claudia recently?"

Taka didn't bother with social niceties either—he recognized by Bishop's voice that things were at a crisis level. "Not for five days. She said she was going to the mountains on Hokkaido, but there's no way to prove it."

"Shit."

If Claudia had decided that Madsen's edict against killing immediate family no longer pertained to Evangeline, then she was as good as dead. Claudia was one of the best assassins the Committee had ever had, and she had absolutely no compassion or morality. She was a true sociopath—the best kind, untroubled by emotions. She simply did the job.

Maybe she'd seen the writing on the wall, knew her days with the Committee were numbered, and she'd decided to act. She had a long memory, and she had never forgiven James for getting Evangeline out of her line of fire. Maybe Claudia had decided to make the break herself.

It wasn't as if her skills weren't highly marketable—she might already be working for the Corsinis. At least that settled things as far as Bishop was concerned. He was going to kill his occasional partner. He should have done it long ago.

Things were beginning to make sense now. His instincts had been right—Claudia would have known where Evangeline was, Claudia would have set the Corsinis after her. Claudia was capable of anything.

The rain was pounding down, and even in the darkness, he could see white balls of hail bouncing off the ground amid all the rain. Lightning hit close by, momentarily illuminating the yard, and it took only that brief moment to see the muddy path they'd taken. It took him another moment to grab his gun, and he was out the window, after them. If he muttered prayers under his breath as he ran, he wasn't even aware of it.

The pain came first. Evangeline felt as if she were being pulled apart—her shoulders burned, her wrists stung, her head felt like a black hole of misery, and she was wet and aching and blind. No, not blind. It was pitch black, but as her eyes slowly grew accustomed to it, she could make out her surroundings. She was in some sort of shed, and she was hanging from her bound wrists, her toes barely touching the ground. She squirmed, trying to release her hands, but she'd been tied with something that felt like wire, and it was cutting into her wrists.

"Don't bother." The voice that came out of the darkness was almost ghost-like. It had no gender, no accent, no age to it; it was just a disembodied threat from the rain-swept darkness.

The cold had finally penetrated her thin dress, and she had started to shiver. The eerie voice didn't help, but she bit her lip, trying to force some strength into her body, some justifiable rage as she hung suspended.

"Who the fuck are you?" The tone was good, she thought, snappish without sounding petty, and only slightly marred by her chattering teeth. "Let me down."

"In the words of the immortal Dirty Harry, I'm your worst nightmare," the voice said, and she began to make out a form in the murky darkness. He was of average height, thin—after that she was lost.

She struggled, trying to move away from the menacing figure, and her body swung slightly. "Why?" Fear was making the cold even worse, but she tried to keep her voice even. "What do you have against me? If you think James will come after me, you're dead wrong. He'd probably be happy to get rid of me."

The man laughed quietly, the sound both charming and impossibly creepy. "You're not very bright, are you, no matter how many degrees you have. I have no interest in James—I sincerely hope he doesn't find your body until I'm long gone, or I'll have to kill him too, and he's too good a tool to throw away. No, I'm afraid it's you I want dead, and I'm hoping I can take my time with it, enjoy myself. Strung up like that, you're a perfect canvas for my creativity—otherwise you'd already be dead."

The soft words were madness, and yet he sounded so matter of fact. "But why?" she said again. "If I'm going to die, you could at least tell me why."

He snorted, a genteel sound she barely heard over the pounding rain. "What do you think this is—some sci-fi epic where the villain tells all, wasting enough time for the knight-errant to rescue the fair damsel?"

"You're mixing your genres," she snapped. Her arms felt like they were being pulled out of their sockets, but she refused to show pain.

Again the eerie laugh. "And you have no sense. You don't piss off the villain in the tale. If you think I have some desperate urge to confess my darkest sins, then you've definitely been watching too much television. I think the fact that you'll die without ever knowing why is very satisfying. Telling you would be too easy."

They must have realized she was gone by now. Merlin would have made a huge fuss once he heard someone in the house, and he'd alert James. The two of them would be searching for Evangeline and her assailant at this very minute, and this patch of land between the river and the creek was too small for them to hide very well. "They'll find us," she said, her voice shaking from the cold. "They'll find us and they'll kill you."

"They? Oh, you mean the dog. I'm not worried about him. I gave him enough drugs that I doubt he'll survive. I don't have any sentimental qualms when it comes to children or animals—if they're in my way, they're fair game."

"You drugged Merlin?" Her voice was no more than a dead whisper, and then she exploded, struggling, kicking, screaming at him. "If you've hurt my dog I'll kill you! I'll rip your fucking heart out, you bastard, I'll . . ."

She felt his fist crack across her face, sending her swinging even more wildly, and then he put his foul hands on her, settling her, and for a moment there was nothing she could do, no way to fight back. And then she spat in his face.

The monster laughed. "He might survive, depending on how much he ate. I had to dump the stuff in his dog food, and that's one big, scary dog. Maybe he'll be fine. I'm afraid you'll never know. And you can forget about Bishop coming after you."

"Don't tell me you killed him too! I won't believe you!"

"Not yet. Bishop trusts me. If I tell him I wasn't anywhere near here, he'll believe me." He caught her, stilling her as she swung gently in the breeze. His hands were strong, and they were gloved, to leave no trace. She was in some sort of shed—she felt the rough wood against her back—but whatever roof the structure had, it was more holes than a cover, and water was running down her back, adding to her chills. Or maybe it was simply that she was terrified.

"Let's take a quick look at you," he murmured affably, and for a moment she was blinded by the flashlight. It was sheer discipline that kept her from squirming away from the glare, and she could see more of the man behind the light. He had a shaved head and a beard, but his eyes were simply dark holes in the dimness, and while there was something oddly familiar about his face, she was sure she'd never seen him before.

"Having trouble looking at me, sweetie?" he said with a laugh. "Here you go." He turned the flashlight on his own face, giving her plenty of time to take stock. His eyes were hazel, and incredibly beautiful, with the lush lashes only men seemed to have. His nose was narrow and straight, his cheekbones high above the scruff of beard, his lips thin and almost feminine. "Do I look familiar?"

She stared. "Yes," she said, "but I don't know you."

"Of course you don't. Too busy with your nose in a book to learn to observe real life."

That wasn't true, and it was enough of an insult that she looked closer, racking her brain for the source of familiarity. She didn't know him, but she knew someone related to him—a brother or sister. Someone with a strong family resemblance.

He switched off the light, plunging them back into darkness once more. "Can't risk having Bishop see the light. Not that I'm worried. If he even realizes you're gone, he's never going to find you. There's no need to hurry, but I don't want to take foolish chances."

"And how are you going to enjoy killing me if you can't see me?"

"Oh, sweetie, I can slowly rip you apart with my eyes closed. Don't worry about me. And I wouldn't bother fighting against my restraints. That's a garroting wire you've got twisted around your wrists. You'll cut your hands off before you break free."

Garroting wire? Why did that sound familiar? She tried to keep calm. She refused to believe Merlin was dead. It would take more than a slimy pissant, like the man who had her strung up, to kill Merlin. He'd find her. Even if they were so well hidden James wouldn't get here in time, Merlin would find her. "Does your vow of silence include not telling me where we are?"

She was growing used to the murky light, and she could see his face. Which meant he could see hers, and she managed an emotionless expression. "Tut tut. You're being very sarcastic, aren't you?

We're in the remnants of a chicken coop, if my sense of smell serves me. At some point a tree fell across it, and it looks like a splintered pile of wood, but there was just enough room for the two of us, all nice and cozy, and you look so pretty, all strung up like that."

For some reason she felt no sexual threat in his words. Merlin would find her. It was a mantra in her mind, and she wanted to throw it in his face, but it might make him speed things up. She tried to clear her throat, to sound normal despite the fact that he had her captive. "I wouldn't call this cozy."

"Ah, you're used to more elegant surroundings, aren't you? I'm afraid this was the best I could do on short notice—I wasn't going to wait until you reached New Orleans, though if there was ever a city where murder is easy, that's the one." The man moved closer, pushing his face up next to hers, and she saw he held a stiletto in one thin hand. Evangeline glanced at the weapon dispassionately and then back at his face. If she was going to die, then she wasn't going to give him any satisfaction.

She had a good memory for faces—so much for the fuckhead saying she was unobservant—and she finally recognized who he resembled. Someone she hadn't seen in more than five years, and then only briefly. He looked eerily like the woman who'd been with James at the hotel in Tuscany. He must be her brother . . .

Realization hit, startling a little sound from her before she managed to shut down her reaction. The man spoke. "What's up, buttercup? You think you hear Bishop coming to rescue you? I have better hearing than you do, and I've got the doors wired. I'll know the moment he leaves the house."

Evangeline leaned back against the flimsy structure, forcing her body to relax, and she could see the man's beautiful eyes narrow. "Maybe," she said evenly. "Do you mind telling me how you're going to kill me? Since it's supposed to take a long time, I can't quite imagine how you're going to do it. I did read somewhere about the

Chinese Death of a Thousand Cuts, but I don't think you have time for that. Are you going to hack off body parts while I scream? But that might draw Bishop's attention."

"You are a cool one, aren't you?" There was clear admiration in the man's voice. "No wonder James is in love with you."

The words hit her like a blow, far worse than anything else he could have done. "Don't be ridiculous."

"I told you you were unobservant. The man is obsessed with you, though even he refuses to face it. The two of you are like some idiot pair of Shakespearean lovers, bumbling around."

"Ah, a scholarly bent, I see," Evangeline said acidly. "And I agree completely—I'm completely unobservant and idiotic. Look at how long it took me to realize who you are."

He didn't even blink, his thin lips curving in a smile. "I sincerely hope that you do. I tell you what—we can play Rumpelstiltskin. I'll give you three chances to tell me who I am. If you get it right I won't kill you."

"Rumpelstiltskin," she said promptly.

He toyed with his knife, letting her observe its perfect blade. "One down. Try another."

"Jimmy Hoffa."

"Now you're not even trying," he chided, sounding disappointed. "Last chance, Evangeline, and then I'll cut your throat first so you can't do anything but gurgle while I play with the rest of you."

"Fair enough," she said sweetly. "Did you get that knife in Italy, Claudia?"

His expression was almost comical, like that of a child whose balloon had been popped. He seemed almost affronted, but it only took him a moment to pull himself together. "Actually I go by Claude when I'm dressed like this. And I have a surprise for you."

"And that is?"

"I lied." He came at her then, but Evangeline could read body language; she hadn't trusted him for a moment, and she tried to dodge him, kicking out at him. To her amazement she connected, and he went flying, crashing against the wall. The rotting wood splintered around him, around them, and she heard the creak and groan of the ancient structure as it began to collapse, and then she was down in the mud, covered with wood and debris.

She screamed for James, knowing it was useless. The rain was pounding down, drowning out any sound she could make, and the wind was whipping the cottonwood trees overhead, adding to the noise. He wouldn't hear her, he was safe in the confines of the house, his face glued to the goddamned computers, and Merlin was dead. She screamed again as Claude began to rise from the debris. He reached for her ankle, trying to drag her back, and she kicked at him with her bound ankles.

"Bitch!" Claude screamed, his husky voice higher-pitched in his fury, and he slashed at her with his knife.

She kicked again, kicked as hard as she could, ignoring the slashing blade, and she felt her foot connect with his face, hard enough to hear bone crack. She did it again, twice, so fast he couldn't move out of the way; then she managed to roll out from under the collapsed chicken shed, where she was faced with the fallen trunk of a massive tree. She dove over it, rolling in the mud, just managing to get to her feet with her hands still bound in front of her, and began to hobble forward in the inky darkness.

She slammed into him, so hard she almost knocked herself unconscious, and she opened her mouth to scream again, when he caught her, turned her, and slapped his hand over her mouth, silencing her. How the hell had he managed to get ahead of her? She kicked and fought desperately, digging her teeth into his hand, when his arms tightened, and she knew . . .

It was James. James had found her; James was holding her. She let her body sag against him, exhaustion pouring through her. She didn't even care if she died now—not so long as he was there, holding her shaking body.

A bolt of lightning illuminated the landscape, sizzling in the air, and she could see Claude only a few feet away, the knife in his hand, his face covered with blood. She had no idea whether she'd done it with her kicks or if it had been the result of the collapsing structure, but she hoped she could take the credit.

"Did my woman do that to you, Claude?" James asked in a deceptively calm voice. "I probably didn't even need to come after her. She's very good at taking care of herself."

And how could she possibly hold on to the words, "my woman" at a time like this? But she did, and the bitter cold that had settled in her bones began to warm, just a bit.

"You don't need her and you know it," Claude answered, his voice both nasal and muffled from the broken nose. "You should have let me take care of her five years ago, and we could have avoided all this. Tell me she hasn't been a pain in your ass from day one."

"I'd never lie to you, Claude. Being a pain in the ass isn't a reason to kill someone."

"I don't need a reason. No witnesses, remember. Collateral damage is a fact of life."

"Not in this case." He'd shifted her, so she was partly shielded by his body. "The only collateral damage in this case is going to be you."

"How do you think Madsen would like that? I'm his best, most reliable weapon," Claude taunted.

"You're a nutcase, and if he doesn't like it, he can fire me."

"And just how do you intend to kill me? You know how good I am with a knife. I could land it between your eyes before you got one shot off. I assume you came armed."

"I did. And we'll just have to see about that."

ANNE STUART

"Of course, I could aim for your girlfriend and then shoot you as she collapses in your arms," Claude mused. "In fact, I think that's the best possible plan. I really didn't want to kill you, James, but you're just too damned good."

She could feel the tension in James's body. He had her tucked under one arm, and she considered diving to the ground, but that would free Claude to throw the knife at James, and she had no doubt at all that he would succeed. She held very still.

"So we're at a standstill?" James said in an even voice.

"You could look at it that way. I might suggest a truce. You let me go and I'll let the bitch live. For now."

"Now you had to go and ruin a perfectly acceptable compromise. Not that I would ever have believed you, but you could have at least made the effort." James's voice was lightly mocking.

"Ah, you never would have believed me. I will tell you one thing. You leave me the girl and I won't kill you. I'll even promise to make it fast and painless for her. You know I can do that, don't you? I'm a far better killer than you ever were."

"But you know I'd come after you, and for you I wouldn't make it fast and painless. There's only one acceptable outcome to all this."

Thunder rumbled overhead, and the rain was lashing around them, plastering their clothes against their bodies. "Acceptable to you, perhaps. I think my best choice is to disappear for a while. Whether I show up to finish the job is anybody's guess."

"I can't let you . . ." Before James could finish the sentence, Claude had vanished into the storm. James shoved Evangeline away and dove after him, not pausing when she went sprawling in the mud. She didn't try to get up—she simply lay in the mud and the cold in misery. The two men had disappeared into the darkness, and she could hear the rushing of the water all around them. The formerly calm creek had risen, moving across the land, and she could see it inching toward her. She'd have to find the resources to get to her feet one more time, to stagger toward the house if she could even guess what direction it was in. Her chances of finding James were almost nil—she could hear nothing over the roar of the storm, and she knew she'd only prove a liability.

She had to find some way to move. She felt the cold water touch her toes, and it should have been enough to galvanize her, but she lay still. She tried to push back with her bound hands, but she couldn't summon enough energy to get to her feet without something to push against. She was shaking too badly, was weak and disoriented, and couldn't move.

She almost didn't recognize the sound in the distance. It was the sound of a dog barking, and she almost wept with relief. Merlin was alive. He sounded strange, probably the result of the drugs Claude had given him, but he was alive.

She didn't know how long it took him to find her. The water had reached her knees, and she'd made a desultory effort to inch herself forward, away from the encroaching river, but her energy had failed her, and she was content to lie where she was. Either James would come back and get her or Claude would win, in which case she'd rather drown than let him get his hands on her.

Merlin's hot breath was all around her, snuffling, whining, pawing at the ground. "Good boy," she said in a croak. "Go find Bishop."

But Merlin wasn't moving. Maybe he didn't know who Bishop was—who knew what name Merlin's dog brain had given to his original trainer, and Evangeline couldn't be bothered to figure it out. Merlin had gone from whining to barking, and she tried to push herself forward, away from the water, but with her hands and ankles bound, she could barely move.

She felt his huge jaws close around her neck, so gently that she could have been a helpless puppy. His teeth dug in, just a bit, and he began to drag her, slowly, carefully, out of the water, well onto dry land, before releasing her, licking her neck with his huge tongue to soothe any pain he might have caused her.

And then he was gone into the darkness, heading after Bishop, and she realized he didn't need to be told. He would know there was trouble, and all the drugs in the world wouldn't keep his sense of smell from telling him where to find it.

She heard the scream from a distance, the sound of a gun being fired, and the thunder shook the earth once more. When the rumbling had died away, there was nothing but the sound of the rain and the rising river.

She closed her eyes and prayed.

Chapter Seventeen

Bishop had to rely on the intermittent flashes of lightning to follow Claude's desperate race through the rain—the sound of the wind and weather drowned out any noise he might have made. He'd left Merlin's body on the porch, hoping the cold rain might counteract the drugs in his system enough that he'd be able to come after them, but Bishop couldn't hear a thing. He had to take it on faith that Evangeline was safe for the moment, despite the rising water. If he didn't finish Claude here and now, Evangeline would never be safe again.

Before he realized it, he'd made it to the edge of the river, which was much higher than it had been before, and he almost turned back. The remnants of an old bridge hung suspended across the water, the rickety structure barely strong enough to support a man.

But in the next flash of lightning he could see the outline of someone on the decaying surface, and he knew he'd found his quarry.

A moment later everything was plunged into darkness again, and he hadn't been able to see well enough to know if the bridge reached the opposite side of the rising river. He was an excellent shot, but no one could hit a blind target, and he crouched down, aiming, while he waited for the next flash of lightning to give him some clue where Claude might be. He wouldn't have long to find his target and make his shot, and every second counted.

It seemed to take forever for the next flash of light, and to Bishop's fury there was no sign of Claude on the bridge, no sign of him anywhere. Cursing, he rose, moving forward, when he heard the muffled sound of heavy breathing, close, too close, and he spun around just as Claude leapt at him.

They went down in a tangle. Neither of them let go of their weapons, but they were well matched: Claude couldn't get his blade close enough to cut, nor could Bishop manage to fire his gun. They rolled and grappled, cursing each other, and Bishop tried to control the murderous rage that filled him. Emotion weakened him—he need to be cold and calm to get the better of a sociopath like the person currently wearing the persona of Claude, but he couldn't fight the fury and the man at the same time.

Claude was experienced enough to take full advantage of that, and even though Bishop was bigger and stronger, he found himself on his back, Claude straddling him, one knee pinning Bishop's gun hand to the muddy ground. "Always a mistake to fall in love, Bishop," Claude panted. "Didn't I warn you about that five years ago?"

He wanted to deny it, but there was the very real possibility that he was going to be dead in the next few moments, and there was no need to make his last words a lie. Instead he said, "Fuck you, Claude."

Claude laughed. "You know that's not my style." He raised the knife, ready to plunge it into Bishop's throat, when something huge flew at them out of the darkness, knocking Claude off him, and a moment later Bishop was back on his feet, his gun in hand, watching the shadowy forms of Merlin and Claude as the dog wrestled with him, his huge jaws clamped over Claude's right hand.

The knife fell, and normally Merlin would have backed off, but the dog's rage was equal to Bishop's. Claude was screaming, shoving at him, and a moment later he tore himself away, starting back across the bridge to safety, another flash of lightning illuminating his mangled hand.

Bishop took aim and fired three times, hitting him right in the center of his back, and Claude froze for a moment, turning. Then he collapsed over the side of the ruined bridge, into the churning river, while Bishop watched him being carried down the raging torrent. Claude didn't scream again—with three bullets center mass he still wasn't dead—and he was trying to hold his mangled hand over his head as he struggled against the current. He went under, surfaced again, and lightning lit the sky, turning everything to daylight for a brief, endless moment. He could see Claude's eyes clearly—Claudia's eyes, mad with fury—see the hand that Merlin had savaged, and then Claude went under as everything darkened once more, followed by ground-shaking thunder.

He didn't surface again, and Bishop couldn't waste time watching for him any longer. Merlin was dancing around, clearly wanting to dive into the river after him, but he'd already done his job. If Claude could survive the raging waters with one useful hand and a body riddled with bullets, then he was superhuman, and Bishop had learned long ago that no one was superhuman. A moment later the last of the bridge collapsed into the raging torrent, following Claude's body into oblivion.

"He's gone. Good job," he said, but Merlin was still dancing, heading away from him, then circling around and coming back, whining. *Evangeline.*

He found her lying in a crumpled heap, the overflowing river almost at her feet. Her wrists and ankles were bound, but he didn't bother loosening her. More lightning, and the distant lights of the house went out. He cursed beneath his breath as he knelt down and hoisted her into his arms. Even the best of security systems and generators were no proof against a direct hit by lightning, and it looked as if they were stuck in darkness.

She cried out in pain. "Just hold on," he said grimly, his voice barely audible over the thunder. "I'll cut you free as soon as we get back to the house."

Her teeth were chattering, and she was shaking. "M . . . M . . . Merlin?"

"He's with us. He's fine. Claude's dead."

She asked no more questions. Her body was stiff with tension and pain, but she put her face against his shoulder to block out the rain, and he took off in a run.

The old farmhouse loomed up sooner than he expected, and he felt an uncharacteristic sense of relief. He kicked the back door open, shouldering her in, with Merlin at his side in perfect formation despite the worried sounds he made. The house was in complete darkness, but he knew enough about the infrastructure that he was reasonably certain the gravity-fed pump and huge hot water tank would provide enough bathwater to warm her.

He carried her into the bathroom and set her down on the commode, ignoring her cry of pain as he turned to start filling the large tub. The air-conditioning was already dissipating, the hot Texas night infiltrating the house, but Evangeline was shivering.

He knelt down beside her, his knife out. "This is going to hurt," he said gently.

Her only response was a shattered laugh, as he cut through the thin, vicious rope binding her wrists and ankles. There was blood around both, and it felt like a blow to his stomach.

He knelt in front of her and for the first time in his life he didn't know what he could do. "It'll be better in a moment. A hot bath will do the rest. The lightning must have hit the generator, and once I get you settled, I'll see if there's a backup, but in the meantime we need to get you into a hot bath or you'll go into shock."

"I'm . . . n . . . n . . . not that b . . . b . . . big a pussy," she managed to protest in a mere shadow of her usual fierce voice.

He found he could laugh. As long as she could fight back, she'd be fine. Merlin was sitting on his haunches, his head in her lap, and Bishop was about to order him away when Evangeline lifted her hand and caressed his head. "Good baby," she whispered.

"Baby," he echoed in mock distress. "My poor dog."

"My dog."

He rose, checking the huge bathtub. It was already filled with steaming water. He turned off the tap, then went back to her. She was still wearing the dress, though it was ripped and covered with mud, and her face was just as bad. He didn't bother with searching for buttons or zippers—he simply took the knife and sliced through the shoulders of the thing, then ripped it down the front. The wet fabric only resisted for a moment—at that point his adrenaline was still pumping enough that he could have torn through steel to free her from her clothes.

She didn't make any effort to cover herself—maybe she thought it was too dark for him to see anything. She was wrong. He could see her pale skin, her sweetly rounded breasts, the healing wounds from Clement's knife. "Did he hurt you?" he demanded, trying to ignore the heat that was filling him. Filling his cock. He was a pig, and he was going to ignore his desperate need to fuck her, hard, claim her, ride her until they were both too shattered to think or move.

She shook her head, her hair hanging down in limp strands around her face. She was lying—he'd seen the bruise on the side of her face—or maybe shock was setting in and she really didn't know what he had or hadn't done.

She hadn't been raped—Claude/Claudia's affectations didn't include sexual desire of any sort, unless he had to establish an alibi, which was some blessing. He had no idea how long Claude had her—from the time she'd left him at his computers to the time he finally realized something was wrong could have been anywhere from a few minutes to a few hours.

And what the hell had happened to his usually infallible instincts? He'd never missed danger when it was lurking—he had a sixth sense for it, finely honed.

But he knew the answer. It was Evangeline. She threw everything off. He spent so much time worrying about her that he could no longer trust his instincts, and so he'd ignored them.

He slid his arms around her and scooped her up quite easily. She hadn't been eating enough—she was lighter than she had been in Italy, lighter than she'd been a few days ago. He was going to have to feed her. Fortunately New Orleans had the best food in the world.

"This might hurt," he said, and once more she gave that rusty laugh as he set her into tub, the steaming water coming just up to her breasts. She was still shivering, and he realized it wasn't the cold that was the problem, and all the heat in the world wouldn't fix it.

It took him less than a moment to slip out of his clothes, and he doubted she was even aware of it, aware of anything until he slipped into the tub behind her and pulled her against him. He expected her to struggle, to complain, to lash out, but she sank back against his chest as if it was where she belonged, resting her head against his shoulder as he put his arms around her. For the first time he felt some of his own tension begin to drain away, felt his heartbeat slow, his adrenaline sinking back to normal levels, and he slid down in the tub, taking her with him, leaning his head back against the porcelain edge. He could feel when her trembling slowed, stopped, when her icy skin warmed. He knew when she became aware of his hard dick pressing against her backside, and he expected her to sit up, to push away from him in disgust. She didn't move.

He took the soap from the tray beside the tub, wetting it before he touched her arm with it, letting her get used to the feel of his hands, of the soap. After an initial start she relaxed again, and he soaped her, slowly, lazily, her arms, her stomach, her breasts with their tight little nipples . . .

She was warm. The water was steaming—why were her nipples hard? He rubbed the soap around one soft, plump little breast, rubbing his thumb against the nipple, and he felt the reaction slip through her body.

He stopped thinking—he'd thought enough during the last four days. He let the soap slide down her stomach, between her legs, and she deliberately lifted her hips, spreading her thighs for him as he soaped her, gently, tenderly, when he wanted nothing more than to turn her over and put her astride him, shoving up inside her and fucking her until his mind went blank. He set the soap back on its dish, then put his hand where the soap had been, parting her folds, his fingers sliding down, circling her clitoris, waiting for her protest.

She was mute, tense, demanding, and he knew what she needed, knew how to take care of her. After all, hadn't that been what he'd been doing for the last five years, mostly from a distance? This wasn't about his own needs; it was about taking care of her, the woman who'd been dragged into his clusterfuck of a mess by accident. Taking care of her and then letting her go.

He wanted to go down on her, but she didn't need that. He could do this much for her, as he used his thumb, circling, pressing against her.

She climaxed quickly, arching her body, her only sound a soft, keening wail. Merlin didn't move—the smart dog knew that sound. Bishop wasn't going to think how he knew—there'd been no one in Evangeline's life since her rat of a fake husband.

He could rub against her—it wouldn't take much to bring him off as well. Death always did this to him—brought the need to affirm life on its most elemental level. She might not even notice.

But he wasn't going to. He let her fall back against him, weak, limp from her climax. He slid out from behind her, climbing out of the bath. For a moment he considered wrapping a towel around his waist to hide his throbbing erection, but he decided, fuck it. She'd seen a cock before; she'd seen his cock before. Besides, she wasn't in any condition to pay attention to it.

He knelt by the tub with a washcloth, dipping it into the hot water and carefully washing her muddy face. She winced, and he moved more gently, clearing away the dirt to expose a cut, surrounded by a huge bruise on her left cheekbone. He picked up her wrists, darkened by bruises. The places where the thin, strong rope had cut through her skin were closing, and her ankles were only bruised.

He could sense her looking at him, but it was too dark for normal people to see much, and she wouldn't know the utter rage that suffused him. "Will I live?" she said, trying for humor and failing.

"You will," he said. "If I could, I'd kill him all over again."

"You're sure he's dead?" Her voice wasn't shaking, but it was small, quiet.

Bishop wasn't sure of anything in this world, including how he felt about this woman, but a lie was easier. "Absolutely positive." It would take a miracle for Claude to survive, and Bishop didn't believe in miracles.

And he needed to go someplace and jack off. "Do you need help washing your hair? It's caked with mud."

Slowly she shook her head, reaching up to touch her matted strands. "No," she said, "I'll be fine. You go do what you have to do."

Did she have any idea he needed to get away from her before he hauled her out and took her on the bathroom floor? Probably not—she still held a certain naïveté despite all she'd gone through.

"Good," he said, and moved away from her. Merlin stayed to guard her, though the dog's reactions were still a little off from the drugs Claude had fed him. It was sheer luck the dose hadn't been lethal—Claude wouldn't have given a shit if he'd killed him.

The rain was still pouring down, though the lightning had died back, and the distant rumble of thunder told him the storm was moving off. He stepped out into the night, letting the cool rain wash down his body, reaching for his cock. But then he laughed. He could jerk off a dozen times and still be hard for her. Why waste his time?

He managed to find a pair of shorts in the darkness, and he pulled them on before heading back to the pitch-dark bathroom, his libido under stern, albeit rebellious, control.

She was leaning back against the bathtub, her hair clean, her eyes closed, sound asleep. The water had to be cooling by now, and he didn't want her to get another chill, so he slid his arms beneath her, lifting her drowsy body and holding her against him, all wet and soft and smelling like gardenias.

He was going to carry her into her bedroom, settle her in, but one look at the open window changed his mind. Instead he took her to his room because he knew the bed was big enough, the sheets were clean, and it had a comfortable chair where he could sit and watch her. Merlin padded along behind them as he nudged open his door.

He managed to pull the covers down while he held her, and a moment later he set her on the mattress, watching as she curled up sleepily, all defenses and prickles. He pulled the covers up, and she let out a soft sigh and sank back into a deeper sleep. So much for any lingering fantasies that she'd put her arms around his neck and pull him down with her. She needed sleep more than anything. And he'd given up, hadn't he? The more he touched her, the more he needed her, and he couldn't afford to need anyone.

Merlin sat guard while Bishop went into the darkened kitchen, unerringly found his favorite Scotch and a glass, and carried both back into his bedroom. He had a lot to think about, and a glass of Scotch would keep him company while Evangeline slept like a virgin in his clean white sheets.

Damn everything.

Chapter Eighteen

The darkness surrounded Evangeline like a cocoon, thick and warm and smothering. The air was hot and humid, and somewhere in the distance she could hear the soft patter of rain overhead. She didn't know where she was—but it was not in the bed she'd started out in, the bed she'd been taken from.

Claude was dead. She knew Merlin was lying in front of the door—she could hear the steady sound of his breathing. She could smell Scotch, but it wouldn't have taken that to know that James was nearby. When had he become James again, and not the snide "Bishop"? When had she wanted to know he was near?

Always. She was a casualty of his murderous business, one she still didn't comprehend, and he had an overdeveloped sense of honor, a need to keep her safe that had nothing to do with real emotions or caring. She was collateral damage, all right, and for some reason he felt it was his duty to save her.

"Go back to sleep." His voice was soft in the inky darkness. "You think too much."

She started, feeling guilty, almost as if she'd spoken her thoughts out loud. "It that possible?" Her low tone matched his.

"To sleep, or to think too much?"

She ignored his response. "I make my living from thinking. It's the way I solve problems, put my life in order."

"I use a gun for that." The words were flat, emotionless.

"He's dead, isn't he?" The question came from nowhere.

"I told you he was."

"He drowned? In the river?"

"He drowned," James agreed in a lazy voice. The Scotch must have relaxed him, at least marginally. "After I shot him and Merlin tore half his gun hand away. He'd have to be Rasputin to survive."

"Good dog," she murmured, perfectly comfortable with the gory image, and she heard Merlin's tail thwap against the floor in response.

"We'll leave at first light for New Orleans. It's a short drive—you can sleep in the back while I drive. As soon as we get there I'll pass you off to Ryder, who'll have a safe house for you."

She ignored the pain that hit her. He'd pass her along, first chance he got. Of course he would. "Why do I need a safe house? If Claude is dead, then I should be fine. I could go back home."

There was a hesitation, and she tried to guess what was going through his mind. Maybe he was trying to find a way to tell her that he didn't want her to go, that she needed to stay for some trumped-up reason, that he needed her . . .

"The bad news, Angel, is that Claude had absolutely nothing to do with Clement's attack, so that's still an issue."

"What is?"

She heard him sigh. "The Corsini family wants to get its hands on me in the worst way, and they know the best way to do it is through you, thanks to Claude's help. He wanted you dead for the last five years, ever since you stumbled into Corsini's execution in the church in Italy, and I refused to let him kill you. I should have realized he was no longer going to play by the rules."

"Rules? There are rules in what you do?"

It was odd, talking in the dark like this. It was as if they were old lovers, curled up in bed together in the middle of the night, able to say anything they wanted. Except they weren't lovers; they weren't even touching, though he was closer than she'd first thought. He couldn't see her face; she couldn't see his. What was said in the dark, stayed in the dark.

She slid up in the bed, realized she was stark naked, and slid back again. Her face hurt, her shoulders ached, but she felt warm and clean and safe. Vaguely she remembered the bathtub, his hands on her, but then it was all a blur.

She heard James shift in the chair, the clink of a bottle against the lip of a glass, the splash of liquid; then the rich aroma of Scotch filled the air.

She had the suspicion he was killing time, putting off answering her question, but she was warm, relaxed, and infinitely patient. "Believe it or not, the organization I work for has certain rules."

"The Committee, you said."

He made a disgusted sound. "I told you that, did I?"

"What kind of rules?" she persisted. "You don't kill women?"

His laugh was utterly mirthless and should have chilled her, but right then nothing he said or did could horrify her. "No. We don't discriminate, and evil comes in all genders."

"All?"

"Claude," he said simply.

He was trying to distract her, but it wouldn't work. "What rules would he have broken if he'd killed me? You yourself said that collateral damage was an unfortunate necessity. Why wasn't I an unfortunate necessity?"

"Because the Committee has an iron rule that you leave family members alone. If a family member manages to infiltrate the organization, then it's up to the agent himself to terminate that person."

"What are you talking about?"

She could feel his eyes on her, even in the darkness. "That's why I married you. Because it meant that Claude couldn't come after you."

The silence in the room seemed almost like a living thing, and it took her a while to speak. "You mean that marriage was actually legal?"

"Yes."

"And my marriage to Pete?"

"Bigamous and totally fake. If you'd looked happy I would have done something about it, pulled a few strings and gotten a back-dated annulment so you could have your perfect little happily ever after, but one look at that slimy bastard and I knew you'd be done with him in less time than it would take me to get the annulment."

"One look at him?" She felt her breath catch in her throat. "When did you see him? When did I look unhappy?"

"On your so-called wedding day, Angel. You don't think I'd miss an occasion like that?" he said lazily. "It's not every day your wife gets married."

"You were there? I didn't see you." What would she have done if she had seen him? Thrown her bouquet over her shoulder and run after him like something out of a screwball comedy from the 1930s?

"It's my business not to be seen."

She digested this. She heard him take a sip of the Scotch. "Could I have some?"

"Some what?" He sounded almost irritable.

"Some Scotch. You don't need to hog it all to yourself."

"I only brought one glass."

"I think I'll survive the germs," she said, irony thick in her voice.

He moved, a looming shadow in the darkness, and the mattress dipped beneath his weight as he handed her the glass. "Drink it slowly," he said. "You're not used to it."

Irritation flared, not the least because he was so damned close and she couldn't, wouldn't touch him. "How do you know what I'm used to? I had a bottle in my trailer, didn't I?" she shot back, wrapping her fingers around the glass. Her hand brushing his. Did his linger for a moment?

"It was opened but untouched, and you bought it in Wisconsin. You've been on the road for months—that's a long time to carry around a full bottle of Scotch, and I'm pretty sure you weren't expecting guests."

"I got them, though, didn't I? What makes you think I bought it in Wisconsin?"

"Tax stamp on the bottle," he said briefly. "It's the same rare single malt that I like, and I'm surprised you can even get it in the Midwest."

She'd special ordered it, but she wasn't about to tell him that. No, she didn't drink it. But every now and then she'd uncap the bottle and breathe it in, pretending he was there. A brazen lie was the best. "I bought it to prove to myself that I was over you."

"Sure you did." His voice was low, hypnotic, and she wanted him to touch her, she wanted him to get the hell away from her.

She took a tentative sip of the Scotch, letting it burn pleasantly, the rich, peaty taste of it filling her senses. She remembered the burn of the chili in his kiss. What would a whiskey kiss taste like?

She started to edge away from him on the bed, but his hand shot out and caught hers, holding her in place. "Where do you think you're going?"

"I think you know a little too much about me. All I know about you is your name, and I'm not even sure I believe that."

"You know my name, you know the name of the organization I work for."

"Great basis for a marriage."

"We're not going to have a marriage. Now that Claude's dead I'll arrange for an annulment. Since we went through the Catholic Church in Italy it'll be too complicated for you to handle, and take too long. We have people who can take care of those things."

"Speed is of the essence," she said, trying to keep the sarcasm out of her voice. She took another sip of the Scotch, too big a one, and began coughing. She felt him take the glass out of her hand and set it down on something as she choked, and since he was sitting in front of her, he pulled her against him to pound her back. All polite and necessary.

"I told you not to drink too fast," he said in her ear.

She closed her eyes, breathing him in. Clean, fresh skin, rainwater, Scotch, a heady combination. It was dark, there was no one to see, not even James, not even her. She put her face against his bare shoulder, burying it against his skin, wanting to disappear into him. She wanted everything to go away, everything to stop, she wanted to stay in this thick, warm darkness with him forever, no matter what lies he spun her, no matter what game he was playing, no matter whether he cared for her or whether she was some demented charity case. She didn't even realize she'd slid her arms around him, that the sheet had come down to her waist and her breasts were pressed against his warm flesh.

She half expected him to pull back, set her gently away from him. He was being so kind, so polite, so understanding. Such a gentleman, such a tender, vanishing lover, and her impervious, stone heart was breaking.

She was the one who pulled away from him, staring up at him in the darkness. She wasn't going to let him disappear. She slid her hands up, cupped his face, and dragged his mouth down to hers for a hard, desperation-tinged kiss.

He caught her hands and stopped her, and she wanted to scream, to weep. She tried to yank away, tried to kick him off the bed so that she could curl up in a miserable little ball, but he held on, subduing her quickly.

"Stop it!" he snapped, his Scotch-sweet breath exploding on her face. He shook her, just slightly, and his fingers were digging into her upper arms, so tightly there'd be bruises, and she was glad of it, glad she'd have something of him for at least a little while longer.

"Angel," he said, and there was desperation in his own voice. "I can't keep doing this. I can't keep fucking you and disappearing."

"Then don't disappear."

The moment was endless, breathless between them. "If I touch you I might hurt you. I won't be gentle. I can't. Not if I've killed someone."

She understood. "Then don't be gentle. I don't break."

She heard his deep intake of breath. "No, you don't, do you?" He pushed off the bed, and she thought he was going to take off the rest of his clothes and come to her. Instead she heard him heading to the door.

"Where are you going?" She shouldn't have asked; she shouldn't have said anything.

"Away from temptation. I'm as bad for you as you are for me and you know it."

She heard the determination in his voice, heard the door open, and she was out of the bed, reaching him, shoving the door shut before he could leave.

He leaned against the door, keeping very still. "Why?"

"You know why." She wasn't going to put it into words. She'd told him she loved him, so many times in so many ways, and had it thrown back at her. That his motives had been honorable didn't change things. "You seem determined to do the right thing for me. Why don't we do the wrong thing for a change?" She put her hands on his chest, sliding them up his shoulders, his warm, sleek skin, and she wanted to drown in him, devour him, die in him. She moved on her tiptoes, brushing his mouth with hers, softly, luring him. She kissed his hard jaw, his throat, moving down his chest to lick across one flat nipple. She felt the shudder run through his body as he tried not to react, and then she went for the other one, letting her teeth brush across it.

"Angel . . ." he groaned, not touching her, his hands fisted at his sides.

She kissed his hard stomach, rubbing her face against him like a contented kitten. And then she sank to her knees, her hands in either side of his waistband, and she pulled his shorts down, letting his erection spring up, and she felt him freeze.

She put her hands around him, the thickness of him, letting her sensitive fingers run along the silky flesh, the thick veins that bulged along the side, and a fierce hunger ran through her, from her mouth to her sex. The thought of this had always disgusted her, but now she wanted the taste of him more than anything in the world.

She leaned forward, resting her forehead against his flat stomach, his hard-on brushing against her, and then she put her mouth around the head, tasting the salty sweet liquid there.

"Jesus!" he groaned, and he put his hands in her hair and pulled her away. She wanted to scream at him in her fury at his denial.

"You don't want to do this, Angel. I know you don't. It won't make any difference." His voice was bleak.

She stayed on her knees in front of him as she reached up and pulled his restraining hands away from her. "How many times do I have to tell you that you don't know shit about me?"

"You mean you learned to suck dick after I left you?"

She wanted to cringe at his deliberately crude words. "No. I mean that right now there's nothing I want more than to take you in my mouth. And you know as well as I that I've never willingly done it before. Never wanted it before." She leaned forward again, grasping him, trembling, and took him into her mouth.

She heard another curse in the darkness, but this time he didn't push her away. She let the length of him slide into her throat. He was much too big to fit, so she wrapped her hands around the base as she took all of him that she could, savoring him, closing her mouth around him.

"Angel," he said in a choked voice, but she ignored him once more, drinking in the taste of him, the texture, the iron-hard erection beneath the strangely soft skin, and she wanted so much more. She wanted to pull him in so deep her face was against his stomach, she wanted him to pour himself into her mouth, she wanted to swallow him, keep him.

She felt his hands on her head, his fingers threading through her hair, but now they were soft, caressing, not pulling her away, and she responded to his subtle guidance, changing the rhythm as he wanted, letting his soft instructions curl in her stomach with a fierce heat. "Relax your jaw," he whispered. "That's better," when she did, and found she could take more of him. "Harder now. Harder."

She accidently let her teeth graze against the side of him, and if anything he seemed to grow even bigger in her mouth as he shuddered with pleasure. She reached beneath him and cupped his balls. They were drawn up tight to his body, so she knew his orgasm was close at hand, and she gloried in it, so turned on she thought she might climax without touching herself, without being touched, just from the sheer eroticism of his cock in her hungry mouth.

"You like it." His voice was soft. It was the only soft part of him, and she could feel the pressure build within him beneath her tongue, her deep, sucking gulps, and then suddenly he yanked her head away from him, setting off a deep wail from her.

"No!" she cried, reaching for his hips, trying to get him back. "I want it. I want it all."

"Next time," he said, lifting her up and turning her till she was up against the door, her feet dangling down. "I need to be inside you." He drew her legs up around his hips and slammed into her, so hard and deep that she yelped and then climaxed with a deep shudder. Her entire body was on fire, shaking, as he thrust into her, over and over again, until his own climax set off a another round of powerful convulsions, and all she could do was cling to him, her eyes closed tightly in the inky darkness.

They stayed that way for a long time, and then he moved, still holding her, swinging her around to the bed, and she realized with shock that he was still hard inside her, despite the heat of his ejaculate. The mattress was beneath her, he was on top of her, with short, sharp thrusts, then longer, slower, deeper ones, as it built once more. She dug her fingers into the sheets beside her, rocking against him, and then suddenly he reared up, pulling her with him, sitting back with her astride him. She clung to him, and his thrusts were different, hitting different parts of her, filling her so deeply that all she could do was hold on to him, shaking, until she came apart in a soundless scream.

He held still while she convulsed around him, cradling her gently, and when the spasms finally slowed, he laid her back down on the bed again, pulling out. He was still hard, and she responded to his loss with a cry of distress, until his mouth closed over her breast, sucking it in deep, his teeth a sharp delight of pain and pleasure, and she cradled his close-cropped head, unbelievably wanting more. He pinched her other nipple between his long fingers, and she made a sound of mindless pleasure, and then his hand went to the slippery wetness between her legs, the mixture of both of them, as he sucked long and hard at her nipple, his tongue playing with her. She could feel the desire, so recently sated, rise again, but she was overwhelmed.

"Please . . ." she gasped, as he rubbed her clitoris, her entire body vibrating with frustrated need. "It's too much."

He let go of her breast with a sucking pop, and unbelievably the sensation brought another sharp stab of desire. "Nothing's too much," he growled, pulling back. Before she realized what he was doing he'd flipped her over, pulled her onto her knees at the edge of the bed, and he pushed into her from the back, past her wet, swollen tissues to the very heart of her, so deep, so deep, and she buried her face in the sheets that smelled of their sex, clinging to them, panting. He pounded into her, over and over, driving out his demons and hers, and she went past desire, past pleasure and pain and love into some dark, wonderful place where there was nothing but the rutting need between them, and then she was gone, past anything but the climax that finally ripped her into pieces, shaking, sobbing, lost.

Until she felt his body wrap around hers, his mouth on the back of her neck, the tightness of his muscles as he emptied himself into her, the hot flow of his semen, claiming her as nothing else could.

She let out a soft cry when he pulled out of her, then came back down on the bed with her tightly in his arms. He turned her until they were lying face-to-face, their sweat-slick bodies plastered up against each other, and he was holding her, suddenly tender, his fury past, kissing the tears from her face, tasting them.

IloveyouIloveyouIloveyou was a mantra in her brain, and she knew she should struggle to find something of herself once more, but there was nothing left. Only her love for him, unspoken and soul-crushing. She didn't want to sleep. This would be the last time she lay in his arms—in a few hours he would hand her off and she'd never see him again, and she needed to feel his heart pounding beneath her head, needed to face his raw gasps as his body finally settled down. She wanted him to sleep so she could lie in his arms and store up every memory, every sensation, for the long cold nights ahead of her.

But James didn't sleep. He lifted one hand, brushing back her hair that clung to her tear-damp face, gentle, tender, and she felt his lips against her forehead.

"Sleep," he whispered. And she did.

Chapter Nineteen

It felt as if her eyelids were glued shut, Evangeline thought, as the bed rocked and rolled beneath her and the rumble of an engine filled the air. She tried to sit up, but the motion threw her back on the mattress, and she felt a blazing heat at her back, fiercer than the sun.

She pried her eyes open, and the world was oriented once more. She was back in the camper—he must have carried her out to it while she slept—and the vehicle was moving at breakneck speed away from the fiery conflagration that had once been the farmhouse.

She caught hold of the railing, noticing the bandages that were wrapped around her wrists before hauling herself up, and Merlin rose from his place on the floor to nuzzle her happily. "What is going on?" she cried, forgetting that she'd meant to keep away from him as best she could until he abandoned her in New Orleans. They'd said and done everything last night—or was it this morning?—and she wanted to keep that memory with her, not let him ruin it.

"Lie down!" James snapped, the lover gone. Forever. "I can't worry about you being knocked around the place. We're going to have a hell of a time crossing the river after last night's storm, and I don't want you distracting me."

She slid off the bunk onto the floor, cradling Merlin for a moment.

"What happened to the house?" she persisted, crawling forward as carefully as she could while the RV lumbered back and forth over the rocks and small trees. She didn't want to distract him from his intense concentration, but she wasn't going to hide back there. She wasn't going to hide anymore. "Did Claude come back?"

"Claude is dead. I had orders to set the house on fire," he said, never taking his eyes from the road. "We've got to get out of here before someone alerts the local fire department. Not that it'll do any good—there's no way a normal fire truck could cross that river now, and as far as anyone knows, it's a deserted building that's going up in flames. But they might come out to take a look, and we can't be seen." He shoved the engine into a lower gear. "And for future reference, don't ever try to sneak up on me. I tend to attack first and ask questions later."

She stopped her stealthy approach. "I didn't want to distract you," she said, feeling foolish. She really didn't want to talk to him, to look him in the eye, not when she remembered that the last time she'd looked up at him, he'd been looming over her, inside her, and she'd been lost in such a dark, crazed pleasure that even the memory of it made heat flood her cheeks. But she wasn't going to stay back there and risk being swept to her death without seeing exactly what they were doing. Not without being beside him.

"No one could sneak up on *you*, particularly not me," she added in a deceptively calm voice, hauling herself into the passenger seat and putting the seat belt on. It was only then she realized what she was wearing—a huge flannel robe made for someone twice her size. He must have pulled it around her before carrying her out.

She felt sticky, sore, and embarrassed. She'd never lost her soul so completely, even on their so-called honeymoon. She would have done anything he told her to, *had* done anything he wanted, and most shameful of all, she'd initiated it. He'd been trying to leave her, and she'd gone up to him and . . .

She made a mortified sound. She remembered exactly what she had done, the feel of him in her mouth, and she started to unfasten the seat belt when he slapped his hand over hers.

"Leave it," he said sharply. "You chose to come up here in the first place, you can stay put. I can't be worrying about you being bounced all over the inside of the camper because you're suffering from a case of postcoital regret. Frog in a blender, remember?"

She turned her face away to hide her expression, staring back at the burning building. Trust Bishop to put it right out there—everything she wanted to keep still and sacred in her heart. Next thing she knew he'd accuse her of raping him.

"Merlin, down," James said in a voice of unshakable command, and Merlin immediately dropped down, putting his head on his paws. Evangeline turned back to the path ahead of them and let out a strangled cry of horror.

The shallow patch of river where they'd crossed was now a raging torrent, carrying tree limbs and debris in its wake. "If you're going to scream then go lock yourself in the bathroom," James said coolly, idling the engine for a moment while he surveyed the flooding water.

"We'll drown."

"Oh, ye of little faith," he mocked. "I can drive through this blindfolded."

"Please don't."

He glanced over at her, the engine idling, revving. "I told you I'd keep you safe, didn't I?"

"I don't think you're much good at controlling forces of nature." She managed to keep her voice from shaking, but just barely. She was terrified.

He grinned, and she realized with a kind of dazed wonder that he was enjoying this. *Bastard.* "Trust me, Angel."

She wanted to tell him never in this lifetime. She wanted to laugh in his face at the absurdity of it. The words came out before she realized what she was saying. "I trust you," she said, and she knew it was the truth.

His smile vanished as he looked at her. "I actually believe you do."

"Then get moving. You're not Charlton Heston and this water isn't going to part like the Red Sea."

Without another word, he gunned the motor and they went flying, hitting the rushing river with a huge upsurge of spray. She could feel the tires slip, feel the camper begin to lift in the water, the back end swaying.

Evangeline covered her mouth with her hands to keep from screaming, as James managed to move the vehicle forward, somehow, some way. And then suddenly the huge box of a vehicle found purchase again, and a moment later he had pulled them onto dry land. The dusty road they'd followed to the farmhouse was now a muddy track, but mud was more manageable than water, and after a few minutes they were on blacktop, heading south as siren-screaming fire trucks passed in them the oncoming lane, heading for the ball of flame they had left behind.

Evangeline realized she'd been gripping the sides of the seat so tightly her fingers were cramped, and she had to force herself to loosen them. She sank back, shaking in relief.

"Good thing you trusted me," he said dryly. "Think what kind of shape you'd be in if you had any doubts."

She unfastened the seat belt and started to head toward the back in silence when the edge of her robe caught on something and fell open, giving James a full view of her body.

"Not right now, dear," he drawled. "You'll have to wait till tonight for me to take care of your needs."

"You asshole," she said, anger flooding through her, wiping out the lingering tenderness.

"That's getting old," he said. "Why don't you come up with another epithet for me? Surely there are some more creative insults."

"Fuckhead. Dickwad. Shit for brains," she readily supplied.

"Now I object to the last one. I'm actually quite smart, even if I do stupid things."

"Like what? I thought you didn't admit to mistakes," she said bitterly.

"Mistakes like you, Angel."

How could she leave herself open like that? She jerked away the moment the words left his mouth, shaking with fury and despair. How did he manage to get past her defenses each time? How did he manage to talk her into lowering them long enough for him to deliver some stinging emotional blow?

It was a good thing he was dumping her—she had to get away from him. She'd forgotten that need in the turmoil of the last few days. He'd hurt her and broken her heart, made love to her and then rejected her, and she'd lost the ability to think clearly. Even now she wanted him to pull the vehicle over, to take her in his arms, to make love to her even if he couldn't love her.

But it was never going to happen.

She headed toward the back of the RV. At least she'd find some privacy in the bathroom. "I don't suppose one can take a shower when the RV is on the road?" She used her iciest voice.

"One certainly can," he mocked. "Just go ahead and try to scrub every trace of me off you. And inside you."

She'd never considered him particularly cruel, but now she wasn't so sure. "Let's just hope there's plenty of water," she said, closing the door on the tiny bathroom quietly behind her.

Jesus, he was an asshole, Bishop thought. Evangeline had it right in the first place, along with the other insults she'd hurled at him. He couldn't remember a more intense twelve hours—from the moment he discovered her missing, right through to her falling into a damp, exhausted sleep in his arms. He always thought he'd had the best sex of his life when he was with her, and yet somehow it always managed to get even better. Last night had damned near killed him.

He hadn't been counting, but it seemed as if he'd come three times on the same erection, something he would have considered a physical impossibility. But Evangeline managed to confound the laws of physics. If she hadn't seemed on the edge of passing out he could have kept going. He was as sexually driven as any man, but his wife took him to places he'd never known existed.

She'd laugh if he ever tried to tell her that. She'd never believe him. He'd worked so hard to keep her at arm's length that she had to think he was nothing more than some horny bastard who shagged anyone he could find.

No matter how cruel it was, this was still the best possible thing to do for her. There was no way he could ever stay with her. It may have worked for Madsen, with the full power of the Committee behind him, or for Taka and Reno with their Yakuza connections. If he tried to keep Evangeline with him, it would be putting a target on her back.

Now that Claude was dead, there was no reason to let the marriage stand. Breaking the connection would only help when it came to people like the Corsinis and all the other enemies he'd racked up in a lifetime of doing bad things for good reasons. Madsen could arrange the annulment, no questions asked, and she could go on to a life of academic boredom and another jackass of a husband, this time a real one.

And he'd snap the bastard's neck.

It was no wonder he was such a jerk—he couldn't keep her and he couldn't let her go.

He wasn't going to have to worry about it. He'd been such a bastard to her that there was no way she'd forgive him, no reason she'd want to. He'd made sure of that, and the only thing he could do as penance was to let her keep Merlin.

He hadn't been brought up to love anyone. His father had been an even bigger bastard than he was, a lieutenant colonel in the military with the compassion of a snail. Too bad his mother had died in a car wreck coming home from a night spent with her lover—she might have softened the old guy. It was just as well Bishop had had no siblings for the colonel to take his rage out on—it was easier taking the punishment himself than worrying about others.

Last time he'd checked, his father was still alive somewhere, but that had been long ago, and he'd probably succumbed to a lifetime of cigarettes somewhere along the way. If he was still alive, he'd think his only son had died in Afghanistan. Bishop had tried to talk Madsen into making it look as if he had deserted because of cowardice, a final blow to the old monster's pride, but Madsen had refused, telling Bishop he'd eventually regret it.

Madsen hadn't known his father.

Merlin was the first creature Bishop had allowed himself to love. No, maybe that wasn't quite true, not if he wanted to be strictly honest with himself, something he'd rather avoid. Merlin was only four years old—he'd met Evangeline more than five years ago.

Not that he loved her, he reminded himself. He couldn't afford to love anyone, not even his damned dog.

The door to the bathroom opened and the RV was filled with the aroma of gardenia soap, the same that had been in the farmhouse. He'd told Madsen's assistant what to stock in the camper—he remembered everything about Evangeline, and in those intervening years, she still favored the same toiletries. The familiar scent that filled the interior of the camper made him hard.

He glanced at her in the rearview mirror. Her eyes were red. The cut on her cheekbone from last night was blossoming into a black eye, and he wanted to kill Claude all over again. At least

Merlin had ripped away half his right hand before Bishop's bullets had sent him over into the raging river.

He could mock the tears she tried to hide, just to be even more of a prick, but he kept his mouth shut, focusing on the highway ahead. They'd be on the outskirts of New Orleans by early evening, and he could let go of her, place her in Ryder's capable hands. Not only could, but had to.

Ryder had already established a safe house while he scouted locations for the new office—Evangeline would be safe there until they finished with His slimy Eminence and the men who were literally his acolytes. The Corsinis' sex trafficking couldn't be crushed that easily—it had been going on for decades—but the center of operations could be smashed, and the person in charge eliminated.

Once the endless ordeal was finally finished, she'd be free. No one but the Corsini crime family could connect her with the shadow operative who sometimes went by the name of James Bishop, and that connection would be severed.

He glanced back at her. She was wearing cutoffs and a baggy T-shirt, and he could see the outline of her breasts beneath the loose fabric. He yanked his gaze back to the road. He couldn't afford to get distracted. Last night had been as good a way to end things as possible. Each time he touched her, he went a little farther down a path that could destroy them both, and his cruelty this morning would keep her away from him. What was the good in hurting her if he only . . .

He pushed the thought out of his mind. They were as safe as they could be right now. The Corsinis might guess that Clement was dead but they couldn't be certain, nor could they know whether he'd managed to kill Evangeline or not. Bishop had made sure they'd left absolutely no trace behind, and by the time Claude's battered body washed up, he'd be unrecognizable. There were no DNA, fingerprint, or dental records on file for him anywhere. He'd be a John Doe, the worst kind of epitaph for a prima donna like Claude.

He smelled coffee, and he would have given his left nut for some, but chances were if he asked Evangeline, she'd put rat poison in it. He could make it the final six hours without caffeine, though it would be harder.

He was acutely aware of her coming closer, and he gripped the steering wheel tighter for a moment before relaxing his hands. From his peripheral vision he could see the insulated bottle she held out to him. "What's this?" he said. "A peace offering?"

"Insurance that you don't fall asleep at the wheel and kill us both," she said. Someone else might have thought her gesture was completely casual, but he could hear the rawness in her voice, both from her recent tears and her screams last night. Screams for help when Claude had taken her. Screams of pleasure when he'd . . .

"Thanks," he said briefly, taking it. "Sure you didn't add rat poison to it?"

"I'm trying to stay alive, remember? And I didn't see any rat poison in the cupboard, or I might have been tempted."

Against his will he laughed. No matter how bad things were, she always managed to summon up some fight. Here was a woman who wouldn't let life get the best of her, even if it brought a scaly bastard like himself.

"I'm going to sleep," she said with an entirely unconvincing yawn. "Wake me when we get to New Orleans."

He nodded, sipping at the coffee. One sugar, lots of cream. The way he'd always taken it, something she had to have remembered from Italy. If he had any choice, he would have jerked the wheel to the right, parked by the side of the road and grabbed her. He didn't glance at her.

"Sweet dreams."

Her derisive snort made him smile to himself.

Chapter Twenty

Evangeline lay on the bunk with her eyes open. She'd managed to bury herself in sleep during the last few crazy days, but that escape had finally abandoned her, and she lay still, hugging herself, staring out at the landscape speeding by. James was up in the driver's seat, concentrating on the road, listening to jazz again, and it suddenly occurred to her that from now on the sound of cool, cerebral jazz would make her want to throw up.

Half a dozen times she'd been about to push herself off the mattress, head to the front of the camper, and start an argument with him. By tonight he was going to be out of her life. Forever. Some small, self-destructive part of her wanted to hold on to anything for the last short time she had, even a fight. She didn't move. The sooner he was gone from her life, the sooner she'd start to let go, and she wasn't going to bother with any more questions, questions that he'd never answer. As far as he knew she was sleeping, and that made it easier on both of them.

He stopped once, to let Merlin out to pee, to make himself another cup of coffee, to glance at her supposedly sleeping body before heading back to the driver's seat. By the time they were back up to speed, Merlin had paced back to her, nuzzling her face. Unlike

James, he wasn't fooled by her feigned slumber, and he wanted cuddles and games and attention, but she remained motionless. Finally, with a sigh of canine acceptance, he climbed up onto the bunk and curled up at her feet, taking a good third of the narrow bed. It was the first time he'd ever relaxed his guard enough to get on the bed with her, and it was almost enough to bring silent tears, the ones she'd fought since she'd left the shower. She slid a surreptitious hand down to scratch his head and he sighed blissfully. If there was only some way her life could be that simple.

It was growing dark earlier and earlier, particularly the farther south they went. Over the Canadian border the sun had been going down around 8 p.m.—it was a full hour earlier as they neared the Gulf of Mexico. Small night lights came on automatically in the back of the RV, but she and Merlin lay mostly in shadow; even the renewed sound of heavy traffic, the stop and start of the caravan, the street noise and raucous music wasn't enough to make her lift her head, though it made Merlin jump down and pace to the front to sit at James's side. They were in the city. They were near the end.

She wasn't going to make it any easier for him, she thought, dry-eyed. He'd carried her into the camper—he could carry her out. He could set her on her feet and turn his back on her. If he could.

When the Winnebago finally came to a halt, she wanted to groan. Her body was aching from her enforced stillness, not to mention the activities of the night before, all she'd been through, the brutal and the beautiful. It took all her strength of will to lay perfectly still, to keep her breathing even. The lights came on fully, but she didn't let her eyelids quiver, and she felt him approach her, then stand over her, looking down at her for an endless moment, as if deciding what to do with her. Would he pick her up and carry her inside? He seemed to have no trouble carrying her around—he was a lot stronger than his lean frame suggested. Or would he join her on that narrow berth, cover her body with his in a final joining . . .?

He did neither. "Merlin, come," he ordered in a soft voice. And a moment later she was alone in the RV, in the darkness.

She pushed herself into a sitting position, leaning against the wall of the van, staring sightlessly ahead of her. So that was that. It was over. She should thank him, really she should, for not prolonging matters. A clean break, fast and sharp, was the best way to deal with things. She drew her knees up, hugging them. Already she could feel the muggy heat of Louisiana infiltrate the camper as the artificially chilled air began to dissipate, and she wondered whether he'd locked her in. Maybe she'd die of asphyxiation before he could decide what to do with her. That would be just fine with her—she'd lost everything. Annabelle, her beloved camper, a goodly amount of her research, possibly even her job. She'd had a grant for the work she'd been doing, and it had all hinged on the last two American sites. Without that research she would have nothing to publish, and the college was going to take a very dim view of things. Which mattered less than she thought. She had money of her own—maybe she'd just disappear. She'd told herself she'd never go back to Italy—maybe it was time to lay that particular ghost.

She heard her own cynical laughter. In fact, she'd spent the last few days doing just that—laying that particular ghost. It was time to exorcise him for good, and a week or two in Venice should do the job nicely.

This time there would be no need to try to drive him from her mind and her body with a series of unsatisfactory love affairs. She'd accepted the truth, looked at it clearly and without sentiment. Something happened when they were in bed together, something unlike anything she'd ever experienced, and she knew perfectly well what the magic ingredient was. Not his remarkable prowess and inventiveness or even his sheer gorgeousness.

It was the stupid, incontrovertible fact that she loved him.

She could only hope the condition wasn't terminal.

She hadn't heard the footsteps outside, and when the door opened and the lights flooded the space, she didn't have time to slide down into the bunk again. It didn't matter. The man who stood there was a stranger.

"Dr. Morrissey?" He stepped up into the camper and shut the door behind him, pushing the switch to keep the lights on. "I'm Matthew Ryder. Bishop has asked me to look after you."

She blinked, unable to come up with a response for a moment. "Where has he gone?" she said before she could stop herself.

"He's taking care of some legal business that was waiting for him. In the meantime I'm going to transport you to a safe place for you to stay for the duration."

"The duration of what?"

Matthew Ryder looked vaguely annoyed, not at her, but at his absent friend. "He didn't explain things to you?"

"Not much. Why can't I just go home?" Now she was sounding positively plaintive, and she wanted to kick herself. She was made of stronger stuff than that, and she wasn't going to pancake simply because James had finally done what he'd always done: abandoned her.

"I'm afraid we're still in the midst of a very sticky situation, one that leads all the way back to when you first met James in Italy," Ryder said. "The man who tried to kill you in Montana worked for a major crime family, one which has a large contingent of members and a very profitable business centered in this city, and they'd like nothing better than to get their hands on James. They blame him for the execution of Dimitri Corsini."

She thought of that seemingly sweet old man. "I thought Claudia . . . er . . . Claude killed him?"

Only the lightest twist of a smile touched Ryder's impassive face. She stared at him, trying to memorize his features, but he kept in the shadows, and she could find nothing particularly interesting or memorable about him. In fact, he looked like a pencil pusher, a civil servant of some sort, totally bland and forgettable. She suspected he was anything but.

"I'm afraid Claude knew his usefulness to the Committee was coming to an end, and he decided getting rid of you was a good idea," he said smoothly. "If anything, you're in even more danger than you were before, and I've promised James I'll make sure you're safe until this is dealt with. With luck it will only be a few weeks . . ."

"A few weeks?" she said, her resignation fading. "I can't stay here that long! I have to start classes at the end of the month, I have to do something about salvaging my work."

"Don't worry, Dr. Morrissey." His bland voice was soothing. "We've got it all in hand. You've got a leave of absence from your teaching position, and I promise, the time will fly."

She stared at him in patent disbelief. "Don't call me doctor," she said finally, for lack of anything else to say. "I've got a PhD, and it's pretentious. I'm Evangeline."

"Bishop's Angel," he murmured, and she turned away so the man wouldn't see her flinch of pain. "I hope I can count on your cooperation in this. It's to keep you safe."

"And if I don't cooperate?"

His smile was very cool. "I'm afraid you'll be doing it anyway. Bishop wouldn't like it if I had to hurt you, but personally I wouldn't hesitate."

She looked into his eyes then; they were flat, black, and completely soulless. He was another man like James, one who did what he had to do with no remorse. "Would you kill me?"

"It wouldn't come to that. I'm too good at what I do." He held out his hand. "It's getting hot in here, and there's a nice apartment with clean clothes and food and cable TV awaiting us across town."

"What makes you think I watch TV?"

He didn't blink. "James has briefed me thoroughly. You have a preference for twisted mysteries and love stories and you don't like sitcoms unless they're British. Plus, New Orleans has some of the best food in the world and I've made arrangements to have meals delivered from any restaurant that takes your fancy."

She swung her legs off the bunk, ignoring his proffered hand. "Where's Merlin?"

"I'm afraid he can't come with you. He's too easy to track. Once everything is taken care of, you'll be able to take him back to Wisconsin with you."

For a moment she didn't move, but then she did what she had done so long ago. She simply turned everything off, all feeling, all interest, all longing, regret, or memory. "I don't have any shoes," she said, as if that were the most important thing in the world.

"That's all right. It's only a few steps to the car. There'll be shoes waiting for you."

"And how do I know you aren't one of the people who has tried to kill me? Why should I trust you?"

Ryder's smile this time was less of a grimace. "James said you'd ask that. He said to give you these." He took her hand and placed something in it, closing her fingers around it. She knew what it was, even before she looked.

Her aunt's diamond earrings, the ones he supposedly stole in Venice. She wanted to fling them at him.

But then, he wasn't Bishop. So instead she calmly put them on, sliding them into the piercings and fastening them. She looked Ryder straight in the eye. "I'm ready," she said.

***

"How did she look?" Bishop was sprawled in the apartment where Ryder had been living the last month, partway through a bottle of

Scotch. He'd spent the last few hours signing paperwork, checking in with Madsen, prowling around the ramshackle building Ryder had chosen, and he was in a thoroughly foul mood. Merlin had risen the moment Ryder had come back in, whining in anticipation, and then sank down on the floor with a sigh of disappointment when he realized Evangeline wasn't with him. Bishop knew just how he felt.

"Your Angel? Just fine, particularly when she saw all her research papers and her laptop waiting for her. Jenkins and Thomas have the first watch, and Thomas had already stopped in at Commander's Palace for food. She looked quite happy to be rid of your sorry ass, though I think she misses the dog."

"Thanks," Bishop said with just the trace of a snarl. "She didn't argue?"

"Just a little. You were right, though. Once I handed her the earrings, she shut right up. Nothing like diamonds to make a woman behave."

"You don't know shit. Those were her diamonds." Stupid idiot that he was, he'd carried them with him, ever since he left her in Venice. He'd kept meaning to give them back to her, but something had always stopped him. Now he had nothing tying him to her, apart from the legal trifle of a marriage. Now he could let go of her. "I took care of the paperwork. This wreck of a place officially belongs to the Committee on the Preservation of Democracy. How's that for a bullshit title?"

"It'll do for now, as long as we don't have any skinheads crawling out of the woodwork. Now that you've finally gotten your ass here we can start work on retrofitting the place, plus I've bribed the right people. Considering New Orleans's reputation, it's surprising how twitchy the city gets about their old buildings."

"You could have chosen a high rise," Bishop said.

Ryder shrugged, unmoved. "I don't like them, and neither do

you. We'll have an easier time keeping things on the down low here in the Garden District. You gonna see her again?"

The last bit was such a change in subject that Bishop snarled before he could control himself. "You said it. She's better off without me."

"Think about business for a change, why don't you?" Ryder said, totally without sympathy, but then, he'd always been a cold bastard. "We've only got circumstantial evidence against His Eminence, not even enough to warrant an official investigation, and in the meantime ships go in and out of port, filled with cargo."

"Human beings aren't cargo." Bishop took another drink. He could hold his liquor, which was unfortunate when he wanted nothing more than a few hours' oblivion.

"Not to His Eminence and the Corsini family. And we can't even get close enough to take him out. He keeps that cadre of priests around him at all times—the only chance we'd have would be to kill all of them."

Bishop looked at him. "Why haven't we?"

"Two reasons. You and I are sanctioned—the others aren't—and I'm not sure you and I are enough to handle it. Plus, not everyone in the Cardinal's entourage is dirty. You were raised a Catholic—how'd you like to face your God after murdering an innocent priest or two or three?"

"I'm not likely to face any God at all after the things I've done. And I'm a recovering Catholic. If I'd still kept any doubts, this whole mess would have put a stop to it."

"You shock me!" Ryder's voice was mocking. "Even with your nice new pope?"

"He's not my pope, and he's probably a Corsini too," Bishop said bitterly. "And I really wouldn't mind beating the shit out of you, so just keep at it."

Ryder laughed. "You and what army?"

Bishop leapt for him. It didn't take long, and as usual it was a draw. The two of them lay side by side on the floor, broken furniture around them, and Bishop passed Ryder the bottle he'd managed to salvage before their brawl. He took a long pull, then passed it back. "You have to get over her," Ryder said.

"I can hit you again," Bishop growled.

"It's not me you want to hit. Just keep your mind on business and it'll be over. The sooner it's done with, the sooner she's gone, and you can go back to living a normal life."

Bishop closed his eyes. He didn't feel like moving—there was a broken chair leg under his back and he was bleeding from a cut on his forehead, but he was just as comfortable where he was. "Sure I can," he said morosely. He glanced over at Merlin, still lying by the door, paying absolutely no attention to their short, furious battle. "*Laissez les bon temps rouler.*"

⌣

With great dedication Evangeline threw herself into ignoring the passage of time. She had plenty of things to keep her busy—the sheer mass of data she'd acquired during the summer required organization and editing, plus there was a goodly amount she hadn't transposed onto the computer yet. She played gin with her bodyguards, watched old movies, managed to keep a false veneer of Zen-like calm around her. Bishop wouldn't have believed it, but Bishop wasn't anywhere around her. He'd disappeared—as far as she knew he wasn't even in the country, much less in New Orleans. She didn't miss him, not for one moment, she told herself every morning when she woke up in the huge, king-sized bed, and every evening when she climbed back into it, alone. She just missed Merlin.

She wasn't any too fond of the man called Ryder. He showed up occasionally, when she least expected him, and she never could figure out why. She missed freedom; she missed fresh air, even if it was the sultry heat of the Crescent City. She missed her camper, she missed her house in Wisconsin . . .

Fuck that, she didn't miss any of those things. She just missed Merlin, and his asshat of an owner. No, she was his owner now, she reminded herself. Meaning she had no connection left to the man she'd unwittingly married. He'd probably disappeared to end that particular travesty, and once it was done with, she'd be released to the wild once more, like some captive animal.

She hadn't spent much time in New Orleans in the past, and what little she could see out of the shuttered windows didn't give her much of a clue as to which area of town they'd stashed her. It was close to the heart of the city, she could tell that much from the noise that filtered through, the buildings that were crowded together, the general sense of grunge. Occasionally she considered trying to escape—she had no illusions that the guards were simply there to protect her. They were there to keep her from leaving as well, and she was getting very sick of it all. She had no access to the Internet, no phone, and despite Ryder's empty promises, the only television available to her was only for streaming movies. In the past three years of living alone, she'd watched a lot of movies, and the only ones she'd loved enough to want to see again were fucking romances, the last thing she was in the mood for.

So she sat, and she worked, and she waited. When it was all over, when she was finally safe, would James be the one to bring Merlin back to her? Or was he really gone forever this time?

It was Thursday, and she'd been cooped up in the small apartment for a week. Her research was turning into a frustrating pain in the butt—there was too much for even a lengthy paper but not enough for a book, and she was heartily sick of it. She was half tempted to just send the whole fucking thing to Pete so he could keep plagiarizing. At least there'd be some consistency in the writing.

She was just as sick of the rich food, no matter how much she'd loved it the first few days, sick of coffee with chicory in it, sick of playing gin, sick of everything, even beignets, which she would have considered an impossibility. Finally, in an act of great rebellion, she'd sent Jenkins out to the nearest fast-food restaurant for the greasiest cheeseburger and fries she could get, complete with a milkshake and a gallon of Diet Coke, as she prepared to enjoy a total debauch of junk food. Maybe the taste of ordinary Americana would help remind her there was another life waiting for her, back in the heartland.

"What's taking him so long?" she asked Odila, one of the six guards in rotation to watch her. Odila was a young father and a lousy gin player, two things that recommended him, but he was almost impossible to lure into conversation. His expression was entirely neutral, but she'd become very observant, particularly with nothing to watch but the limited confines of the apartment and her cadre of guards. He looked worried.

"Probably long lines at the burger place. You said you wanted the best cheeseburger in the Big Easy," he said.

"Probably," she agreed. "Or maybe a vampire got him," she added with a weak attempt at humor.

"Vampires aren't real," Odila said repressively.

"Yes, but you have to admit that if they were, they'd live in New Orleans."

Odila wasn't admitting anything. "I'd be more likely to believe in Voodoo," he said. "There's a stronger history. Everything else just comes from a crazy lady in the Garden District."

"Blasphemy!" Evangeline summoned up some humor. "I love Anne Rice."

Odila's response was monosyllabic and profane. They sat in an uncomfortable silence for minutes longer. It was getting late, though anything before two in the morning was early for New

Orleans, and a brief rain had ended, already swept out to sea, leaving the streets wet and shining in the lamplight. "Maybe I'll take a look outside and see what's keeping him," he said finally.

"Can't you call him?" For some reason she felt uneasy. Here was her perfect chance to escape her mink-lined prison, and instead she didn't want to be left alone.

Odila shook his head. "No phones. Too easy to track them."

"Not if you use burner phones."

Odila gave her a pitying look. "If we can track burner phones, then they can too."

"Then how do you let Ryder and James know if something's wrong?" She put James's name in there as a test, to see if Odila would admit whether he was still around or not.

"We're good enough at what we do." He shoved himself to his feet, giving nothing away. "I'm going to check on Jenkins. Don't let anyone in, including me, unless I give you the password."

"Which is?"

He hesitated for a moment. "Vampires," he said finally, giving in.

She laughed. "Sounds good. I'm really looking forward to that hamburger."

Across town, the empty house in the Garden District had lights on for the first time in years. "You know you're a pain in the butt, don't you?" Ryder said, throwing himself into one of the folding camp chairs they'd brought in. "If I had any idea you were going to be such an asshole, I would have told Madsen to send someone else. Being cooped up with you has to rank with one of my worst assignments . . ."

"Not likely," Bishop said, glancing up from the schematics he was looking over. The moldy Gothic mansion in the Garden

District was going to need a complete gut job, both for the damp and the complicated infrastructure needed for any outpost of the Committee, and he'd been staring at the sketches spread out on the makeshift table for hours without really seeing anything. "You forget, I was with you in Chechnya, not to mention that mess in Lyons. We barely made it out alive."

"I'd take being shot at over putting up with a lovesick idiot."

"Fuck off," Bishop snapped, pushing the papers away from him. "The only reason she's still here is that you haven't taken care of business. Find one way for me to get a shot at His Eminence and this will all be over."

"I think that was going to be Claude's job," Ryder pointed out.

"Well, Claude isn't here, is he?" Bishop's voice was like ice.

"No, he's not. And if you think the Corsinis don't know exactly where you are, then you're even more of a fuckhead than I thought. There's no reason to keep your little wife on ice . . . They don't need her to get to you and you know it."

"Shut up about my wife," Bishop snapped. "It's not safe."

"Yeah, right. You going to tell me you aren't just as much a fool for that woman as your dog is?"

Merlin lifted his head. He'd taken to sleeping by the door, clearly waiting for Bishop to take him back where he belonged, with Evangeline. Since no one was heading in his direction, he dropped his head back with a heavy canine sigh.

"If I were fool enough to let myself get emotionally twisted over some damned woman, I'd have been dead long ago," Bishop said repressively.

Ryder laughed. "You didn't fall in love before. Don't bother denying it—I recognize the signs. I've seen far too many good men laid low by it. If I thought there was a chance in hell of curing you, I'd do it, but you're too far gone. It's a chronic condition and you'll never get rid of it, so you may as well get used to it."

"Give me a break. You know as well as I do that there's no room in our lives for normal relationships."

"Shit, I don't think you'd know a normal relationship if it came up and bit you on the ass. No offense, Merlin," Ryder added when the dog lifted his head again. "Neither of us is cut out for a normal life, but you let your guard down, and now you're moping around like some fucking teenager . . ."

"Don't annoy me." There was no missing the very real danger in Bishop's voice.

"Look, we're wasting our time. We need to concentrate on shutting down His Eminence, not arguing about who wants to go steady with his best girl. Shit or get off the pot. You're in love with her. Either take her or let her go."

"She'd end up with a target on her back . . ."

"She already has a target on her back, Bishop," Ryder said, clearly exasperated. "And she always will, no matter how far away from her you keep yourself. The safest place for her to be is with you—you're about the only one who can protect her. Well, I could, but I'm not interested in the job."

His sudden surge of jealous rage shocked Bishop. "Go near her and I'll cut your throat."

"Did you hear me? Not interested. Never will be—women have two uses in this life: to sleep with or work with. That's it, and the two lines don't cross. If you don't get your ass in gear and do something about her then I will. If you aren't going to take her, then it's time for her to go back to Iowa or wherever she comes from."

Bishop controlled his temper with an effort. "And what the hell makes you think she'd come back with me? I've done everything I could to drive her away."

"You'll never know until you find out." He pushed back from the table. "You coming with me?"

Chapter Twenty-One

Odila didn't return. Evangeline tried not to look at the clock, but she knew that Jenkins had left around eleven, and it couldn't have been more than two hours later that Odila had gone after him. It was almost three in the morning now, the noise of the city was dying down, and she was still alone.

Maybe it was simply Bishop's way of getting rid of her. He'd called off his watchdogs long enough to let her escape so he wouldn't have to be troubled with any messy scenes. This way he could keep Merlin and never have to deal with unpleasant trifles like emotions and a lovesick female.

Lovesick? She wanted to laugh, but she couldn't really find it funny. She'd had a lot of time to think during the past week—and she'd twisted herself inside out trying to avoid the ugly truth, but it just kept popping up again, inescapable. No matter how big a bastard he was, no matter how he tricked and lied and manipulated her, no matter how clearly hopeless any kind of future was, she still loved him, and had never stopped, even when she thought he'd seduced her only to rob her.

She reached up and touched the diamond studs in her ears. Why had he held on to them? Clearly he hadn't needed the money or he would have sold them—he'd simply needed an excuse to ditch her. But why keep them with him?

If he thought she was going to run away the first chance she got, then he was mistaken. He might be an emotional coward, but she wasn't. She'd fucked up her life good and proper five years ago, and never had any closure. Oh, she could blame him, and God knows he'd been the one to instigate it, to lie and trick her.

But she wasn't a victim. She had been dazzled by him, she'd tossed away all practicality and gone with him the moment he'd beckoned, and instead of giving herself a good kick in the ass and moving on with life once he left her, she'd moped and thrown herself into even worse relationships, culminating with her marriage to Pete.

Which apparently wasn't a marriage at all. She could take some pleasure from that, at least. And she'd really been trying to move ahead for the last three years. James Bishop's reappearance had shown her just how little progress she had made in that direction. He'd gotten her back in bed in just about the same amount of time.

No, she reminded herself. He hadn't gotten her back in bed. She had gone with him, willingly. If she was ever going to move past this she needed to take responsibility, and she was tired of feeling helpless.

Tired of being a prisoner as well, even if it was ostensibly for her own protection. She should open the front door and peer out. She should put on her shoes and go out looking for them, but something kept her from heading for the front door. Her instincts were clearly useless—she'd had no idea James had been using her, no idea that Pete was a lying, cheating plagiarist. How the hell could she trust whether she was in trouble or not?

It didn't matter. As long as there was any chance of danger, she'd need to be careful. Ryder and his men might think they were the crème de la crème of operatives, or whatever they called themselves, but she'd spent the last week working on the decorative iron grille over the bathroom window and no one had noticed. A nail file had gotten it started, and each time she could reasonably disappear into the tiny room she'd worked on it. It would be a tight fit, and she would have to be able to set the grille down on the narrow iron walkway outside the window without attracting any attention, but right then it seemed like the smartest thing she could do. She had no ID, no money, no credit cards, but it didn't matter. There was always the police, though from the stories she'd heard they might not be any better than the crime family Ryder had warned her about. One thing she wasn't going to do: stay in this apartment like a sitting duck, waiting for someone new to try to kill her.

She moved over to the door as quietly as she could, pressing her ear against it. Was she imagining faraway whispers, or were people really out there? People who didn't want to alert her to their presence?

Her indecision vanished. She slipped into the bedroom and locked the door, then dragged a dresser in front of it. Grabbing her sneakers, she then went into the adjoining bathroom and locked that door before climbing up onto the toilet. The moment she opened the window muggy night air swept into the air-conditioned room, but for some reason she shivered. The grille needed one more shove at the upper corner, but when she gave it one, it slipped out of her grasp and went crashing onto the narrow metal balustrade, bouncing off it and landing on something below, something that sounded sickeningly like a car.

She couldn't hesitate. Shoving herself up, she dove through the window, wiggling herself through it as she clung to the railing, and when she finally pulled her feet through, she reached back and shut the window behind her.

It was only then she realized she'd left her shoes in the bedroom. She could hear noise from the apartment, a banging sound.

Someone was trying to break down her bedroom door, and whether it was Odila or someone far more dangerous, she couldn't afford to squat there on the narrow railing and wait for that person to get to her. The moon had come out again, illuminating the night, but she didn't dare run on the flimsy little balcony and draw any more attention to herself.

She had no idea whether there would be a fire escape off this thing or if she was still trapped, but she headed for the back of the building, reasonably certain that if there was any way to get down to the street, it would be back there. *Please please please*, she muttered beneath her breath, as she heard the muffled sound of something crashing beyond her. She had made it around to the back of the building when she heard the breaking glass, the shouting; suddenly, like a deus ex machina, a fire escape appeared, and she practically threw herself down the ladder's two flights, her bare feet slipping on the rusty metal.

She landed in a dark alley, which was dimly lit from the street-light out on the main thoroughfare. She had no idea where she was—it had been dark when Ryder had brought her here, and she'd been too angry and miserable to pay attention—and naturally her rotating cadre of protectors/wardens refused to answer any of her questions. She could be in the French Quarter or down by the once-savaged levees, and she had no idea where to go.

No, not the French Quarter—it wasn't bright or noisy enough. Probably not the once-flooded part of the city either—surely there'd still be a smell of lingering damp? She hesitated, and then heard the thundering footsteps overhead. She couldn't afford to wait.

Heading toward the light would be the obvious choice, so instead she turned and sprinted down the alleyway, into the darkness. The ground was rough beneath her feet, and she knew it would only be luck that would keep her from slicing her foot open on something. The alley smelled of beer and piss and puke, and she could hear the thunder of footsteps racing down the rickety metal stairs. It sounded like an army was coming after her, and she knew it wasn't anybody from Bishop's mysterious Committee after all. Whoever it was wanted to harm her, wanted to kill her, and she wasn't ready to die.

She turned the corner and slammed to a halt: wire fencing went up twenty feet or more, blocking the exit. They were coming closer now, and she looked around for a place to hide, desperate. There was nothing—no convenient Dumpster, no abandoned car, nothing to hide behind. She was well and truly trapped.

She looked back at the fencing, wondering if she could climb over it, just as strong lights speared into the alleyway; they missed her as she ducked down, but briefly illuminated a door in the brick wall she'd thought was solid. The beam of light swept back, and she jumped, not hesitating, reaching the door before the light returned.

For one desperate, breathless moment she thought it was locked, and she wanted to scream, to cry, to yank at what she believed was an immovable doorknob. But it moved, opening inward, and she stumbled into the darkness, down, down, managing to kick the door shut behind her as she fell.

———

Merlin found Jenkins's body underneath the stairs. Bishop might not have noticed, but the smell of blood and body fluids hit him a moment after Merlin leapt forward.

Ryder pushed past him. "You go on," he said brusquely, kneeling down by the corpse as Merlin began scrambling up the flights of stairs in search of Evangeline. Odila's body was crumpled in a corner of the third-floor landing, but the dog didn't slow down, his nose taking him straight to the apartment door, and Bishop didn't stop to check whether he was dead. The Corsini family never left anything to chance. He followed Merlin and saw the apartment door standing open. Whoever had come after her hadn't had to kick it in—they'd have taken the keys from Odila, and Evangeline would have had no idea that she was about to die.

He didn't hesitate, crossing the hallway with a few strides. Merlin was already inside, growling, and he knew she was already dead. She wouldn't have had a chance, and it was all his fault . . .

Merlin's growl turned to a bark, and Bishop sped up, slamming past the open front door, certain he was going to find her body, but there was no sign of her. The door to the bedroom had been smashed in, and he could see she'd tried to push the bureau in front of it. Smart girl—she hadn't been caught unawares after all.

She was still no match for hired killers. Merlin had already leapt through the remnant of the door, and Bishop followed. No sign of her there either. The dog was already in the bathroom, barking loudly, the sound echoing off the tile.

He steeled himself, but the small room was empty. Someone had taken the grille off the window, and he knew it had to have been her. It would have been a slow, painstaking job, and it would have taken her days to work on it. She was a fighter and she never gave up. Thank God she didn't trust him—otherwise she would have been trapped in there.

Merlin was trying to jump high enough to get through the window, but with a short command, Bishop called him back. The only way they could find her was through Merlin, and the chances of Evangeline being out on the narrow balcony were nil. Ryder was already at the door, his face the same expressionless mask he always used on assignment. He took one look at James and allowed just a glimmer of reaction before he shut down again.

"She got out?" he said.

Bishop nodded. "Sneaky little thing spent the week unfastening the bathroom grille. She got out that way."

"But how far?" It wasn't a question—Ryder knew that Bishop would have no more answers than he would. He also knew that time was running out.

"Merlin will find her," Bishop said.

"In time?"

Bishop just looked at him, and Ryder shook his head. "We'll be in time, James," he amended. "If the mighty James Bishop is going to fall, then I'm damned well not going to let some half-ass mob family get in the way of love's young dream."

Bishop didn't bother replying. If Ryder had any control over the situation, they'd get her back safely. But they both knew that some things were out of their control.

Merlin barked. "You're right," James said to the dog. "We're wasting time. Find her for me."

A moment later Merlin had disappeared down the stairs, with James and Ryder in close pursuit.

Chapter Twenty-Two

She couldn't breathe. Alone in the deep, cocooning darkness she thrashed and struggled, unable to make a sound, and she was going to die alone, never found, her body rotting and eaten by rats . . .

Her breath returned with a giant whoosh, and she collapsed on the floor, then immediately shoved herself up again. She'd had the breath knocked out of her, and now she was lying in a pool of foul-smelling water, trying to find the strength to get to her feet.

Pain radiated from every part of her body, and she wanted nothing more than to curl up in a ball and weep, but she didn't dare. She could hear them, or maybe she was imagining it, voices, footsteps, so she started to run, straight into the darkness, into cruel hands that waited, clamping down on her. She opened her mouth to scream, but a meaty hand slammed over her face, and she didn't make the mistake of thinking it might be someone who wanted to help her. She fought, twisting in their hands, kicking, desperate, but she was helpless. There were at least two men holding on to her, impervious to her blows. Steeling herself, she bit down on the hand across her mouth, hard, and the man loosened his hold for a fraction of a second, cursing.

It was all that she needed. She tore herself away from them, throwing herself into the shadows. Her eyes were becoming accustomed to the inky blackness and she could see shapes well enough to avoid them, a glowing red light in the distance that she hoped and prayed was an exit sign.

She darted through the impenetrable darkness, hiding behind piles of crates, avoiding the steel pillars that seemed to be holding the place up. The stink of it made her gag—the old building had been used as a toilet—but she didn't have time to think about that, only that she needed the fresh night air, that she needed to get away from the men who were hunting her. She tripped, going down again, but this time she held still, squatting low in the darkness, as the flashlights beamed over her head.

"She's gone out there." The voice was gruff, foreign sounding, and a moment later the exit door slammed open, letting in marginal light from the night outside. She counted three of them—bulky figures, holding guns—as they poured out the door, and it slammed shut behind them, closing her inside.

She didn't make the mistake of moving. Had all of them left, or was it simply a trick to lure her out? She held her breath, listening, and a scratching noise came from her left. Soft, scuffling, it was a noise that could only come from rats.

Evangeline froze. They wouldn't come closer, would they? If she stayed where she was, unmoving, would they think she was just another piece of meat to gnaw on? Did she dare stay where she was for long enough to catch her breath, or was someone else inside with her, waiting for her to make another mistake?

The scrabbling came closer, the only sound in the dank basement aside from the slow drip of water, and she knew she couldn't wait any longer. If something touched her, she'd start screaming and she wasn't sure she'd be able to stop.

Were they waiting outside the door, watching for her, guns drawn? No, they hadn't shot her when they had their hands on her. They didn't want her dead—at least, not right away—or they would have already shot her. She'd escaped once—if they were waiting for her, then she could escape again.

She wasn't even going to think about what she was walking through on bare feet. Cut feet were really the least of her worries— a cut throat would be permanent. As she edged closer to the door, none of the shadowy forms around her moved.

She found the door by feel alone, and she rested her cheek against the cool, sweating metal, listening for the telltale sounds of voices, for traffic, for any sign of life. She was at the opposite end of the alley from where she'd been trapped—with any luck this door would open onto a major thoroughfare, and she'd take her chances with the police. Or maybe, just maybe, James would have discovered she was missing, and he was coming after her, coming to rescue her once more, as he had so many times before.

Or maybe he'd finally given up. She couldn't count on rescue, either way. All she could do was try to rescue herself. She pushed at the bar across the door, and it opened slowly, with a creaking sound so loud she thought it would wake the entire neighborhood. She peered outside, ready to yank the door shut again, but all was silent. She stepped forward into the night and let the door close behind her, realizing too late that there was no way to get back in if she needed to.

She looked around her. The streets were still wet from the earlier rain, steam rose off the pavement, and the streetlights glistened in the puddles of water left from the drenching. She was in some sort of cul-de-sac—there were shuttered storefronts, a bar with noise and light streaming from it, and a small white Catholic church built of stone in such a state of disrepair it looked as if it had been abandoned years ago.

There'd be a phone in the bar. Someone could call the police for her. She started toward it, when three figures darted from the entrance, the overhead light illuminating their cold faces, and she knew they were the men who'd followed her into the basement of the abandoned building, the men who'd been after her since she'd escaped the apartment.

She froze, and it seemed to her she could see into their flat, dead eyes, even though that would have been impossible given the distance and the dark. She could recognize the silhouettes of guns though, and her immobility shattered. The church was her last chance—she sprinted across the littered street, ducking into the shadows, moving as swiftly and silently as she could, ignoring the shooting pain in her foot when she finally stepped on something sharp, stumbling up the front steps of the church and flinging herself at the doorway.

She half expected it to be locked, and when it opened beneath her icy fingers, she wanted to fall inside and fling herself on the floor crying "Sanctuary!" like some medieval thief. The door closed with a heavy thud behind her, and she staggered forward into the light.

It was a small church, with only a dozen rows of pews, but it was far from abandoned. The altar was filled with tall brightly lit candles and a black-robed priest stood there praying, his back to her. He turned at the sound of the door shutting, and looked at her ragged, barefoot appearance without any surprise at all. Then again, maybe she wasn't that strange-looking for New Orleans in the small hours of the morning. There must be a need for a priest to be on duty.

"My child," he said in a gentle, welcoming voice. "Are you in some kind of trouble?" He started down the aisle, his long robes swishing on the stone floor, his elderly face full of compassion. "You've hurt your foot. Give me your hand and I'll help you to a seat."

"I need you to call the police, Father," she said, her voice cracked and shaking. "There are some men after me—we need to lock the church doors or they might hurt you as well."

He smiled at her. "There's no need. These streets are lawless, but everyone knows that the Church of the Blessed Martyr is protected. Come and let me see to your feet." He took her hand in his. The skin was soft, but the hand was surprisingly strong, and he pulled her along to the front of the church, setting her down gently in the front pew. Candles were burning on the altar, a soft, reassuring glow, and she gasped in awe at the candlesticks. They were tall and ornate, and looked as if they might be solid gold.

"Is it safe to use those candlesticks? Won't someone rob you?"

He glanced behind him, as if he'd forgotten them, and chuckled softly. "No one would dare rob this place. And you have a good eye, my child. Those are very old—from the time the French ruled New Orleans. Their value in gold is estimable, their historical value is beyond calculation. But no one would dare such sacrilege. Now you sit here while I get something to bathe your feet and call the police."

"But if those men find me . . ."

"Don't worry, my child. Trust me." He disappeared, and she leaned back against the pew, trying to catch her breath and calm her racing heart. Would murderers and members of organized crime really respect the boundaries of a church? James and Claudia . . . Claude . . . certainly hadn't when they carried out an execution in the tiny mountainside church.

Evangeline had left bloody footprints up the narrow center aisle of the tiny church. Her feet were filthy—if the men didn't storm the church, she'd probably die of typhus or some hideous disease anyway. She ought to leave. She was putting that sweet old man in danger. Surely there'd be a way out the back, and she could keep running . . .

And leave a trail of blood wherever she went. She was about to rise when the old priest returned, this time with a richly embroidered drapery over his black robe, and he carried a tray with a heavy silver bowl of water, a little ewer of oil, a box, and a pile of linen cloths.

"I've called for help," he said. "And now you must let me tend to you." To her absolute horror, the old man knelt at her feet, placing the bowl in front of her.

"Father, no!" She protested, trying to rise, but he was in the way and she could scarcely knock him over.

"My daughter, this is a rite as old as time," he said calmly, dripping some oil into the steaming water. "Just relax." He took one of her feet and placed it in the basin, scooping up the water with his hands and pouring it over her. "Tell me, my child, are you a Catholic?"

"I'm afraid not. I wasn't brought up in any particular religion." She glanced nervously behind her, but the doors to the street remained shut. "Perhaps you shouldn't . . ."

"Nonsense. Your parents' failings were not your fault. Do you repent of your sins?"

At the moment she couldn't think of any, except being stupid enough not to tell James she loved him. She hated the thought of dying without him knowing, but then, if she didn't make it through the night, it would probably be easier on him if he didn't know.

Then again, she didn't want to make her death easy on him, and surely that was a sin in itself? She needed to humor the old man, though, or he'd never let her go, and they'd both be sitting ducks. "Yes, Father."

"Then you are absolved, my child." He made the sign of the cross, then removed her foot from the water and wrapped it with a heavy linen towel. He set it down on the stone and reached for her second foot. Blood filled the water, and the cut stung. The priest continued talking in a calm voice. It took her a moment to realize he was speaking in Latin, but the sound of his voice was as soothing as the touch of his hands. When he finished with her wounded foot and lifted it from the bowl, she could see the cut wasn't nearly as bad as she feared, though it was still oozing; she wanted to protest that it was ruining the beautiful linen but decided it was a waste of time.

The priest had his own agenda. She wondered what he was saying in Latin. Some blessing or prayer for healing, she imagined. She'd studied Latin—her parents had insisted on it—but she hadn't heard it spoken conversationally, and she had no idea what he was saying.

He dried his own hands on another towel—she felt sorry for the parish laundry—and then reached for a small case that lay on the tray. Opening it, he took out a small piece of almost paper-like substance. "Open your mouth, child, and let this dissolve. Don't use your teeth."

She looked at it warily. "I don't want painkillers."

His laugh was warm. "The only painkiller this contains is the Holy Spirit. Open."

He had the voice of authority beneath his kindly tones, and she figured she needed all the help she could get as he placed the wafer into her mouth, continuing in Latin. Next came a tiny glass of sweet wine, and she decided this must be some Catholic form of healing. Odd that the priest would give communion to a non-Catholic, but she decided he must be a very sweet man. The act of kindness made her want to weep in her exhausted state, but she simply went along with his directions, unable to summon the energy to protest.

Where the hell were the police? He said he'd called them—how long could it possibly take? The priest kept on with his Latin, and some of it began to sound familiar. *Mea culpa, mea culpa, mea maxima culpa.* What sin had the priest committed? Oh, no, he was praying for her sins, wasn't he? It was a good thing he didn't know what she'd been doing with James Bishop or she'd probably be doomed to the fiery reaches of hell, at least according to the church.

When he was finished, she would leave. Even in the sanctity of a church she didn't feel safe, but at the moment she couldn't make herself move. She simply stared at the candle flame, mesmerized.

She could hear muted voices, and she sat up. "Is someone here?"

The priest finished the rest of the wine and put the small bottle back in the heavy silver case, which was ornately engraved and monogrammed. "Only some of my helpers." He took the little ewer of oil again, poured some on his hand, reaching up to make a mark on her forehead. Blessing her, she supposed. She knew that the Catholic faith was big on ceremony but even this seemed extreme to her, and she was about to protest when he began speaking again in what was clearly a prayer, and she dutifully bowed her head, not wanting to seem ungrateful.

He'd switched to English somewhere along the way. "Through this holy unction and through the great goodness of His mercy, may God pardon thee whatever sins thou hast committed . . ."

He'd already pardoned her so-called sins. "Unction?" she interrupted. "What are you doing?"

For a moment the old priest looked cross, interrupted midspate. "I am performing the holy rite of extreme unction."

The tiny amount of wine in her stomach threatened to erupt. "Extreme unction? Isn't that the last rites? Do you think I'm going to die?"

He made the sign of the cross over her, rising again. "No, my child," he said kindly. "I know you're going to die."

Panic sliced through her, and she surged to her feet, shoving at the old man, but he remained solid and immovable. "I have asked my men to make it painless," he continued in his entirely reasonable voice. "It's an ugly business, but a necessity. The Committee must learn to keep out of our affairs and we will keep out of theirs. Your friends will come searching for you, but it will be too late: you will be dead, and when they touch you, this entire building will disappear."

"By magic?" she said stupidly.

"No, dynamite." He moved away from her, heading back to the altar, and when she rose, ready to run, she saw that the doors were now open, and the men were advancing down the center aisle, some in priests' garb, some in street clothes, but they moved as a unit, purposeful, deadly.

She must be imagining the sound in the distance. Was it real, or had her mind simply given up in terror and she was hallucinating? Merlin would do anything to find her—she trusted him. If James and Ryder realized she was gone, they'd let Merlin out to find her.

She heard the bark, closer now, and she knew it was real—the familiar bay of a dog on the scent. The men had their guns drawn, even the three priests, and she had to find some way to stop them, to slow them down, long enough for Merlin to find her.

She rushed the altar, shoving the old man aside as she grabbed one of the heavy candlesticks. Wax dripped onto her hands and the ornate carving bit into her fingers, but she didn't hesitate. "Come any closer and I'll bash his head in, you motherfuckers."

The priest looked up in shock. "This is a place of holy worship! You watch your language, young lady!"

She wanted to laugh, and she realized she was getting hysterical. The old man rose to his feet, but she kept herself behind him, out of range. They couldn't shoot her without risking killing the priest, and she knew they wouldn't.

The old man grabbed for her, but she kicked him. Big mistake—he went down, and she was an open target for the men advancing on her. One of them raised a gun at her, and she ducked behind the altar, rolling onto the floor, still clutching the huge, ornate candlestick, when she heard the eruption of gunfire, the familiar snarl of a furious animal, and she flattened herself against the stone.

"Angel!" James's voice was laced with desperation.

"Angels won't help you now, Bishop!" she heard the priest cry out, and she felt the hysterical laughter rise again. There was the sudden howl of a man in pain and she edged along the floor on her stomach, around the side of the altar.

It looked like a war zone, the blood and gunsmoke and bodies and noise. One of the younger priests lay spread-eagled in the middle of the floor, lying in a pool of blood, a gun near his outstretched hand, while another man was trying to fight off Merlin's jaws clamped around his forearm. James was circling a priest, both of them armed with knives, the holy father looking even more dangerous than her murderous lover, and she almost screamed when the man lunged, slashing across James's stomach, ripping through his shirt and drawing blood.

He'd made a mistake, though, overbalancing, and James caught his arm and pulled it straight up behind him, the sickening sound of cracking bone warring with the man's scream of pain. He went down in a welter of black, and then James was on top of him, grappling with him. There was no sign of the old priest.

She could make out Ryder at the back of the church along with two of the men who'd taken turns guarding her. They were in the midst of a pitched battle, and she ducked her head in horror as one man fell back, his head seeming to explode from a hail of bullets. She couldn't hide forever, and she scrambled to her feet, limp with relief when she saw Merlin astride the man he'd been chewing on, growling fiercely. She saw James slowly, methodically beating the shit out of the man who'd knifed him, though the priest wasn't putting up much of a fight by this point; then she caught a glimpse of the black robes from the corner of her eye.

It was the old man, the priest who'd given her the last rites before he planned on killing her. He was so intent on James he didn't notice her, and there was a gun in his hand. She wanted to call out, warn James, but there was no time. If she screamed the old man would probably shoot her and still manage to kill James.

She had no choice. All conscious thought left her mind then, as something outside of her seemed to take over her body. She lifted the heavy candlestick high over her head and brought it crashing down on the old priest's skull.

He collapsed on top of James and the man he was beating; blood and brain matter splattered everywhere, and all feeling and strength drained from Evangeline. She sank down on her knees, just as Merlin leapt forward, whining with relief and love, licking her face, her hands, licking the gore off her while she stayed there, dazed. She hugged him, dry-eyed, in shock, ignoring the blood splatter on her bare arms. It was over.

Everything was over.

Ryder was the one who came to her. At first Merlin didn't seem like he'd let anyone close to her, but a one-word command came from a few yards away, the only proof that James was alive and unharmed, and Merlin sat back, a warning growl still rumbling in the back of his throat.

"I'm getting you out of here," Ryder said in his cool, emotionless voice. "You don't need to be tied in with this, and it would be better all-around if you weren't." He had taken her arm, half supporting her, and she didn't want to think what she was walking through as he led her away from the altar, toward the back of the church. She tried to turn, to find James, but Ryder was too strong.

"He's fine," Ryder snapped. "And he can't afford to be distracted by you. You'll see him as soon as he's taken care of business."

"I don't give a flying fuck," she said bitterly, but the words came out in no more than a whisper, and he ignored her. Merlin was pacing by their side, and Ryder stopped.

"Call the fucking dog off, Bishop! I can't bring him with me to the hospital."

"I don't need . . ." Evangeline began.

"Shut up," Ryder snapped. "Call the dog."

"Merlin, come." The only words she heard from him. The last words she would ever hear from him, the heartless bastard. She could walk away from a hospital, walk away from Ryder, who would no longer give a damn what she did.

Merlin protested noisily, sitting on his haunches and whining. But he obeyed James, and she knew she would never see Merlin again either.

Ryder's manner was brusque but his hands were gentle as he pushed her into a dark sedan. "Put your seat belt on," he said, climbing in the driver's side. "I need to get away from here fast, before New Orleans's finest show up."

"What about James?" She wanted to kick herself the moment the question came out. She didn't care about him. He didn't care about her.

"He and the dog will be gone by the time they show up. He just has to take care of a few things, and it's better if I look after you."

"Why?" She told herself she didn't care, but her questions kept coming.

"Because you distract him, and he's already furious with himself for letting this happen. I want him to take care of business, not get distracted. Things need to be cleaned up as quickly and efficiently as possible, and he's better off where he is."

She wanted to ask why again. Why would she distract him, what the hell did it matter, but she finally had the sense to shut up, to shut down. She didn't care. She wanted to go home. She wanted her dog. She wanted the man she loved. She wanted to run away.

She leaned back against the seat and closed her eyes. She wasn't going to think, to feel, to remember. She just wanted to shut everything out, the sickening feel of the old man's skull cracking beneath the candlestick, the mess, the smell, the unbearable hideousness of it. She was past crying, past fear, past everything.

But curiosity got the better of her. She at least needed some answers. "Will you tell me what was going on? Why were those men pretending to be priests? Why did they want to kill me?"

"They weren't pretending," Ryder said grimly. "The man you did such a fine job with was a man we call His Eminence, one of the bishops in New Orleans named Raphael Corsini. He was a monster—that's all you need to know. You did the world a favor."

"That's not all I need to know. I killed a man tonight. I have to know why." Her voice sounded desperate, and she decided she was glad that James wasn't there to hear her break down.

"He was going to kill Bishop. Wasn't that enough reason?"

She remembered the sickening sound of the ornate candlestick crushing the man's skull. "Reason enough," she said, thinking of James.

Ryder sighed. "Okay, I can't tell you much. Corsini was in charge of human trafficking for the crime family. It all started when he was a young priest, assigned to a small town in South America. It was easy enough to send the young girls and children to the States, supposedly to devote themselves to the church and live better lives. Of course, they never saw the outside of the container ship until they reached their final destination, where they were to work either as sex slaves or cheap labor, and the villagers never asked questions. It worked so well that Corsini expanded the operation, bringing promising young men into the priesthood to help him branch out his activities, and when the family moved him up to New Orleans, it made a perfect headquarters for the operation. We've been after them for more than a decade, and this won't end their business, but it will put a big crimp in it. The man Claudia killed in Italy was in charge of bookkeeping for the operation, and we'd hoped his elimination would screw things up enough for us to take everyone down, but the Corsinis are more resilient. And that's all I'm going to tell you, and it's a hell of a lot more than I should have, so don't bother asking me any more questions. Just know you delivered payback for a lot of women and children who lived lives of abject misery and died before their time. And you kept Bishop alive while doing it, though I'm not sure whether you think that was a benefit or not."

She could see his face as he drove through the still-lively city, and it looked cold and brutal in the reflected lights. "Just one more question."

"No, I don't know when Bishop will come and see you, if he will at all. He's an idiot."

"Yes, he is," she said. "But that wasn't what I wanted to ask. Where is Odila? And Jenkins?"

Ryder hesitated. "They didn't make it."

And then, finally, she wept.

⌣

"Where the fuck is she?" Bishop snarled. He hadn't slept in three days; instead he'd flown to London to report to Madsen, paid off all the necessary people, had the already deconsecrated church torched, dealt with Merlin's extreme case of the sulks, and worked out help for Odila's family and Jenkins's brother, all the time expecting to find Evangeline waiting for him when he finally got back to the shell of a house that was slowly being renovated and retrofitted for their headquarters.

She wasn't there, and Ryder wasn't saying anything. In fact, he did his damnedest to always be around someone else so Bishop couldn't demand to know where she was. Bishop ended up lying in wait, and when Ryder was finally alone, he slammed the man against the crumbling wall of the old house in the Garden District.

"You know I let you do that, right?" Ryder said. "You're just lucky I knew it was you or you'd be dead by now."

"One of us would. Where is she?"

Ryder's smile was cool and inscrutable. "That all depends what you want with her."

It was the last thing James was expecting. "What the fuck business is it of yours?"

"Because I know where she is, and I have no intention of telling you if you're just going to keep putting her through the wringer. She's good people, Bishop. You know it and I know it. She deserves better than you, but for some reason it's you she wants. She's in love with you, and if you aren't going to do right by her, then leave her the fuck alone."

Bishop blinked. "She's not in love with me," he said instinctively. "How could she be?"

"Beats me. I never said she was levelheaded. In fact, she's a fool for you, and if she can't protect herself, then I'll protect her from you. So I'll ask you again. What do you want with her?"

"We're still married," he said stubbornly.

"You said you were going to have Madsen take care of that. Did he?"

"What business is it of yours?"

"Did he?"

"No!"

"Why not?"

"I could break your jaw, you know."

"We've already tried that," Ryder drawled. "We're evenly matched. Evangeline has been through hell and back, and there's only one thing she wants and deserves after all the shit she's put up with."

"The dog," Bishop said flatly.

"Okay, make it two things, and the dog's the more important one. What are you going to do about it?"

"I'm no good for her."

"Agreed. She still wants you. Give it up, Bishop, and stop acting like an asshole. What are you going to do?"

Bishop just looked at him, wishing to hell he could summon enough self-righteous fury to slam him across the jaw. "What do you think I'm going to do?" he growled. "I'm going to buy her a fucking Winnebago."

Chapter Twenty-Three

The new school year had started, but Evangeline didn't care. She was still supposed to be out on sabbatical, and it was easy enough to hand in her notice, much to the shock of the dean. After all, she was tenured, well respected—one didn't just throw that away.

But that was exactly what Evangeline was doing. It had been two weeks, and there was no word from Bishop. She'd put the house on the market, prepared for it to take months or even years to sell, but to her shock it sold in three days, leaving her essentially homeless in less than a month. Her research had shown up at her house one day, already preloaded on a brand new Mac, and she knew she could thank Ryder for that. Bishop had already forgotten about her.

She still couldn't decide whether she was married or not, but since she never planned to go near any man again, it hardly mattered. Everyone who wanted her dead was gone—the members of the Corsini family, including that wretched old man, were out of the picture, and Claude had drowned in Texas, though as far as she could tell his body had yet to turn up. She was safe to continue on with her life, just as if James hadn't walked back into it.

She wasn't sleeping well. She missed Merlin, she told herself, knowing full well there was more than that troubling her. Maybe

Ryder could get him back for her. Bishop was probably incapable of caring about anything, including an animal, but Ryder seemed reliable, at least. Or maybe she was wrong. Maybe Bishop could love something. Merlin, not her.

———

It was only seven o'clock when Evangeline dragged herself out of bed one late-September morning. She'd fallen asleep sometime after three, and she wanted nothing more than to bury her head under her pillows and shut everything out again.

But something had woken her, some unexpected noise, so she dragged herself out of bed, threw on a pair of sweats and an old T-shirt, and headed downstairs for her first cup of coffee, dodging all the packing boxes that blocked her way. She still had no idea where she was going—her current plan was to put everything in storage and simply take off. There was no reason to make any plans, no one else who mattered in her life. Everything was up to her. She ought to revel in the freedom.

She brewed a pot of Sumatran coffee, poured herself a nice black mug of it, and leaned against the kitchen sink to take her first sip.

Suddenly she dropped the mug into the sink with a crash, splattering herself with scalding coffee. She leapt back, cursing, before looking out the window once more.

There was no sign of the boring car she'd bought to replace her lost pickup. Instead there was a brand-new dark-blue extra cab Silverado, with the most beautiful vintage Airstream trailer attached to it. It was bigger than Annabelle had been, it would be a bitch to maneuver, and she was in love.

She didn't bother putting on her shoes, ignoring the chilly ground as she ran down the back steps and around the side of the camper, staring at it in awe and wonder. It was a thing of beauty, and she was almost afraid to touch it. But then, she wasn't afraid of anything.

She opened the door and stepped up into the camper.

He was there, of course. She barely had time to see him before Merlin launched himself at her, smothering her with doggy kisses and whines of delight, and she hugged him, determined not to look up. She got down on her knees and wrapped her arms around him, saying all sorts of silly doggy things to him.

"Oh, God, don't call him a puppy!" came Bishop's pained voice. "You've already turned him into a major wuss."

She had to face him, sooner or later, so she lifted her head. He was sitting at the dinette, a cup of coffee in his hand. He looked entirely at ease, cynical, sarcastic, the man who'd abandoned her. But his hand was shaking, just slightly, and that cynical smile was just slightly off, and suddenly she knew it was going to be all right.

Once she made him crawl through the mud on his belly like a reptile.

"What are you doing here?" she said coolly, rising to her feet. He'd made a pot of coffee, and it smelled divine. He'd always made good coffee, she remembered, so she walked past him, found the mugs, and poured herself a cup.

"I told you I'd replace your truck and camper."

She raised an eyebrow. Up close he looked even more nervous. There were shadows under his beautiful eyes, as if he hadn't slept. Good. "Did you, now? I seemed to have forgotten that little detail. You decided not to give me a choice in the matter?" He'd picked exactly what she would have wanted but couldn't afford—something funky and stylish and comfortable, something with soul. The inside of the vintage trailer had been rebuilt with hardwoods and rich textiles, like a gypsy caravan crossed with a rock star's tour van, and she could see the bed behind him. Wide, comfortable, curtains all around it.

He was buying into all of this. "If you don't like it I can get you something else," he said stiffly, and she wanted to laugh.

Sliding into the seat opposite him, she kept her face impassive as she took a sip of coffee. Sumatran, of course. He really did know her so well, even if he didn't seem to understand she was so in love with him she was probably going to die from it.

She shrugged. "It'll do," she said smoothly. "What were your plans?"

"Get a taxi to the airport. I couldn't get away from New Orleans until now, and I expect Ryder wants me back as soon as I can make it." He was cool now as well, and she was suddenly uncertain, not knowing whether she'd imagined his nervousness. Was it wishful thinking?

"Oh," she said lamely. She glanced around her. "This is bigger than Annabelle was."

"Don't worry—the truck's big enough to handle the extra load."

She nodded. "Okay," she said, suddenly defeated. "Do you want me to give you a ride to the airport?"

He leaned back, his long fingers cupping the mug, the long fingers that had touched her with such exquisite cleverness. "I don't think so."

So that was that. Once more she'd let herself hope for the impossible, and once more she'd lost.

"In fact," he said, "I'm not sure you're up to driving such a big camper without some practice. I wouldn't feel right leaving you without knowing you were up to the challenge."

Her eyes met his. His blond hair had grown out a bit, his scruffy beard made him even sexier, and his blue eyes were staring into hers. "You wouldn't?" she echoed.

He shook his head. "I think I need to make sure you're qualified to handle something like this. This is the sort of thing that could take a lifetime to master. That is, if you even want to."

He wasn't talking about the camper anymore. "I want to," she said. "I love . . . campers." Her courage failed her at the last minute.

His grin was slow, devastating, as he slid from behind the table and pulled her out into the walkway. "I love . . . campers too," he said, his mockery light and gentle. He brushed his mouth against hers, and she wanted to breathe him in, like he was the oxygen she'd been deprived of for too long.

She slid her arms around his neck, pulling him closer to her, and she could feel his body hard against hers, the familiar bone and muscle, the erection pressing against her stomach. He lifted his head to look down at her, and there was a questioning expression in his eyes. "I made sure they put a good mattress in for you."

"Maybe we'd better check . . ." she began, but before she could finish, he'd picked her up and set her down on the wide mattress, gently, carefully, as if she were breakable and the most precious thing in the world. She reached up and pulled him down with her, reveling in his weight on top of her, his legs between hers.

They took it slow and easy, taking joy in each other's body, sliding over the thick mattress and the expensive sheets he'd gotten for her. She took him in her mouth—she'd been dreaming about it for weeks, wanting the taste of him again—and he moved her into the positions he wanted, taking his time, loving her so exquisitely she almost thought she might die from sheer bliss. And then they went faster, harder, deeper, and no sooner did she begin to come apart than he joined her, shaking with the power of his climax, and they sank against each other, replete.

James rolled off her, onto his back, but he took her with him, his strong hands stroking her back, keeping her against him. They had said nothing as they made love, but now he spoke. "Maybe I ought to mention that I love you."

There were a thousand things she could say. *What took you so damned long? Where the fuck have you been? What made you finally realize?* She said nothing, smiling up at him. "Really? You're not just trying to get my dog away from me?"

Merlin had been sleeping peacefully on the floor at the side of the bed, discreetly keeping his head on his paws, but at the word "dog," he lifted his head for a moment. Apparently content with what he saw, he dropped it back down again.

"Don't forget the camper," James said. "Not to mention Ryder would kick my butt if I showed up without you. He says you're in love with me."

Her heart was so full she could barely speak, but he could read it in her eyes. She wanted to sound cool, flippant, but she was breathless, tears in her eyes, dying for him. "And what do you think?" she whispered against his damp skin that smelled so divinely familiar, his own special scent that she could surround herself with forever.

He smiled down at her with such tenderness, her tears spilled over onto her cheeks. "I never had any doubts, Angel," he said, pulling her tight against him.

From the floor beside them, Merlin began to snore.

About the Author

Anne Stuart is a grand master of the genre—winner of Romance Writers of America's prestigious Lifetime Achievement Award and survivor of more than forty years in the romance business—and still just keeps getting better.

Her first novel was *Barrett's Hill*, a gothic romance published by Ballantine in 1974, when Anne had just turned twenty-five. Since then she's written more gothics, regencies, romantic suspense, romantic adventure, series romance, suspense, historical romance, paranormal, and mainstream contemporary romance.

She's won numerous awards, appeared on most bestseller lists, and speaks all over the country. Her general outrageousness has gotten her on *Entertainment Tonight*, as well as in *Vogue, People, USA Today, Woman's Day*, and countless other national newspapers and magazines.

She's just celebrating her fortieth wedding anniversary with her luscious husband, and she lives by a lake in northern Vermont, where she enjoys an empty nest, fabulous grandchildren, and over-acting in local theater. She has so many books she still wants to write that she plans to live forever.